A CORDELL LOGAN MYSTERY

FANGS OUT

ALSO BY DAVID FREED

Flat Spin

A CORDELL LOGAN MYSTERY

FANGS OUT

DAVID FREED

The Permanent Press
Sag Harbor, NY 11963

For information, address:
  The Permanent Press
  4170 Noyac Road
  Sag Harbor, NY 11963
  www.thepermanentpress.com

Library of Congress Cataloging-in-Publication Data

  Freed, David—
    Fangs out / David Freed.
        pages cm. — (A Cordell Logan mystery)
    ISBN 978-1-57962-333-3
        1. Murder—Investigation—Fiction. 2. Pilots—Fiction.
    3. Mystery fiction. 4. Suspense fiction. I. Title.

  PS3606.R4375F36 2013
  813'.6—dc23   2012048034

Printed in the United States of America

For Elizabeth

Acknowledgements

My thanks to master aircraft mechanics Dan and Brian Torrey for their insights on all things mechanical, and to editors Barbara Baker, Barb Hallett, and Joslyn Pine for their expertise. Thanks also to esteemed writer and friend Sara J. Henry for helping keep my prose honest. To cover designer Lon Kirschner, website guru Kevin Pacotti, my agent extraordinaire Jill Marr, and publishers Judith and Martin Shepard, I am deeply indebted, as I am to the many family members and good friends who have opened their hearts, doors, and, not infrequently, wallets, in my pursuit of the writer's life. My gratitude also to those anonymous intelligence professionals, true heroes all, who each day help keep us safe without expectation of reward. You know who you are.

Pilots take no special joy in walking. Pilots like flying.

—NEIL ARMSTRONG

The dead man wanted Lobster Thermidor and a good bottle of Pinot Noir.

"Who does he think he is," the warden said, "Wolfgang Puck?"

They compromised on a bacon cheeseburger, onion rings, and two cans of cold Pepsi from the roach coach parked out in the visitors' lot, the aroma of sizzling grease wafting through the exercise yard like a tantalizing reminder of freedom itself. Thankful at having avoided a dust-up over last meal menus, the warden threw in what remained of a carrot cake left over from his executive assistant's baby shower.

"The upside of capital punishment," the dead man said as he licked cream cheese frosting from his fingertips. "No more worrying about bad cholesterol."

Dinner concluded at 5:30 P.M. Last rites were performed half an hour later, courtesy of a junior priest from one of Terre Haute's lesser parishes who'd volunteered for the task. The rest of the evening was spent writing farewell letters and playing five-card stud with the earnest young cleric, who would've lost his collar in smokes that night had the wagering been for keeps.

At 10:30 P.M., a nurse practitioner exuding all the warmth of a turnpike toll booth collector arrived from the prison infirmary with a syringe of diazepam. "To relax you," she said.

The dead man refused the injection. Few people, he said, can ever know in advance the precise moment at which they will cease producing carbon dioxide. He had every intention of experiencing it with a clear head. Besides, he quipped, he was scared to death of needles. Nobody laughed.

The captain of the guards appeared at 11 P.M., flanked by two underlings garbed in riot gear and built like the junior college offensive linemen they'd once been. The dead man was made to stand. They manacled his ankles, strung a chain through the belt loops of his prison-issued khakis, then locked his wrists to his waist.

"We're good to go," one of the correctional officers said when they were finished.

"Easy for you to say," the dead man said on legs turned suddenly to rubber.

With chains jangling and the priest reciting the Lord's Prayer in his wake, he shuffled through the otherwise tomb-silent penitentiary, officers steadying him, to a small, nondescript building outside the cellblocks. The death house.

"You can dispense with the holy roller nonsense, father," the dead man said. "I stopped believing a long time ago."

"It's OK, my son. We're all God's children."

"Yeah? Tell it to the FBI. They think I'm Ted Bundy."

The execution chamber was hospital antiseptic, its walls tiled in a soothing asparagus green. Guards hoisted him onto a futuristic gurney padded black and bolted to the floor in the center of the room. They unhooked his wrists, then strapped him down with five Velcro restraints, lashing his arms, palms up, to two perpendicular extensions, like a horizontal Christ on the cross.

The nurse practitioner reappeared wearing latex gloves. The dead man watched with strained bemusement as she tied off his forearms with surgical tubing, found two good veins, and expertly slid a needle into each wrist.

"No alcohol wipe? What if I get an infection?"

"The least of your problems right now," the nurse practitioner said, taping down the catheters through which the chemical cocktail would soon flow, stopping his heart.

The dead man tried to smile but couldn't. Gone, finally, was the false bravado. He would take his last breath one minute after midnight, on May 28—Amnesty International Day, it said on the wall calendar they'd allowed him to keep in his cell. The irony of it, dying by the government's hand on a day honoring human rights. Tears sluiced down his cheeks.

The witnesses were ushered into two rooms flanking the execution chamber. They would watch him die through bulletproof glass—his defense attorney, eight federal agents, five pool journalists, and the three-member U.S. Justice Department team that had prosecuted him. Family members of his former girlfriend, a lithe, brilliant Annapolis graduate he'd been convicted of butchering nearly a decade earlier, would look on via a closed-circuit video feed from more than 2,000 miles away, in San Diego, not far from the beach where her body had been found.

The warden, a one-time rodeo rider, entered as if on cue at 11:55 P.M. Those who worked for him said his weathered features resembled a used sheet of sandpaper, though never to his face. From the breast pocket of his suit he removed an index card, cleared his throat, and read aloud in a keening tenor.

"Dorian Nathan Munz, you've been found guilty of the crime of capital murder and condemned to death by order of the court. Is there anything you wish to say before your sentence is carried out?"

The dead man slowly gazed up at the video camera aimed down at him from the ceiling.

"Funny," he said in a voice tremulous with rising fear, "you should ask."

One

A pilot was in trouble. For once, it wasn't me.

He'd radioed approach control that his vacuum pump had quit, rendering his directional and attitude indicators useless. He was also running precariously low on fuel. Probably no more than ten minutes of flying time left.

None of that would've mattered much had Rancho Bonita been enjoying its usual postcard-perfect weather. You don't need many gauges or even a working engine to land an airplane safely when the skies are crystalline and you can see the runway from miles out. You simply glide in. But this was June, and June on California's central coast means fog, along with 300-foot cloud ceilings that can hang around for weeks like your couch-surfing, unemployed brother-in-law.

The airport was socked in.

"Mooney Seven Seven Delta, do you wish to declare an emergency at this time?" the controller asked over the radio like it was just another day at the office.

"Affirmative," the pilot responded calmly in a slow Georgia drawl.

My eyes no longer tested 20/10 like they did when I was on active duty, but the old peepers were still plenty good enough to spot his airplane from afar. He was at one o'clock high and about three miles off the nose of the *Ruptured Duck*, my scruffy Cessna 172—a dark speck that stood out against the unbroken batting of soft white stratus like the mole on Marilyn Monroe's cheek. The carpet of clouds stretched horizon to horizon beneath our two small ships. To survive his predicament, the Mooney pilot would have to descend through that half-mile-thick overcast—no easy task without fully functional flight instruments. Even the most skilled airman can become disoriented when his eyes are deprived of the ability to distinguish heaven from earth, up from down. A touch of vertigo and pretty soon they're digging your charred carcass out of the abstract sculpture that used to be an airframe.

Nobody said it, but everybody listening in on the radio, including the Mooney pilot, knew that there was a fair chance he might soon be participating in that process known uniquely to aviators and agricultural brokers alike as "buying the farm."

I was in no mood to play Good Samaritan. What I wanted to do more than anything was land, then go chill out with a long walk on the beach after an emotionally taxing weekend discussing possible reconciliation with my ex-wife at her home down the coast in Los Angeles. Unfortunately, given the urgent needs of a fellow airman, not to mention the Buddha's insistence that true contentment can never be realized without embracing a reverence for all humanity, I suppose somebody had to goddamn do something.

"Rancho Bonita Approach, Four Charlie Lima has a visual on the Mooney," I said, pressing the push-to-talk mic button on my control yoke. "I can shepherd him in."

Static in my headset. The *Ruptured Duck's* radios were acting squirrelly again. Small wonder considering they were ancient enough that Marconi probably designed them himself. I smacked the audio panel where I always smacked it and tried radioing again.

"Approach, Cessna Four Charlie Lima, how do you hear?"

"Four Charlie Lima, Approach. Loud and clear. How me?"

"Loud and clear. Four Charlie Lima has the Mooney traffic in sight. If he orbits left and throttles back, we can form up and he can follow me down on the ILS."

"You ever done any formation work, Charlie Lima?" the Mooney pilot asked me.

"Some," I radioed back. "I flew A-10's in the Air Force."

"A *Warthog* driver?" He said it like it was some kind of disease. "Y'all're into close-air support, not precision flyin'."

"That's true. But the way I see it, you've got two choices. You can wait for the Blue Angels to show up, or you can live to tell the tale. Your call."

He chuckled. "Well, when you put it that way, I suppose I'll just have to take what I can get. Tell you what, Charlie Lima, you get me and my wife down in one piece, the drinks are on us."

"Unable," I responded. "Demon rum turns me into the Incredible Hulk and green's definitely not my color. My makeup consultant says I'm much more of a winter palette."

"All right then, how 'bout dinner?"

I've never turned down a free meal in my life. I wasn't about to start now, not with the sad state of my bank account.

"You're on," I said.

I glimpsed his face as I maneuvered alongside his airplane a mile above the earth. He looked to be about fifteen years my senior, around sixty, graying and gaunt, wearing a sky-blue windbreaker. Rimless reading glasses perched on the end of a long, bony nose. His wife, a sultry blonde who appeared closer to my age than his, rode copilot and gave me a nervous, Queen of England-type wave. I nodded in response. She looked familiar. They both did. But there was no time to play place-the-face. I had to get two people on the ground, quickly, or they would soon be in it.

The pilot angled his Mooney in behind the *Ruptured Duck's* left side and held it there. Our wingtips were separated by less than five feet, as if our two ships were one.

"Looks like you've done a bit of formation work yourself," I radioed.

"Been awhile."

The controller's voice crackled in my headset. "Cessna Four Charlie Lima, flight of two, four miles outside of Jared intersection. Turn right, heading zero-six-five, vectors to final approach course. Maintain 2,000 feet until established. Cleared to land, ILS runway 8. We've rolled the equipment for you, just in case."

I repeated the instructions to the controller, leaving out the part about the "equipment," also known as the airport crash trucks, whose crews rarely get any *real* action to speak of and were probably salivating at the possibility.

The Mooney pilot repeated that his fuel gauge needles were bouncing on empty.

"Think positive," I radioed him. "We'll be down soon."

"Hopefully not too soon," he said.

We started down through the soup.

I wish I could say that it was a descent into hell. That flying blind, we iced up and spiraled out of control, managing to pull out only inches from impact. Or that visibility was so limited, we nearly collided and only by some miracle cheated death. But that would've been the Hollywood version. This wasn't. With the Mooney a wispy ghost glued to my left wing, I centered the localizer and glide slope needles on my VOR and rode them down like I'd done on countless other instrument approaches under far lousier conditions. At 300 feet, the clouds gave way and there was the runway, half a mile dead ahead.

Booyah.

"That's one I owe you," the Mooney pilot radioed.

"Rock on."

I shoved my throttle to the firewall, informed the tower I was initiating a missed approach and climbed back into the soup.

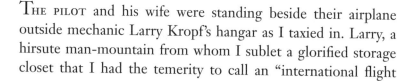

THE PILOT and his wife were standing beside their airplane outside mechanic Larry Kropf's hangar as I taxied in. Larry, a hirsute man-mountain from whom I sublet a glorified storage closet that I had the temerity to call an "international flight school," already had the Mooney's cowling open and was noodling around inside the engine compartment. He was wearing his usual low-riding, blue Dickies work pants, revealing his usual six inches of butt crack, and a faded, oil-smeared gray T-shirt that said on the back, "In dog years, I'm dead."

I toggled off the *Ruptured Duck*'s avionics master switch and pulled the mixture control. The Mooney pilot had my door open and was shaking my hand almost before the propeller had stopped spinning.

"You're one helluva stick, fella," he said.

"If I was, I'd definitely be making more money than I am." He grinned. "You must be flying for a regional carrier."

"He's a flight instructor," Larry said. "A broke one at that."

"Thanks, Larry. I love you, too."

"My name's Walker," the Mooney pilot said, still pumping my hand.

"Cordell Logan."

"Well, it's a damn pleasure, Mr. Logan."

He volunteered that he and his wife were flying home to San Diego after attending a charity fund-raiser in Carmel when his vacuum pump gave up the ghost. Larry had already concluded that the pump was beyond repair and would need replacing. There was also a problem apparently with the fuel sensors on Walker's plane. Even though the gauges had indicated his wing tanks were all but dry, the Mooney, as it turned out, still had plenty of gas left.

"How long you figure it'll take to fix everything?" Walker's wife asked Larry.

"I get the parts in, you'll be on your way tomorrow afternoon."

"Guess it looks like we're laying over in Rancho Bonita." Walker turned to me. "I'd appreciate a hotel recommendation. Something reasonably priced, if there is such a thing around these parts."

"Good luck with that," I said, almost laughing as I climbed out of my plane.

Dwarfed on one side by verdant, 4,000-foot mountains, and cuddled on the other by the Pacific, Rancho Bonita perches on a hilly, south-facing strip of earth that is among the most picturesque and least affordable locales in all of America. An average two-bedroom fixer can run close to $1 million. A gallon of gas costs twenty-five cents more than anywhere else on the mainland. Everything is more expensive in "California's Monaco," as the city's landed gentry like to call it. But the trust fund babies and reclusive show biz luminaries who make up a disproportionate percentage of its population rarely complain. Nor, for that matter, do Rancho Bonita's many other, lesser residents. Surrounded by natural beauty and graced with arguably the most perfect weather on the planet, everybody smiles a lot and counts their blessings, even if it means scrounging for work and slowly draining their life savings in the process.

"I know where there's a flophouse downtown," Larry said, his head still buried in the Mooney's engine compartment. "Put my in-laws up there last time they were in town. It's clean and cheap. They even have Magic Fingers."

Walker's wife gave a quizzical look. "Magic Fingers?"

"You stick a quarter in a machine," I said, "and the bed vibrates your fillings while you tell yourself it feels like a real massage."

She smiled and took my hand firmly. "You saved our lives today. How can we ever repay you?"

A few methods came readily to mind. Amply proportioned in all the right places, Mrs. Walker was dressed in black silk slacks, glossy black pumps with high heels, and a scoop-neck, long-sleeved knit top that matched the honeyed hue of her shoulder-length tresses. She wore a small fortune in gold along with the air of an exceptionally attractive, middle-age woman long accustomed to men drooling over her.

"It was my pleasure, Mrs. Walker," I said, reminding myself she was married and that part of me wished I still was. "I was just happy to help."

"Call me Crissy, please."

Larry yanked his head out of the Mooney's engine compartment like it was on fire. He scrunched up his veined, bulbous nose and gaped at her through the half-inch-thick lenses of his Buddy Holly glasses.

"Crissy Walker? Playmate of the Year? *That* Crissy Walker?" The smile drained from her face. "You must have me confused with someone else."

"C'mon, I know it's you. It *is* you, isn't it?"

She exhaled. "I haven't been *that* Crissy Walker in over twenty years."

"I *knew* it." Larry squealed like a kid come Christmas morning, which would've sounded cute had he actually been a kid. Not so cute coming from a guy who looks like the "before" picture in a Lap-Band infomercial. He wiped his greasy paw on his T-shirt, then offered it to her. "I'm a huge fan," he said. "I used to look at your photo spread all the time. Sometimes three, four times a day."

"Way too much information, Larry," I said.

Crissy shook his hand tepidly.

Truth be told, I'd spent a little time myself admiring Crissy Walker's pictures back in the day. We all did, my fellow Air Force Academy cadets and I. Who could blame us? There she was, stretched out on the wing of a B-17, wearing nothing more than a World War II bomber pilot's cap and a smoldering, come-fly-with-me smile. The years had done little to diminish her emerald-eyed sensuality. But unlike my lascivious friend Larry, I was less awed by the former centerfold than I was by her husband. For the first time I could ever remember, I was truly starstruck.

"You're Hub Walker," I said.

He shrugged and smiled, embarrassed at being recognized. "Reckon I am."

I resisted the urge to squeal myself. Not because Walker was a big deal in film or on TV—why the world slathers adoration on mostly short, insecure people who stand in front of cameras pretending to be taller, self-assured people is beyond me. No, the reason I went weak in the knees was because in aviation circles, Hub Walker was nothing short of a living legend.

He was a natural pilot—talented enough to have flown with the Air Force's Thunderbirds demonstration team. In Vietnam, he'd been a forward air controller, a Southern country boy piloting unarmed O-2 Skymasters at low level over the jungle canopy to purposely draw enemy fire, then directing fighter-bombers in to attack. Twice he'd been awarded the Distinguished Flying Cross for bravery. In 1972, he'd intentionally crash-landed in a rice paddy to protect a Navy pilot who'd been shot down. Though badly wounded himself, Walker held off an entire NVA platoon for nearly an hour with nothing more than a German Luger pistol his father, a World War I doughboy, had given him. For his pluck, Hub Walker received the Medal of Honor.

Ceremonial jobs with defense contractors soon followed. He got paid big bucks to attend cocktail soirées and play golf with Congressional power brokers. He also grew addicted to prescription painkillers. Guilt-ridden at having survived combat when so many of his squadron mates hadn't, he married his psychotherapist, who would die during labor less than a year later giving birth to their only child, a girl Walker named Ruth. A few years later, during a Memorial Day barbecue at the Playboy Mansion honoring America's fighting men and women, he met Crissy.

As I remembered it, she'd grown up Appalachian poor, the tomboy daughter of a veteran Air Force mechanic who'd instilled in her an appreciation of how airplanes worked, and a love of the outdoors. But with the visage of an angel and a body like vice itself, Crissy's ambitions extended far beyond the humble hollers of her roots. She'd attended beauty college for awhile, dropped out to work as a flight attendant, and ended up posing *au naturel* on the pages of America's most popular monthly men's publication.

Walker would later thank Crissy for helping him beat his drug addiction and rescuing him from thoughts of suicide. She, in turn, would credit Walker for giving her life true purpose. Being the loving, supportive wife of a national icon was more than she ever could have hoped for growing up. They eloped to Las Vegas a month after meeting.

Their fairy-tale romance was profiled in magazines from *People* to *Flying*. I remembered reading one especially breathless article in *Cosmopolitan* between missions in our ready room outside Dammam during Desert Storm. The piece was headlined, "The Hero and the Hottie: A High-Altitude Love Story." It made the rounds among my fellow sex-starved fighter jocks as quickly as Crissy Walker's centerfold when I was at the Academy, where those of us on the football team voted her "Most Likely to Make You Feel Funny in Your Jockstrap."

Larry dug a felt-tip pen out of his own pants, lifted his T-shirt, and asked her to autograph his massive gut.

"You've gotta be kidding," she said.

"I'd never kid about what could be the greatest moment of my life."

"Your wife might not think it's so great," I said.

"Mind your own business, Logan. Besides, Doreen'll never know. She hasn't seen me in the buff with the lights on for years. She has a heart condition. The shock would probably kill her."

"I don't sign body parts," Crissy said.

"What if I knocked a hundred bucks off that replacement vacuum pump?"

"No."

"OK. One-fifty. I gotta at least cover my costs."

"No. And no means no. Not at any price. You got that?" She stormed past us, into the restroom of Larry's hangar, and slammed the door shut.

Walker shrugged apologetically. "My wife gets a tad embarrassed over some of the decisions she made in her younger days. I'm happy to pay full price for the pump."

"Suit yourself."

A dejected Larry stuffed the pen in his pocket and went back to work on Hub Walker's Mooney.

That night, over dinner on his dime, Walker insisted on telling me about how his daughter had been murdered, then offered me work that made me wish in hindsight I'd been born rich.

Two

Crissy Walker was in a fish mood. I recommended a cozy seafood place called Hooked at the far end of the municipal wharf where I always ordered the grilled wild sea bass with salsa fresco and a whisper of cilantro. Walker and his wife both went with steamed crab legs. From our table, the street lights onshore were gauzy starbursts, refracted in the mist that had settled thick and damp over the Rancho Bonita waterfront.

"Ask anybody," Walker said, downing his third Jack Daniel's and signaling the waiter for another. "My daughter was a knockout. Smart as a whip, too. Second in her class at Annapolis."

He pulled out his wallet and pulled out a picture of an athletic-looking brunette with strikingly blue eyes. She was wearing Navy whites and flanked by eight other cadets identically dressed, all grinning into the camera and holding hand-lettered signs that said, "Beat Army!" They all looked like they had their whole lives ahead of them, but none more so than Walker's daughter, Ruth. He was right. She was a knockout.

"That's what happens when you raise your kid in a Navy town," Walker said with a bittersweet smile. "She never did want to go the Air Force route like her old man."

"You did good work, Hub."

I handed him back his photo. He looked away, out onto the dark ocean, his eyes moist, hoping I wouldn't notice them.

Crissy leaned her head on his shoulder and stroked his arm affectionately. "I was only her stepmom, which I knew Ruth resented sometimes, but I don't know how I could've loved her any more."

Nearly a decade had passed, Walker said, since two SEAL team snipers out for a leisurely, ten-mile midnight run found his daughter's body sprawled in the sandy bluffs behind Coronado beach, about a half-mile from the Center for Naval Special Warfare, where West Coast SEALs do much of their training.

"She died," Walker nodded, gazing out the windows and into the murk, "on a night just like this."

I asked if her killer was ever caught.

"They stuck a needle in him out in Indiana about a month ago. Ten years of appeals before he finally ran out the clock. The feds offered to pay our airfare so we could come out and watch, but I was worried I might put the sumbitch out of his misery myself. They put us up in a hotel in San Diego instead and put it on closed circuit TV."

"I couldn't watch it," Crissy said.

"I did," Walker said, staring glumly down at his drink. "Enjoyed every minute of it."

Part of me wanted to offer a congratulatory toast. A rabid dog had gotten what he deserved. I'd helped exterminate a few of them myself working for the government, before I burned out, and before Savannah left me. After we divorced, I did some serious soul-searching and went looking for a new line of work. That's when I found civilian flight instruction and the Buddha, who tends to frown on anything that smacks remotely of the kill-'em-all, let-God-sort-'em-out mind-set with which I'd been leading my life. I wasn't sure where I stood anymore on the debate over state-sanctioned execution, only that I was glad I wasn't the one to decide when to flip the tap.

Our tattooed, ear-studded, twenty-something server, who'd introduced himself at the outset of the evening as Gary, arrived with a fresh tumbler of whiskey for Walker. He ignored my empty water glass and tried not to stare at Crissy's breasts.

"Another wine for the lady?"

"Please."

The waiter's lips curled in a leering smile as a thought came to him. "Excuse me for asking, but didn't I see you in *Playboy*, like, twenty years ago?"

She raised her gaze to meet his, her eyes suddenly hard like jade.

"You have no idea," Crissy said, "how often I get that."

Gary got the hint and swallowed hard. "Be right back with that wine."

"I could use some more water," I said, but the waiter apparently didn't hear me, or pretended not to, as he headed for the kitchen. I thought of going after him, putting him in a wrist lock or an arm bar and making him refill my glass. But that would've been bad karma. I'd probably come back in the next life as Gary's busboy or, worse, his tattoo artist. I excused myself and fetched a water pitcher sitting on a shelf near the cashier's stand. When I came back to the table, Walker was weeping whiskey tears.

"Losing a child, that's something you don't ever get over," he said. "You wake up with it every morning. When your head hits that pillow every night, it's the last thought on your mind."

Crissy rubbed his shoulder and told him everything was OK.

"It's not OK, Crissy. It'll never be OK." He swiped tears with the back of his hand and looked at me straight. "I want to tell you how she died."

Not to sound insensitive, but I didn't want to hear it. We mere mortals prefer our heroes unscathed by the kind of tragedies that randomly befall the rest of us, none being greater than having to bury a child. I didn't know why he felt compelled to confide the painful details of so substantial a loss with someone he'd known all of one day, but changing the subject was a nonstarter. Hub Walker owned a Medal of Honor. Who was I to tell him no?

"Ruthie was a systems engineer, computers," he said. "Served on a guided missile frigate after graduation. She didn't much like sea duty, though. Never got past the throwing-up part."

After she left the Navy, Walker said, he'd helped her land a job by introducing her to Greg Castle, the president of Castle Robotics, Ltd., a small but upcoming defense contractor headquartered east of San Diego in the hardscrabble suburb of El Cajon. Castle Robotics developed aerial drones for the Pentagon. Walker had done some promotional work for Castle's company, and Castle was only too happy to hire Ruth as a computer design specialist. It was in that capacity that she met and began dating a cocky young engineer who worked for one of Castle Robotics' main competitors, another San Diego-based contractor, Applied Combat Systems. Ruth's new beau came from old money in Marin County. He'd gone to Stanford and boxed middleweight on the university's intramural team. His name, Walker said, was Dorian Munz.

"They broke up, but not before Ruth got pregnant," Walker said, blowing his nose with a cocktail napkin. "Munz didn't want her having the baby. Told her he wasn't about to be making child support payments the rest of his life. That's when she told him it wasn't his baby anyhow."

Ruth would give birth to a girl she named Ryder. Munz grew convinced that the infant's father was Ruth's married boss, Greg Castle, who already had four children of his own. Castle dismissed Munz's claim as "laughable."

"Ruthie never would tell me who the real father was," Walker said, "only that it was her own damn business and nobody else's. She was a hardhead. Just like her old man."

"That was Ruthie," Crissy said, smiling wistfully, "always doing things her own way."

According to Walker, Munz became suspicious that Ruth was spreading rumors about him: that he'd become fond of cocaine; that he'd developed a taste for high-end hookers. True or otherwise, they were the kind of rumors that can cost a man his top-level security clearance and his career in the defense industry. Dorian Munz would soon lose both. He started threatening Ruth over the telephone, Walker said, then began stalking her. Ruth took out a restraining order. Munz ignored it. He shadowed her to and from work, when she went to the grocery store, on dates.

"Phone records show that Munz called Ruthie the night she got killed," Walker said. "We don't know all of what was said, but the FBI thinks he lured her out by offering some kind of truce. She agreed to meet him on Coronado. That's where they found her. She'd been stabbed."

Because Ruth Walker's body was discovered on Navy property, the case was quickly deemed federal. The U.S. Attorneys' office announced in short order it would seek the death penalty. Munz's lawyer argued that the government's decision was influenced unfairly by the fact that the victim's father was a Medal of Honor recipient. But Hub Walker insisted that his military accomplishments had nothing to do with it.

"The evidence against that miserable piece of filth," he said, "was thicker than maggots on a dead possum."

Southern colloquialisms. People are never merely upset. They're angrier than a pack mule with a mouthful of bees. They're never simply at a loss for words. They're as tongue-tied as a coon hound chompin' peanut butter crackers.

"At least he's no longer taking up space," I said, hoisting my glass. "To closure."

"There's no such a thing," Walker said sadly.

He stared into the night, grieving over the loss of an only child, and all I wanted to do was get the hell out of there. I'm the first to admit, comforting others is not one of my strong suits. We're born alone, we die alone, and in between, with rare exceptions, people invariably disappoint and deceive us. In the end, even in combat, the only human being you can count on is you. But the Buddha is all about understanding, and I'm all about trying to be a more compassionate, understanding human being, no matter how impossible the task might seem at times. And so, reluctantly, I swallowed down the urge to un-ass myself from my chair, and reached over and gripped Walker's thin arm supportively.

"What's done is done, Hub."

"I only wish." He looked over at me, fisting tears from his eyes. "After you left the airfield today, your mechanic buddy, Larry, told me you used to work some kind of intelligence assignment. Said he didn't know much about it. Said the Los Angeles police couldn't figure out who killed your ex-wife's husband and you did. That true?"

Where to begin? Yes, it was true that after my fighter pilot days were cut short by a gimpy knee from days playing football for the Academy, I was transferred to Air Force intelligence and eventually to a Tier One Ultra unit within the Defense Department code-named "Alpha," where operators were referred to as "go-to guys." We functioned essentially as human guided missiles, hunting down terrorists abroad. That was before the White House got wind of our operations and shut us down for fear of political backlash. And, yes, it was true that I'd reluctantly agreed to assist in the murder investigation of the lowlife my ex-wife, Savannah, had left me for—Arlo Echevarria, my former Alpha commander—but only because her father had offered me $25,000 to do so. I'd subsequently spent most of that money covering an engine overhaul on my airplane, and paying Larry some of the back rent I owed him, which more or less put me back in the financial doghouse. Hub Walker, however, didn't need to hear all that. So I responded to his question with what I concluded was a brilliantly deflecting one of my own:

"What's that got to do with the price of eggs?"

"I want you to help prove that Greg Castle had nothing to do with my daughter's murder."

I looked at him, not understanding. "Unless I'm mistaken, Hub, you just said the evidence against this guy, Dorian Munz, was 'thicker than maggots on a dead possum.' I assume the jury must've agreed, or else they wouldn't have put him on the bus to hell. Or am I missing something here?"

Apparently I was.

As Walker described it, when Munz was asked if he had anything to say before being executed, he said plenty. He had proclaimed his innocence, as he'd done many times before. Only this time, he asserted that Ruth Walker had been murdered after discovering that her boss, Greg Castle, had been bilking the Defense Department out of millions of dollars in fraudulent overcharges. According to Munz, Castle killed Ruth—or paid somebody to kill her—before she could go to the feds with proof. While Munz's allegations failed to produce the reprieve that he'd hoped for, they did generate widespread news reports in San Diego.

"The press," Walker said, "lapped it up."

The result was a public relations nightmare for Castle Robotics and for Castle personally. The company's chances of securing Defense Department contracts were in jeopardy, as was Castle's marriage.

"I've known Greg Castle for years," Walker said. "He's a good family man. Honorable as the day is long. I *know* he had nothin' to do with Ruthie's murder. But that's not the impression everybody in San Diego has, what with everything Munz said before he died. You spend a week or so snooping around, get me something I can throw the news media, something to show that Munz was talking out the side of his filthy, lying mouth before they executed him, and I'll pay you $10,000, plus expenses."

"I'm a flight instructor, Hub, not Kojak."

"But you *did* used to work intelligence assignments, correct?" Hub said.

I shrugged.

"Well, that means in my book you *were* an investigator. And I got an inclination that if you were as good at investigating as you are flying, it'll be money well spent."

"Come down to San Diego," Crissy said. "You can stay with us. We have a very nice place in La Jolla. Bring your wife. I'm sure she'd enjoy a little vacation."

"I'm not married."

"Well, you must have a girlfriend."

I shook my head.

"*Boy*friend?" Walker said with one eyebrow raised.

"Not that there's anything wrong with that," Crissy quickly added.

"What I have is a cat. And that relationship is definitely on shaky ground."

"Sounds to me like what you need is *The Cat Communicator*."

I looked at her.

"It's a reality show," Crissy said enthusiastically. "He's like *The Dog Whisperer*, only he deals with badly behaved cats. People call him up when they're having problems with their kitties. He comes over and straightens them out."

"*The Cat Communicator*. Can't say I've ever seen it."

"That's because it's still in development. That's what I do. I'm a TV producer—trying to be, anyway."

I wondered how many episodes of *The Cat Communicator* would involve issues such as retaliatory scratching and urination.

"Here's the deal," Hub said, "Larry told me you're short on flight students right now. We both know you could use the money. Plus, it'd be a way for Crissy and me to pay you back for all that you did for us today, helping us get through that cloud deck and all."

A quote from Thoreau bubbled up from the tar pits of my brain, an artifact from my Air Force Academy days. The first time I'd heard it was during my doolie year, when a fourth-year cadet upbraided me in a hallway after I deigned to point out that being a military pilot afforded certain privileges, not the least of which was earning a livable wage. Leaning in close, his nose squishing mine, the upperclassman reminded me that one joins the armed forces of the United States to serve his country, not to service his bank account. "Money," he seethed, "is not required to buy one necessity of the soul."

Maybe not. But money *is* required to cover the bills, of which I unfortunately had plenty.

Hub Walker jotted down his cell phone number on his wife's cocktail napkin and slid it across the table. I said I'd sleep on his offer and get back to him in the morning.

<hr/>

KIDDIOT, THE world's dumbest cat, sniffed his dish as if the chow I'd just served him had been stored in a Cold War-era fallout shelter.

"Ten million cats starving to death in China, who would all *kill* for a can of Savory Salmon Feast in Delectable Gravy, and you act like the health department's gonna come barging in here any minute and arrest me on code violations."

Kiddiot flicked his orange bottlebrush tail like he was annoyed, which was his default state, and climbed out his cat door, departing the converted two-car garage apartment that was our home. I couldn't much fault his disinterest in the *plat du jour*. My eighty-eight-year-old landlady, Mrs. Schmulowitz, a retired elementary school P.E. teacher, frequently served him chopped liver with fresh Nova Scotia lox—on fine china, no less. I probably would've turned up my nose at canned Savory Salmon Feast, too, gravy or no gravy.

I showered and shampooed, flossed and brushed, trimmed my beard, eased into bed, and turned off the light. Mindful of my breathing, I tried to relax my mind, to reach that elusively transcendental state of enlightenment that real Buddhists are always clucking about, the one I've never come close to reaching, the one that would've allowed me to consider Hub Walker's offer of employment with complete, objective clarity. That was the plan, anyway. I was asleep before I knew it, dreaming about the only man I ever stabbed to death.

He was toking on a hash pipe, standing outside the alley entrance of an Amsterdam brothel where two Algerian brothers, both al-Qaeda financiers, were enjoying an evening out. To eliminate the brothers, my Alpha team members and I would first have to dispatch their bodyguard. I drew the job. My heart pounded in my ears as I eased in from behind and crooked my arm around his chest to stop him from reaching his shoulder holster, then thrust the tip of my blade into the side of his neck, slicing outward to hopefully avoid the blood spray and prevent him from shouting out. I was lowering his limp body to the ground when my cell phone rang me awake.

"You asleep?"

Groggily I glanced at the digital clock sitting on the wooden orange crate that doubled as my nightstand. It said 3:30 A.M.

"Who sleeps at this hour, Savannah? I'm out clubbing. I'm dancing the rumba."

"You don't dance, Logan. If dancing were any easier, it would be called football. Isn't that what you told me once?"

"Possibly." I rubbed my eyes. "You doing OK?"

"Fine."

"Then why are you calling me at 3:30 in the morning?"

"Just to talk."

"We talked all weekend."

"That wasn't talking, Logan. I believe that would be defined as 'heated debate.' "

"I stand corrected."

Our weekend together, in which we'd agreed beforehand to sleep separately in the exquisite villa Savannah's father bought for her high in the Hollywood Hills, most certainly had its moments. We smiled over tender memories. We exchanged a few soulful gazes over candlelit dinners at her kitchen table, the kind that can prod a man's glands to action without it even dawning on him that he has glands. Our hands brushed. We may have even come close to kissing once or twice. But mostly we bickered, hurling accusations and occasional insults at each other like so many pie tins.

You left me for another man.

You left me no choice. You checked out on me emotionally long before I ever packed my bags.

Gum surgery would have been more pleasant.

Nearly seven years had lapsed since the end of our marriage. Not a day had gone by since when my stomach did not grind over the realization of how big a mistake I'd made, letting her go as easily as I did. Savannah Carlisle Logan Echevarria was intelligent, compassionate, and indisputably beautiful. There were times when I could not look into her depthless mahogany eyes for fear that I was not worthy of such a view. Plus her wildcatting oilman father was obscenely wealthy. She was, in other words, the ultimate catch, the proverbial total package.

Don't get me wrong. The total package was not without its flaws. At forty-three, Savannah could be strong-willed beyond all reason and argumentative just for the hell of it. There was also that small matter of her having dumped me for my former Alpha team leader, Arlo Echevarria. True, as she complained, I'd grown increasingly distant back when I was working for the government; I was no longer "there" for her and Echevarria was. That alone should've canceled out all of her awesomeness in my memory. And yet, somehow, it didn't. I kept hope alive that someday, maybe, we would find ourselves together again. My desire to recapture what we once enjoyed was a feeling to be both savored and loathed all at once—savored because it reminded me of a time in my life when I was never happier; loathed because it was a time in my life when I was never more vulnerable. The yin and the yang. I wondered if Savannah didn't suffer the same ambivalence.

"I've been thinking it over," she said, "and I think I know what our issue was this weekend."

"I happen to dislike bananas and you love them?"

"Not bananas."

"Fruit should be round, Savannah, not shaped like phallic objects. I'll just let it go at that."

"I'm trying to be serious here, Logan."

"OK, what was our issue?"

"Location. We were in my house. I used to live with someone else in this house. So, naturally you were going to be on edge, which put me on edge. By reenacting our perpetual relationship gridlock on an unbalanced stage, we fell into antagonistic patterns of communication. Clearly, it was a recipe for disaster."

"That's very impressive psychobabble, coming from a fashion model."

"I don't model anymore, Logan. I told you. I'm a life coach."

"A life coach. How does that work exactly? You send off for some mail-order certificate that gives you license to tell people how to manage their lives?"

"I didn't send off for *some certificate*, Logan," she said, the rising agitation in her voice hard to miss. "I earned a master's degree in psychology from UCLA. I've also done extensive postgraduate reading."

"I could check out every book at the library on rocket telemetry. It wouldn't make me Wernher von Braun."

Cold silence filtered from the other end of the line. I'd overstepped. Yet again.

"I'm sorry, Savannah. I didn't mean to offend you."

"Like hell you didn't. That's always been your problem, Logan. You think you can say anything to anybody and get away with it. Is that who you are deep down? Somebody who enjoys hurting people for no reason?"

"Not usually. Having a reason helps immeasurably."

"You're so full of crap, you know that? I don't even know you anymore. I'm not sure I ever did."

"You knew me."

"Nobody knows you, Logan. They only know what you *want* them to know. You put up walls. You let no one in. We were married for eight years, eight *years*. I never even knew what you did for a living, what you and Arlo *really* did—and I was your *wife*, for god's sake."

"We've been over and over this, Savannah."

"Have you considered seeing a therapist? Therapy would do you a ton of good."

"Pay some guy two hundred bucks an hour so he can tell me my problem was that I wasn't breast-fed? Thanks, I think I'll pass."

"You have trust issues."

"I have trust issues. Gosh, Savannah, do you think it could *possibly* have anything to do with my wife having dumped me for my best friend?"

She said nothing. There was nothing to say.

Check and mate.

I'd undergone regular psychoanalytical assessments as a member of the military. When the government of the United States authorizes you to kill other human beings, it wants to be assured that you'll be reasonably selective when doing so. Sitting across the desk from a military shrink, you learn quickly what answers he or she is looking for, how to game the exam, because you both know that too much has been invested in your training, and that you're too lethal a weapon to be shelved. *I kill because it's my duty, Doctor, not because I'm addicted to the hunt. Do I see them in my sleep, the dozens whose lives I've extinguished, some more gruesomely than you could ever imagine? Sometimes. But who doesn't have an occasional nightmare? Nature of the beast, right, Doc?* I passed every mental evaluation I ever took. But that didn't mean I didn't give serious consideration to Savannah's suggestion.

Though she didn't know it, I'd actually gone to a psychiatrist when our marriage was foundering. I'd selected him randomly from the Yellow Pages, a corpulent, middle-aged man who maintained his practice on a houseboat in Sausalito and whose hands trembled all the time, like he was living atop the San Andreas Fault. He spent forty-five minutes asking me how I felt about having been abandoned at birth by my heroin-addicted teenaged mother, and how I felt about having been brought up mostly by strangers, bounced among more foster homes than I cared to remember. I told him I was fine with all of it. You can't change the past, I said. All you can do in life is move forward. The shrink recommended we commence twice-weekly counseling sessions immediately. I never went back.

"What if we met on neutral turf next time?" I told Savannah. "Some place that doesn't remind me so much of Arlo."

"Somewhere that doesn't engender ingrained resentments. That's an excellent idea, Logan. Any place in particular you have in mind?"

"What about Costco? I'm running low on cat food. We could meet at the one in Burbank. That's pretty close to your house, is it not?"

"You want to talk about reconciliation at Costco. Can you be serious, Logan, please, for once in your life?"

"I am serious. I don't feel at all resentful at Costco. In fact, I usually feel pretty great at Costco, especially when they're handing out lots of samples. You know the expression, 'There's no such thing as a free lunch?' Whoever said it has never been to Costco."

"I'm hanging up now, Logan."

And she did.

I tried going back to sleep but I couldn't. The fog had dissipated, giving way to a dinner plate moon that bathed Mrs. Schmulowitz's small, perfectly tended backyard in a creamy luminance no mini-blinds could filter out. The coyotes were yipping up in the hills above town. Sometimes, they ventured down to prowl Rancho Bonita in search of four-legged midnight snacks. I debated going out and trying to convince Kiddiot to come inside, but I knew he'd only blow me off.

We'd first met one morning when I went outside to get the newspaper and found him curled asleep on the hood of my truck. When I tried to pick him up to put him on the ground, he growled softly without bothering to open his eyes. So I left him there. He was doing no harm, I figured. I came back out a half-hour later to head up to the airport and he was gone.

That evening, I was reading—Bertrand Russell, if I remember correctly—when something banged loudly against the wall of my converted garage apartment. I put down my book, grabbed my revolver, flung open the door, and found Kiddiot sitting there in all of his oversized orange glory. He trotted in as if he owned the place. I poured a little milk into a mug and offered him part of a leftover chicken burrito. He approached, sniffing them like they were both radioactive, then hopped up on my bed, stretched out, and went to sleep on my pillow with his tongue hanging out. He wouldn't leave after that.

I posted "cat found" notices around the neighborhood, but no one ever called. Where he came from, I couldn't say. I dubbed him Kiddiot because he seemed unwilling to comprehend anything, including his new name, even though I am certain he understood everything I ever said to him. Mark Twain once said that a man who carries a cat by the tail learns something he can learn in no other way. I learned that Kiddiot didn't give a damn what anybody thought. He led life on his own terms, wholly and unapologetically. You've got to admire that.

He'd be fine, I told myself.

I punched my pillow and flopped from my left side to my right, trying to find a comfortable position, but sleep eluded me. My insomniac thoughts swirled around Savannah, as they always did. Maybe on neutral turf, we *could* work toward something approaching what we once had. I thought about the temporary employment Hub Walker had offered me. Getting paid to roam around San Diego for a few days while getting reacquainted with Savannah? The idea grew on me.

I called her back.

"Forget it, Logan. I'm not going to Costco with you."

"OK, forget Costco. What about San Diego? I've been offered a gig down there. Should take less than a week. We could hang out."

"Could we go to SeaWorld? I've never been there."

"If that's how you want to spend your time."

"What's wrong with SeaWorld?"

"Who said anything's wrong with SeaWorld? SeaWorld's fine."

"It's just that you don't sound too excited about the idea of going."

"Did you not just hear what I said?"

"If you don't want to go to SeaWorld, Logan, tell me. It's not like you're going to hurt my feelings. I just thought it would be something fun to do together, that's all. See Shamu. Pet the dolphins."

As evenly as I could, I said, "I'm in."

"When are you planning to go? I'd probably need to re-schedule a few clients."

"As soon as I find out, I'll let you know."

"Fine."

"Good."

Awkward silence.

"Sweet dreams, Logan."

"You, too, Savannah."

The line went dead.

I lay back, my hands behind my head, feeling pretty special about the aspiring Zen me. There are three fundamental rules in Buddhism. The first is that nothing is fixed or permanent. The second is that change is possible. I'd exercised the first rule by my willingness to shelve whatever lingering resentments I harbored toward my divorce, and the second by proposing to Savannah an alternative path toward reconciliation: we would go to SeaWorld. But as I closed my eyes, trying to get my brain to call it a night, I forgot all about the Buddha's third tenet: Actions inevitably have consequences.

Three

The fog and low clouds had returned by the time I rolled out of bed that morning. Kiddiot had not.

Nothing to be worried about, I assured myself as I did my requisite ten minutes of push-ups and abdominal crunches. Cats go missing all the time and Kiddiot was definitely a cat. He would often vanish for the day, venturing who knows where, returning that night as stealthily as he'd disappeared. I would come home to find him dozing on his favorite branch of Mrs. Schmulowitz's oak tree, the one overhanging my hammock, or atop the purple-colored refrigerator in our garage abode. In fact, all of the fixtures in our apartment were purple and secondhand. They'd once been owned by a fading rock star, one among many who reside in and around Rancho Bonita. His career had gotten a big bump after appearing on one of those celebrity rehab shows, allowing him to remodel his McMansion. Mrs. Schmulowitz snapped up his funkadelic hardware for next to nothing at a yard sale.

"You don't see colors like that in nature," Mrs. Schmulowitz marveled as we watched the movers she'd hired unload the toilet and kitchen sink in the alley that day. "They were practically giving them away. Can you imagine?"

I could. Easily. Anyone could have, with the possible exception of Mrs. Schmulowitz, who was recovering from cataract surgery at the time.

I finished my exercises, threw on a clean white polo shirt emblazoned with my flight school logo, laced up my Merrells,

and went looking for my cat. There was no sign of him anywhere in the neighborhood.

Mrs. Schmulowitz emerged from her back door as I returned
through a side gate. She was wearing lime green Nikes, pink
satin running shorts, and an oversized T-shirt illustrated with
a drawing of Muhammad Ali flattening Joe Frazier. With
her birdlike legs and profusion of spiked, thinning hair (this
week's color: harvest gold), she could've easily been mistaken
for Woodstock from the cartoon strip *Peanuts*, had Woodstock
been an octogenarian great-grandmother from Brooklyn.

"You're up early, kiddo."

"I can't find Kiddiot. You haven't seen him around lately,
have you, Mrs. Schmulowitz?"

"Can't say that I have. And lemme tell ya something, a cat
that fat is hard *not* to see. He's a porker, that cat."

"The only reason Kiddiot is overweight is because you
insist on feeding him like he's training to be a sumo wrestler."

"So he doesn't care for the slop you serve him," Mrs.
Schmulowitz said dismissively. "What am I supposed to do,
tell him no when he stares at me with those sad little eyes and
that cute little nose of his? What, you want him to *die* from
malnutrition? The cat has to eat already! Trust me, Bubeleh,
I'd do the same for you."

I told her I would be going to San Diego for a few days.
Would she mind keeping an eye out for Kiddiot and feeding
him until I got back?

"Would I mind? What, you have to ask?" Mrs. Schmulowitz patted my cheek. "Don't give it another thought. Go.
Have a marvelous time."

She crossed her feet and slowly reached down to touch her
toes, stretching for her morning run. "I'll tell you one thing, he
likes what he likes, that cat of yours. Reminds me of my second
husband. *Oy*, that man could eat. Loved frankfurters like they
were going out of style. Tells me one day he's entering the big
hotdog-eating contest on Coney Island. I tell him he's *meshuga*.

Does he listen to me? Mr. Leave Me Alone I Know What I'm Doing? Never! So, of course, he ends up in the emergency room at Bellevue, getting his stomach pumped."

"Was he OK?"

"Oh, he was fine. But they had to cancel the contest. By the time he got done stuffing three hundred hotdogs down that big mouth of his, they had none left. Completely out. It was a new world record."

"And if you expect me to believe that, Mrs. Schmulowitz . . ."

"Look it up on the Googles, you don't believe me."

"I believe you mean Google, Mrs. Schmulowitz. It's singular."

"Not on my Blueberry Blackberry it isn't."

I smiled and drove to the airport.

MY COMPANY, Above the Clouds Aviation Flight Training, Whale Watching and Aerial Charters, may have been teetering on insolvency, but my one-to-one pupil-teacher ratio was beyond compare. As was the enthusiasm of my only student, Jahangir Khan, a fresh-scrubbed, twenty-two-year-old electrical engineer from Punjab who scribbled down every word I said as if I were the combined embodiment of Orville and Wilbur Wright combined.

"The four forces that act on an airplane in flight are lift, drag, thrust, and weight. Weight is also known as gravity which, for your information, Jahangir, isn't merely a good idea, it's the law."

"Yes, yes, yes. Lift, drag, thrust, and the law of gravity. Check."

He was hunched over a spiral notepad, sitting in one of my plastic Kmart lawn chairs, while I stood before an upturned sheet of construction grade plywood that passed for a makeshift chalkboard, using a two-foot length of rebar to point out various relevant aviation illustrations I'd printed out from the Internet.

"To maintain position and direction of flight, a pilot controls rotation around three perpendicular axes that all intersect at the aircraft's center of gravity."

"Three perpendicular axes. Copy that. May I ask, Mr. Cordell, when will I be permitted to pilot the airplane without your kind assistance?"

"Not for awhile, Jahangir. You've only logged an introductory flight. First we've got to get through the basics of ground school."

"The . . . basics . . . of . . . ground . . . school," he jotted down my words verbatim. "Got it. Roger, Maverick."

The kid had somehow convinced himself I was Tom Cruise. Far be it from me to disappoint him. I let him know that I was going out of town and hoped to be back the following week. We'd go flying then.

"Call the ball," Jahangir said.

I had no idea what he meant. I'm not sure he did, either, but it sounded good.

<hr />

You don't salute generals and admirals when you hold a Medal of Honor. They salute you. You receive a monthly pension, free license plates, free travel on government aircraft, an engraved invitation to Presidential inaugurals, and a reserved burial plot at Arlington. Being a military rock star also means you rarely have to cover your own bar tab. Men have been known to sprout giant honking egos fertilized by such perks. They start believing in their own mythical greatness, tossing around their weight, acting like total fools. Hub Walker was none of that. He was a true unaffected hero, a shy, unassuming man who stared at his own shoes when he spoke. And when he did look at you straight on, what you saw was not ego, but anguish. The pain of his daughter's murder festered in his deep, sad eyes like an open wound.

"I gathered up a few names and telephone numbers, people for you to call," he said.

We'd met for coffee at a café within walking distance of the airport-convenient Marriott where he and his former Playmate wife had spent the night. He handed me a slip of paper taken from a hotel notepad along with a check for five grand made out in my name.

"Like I said last night, I don't expect you to reinvent the wheel. Just find me some info I can feed the newshounds to prove that Munz was lying about Greg Castle having anything to do with what happened to Ruthie. I'll give you the other five thousand when the job's done. Plus expenses. Sound fair?"

It sounded more than fair. It sounded like robbery. But considering that my rent was due, the radios in my aging airplane desperately needed refurbishment, and my flight school was on economic life support, I told him thank you very much and pocketed his money.

Hub's list of contacts was all of five names long. It included Greg Castle, CEO of Castle Robotics; Ruth's co-worker, Janet Bollinger, whose testimony had helped convict Munz; Assistant U.S. Attorney Stephen Tassio, who'd prosecuted Munz; and Munz's defense attorney, Charles M. Dowd.

"Munz's own attorney is willing to call him a liar?"

"Mr. Dowd got awful bent out of shape with some of the holes in Munz's story that came out during the trial. I think it's safe to say he was pretty well embarrassed."

"Lawyers don't get embarrassed, Colonel. That would require them to have feelings and a central nervous system. Either would disqualify them from taking the bar exam."

The last name on Walker's list, Eric LaDucrie, was one I recognized. A former major league pitcher known for his knuckleball and ultra right-wing politics, LaDucrie—the "Junk-man" to his fans—had ended his career with the San Diego Padres, then gone into politics. After several unsuccessful Congressional runs as a Libertarian, he'd formed "Eye for an Eye," a San Diego-based lobbying group devoted to preventing the courts from outlawing the death penalty. Anytime any criminal anywhere in the country was about to be executed, you could find the Junkman making the rounds on the morning news shows, spouting his hellfire advocacy.

"You want me to talk to Eric LaDucrie?"

"He should be the first one you talk to," Walker said. "Eric went on TV when some of these other people started protesting Munz's execution and said he had every confidence Munz was guilty. Those were his exact words—'every confidence.' The man's got an entire network of folks out there that feed him inside dope all the time. Liberal media, they won't report what he says because of his politics. You find out everything he knows and hasn't said, and I'll pass it on to the press myself."

Walker handed me a business card and repeated his wife's offer to let me stay in their guest room when I got to San Diego.

"She wanted to have coffee with us this morning, but I let her sleep in. She was fairly shook up over what happened yesterday."

"You mean the emergency landing, or Larry wanting her to sign his stomach?"

"The landing was no big deal. My wife knows enough about airplanes. She's a cool customer when it comes to flying. She just can't stand it when people bring up the 'old her,' the things she had to do back then just to eat, like posing for that magazine. Ever since we got married, all she's ever wanted to be is respected, a pillar of the community. She told me once she'd rather die than have to go back where she came from."

I knew the feeling well. People from the wrong side of the tracks—or, in my case, the feedlot—can spend a lifetime overcompensating, struggling to attain the kind of acceptance and respectability in general society denied them at birth. Crissy Walker hailed decidedly from that camp.

Walker finished his coffee and stood. "I'd like to get on over to the field, see how Larry's doing on the repairs to my plane."

"That's assuming Larry's even at the airport," I said, "and not at your hotel, trying to get your wife to sign who knows what."

Walker grinned.

We walked along a frontage road to Larry's hangar. The gray overcast had lifted a thousand feet or so, still low enough that it obscured the ridgelines of the coastal Rancho Bonita Mountains to the north. I watched a Great Blue Heron standing motionless in a field adjacent to the runways, its long sharp beak tilted earthward over a gopher hole, waiting patiently in ambush. The bird reminded me of how I once hunted terrorists.

"You mind me asking you a question, Hub?"

"Shoot."

"What was it like, getting that medal?"

He thought about it for a couple of seconds. "It's like strapping into an airplane, only you ain't flying it. You're just along for the ride. You got all these people telling you how great you are, tears in their eyes, thanking you for your service, all that happy horseshit, when you know the *real* heroes are the ones who didn't make it home." He dug his hands in his front pockets. "The truth of it is, that medal didn't mean a whole lot to me before, not really. Now, it don't mean a damn thing. I'd trade every decoration I ever got in a New York minute, everything I ever owned in this life, if I could have my daughter back for just one day."

"I read once that all the stars in the night sky are really openings in Heaven, so that all the people you've ever loved and have gone before you can shine down, to let you know they're happy."

"Wish I could believe that." We walked in silence for awhile. Then Hub said, "You got any children?"

"My ex didn't think I was ready. She said it wasn't a good idea, having kids when you're still one yourself."

"They do make you grow up right quick, I'll give your ex that much. I thought Ruthie was gonna be a boy. But you find out that don't matter much, which flavor they come out. You love 'em all just the same."

I told him Savannah and I were exploring a possible reconciliation, and that she was planning to come with me to San Diego.

"Well, I sure hope that works out for you, I really do," Hub said. "Lucky in love. Best luck of all."

I couldn't discern an ounce of disingenuousness about the man. The ancient philosophers knew all too well that legends have feet of clay. They warned as much in the sage words they left for humanities majors like me to absorb centuries later. But I saw no such flaws in Lt. Col. Hubert Bedford Walker, USAF retired, one of fewer than one hundred living recipients of America's highest military decoration. I was honored to be in his company and pleased to be in his employ.

⊶⊶⊶✺⊶⊶⊶

THE BANK teller scrutinized Walker's check with thinly veiled skepticism. She had false eyelashes and looked about twelve, which more or less matched the number of minutes I'd been waiting in line for my turn at her window.

"I may not look it," I said, leaning closer and speaking in a low, conspiratorial tone, "but I'm posing online as a Nigerian prince. The sucker who cut me that check? I've got him convinced it's seed money for an investment that'll return ten million large."

"This check is drawn on a bank in San Diego," she said, like San Diego *was* Nigeria.

"OK, the truth," I said, unable to stop myself, "I'm not really a Nigerian prince. I just found that check in the parking lot."

"Excuse me a minute." She locked her cash drawer with a key dangling from her neck and moved off twenty feet to consult her manager.

They spoke in hushed tones, shooting me questioning glances every few seconds. I assumed they would scrutinize the balance of my bank account, which was starting to resemble the federal deficit, and put a hold on the check for a couple of days until it cleared. No biggie. The manager came over. The hold, she said, would be a full week.

"That's pretty standard banking practice for non-local checks in Nigeria," she said.

She smiled, but not in the nice kind of way.

No one ever said being a smartass was without its drawbacks.

KIDDIOT WAS still gone when I got home. At least he was consistent: a cat who never failed to disappoint. I stuffed some clean clothes into a duffel bag for the trip to San Diego, along with my toothbrush, then telephoned the five people on Hub Walker's list.

My calls to prosecutor Stephen Tassio, Greg Castle of Castle Robotics, and Ruth Walker's former co-worker, Janet Bollinger, went straight to voice mail. I left detailed messages for each.

Eric LaDucrie, the ex-Big Leaguer-turned-death-sentence pitchman, answered after about ten rings. He sounded like he was in a cocktail lounge. I could hear the tinkle of a piano somewhere behind him and people laughing, talking loud. I told him that Hub Walker had hired me to dig up dirt on Dorian Munz, and that I wanted to talk to him.

"I might be able to help you out," the Junkman said, "only I'm in Washington. I'm back the day after tomorrow. Can it hold 'til then?"

I said it could and gave him my number.

My last call was to Munz's defense lawyer, Charles Dowd. He sounded inner-city African-American and harried.

"My client has passed," Dowd said. "The case was adjudicated. There's nothing more to be said beyond that."

"All I need is a half-hour of your time, Mr. Dowd. Just to clarify a few points."

"You say you're who again?"

"Cordell Logan. Hub Walker, the father of the young woman your client was convicted of killing, hired me to look into the case."

"What exactly is it you're looking for, Mr. Logan?"

"Your client, Mr. Munz, made certain allegations against Ruth Walker's boss, Greg Castle, shortly before Munz was executed."

"I'm well aware of those allegations. I believe I was there. You still haven't answered my question."

I explained how Hub Walker and Greg Castle were friends—something I was certain the attorney already knew—and that Walker hoped to help repair the damage done to Castle's reputation by Munz's spurious allegations.

"Mr. Walker would like me to gather a few statements from knowledgeable people who can affirm your client's guilt in Ruth Walker's murder. Mr. Walker would like to then pass those statements on to the news media in defense of Mr. Castle."

"The jury," Dowd said, "found the evidence against my client overwhelming. All of that evidence was introduced during proceedings in open court. All of those proceedings are available for your inspection in the office of the clerk of the court. Beyond that, again, there's nothing more I can say. Now, if you'll excuse me, Mr. Logan, I have a preliminary hearing to prepare for."

"I'm told Mr. Munz's execution was televised."

"All federal executions air on a closed video loop and are taped. No doubt so that the Justice Department can look back in perpetuity and enjoy their splendid handiwork." The contempt in Dowd's words was *prima facie*.

I asked him if he had retained a copy of the tape in his files. He said he did. I asked if I could see it.

"Why do you want to see it?"

"To determine the specific allegations Munz made against Mr. Castle before he was put to death."

"Go talk to the prosecution," Dowd said. "I'm sure they'd be more than happy to help you."

"I have a call in to Stephen Tassio."

"Steve Tassio's a world-class prick. He won't call you back. You can petition the court for a copy of the tape if you want."

"Mr. Dowd, you and I both know that could take months. I'm trying to salvage an innocent man's reputation. Your cooperation would mean the world to the victim's father and to the memory of his daughter. Please."

The lawyer was silent for a long moment. Then he sighed. "I got two girls of my own. Youngest just graduated Howard."

"You must be very proud."

"I would be if she wasn't living back home, driving my wife and me nuts. I'm trying to get her off my payroll and onto someone else's. No easy task, Mr. Logan."

I told him I could be at his office that afternoon.

"I'll give you ten minutes," Dowd said, and gave me the address. "Be here at two thirty."

My next call was to Savannah.

"I'll pick you up at the Santa Monica Airport in an hour, assuming that works for you. We'll fly down to San Diego from there."

"I've been having second thoughts," she said.

"About . . . ?"

"Quite frankly, you."

"Oh, here we go."

"You seem conflicted about wanting to get back together, Logan. You say you want to give it another shot, but that's not the vibe I'm getting."

"Is this about Shamu?"

"Shamu?"

"You want to go to SeaWorld. I didn't start doing cartwheels over the idea, and now you're punishing me."

"If you're suggesting that I'm exhibiting passive-aggressive behavior, or that I'm somehow being obstructionist as a means of retaliation, you're mistaken. If anything, Logan, I'm employing a classic anticipatory coping mechanism to blunt what I perceive is your apparent reticence."

"I have no idea what you just said, but I do have a suggestion."

"I'm listening."

"I think we should just sleep together. See how *those* coping mechanisms work."

"I'm dealing with someone who's still clearly in junior high."

"Ah, yes, the old junior high scenario. OK," I said, "you be the viceprincipal and I'll play the unruly student who gets sent to your office in need of some serious *discipline*. It could be wildly entertaining."

I waited for her to laugh. I might've even settled on a polite chuckle, but there was only silence.

"I just need a little time to synthesize things in my head, that's all," she said after a long moment.

At that moment, part of me wanted to fire a Sidewinder missile into whatever remained salvageable between us, to say something irretrievably hurtful and blow up the whole ugly mess, so that we would both have reason to walk away for good. The other part, arguably the better part, realized that when it came to my ex-wife, I was incapable of pulling that emotional pin, and probably always would be.

"If you want to retreat to neutral corners," I said, "so be it."

"I'll call you, Logan."

"You do that, Savannah."

Click.

Something churned up bitter and hot from under my sternum and burned the back of my throat. I swallowed it down and started through the backyard, toward my truck, which was parked out on the street.

"Bubeleh!"

Mrs. Schmulowitz was sitting at her kitchen table, wearing her big round Liza Minnelli reading glasses, motioning me excitedly through the window to join her.

"I have something unbelievably exciting to tell you," she said as I walked in.

"You found Kiddiot?"

"Not yet."

I didn't mask my worry well.

"He'll turn up. You'll see. I'll make a nice brisket. That always gets him."

"It always gets me."

"So tell me something I don't know."

Her table was littered with color brochures from various cosmetic surgeons featuring photos of their handiwork—smiling young women in bikinis with radiant faces and flawless bodies. Rancho Bonita was loaded with them.

"So what's the exciting thing you had to tell me, Mrs. Schmulowitz?"

She beamed. "I'm getting a tummy tuck!"

"Women your age don't get their tummies tucked, Mrs. Schmulowitz. They get hip replacements and the senior discount at Denny's."

"Is that so? Well, how many women my age can do *this*?" She pushed back from the table, bent down with her palms planted on the floor and proceeded to do a handstand.

"I might get a little Botox while I'm at it, too, maybe a boob lift, the whole *schmear*," Mrs. Schmulowitz said, the blood draining to her head, her spine crackling like a bowl of Rice Krispies. "Not many eligible bachelors left out there in my demographic. You can't be too competitive these days, you know."

"You don't need cosmetic surgery, Mrs. Schmulowitz. You're perfect just the way you are."

She blew me a kiss standing upside down, then suggested delicately—to the extent that Mrs. Schmulowitz was capable of doing anything delicately—that I might want to think about having a bit of work done on my own increasingly furrowed features.

"Don't get me wrong, Bubelah, you're a total hotsy totsy," she said, "but, let's face it, none of us is getting any younger, with the possible exception of Joan Rivers. Now, you get a little filler, that schnoz of yours straightened out, *oy gevalt*, we're talking total chick magnet."

I might've taken her advice seriously, especially when it came to my sneezer which, no thanks to football and the occasional fist, resembled not so much a nose anymore as it did a geometry equation. But the dents and wrinkles one collects along the way chronicle a record of service and sacrifice, in my opinion, like ribbons earned in battle, each to be worn with pride. The last thing I wanted was a nose job.

"I appreciate the suggestion, Mrs. Schmulowitz, but I can barely afford cat food, let alone a new face."

I helped her to her feet and departed through the back door. I whistled for Kiddiot but got no response. Not that he ever responded to me anyway. Stupid cat.

I was halfway to my truck when I realized I'd forgotten my duffel bag. Back in my garage apartment, I thought I heard him under the bed, but when I got down on the concrete floor and looked, it was only a blue belly lizard, the kind Kiddiot liked to bring inside to play with until he grew bored with them, then forgot. The little reptile skittered away, past my two-inch, .357 Colt Python, which I kept under the bed, within easy reach. Force of habit told me to take the snub-nose with me to San Diego, but for what purpose? Self defense? My days of bad guys were long behind me. If anything, my mission to America's self-proclaimed "Finest City"—validating the innocence of a man falsely accused by a convicted murderer—sounded to me like a paid vacation. To vacation while armed, that was the question.

The Buddha saw no viable purpose in lethal weapons. Which explains why he was the Buddha. I see firearms as tools, as practical as any saw or drill; they can come in quite handy when bad people need killing. This difference of opinion served to underscore how many of the Buddha's precepts, in my flirtation with them, did not come naturally to my Western military mind. How does a man prone to violence by nature and training embrace a religion that preaches peace above all else?

Kneeling there on the floor, my surgically reconstructed knee aching, I debated before forcing the Buddha's teachings down like medicine, the taste of which you hopefully get used to. I stuffed the revolver between my mattress and box spring, then drove to the airport.

The Buddha, in this instance, had no idea what he was talking about.

Four

Air Traffic Control directed me southbound at 9,000 feet across downtown Los Angeles, en route to the Seal Beach VOR. There were planes big and small all over the sky, whose altitudes and headings all seemed to converge with mine. On my GPS, the *Ruptured Duck's* ground track looked less like the crow flies than a game of Pac-Man.

"Cessna Four Charlie Lima, turn right 20 degrees, vectors for traffic, a 7-6-7 at 11 moving to your 10 o'clock position, same altitude."

"Cessna Four Charlie Lima, turn left 10 degrees for a King Air, 12 o'clock, four miles northbound, 500 feet above you. Report him in sight."

"Cessna Four Charlie Lima, descend and maintain 7,000 feet. I've got a Baron at your 6 o'clock, five miles in trail, same altitude. He's showing 40 knots faster."

The air over the City of Angels was hazy brown with smog that reduced visibility to a couple of miles at best. And did I mention the turbulence? By the time I climbed, dove, and zig-zagged my way down the coast to land nearly two hours later at Montgomery Field on the northern fringes of San Diego, my left hand was cramped so badly (all pilots learn to fly using their left hand only, leaving the other free for important activities like adjusting throttles and picking noses) that I nearly had to pry my sweaty fingers from the yoke.

I taxied in and parked on the ramp in front of ritzy Champion Jet Center where a stringy brunette was working the front desk. The gold name tag pinned to her navy blue blazer identified her as "Kimberly."

As I walked in, she gestured out the window in the direction of my forty-year-old Cessna and smirked as if to amuse. "That," she said, "is one homely beast."

Kimberly was a fine one to talk. To be sure, her skin was not trimmed in oxidized orange and yellow paint, or peeling in spots like a molting snake, as was my airplane's. But with her overbite, limp pageboy haircut, and a pointy snout that would have looked right at home on an Irish wolfhound, homely was as homely said. Was I put off by her making fun of the *Ruptured Duck*? Does it rain in Oregon? Nobody insults a pilot's personal plane, even if that plane does happen to resemble a homeless person with wings. I was about to verbally lay her out, but I didn't. I decided I would take the moral high ground, turn the other cheek instead. I was proud of myself. *Maybe this Buddhism thing is working after all.*

"I'd like both tanks topped off, please, 100 low lead," I said with saccharine sweetness. "And I'll need to rent a car for a few days, if you'd be kind enough to make the arrangements."

"Certainly. I'll be pleased to help you with that, sir. I assume you'll be requiring an economy car during your visit?"

"What would make you assume that, Kimberly?"

My accusatory tone caught her off-guard. "Well, I mean . . ." She glanced toward the *Duck*, dwarfed among sleek, multimillion-dollar private jets, then back at me, as if to say, any nitwit could plainly see that I would be needing an economy car given the pile of junk I flew in on.

I planted my forearms on the glossy mahogany counter and leaned deliberately, threateningly, into Kimberly's personal space.

"I'll be requiring a Cadillac Escalade . . . *Kimberly*."

Her tongue darted nervously over her thin lips and she hunched her shoulders—sure signs of fright, which was exactly my intent.

"My pleasure, sir." Kimberly snatched up the phone and called Enterprise, if only to escape my steely gaze.

No one *requires* a three-ton sport utility vehicle whose gas mileage can be measured in negative integers. I had impulsively demanded an Escalade only because I didn't want some washed-out counter clerk who normally catered to zillionaires thinking I was one step removed from personal bankruptcy, even if in truth I was.

⟨⊙⟩

THE ESCALADE was a black gunboat with chrome rims, heated steering wheel, refrigerated cup holders, burled walnut trim, in-dash satellite navigation system, and an imposing rearview mirror presence that screamed, "Get the bleep out of my way." I felt every inch the stylin' pimp daddy as I cruised westbound along Interstate 8 through San Diego's Mission Valley. I had to admit: it was a darned comfortable ride.

I stopped off for a late lunch at El Indio, a hole-in-the-wall Mexican joint where I'd eaten frequently when I was still with Alpha, conducting joint training ops with the SEAL teams out on Coronado. We shared with the Navy guys some of our tactics—wearing ballet slippers, for example, instead of standard-issue combat boots, when sneaking up on enemy outposts. They, in turn, introduced us to their favorite watering holes, and to El Indio. I sat outside under a hazy sun and inhaled four Baja-style fish tacos. Each was as *exquisito* as I remembered. After I'd had my fill, I called and left another message for federal prosecutor Stephen Tassio. But not before I belched. Then I headed downtown.

Charles Dowd practiced law in a twenty-three-story bank tower adjacent to Horton Plaza, which had once served as San Diego's bum central before the strip clubs and dive bars all gave way to swanky eateries and a gentrified shopping mall. I forked over ten dollars and my car keys to an indifferent Salvadoran parking attendant in the basement and rode the elevator to the ninth floor.

Dowd's office was located among a warren of suites with a communal conference room and a shared receptionist—a cost-conscious arrangement intended by independent practitioners like Dowd to convey the scope and power of being associated with a swanky major law firm without actually working for one. The receptionist was bosomy and sharp featured. She put down her copy of *Entertainment Weekly*, pushing a strand of shoulder-length chestnut hair behind one ear and touching the side of her neck with her head slightly cocked.

"May I help you?"

Her gestures conveyed sexual interest. I once might've followed up on them, before Savannah became a constant on my mind.

"Cordell Logan to see Charles Dowd."

"Is Mr. Dowd expecting you?"

"He is."

She picked up her telephone, tapped a couple of buttons with the eraser end of a pencil, keeping one eye on me, and let Dowd know I was in the lobby.

"Down the hall. Last door on your right."

"'Preciate it."

"Anytime," she said with the hint of a smile.

Definitely interested.

Dowd was waiting for me outside his office in his shirtsleeves, red suspenders, and a bright paisley tie, hanging loose. The fingers of his right hand clutched a fat, unlit cigar. He was paunchy, on the north end of sixty, and wore what remained of his hair in a ragged gray Afro that brought to mind an aging, black Bozo. Nobody, however, would've characterized his temperament or intellect as clown-like.

"I appreciate you taking the time to see me."

"As I indicated," he said without shaking my hand, "you've got ten minutes."

His rumpled appearance matched the decor of his office. Case files and law books were strewn about. His desktop looked like the aftermath of a tsunami. The walls were naked but for a battery-operated clock and a framed law degree. The timepiece was hammered copper and shaped like the continent of Africa. The sheepskin was from Yale.

"I've been trying capital cases for thirty-five years," he said as he parked himself behind his desk in a well-worn leather executive chair. "Dorian Munz was as guilty as they get. That doesn't mean the government had the right to do him like it did. No man's got that right."

I sat down in a folding chair opposite his desk. "You said on the phone you'd let me have a look at Mr. Munz's closing remarks."

"You a PI?"

"Flight instructor."

"A *what*?"

"It's a long story and you've got ten minutes. If I could just see the videotape . . ."

He eyed me sideways, firing up his cigar with a lighter shaped like a gavel. "I still don't get what you're trying to get at, Mr. Logan."

"Just trying to bring a little closure to a father who lost his child."

"Closure's vastly overrated."

Dowd dug a laptop out from under a pile of legal briefs on his desk, typed in a few commands, swiveled the computer screen in my direction, checked his watch, then sat back with his feet up, smoking and gazing out at the sailboats plying San Diego Bay.

The videotape was black and white and less than a minute long. It offered few insights beyond what Hub Walker had already shared with me: Munz lay lashed to a gurney, gazing into a camera mounted on the ceiling above him. Through tears, he alleged that Ruth Walker had stumbled upon a billing scam in which Castle Robotics had ripped off Uncle Sam to the tune of nearly $10 million for work that was never performed. Ruth, he said, intended to go to the authorities with what she knew before she was killed. But that wasn't the only reason, he said, why Greg Castle wanted her dead.

"Ruth had a baby, Castle's baby," Munz said into the camera. "He wanted her to get an abortion and she said no, so he killed her—or had somebody do it for him."

Munz acknowledged that his relationship with Ruth had turned bitter but insisted he was no murderer. "I loved that girl," he declared. "I'll always love her."

The tape ended.

"What proof did Ruth Walker have that Castle's company was ripping off the Defense Department?"

"Mr. Munz received an anonymous letter about a month after he was convicted," Dowd said, flicking the ashes from his cigar into a cut crystal bowl on his desk. "All the letter said was that Castle was dirty, that Ruth Walker knew it, and that's why she died."

"Any idea who sent the letter?"

"Not a clue."

Whoever mailed it, Dowd said, also sent copies anonymously to various local news media outlets. The story dominated San Diego's newspaper and TV stations for several days before the press lost interest. Beyond that anonymous letter, Dowd said, his client had no real evidence tying Greg Castle to Ruth Walker's murder, nor for his assertion that Castle had fathered Ruth's baby. The condemned man was merely grasping at straws, hoping to forestall his execution.

"I petitioned for a retrial," Dowd said. "I argued that the letter introduced sufficient reasonable doubt. My motion, however, was denied. The Ninth Circuit held that the evidence presented by the prosecution was, and I quote, 'Overwhelming and irrefutable.'"

"Sounds like you weren't able to mount much of a defense."

Dowd's mood turned on a dime. "I'm a damn fine lawyer, Mr. Logan. Or perhaps you think people of color got no business in a court of law except wearing 'cuffs and a jumpsuit."

"I don't see color, Mr. Dowd. I only see good or bad. I meant no offense."

"Well, I *am* offended. I've been practicing law in this city for more than twenty-five years, and I don't much appreciate some *flight instructor* coming in here, questioning my legal skills." He snuffed out his cigar on the sole of his scuffed black wing tip. "Now, if you'll excuse me, I have a meeting upcoming with my investigator on another matter."

I stood. "What was the evidence against Dorian Munz that was so 'overwhelming and irrefutable'?"

"You'll find the entire case file over at the clerk of the court. You can read to your heart's content." Dowd picked up his phone and waited for me to leave. "I'm sure you can find your way out. Fly safe, Mr. Logan."

What can I say? Some of us have a knack for offending others without even trying. Call it a gift. I thanked the attorney for his time and turned to go.

Standing in the doorway, blocking my way, was a towering, well-built man with mocha-colored skin. Except for his ears, which were abnormally large for his head, he reminded me of a Doberman pinscher. Same sinewy frame. Same darkly menacing features. His untucked, green silk camp shirt bulged subtly at the right hip of his baggy jean, where his concealed pistol rode in a pancake holster. I made him for Dowd's aforesaid investigator.

"Who's this?" he asked Dowd while gazing at me hard.

"This is Mr. Logan. He's looking into the Munz case ex post facto."

"Looking into the case for who?"

"The father of the victim. I believe Mr. Logan was just leaving, weren't you, Mr. Logan?"

"Surf's up," I said to the Doberman. "Wouldn't want to keep Frankie and Annette waiting."

His eyes held steady on mine. In a previous life, I can only assume we must've crossed swords. Whatever the instinct, it was clear that his dislike of me was as instantaneous as mine was of him. At six-foot-four and 220, he had a good three inches and what looked to be about thirty pounds of steroid-fortified flank steak on me. Ah, but what I gave away in height and weight, I more than made up for in wisdom-rich years. Which is to say that if push came to shove, I was likely going to get my sage, unarmed ass stomped—not without getting in a few good thumps of my own, mind you, but stomped regardless.

"Who's Frankie and Annette?" He had a grating, raspy voice.

"Original Mouseketeers," I said. "Annette went on to have a very successful career as a professional virgin."

The human Doberman smiled frigidly. His teeth looked like something unearthed by a paleontologist. "You're a regular comedian," he said.

"My ex-wife would beg to differ."

"Let him pass, Bunny," Dowd said sternly.

Bunny? Who names a Doberman pinscher "Bunny"? I wanted to say something snide, but held my fire.

Grudgingly, Bunny stepped aside. "See you around, funny man."

"Not unless I see you first."

The receptionist winked at me as I walked out.

I might've blushed if only I could've remembered how.

—————

The clerk's office of the U.S. District Court, Southern District of California, was located a block east on Front Street, in the first floor of a modernistic, five-story building named in honor of a federal judge who, if the memorial plaque in the lobby was to be believed, never uttered an unkind word to anyone, including the hundreds of miscreants he'd sent to federal prison for the rest of their miserable lives. It was past 2:30 by the time I got there. I filled out a request form with the case number I pulled from a computer terminal, turned over my driver's license to an indifferent civil servant manning the counter, and waited for someone to retrieve the file—or, more accurately, files.

Excluding subsequent appeals, the government's proceedings against Dorian Nathan Munz filled three banker's boxes. The clerk's office closed in less than two hours. I'd need to do some serious speed reading. Skimming was more like it. I took a seat at a wooden, librarian-style table, on an unpadded wooden chair, and dove into the transcripts of the trial.

The case file made clear that attorney Dowd had pinned his client's defense almost wholly on an alibi constructed from the sketchy recollections of Janet Bollinger, a co-worker of Ruth Walker's at Castle Robotics who described herself as Ruth's "former" best friend. Bollinger had told FBI agents initially that Dorian Munz could not have possibly killed anyone during the approximately three-hour window in which Ruth was believed murdered because he'd spent that entire evening with her. On the stand, however, Bollinger recanted. She testified that she'd gotten her dates mixed up. Upon reflection, she couldn't be certain, she said, if she and Munz had been together the night Ruth Walker was killed, or whether it had been the night before. Munz's attorney pressed Bollinger. Someone had threatened her, he insisted, forcing her to change her testimony, but Janet Bollinger held fast; she'd simply gotten the dates wrong. The defense's case fell apart faster than a Kardashian marriage.

A succession of Ruth's friends and acquaintances testified that her breakup with Munz had been acrimonious, an allegation that Munz himself did not deny when he later took the stand in his own defense. Cellular phone records entered into evidence by the prosecution showed that he'd made several calls to Ruth's office and home on the day of her slaying, each lasting no more than a few seconds. They were hang-up calls, the kind meant to intimidate Ruth, the prosecution theorized. Munz countered that he'd been framed: someone had stolen his phone from his locker at the YMCA, where he swam daily, then made calls to Ruth to incriminate him.

Two prosecution witnesses testified that on the day of Ruth Walker's murder, they observed Munz at the Mystic Mocha coffee shop in San Diego's University Heights, a few blocks from Ruth's apartment. Munz seemed upset about something, both witnesses said. Munz insisted that his presence at the coffee shop that day was far from sinister; he stopped by occasionally for his favorite espresso. As for his agitated mood, he claimed to have been under pressure at work.

Ruth Walker's autopsy found that she'd been stabbed twice in the abdomen. It revealed scrapes and bruises on her hands and arms consistent with the defensive wounds of someone who'd fought for her life and lost. Munz was taken in for questioning four days after her body was found. There were incriminating bruises on the knuckles of his left hand, photos of which were also entered into evidence. He insisted during his testimony that he'd hurt himself trying to replace the oil filter on his VW Jetta. Dowd, his attorney, claimed during the trial that the bruises were proof of Munz's innocence; the accused was right handed.

Though the murder weapon was never recovered, the nature of Ruth's knife wounds showed the blade to have been approximately six inches in length and one inch wide. Munz owned a pricey set of eight steak knives fitting those specifications. The knives, ironically enough, had been a Christmas present from Ruth, given to him before their relationship soured. Dowd argued that the FBI's own laboratory examination showed all eight knives to be in pristine condition, free of any DNA that would've linked any of them to Ruth Walker's killing. Justice Department experts, however, pointed out that a well-made knife can show no sign of wear, even after years of heavy use. As for the lack of incriminating DNA on the blades, the experts testified that Munz could've simply washed off any flesh or blood after fatally stabbing his victim.

There was, meanwhile, no denying the bloody Pima cotton dress shirt that was discovered inside a trash can in the alley behind Munz's condo in San Diego's North Park neighborhood.

The monogram on the shirt's cuff bore Munz's initials. The blood was Ruth Walker's. Munz insisted on the stand that the shirt had also been stolen from his health club locker, and that whoever had framed him had taken the shirt and mopped up Ruth's blood with it.

In the end, jurors professed little interest in Munz's version of events—not with the mosaic of circumstantial evidence laid out by prosecutor Tassio and his team. The jury deliberated less than one day before finding him guilty.

By the time I looked up from the files, it was nearly 4:30. Closing time. My butt was numb. What kind of federal government shells out $2 billion for a single Stealth bomber and not $2 for a lousy seat cushion? I massaged the circulation back into my bottom, stretched my aching lower back, and returned the file boxes to the counter.

A medium-sized man in his early forties with a sallow face, short receding hair and tortoiseshell bifocals entered the clerk's office and approached me. The right sleeve of his conservatively cut gray suit hung limp and empty.

"Are you Mr. Logan?"

"Depends. You a bill collector?"

"Steve Tassio, Assistant U.S. Attorney. You called me."

I shook his left hand with mine.

"How'd you know I was here?"

"The Munz file is flagged, as are all capital cases," he said. "Anytime anyone asks to review documents in the case, the clerk's office contacts me as a matter of routine. We like to know who's snooping and why."

He gestured to the wooden table and the same unpadded chairs where'd I'd just spent the last two hours. We sat.

"I'm afraid you're spinning your wheels," Tassio said. "I can assure you, Greg Castle was in no way involved in the death of Ruth Walker. Dorian Munz most definitely was."

"I never implied Mr. Castle was involved. Just the opposite. Ruth's father wants me to dredge up information that would confirm Munz was lying about Castle before you executed him."

Tassio cleared his throat, peeved. "I didn't execute him, Mr. Logan. The people of the United States did. You'll have to forgive me. I assumed you were attempting to somehow have the case reopened."

"I'm attempting to help restore the reputation of an innocent man."

"I can certainly appreciate your efforts, but, unfortunately, I can't be of much assistance. Anything I'd have to say is already on record and can be found in the case file."

"Mr. Tassio, I'm sure you can appreciate how significantly Mr. Castle was victimized by Dorian Munz's allegations. Mr. Castle is at a considerable disadvantage defending himself against those allegations because his accuser, the man you prosecuted, is now fertilizer, and the case is officially closed."

"Make your point, Mr. Logan."

"From what I understand, the local press had a field day with Munz's last-minute claims. Munz was convicted nearly ten years ago. He was executed last month. The average San Diego resident is not going to come down here, request the case file, and educate himself as to the truth of what actually went down. It would be helpful if you issued a statement saying, in effect, that Munz was lying."

"As I said, Mr. Logan, I appreciate what you're trying to do, but whatever I'd have to say about the Munz case, I already said many times, both at trial and during a very long, protracted appellate process. Beyond that, any information, or any personal opinions I may hold, would be considered privileged and confidential."

He stood. I stood and gave him my business card.

"In case you decide to reconsider."

"Good luck to you, Mr. Logan," Tassio said, extending his left hand once more. We shook.

I watched him walk out, wondering how he'd lost the arm.

The clerk shoved my driver's license across the counter like she couldn't get out of there fast enough and began turning off the office lights.

As I made my way through the courthouse lobby and toward the exit, past a couple of silver-haired U.S. marshals in blue blazers, I sensed someone's eyes on my back. When I glanced over my shoulder, I saw Steve Tassio staring at me from the elevator. Then the doors slid closed and he was gone.

Five

Bunny the Human Doberman was waiting for me when I stepped outside the federal courthouse. The plaza was steaming in the late afternoon sun. So was Bunny.

"Mr. Dowd doesn't much appreciate what you're doing," he said.

"What am I doing?"

"Asking questions. Stirring things up. Making him look bad, like he didn't do his job 'cuz Dorian Munz lost bigtime. There wasn't nothing nobody could do for that dirt bag, anyway. The case was a dog from the git-go."

"You got it all wrong, Bunny. I came to bury Caesar, not to praise him."

Bunny stared at me like I was speaking Swahili.

"Forget it. Have a lovely day."

I tried to sidestep him, but he clamped his paw on the front of my shirt and yanked me close. His breath reeked of garlic chicken.

"Best thing you can do, homeboy, is go get in your ride and go back to wherever the fuck it is you came from, before somebody gets themselves seriously hurt."

"You have exactly five seconds to remove your hand," I said, "or I will. And I guarantee you, you won't like my methods."

"Is that right? Five seconds, huh? Then what, you gonna—"

I reached down, grabbed his croutons, and squeezed like I was muscling the last bit of toothpaste out of the tube.

Bunny grunted involuntarily and held his breath. His eyes bulged.

"That probably wasn't three seconds, was it? Gosh darn. My bad. I'm gonna let you in on a little secret, Bunny—I hope you don't mind me calling you Bunny, it's just that I feel so close to you right now—but really, I wasn't counting. Which is why I was never much good at touch football. One Mississippi, two Mississippi, three Mississippi. You have to *wait* to rush the quarterback? What kind of dumbass rule is that? Now, if you wouldn't mind, I'd very much appreciate you removing your hand from my shirt before it gets wrinkled."

He let go of me, gasping for air, his face the color of egg-plant. And I didn't even have to say please.

"I'm gonna let you down now, Bunny, nice and slow, and we're gonna pretend like we never met, OK?"

He nodded in agony, then vomited. The Buddha must've been looking out for me that day because the spatter missed me entirely.

I lowered him to the ground with one hand still clutching his groin, while unholstering his .50-caliber Desert Eagle with the other. "Holy Moses, what do you shoot with this thing, mastodons?" I released him and started walking. When I was about thirty feet away, I turned and yelled, "Hey, Bunny."

He was curled like a fetus on the sidewalk, moaning, both hands clutching his throbbing love spuds. I made sure he could see me toss his gun into one of those big municipal trash cans—I may be many things, but I'm no thief—then waved bye-bye. The Human Doberman didn't bother waving back.

Whatever became of basic civility?

HAVING A friend and former colleague who works for a big government spy agency means knowing someone who has the resources and savvy to find out virtually anything about anyone. I needed a home address for Janet Bollinger. It was for that reason I reached out to my buddy, Buzz.

"If you think I'm gonna access classified government files and go to Leavenworth, Logan, just so you can go chasing some strange piece of tail, you're dreamin'," Buzz said. "Why don't you do what every other creepy stalker does these days— look her up on the Internet."

"First of all, I'm not chasing some 'strange.' I'm working. Second of all, I'm out of town and I don't have my laptop. I'm not asking you to compromise national security, Buzz. I'm asking you to check open source records and find me an address, that's all."

"You don't have a cell phone?"

"It doesn't have Internet service."

"Everybody has the Internet on their phone these days, Logan. What century are you living in?"

"The one that requires me to make a choice between eating or paying for cell phone service features I can't afford. Are you gonna help me or not?"

Buzz grunted. He was among my oldest friends, a salty, hard-charging Delta vet who had shown me the ropes when I'd first transferred into Alpha. Buzz had done more to help populate the streets of Paradise with demented martyrs than just about any operator alive or dead. He'd lost an eye to an RPG, gunning down the Libyan boy who'd launched it at him. The injuries, both emotional and physical, compelled him to trade field operations for an all-source analyst's post. But neither his wounds nor his desk job dulled the kiss-my-hind end attitude that made him who he was.

"The Three Tenors," Buzz said.

"The Three Tenors?"

"They're opera stars, Logan, you uncultured lout."

"I know who they are. What about 'em?"

"Buy me their concert CD, and I'll run the address for you."

"Since when did you become an opera fan?"

"Since my old lady decided it was high time I stopped walking around on my knuckles. Face it, Logan, you could stand to do a little less swinging from the trees yourself."

"Next thing, you'll be telling me you're into ballet, too."

"Ballet? Me? Christ, no. Ballet's for pussies."

"Your denial's just a tad over the top, Buzz. But that's cool. There's no shame in liking ballet."

"OK, so I like ballet—but you tell anybody, Logan, I swear to God, the fire department'll have to use the Jaws of Life to remove my foot from your anus."

"Chill, buddy, your secret's safe with me. Three Tenors in concert for Janet Bollinger's home address. Fair trade."

"I probably would've run the address for free, you know, you son of a bitch."

"You're nothing if not a true humanitarian, Buzz."

He made a sarcastic smooching sound and hung up.

RUTH WALKER's former co-worker, Janet Bollinger, lived just north of the Mexican border in Imperial Beach, among San Diego's decidedly lesser suburbs. I drove my black rented SUV south down the Golden State freeway from downtown San Diego, got off eighteen minutes later on Palm Avenue and headed west, passing junk shops, tattoo parlors, and various meth heads and other zombies wandering the sidewalks with dazed, whacked-out faces.

Buzz had gotten back to me with Janet Bollinger's address ten minutes after I called him. Though he didn't reveal his sources, it was evident he'd tapped state DMV records—a big no-no in the federal intelligence community if such inquiries are made for other than official purposes, which in truth they are all the time. More than a few analysts and case officers have stepped on their meat running license plates after spotting some sweet young thing in the grocery store parking lot. Buzz, I was confident, had been around too long and was too savvy not to have covered his computer tracks. Along with Bollinger's address, he passed along her recent driving record. She'd racked up one moving violation in the previous six months and been involved in a two-car, non-injury fender-bender in suburban El Cajon. The other car, Buzz mentioned offhand, was registered to one Hubert Bedford Walker of La Jolla.

"You're kidding me."

"About what?" Buzz said.

"Hubert Walker."

"Who's Hubert Walker?"

"Big war hero."

"So am I, Logan, but I don't hear you launching fireworks every time my name is mentioned."

"That fender-bender with Walker, you got any further details? Any idea when it happened?"

"Two-seven May of this year. That's all it shows."

May 27. The day before Dorian Munz was executed.

"Anything else I can do for you today, Logan? Take a bullet for your sorry ass? Lose my pension?"

"Thanks, buddy. The Three Tenors are in the mail."

"Yeah, right. And if you believe that . . ."

Buzz grunted and signed off.

JANET BOLLINGER resided in a tired, two-story four-plex at Calla Avenue and Florida Street. The place was less than a mile from the beach, but about a million miles from anything about which the Beach Boys ever waxed poetic. Steel security grates covered the doors and windows. Black asphalt covered the grounds. Plenty of off-street parking and not a single flower in sight. A home on the downside of life's bell curve. I checked the bank of tarnished brass mailbox slots bolted to the front wall. The mailbox marked "B" had a slip of paper Scotch-taped to it. Printed in a woman's careful hand it said, "J. Bollinger."

Apartment B was on the first floor, on the east side of the building. I rapped on the door. There was no answer.

On the second floor landing directly above Bollinger's apartment, a chubby, brown-skinned dude in his mid-twenties leaned with his forearms on the wrought-iron railing. He was shirtless and in boxer shorts, smoking a doobie. His underwear was blue and was adorned with little yellow San Diego Charger lightning bolts. A likeness of the Virgin, her hands outstretched, was inked across his flabby gut and man boobs. A tat that said "Esmeralda" in cursive script took up much of the left side of his neck. He eyed me with unbridled disdain.

"How do you think the Chargers'll do this season?" I asked with my most disarming smile.

He shifted his gaze dismissively, sucking in some weed, and stared out at the ocean.

"I'm looking for the lady who lives downstairs."

"Wouldn't know nothin' about it."

"You haven't seen her around today, have you?"

Silence.

"I'm not a cop, homeboy."

"Like I said, wouldn't know nothin' about it."

"Well, what *do* you know?"

He turned his head and spit, like it was meant for me, then looked back out at the ocean.

"Guess what? I know something."

He looked back down at me. "Yeah? Whadda you know?"

"I know that the Buddha never claimed to be a god, which has to make you wonder: is Buddhism a philosophy or a religion, because every other major religion entails some essential form of theism, right? But not Buddhism, which many scholars consider non-theistic or even atheistic. Your thoughts?"

"*Mierde.*"

"What's your name, homeboy?"

He glared down at me. "*Pinche marica come mierda.*"

Making friends wherever I go.

I climbed into the Escalade and went to find some coffee. I'd wait for Janet Bollinger to come home.

～•～

THERE WAS a McDonald's on Palm Avenue a few blocks away. I ordered a small cup and took my time swilling it. It tasted like something that could've leaked out of the Exxon *Valdez*. I didn't care. Coffee's coffee. Anything else brewed from a bean is overpriced pretense.

I called Mrs. Schmulowitz to check on Kiddiot. He remained a no-show.

"He's probably got a girlfriend out there somewhere," Mrs. Schmulowitz said. "Don't think I don't know how *all* you tomcats are, bubby. That kitty of yours, he reminds me of Irving, my third husband. Could be he's Irving's reanimation."

"I think you mean 'reincarnation,' Mrs. Schmulowitz."

"Carnation, animation, whatever. I'm telling you, to look at him, you would've sworn Irving had brain damage—'The *Schmo*,' my father called him. But lock the bedroom door and, *oy*, the man was a Hebrew Mount Vesuvius. The bimbos went after him like flies at a picnic. They never bothered me much, though. He'd get tired of the floozies after a couple days and come slinking back to me, just like your kitty's gonna do."

Mrs. Schmulowitz said she'd gone to the market and was already cooking the brisket she was confident would lure Kiddiot home. She promised to call as soon as he turned up.

"Gotta run, Bubeleh. I'm off to the doctor. We're discussing post-op procedures. When this is all done, I'll have the tummy of a thirteen-year-old Nubian princess. Who knows? Maybe I'll finally get bat mitzvahed."

"Give 'em hell, Mrs. Schmulowitz."

Two fork-tailed fighter jets streaked overhead, F/A-18 Hornets climbing in trail out of the Navy's air station at North Island. Somebody once said that piloting a combat aircraft at high speed is like having sex in the middle of a car

~ 73 ~

crash—dangerous, a total rush, and when it's over, it's over fast. They forgot to mention that once you've flown combat aircraft, nothing else compares. The Hornets banked north in a sweeping right turn and headed out to sea. I was watching them wistfully when my phone rang.

"Just checking to make sure you made it to San Diego OK."

"If I hadn't made it, Savannah, your call would have gone to voice mail, would it not?"

"You don't have voice mail, Logan."

She was correct. One more thing I couldn't figure out on my phone.

"You made it down in one piece, though?"

"I wasn't involved in any midair collisions, if that's what you mean."

"Why are you being so obnoxious to me?"

"Why do you think?"

"Logan, Arlo's gone—and my relationship with him began dying long before he did. I feel like I'm ready to move on with my life. I'm hoping you are, too."

"His dying didn't wipe the slate clean, Savannah. Walking out of a marriage isn't some computer game. You don't reboot and start over."

"I understand that."

"No, Savannah. I don't think you do."

I'm not sure I understood, either. If a man is lucky, he meets that one woman in his life and is forever transformed. She becomes all he thinks about, even when she's no longer his. It's like a favorite song you love and come to hate because you can't get it out of your head. I wanted Savannah out of my head. And, at the same time, that was the last thing I wanted.

"In any case," she said, "I have a surprise."

"I hate surprises."

"I'm aware of that, Logan. But maybe you'll like this one."

"Fire away."

"I'd like to come down to San Diego, to stay with you for awhile, see how it goes."

"I thought you wanted to go to neutral corners."

"I did. I thought about it, and now I'd like to try again. We don't have to go to SeaWorld if you don't want to. I admit, I was being . . ."

"Petulant?"

Her tone took a sharp turn. "If you don't want me to come down, Logan, just say so."

I took awhile to answer, my heart thumping in my ears, a thousand disparate thoughts swirling inside my head. But even as I ruminated, I knew what I planned to say.

"I want you to come down."

"You sure?"

"I wouldn't have said it if I wasn't."

"Good, because I already bought a ticket."

She said she was catching an 8:30 P.M. train out of Los Angeles' Union Station, scheduled to arrive in San Diego at 11:15. I suggested she bring along plenty to read, considering that Amtrak in Southern California runs on time about as often as the Dodgers win the World Series.

"Can't wait," she said.

"Makes two of us."

The dinner hour was approaching by the time I returned to Janet Bollinger's apartment building. I parked up the street and walked back, not wanting to arouse the attention of her pot-smoking, gangbanging neighbor for fear he might set off alarm bells, but he was gone. An older, dark green Nissan Sentra with a dented back bumper that had a faded Castle Robotics parking permit on it took up the space directly in front of Bollinger's unit. I could see diffuse light behind the angled mini-blinds covering the front window. She'd come home. I knocked.

"Janet? Hello? Avon calling."

Nothing.

I knocked again, harder this time. That's when I heard it—a moan so faint that at first I mistook it for the breeze blowing in off the ocean. I turned the knob. The door opened.

"Janet?"

I stepped inside. The place was Crate & Barrel tidy. A chamois-colored sofa with modern lines and a matching love seat dominated the center of the living room. There was a small set of decorative wooden shelves crammed with a collection of about twenty ceramic Hummel figurines. Above them on the wall hung a grouping of six family photos in inexpensive black frames. On another wall was a psychedelic-colored poster of San Francisco's Golden Gate Bridge.

"Anybody home?"

From down a short hallway, a woman's voice emanated faintly at the same instant my brain registered the distinctive coppery essence of freshly spilled blood.

". . . Help me."

I ran.

She was lying on her back. Slender, mid-thirties, shoulder-length auburn hair styled in what I suppose you'd call a shag. Her gray, pullover sweater was wet with red, as was the off-white Berber carpet beneath her.

"Please," she mouthed silently, her eyes pleading.

I knelt, careful not to move her, and gently raised the sweater a few inches. Janet Bollinger had been stabbed in the upper abdomen. The seeping knife wound was deep and jagged at the edges, the result of what I assumed was a serrated blade.

"Hang tough, Janet. You're gonna be fine. Stay awake now for me, OK?"

The bathroom was six feet away. I grabbed a hand towel off a rack near the door and yanked the floral comforter off her bed. Using the towel to apply pressure on the wound, I tucked the comforter around her as best I could to slow the onset of shock, then dialed my phone with my free hand.

"Nine-one-one, what is the nature of your emergency?"

"A woman's been stabbed. She needs an ambulance."

The emergency dispatcher took down the address, then asked me my "relationship to the victim."

"Concerned citizen," I said and hung up.

The towel already was soaked with blood. Janet closed her eyes.

"No sleeping on the job. C'mon, now, Janet. Stay with me, sweetheart."

She was too weak to respond. Her face was ashen, her breathing shallow. I stroked her face softly while applying pressure with my other hand and waited for help to arrive.

There was nothing more I could do.

THE PARAMEDICS arrived within three minutes. Janet Bollinger was en route to the emergency room less than five minutes later. Whether she would survive the six-mile drive to the nearest hospital, in neighboring Chula Vista, was anyone's guess. The rescue crew loaded her into the ambulance in grim silence. I shared their unspoken skepticism. Like them, I too had seen my share of gravely wounded individuals.

"You say you knocked on Ms. Bollinger's door the second time you came back and it was unlocked?"

"Unless I'm mistaken, I believe that's what I just said."

San Diego County Sheriff's Detective Alicia Rosario cocked an eyebrow at my insolent response to her question as she jotted notes on a reporter's pad. She was pretty in a cop kind of way. Black slacks, black pumps, black silk blouse, her black hair cut cancer-survivor short. Under her black leather jacket, below her left armpit, a nickel-plated, 9-millimeter Smith & Wesson rode in a hand-tooled leather shoulder rig.

Her prematurely balding partner, Detective Kurt Lawless was decked out in a charcoal gray suit, white oxford-cloth dress shirt, button-down, pink polka-dotted necktie, and burgundy wing tips buffed to a high shine. He looked like a magazine advertisement for Brooks Brothers.

"What I still don't get," Lawless said, studying my driver's license as the three of us stood outside Janet Bollinger's apartment, "is what you were doing down here in Imperial Beach, when you live all the way up in Rancho Bonita."

I wiped Janet Bollinger's blood from my hands with a towelette from Kentucky Fried Chicken I found in my pocket and repeated what I'd already told the two detectives. How Bollinger's testimony had helped send Dorian Munz to death row. How Munz, before he was executed, had implicated Gary Castle in the slaying of Bollinger's friend, Ruth Walker. And how Ruth's war hero father had hired me to help refute Munz's last-minute claim that the wrong man had been convicted of murdering her.

"Ruth Walker," Lawless said. "Never heard of her."

"The story was all over the local news last month, from what I hear. Maybe you were on vacation. Shopping on Savile Row, no doubt. Nice threads, by the way. They must pay you guys pretty well."

Lawless glared and handed me back my driver's license.

It was easy to understand his knowing nothing about Ruth Walker's murder. She'd been killed probably long before either Lawless or Rosario, both in their mid-thirties, became homicide detectives. And even though Munz had been executed only a few weeks earlier, and the story was widely reported, who under the age of seventy reads a daily newspaper these days or, for that matter, watches TV news? Moreover, Munz had been prosecuted by the feds. If you're a local cop, federal cases might just as well be tried on the moon.

"So," Detective Rosario said, "just so I'm clear, you say you're staying with Mr. Walker, you drive down here intending to speak with Ms. Bollinger, to get her to give you some sort of statement saying this Dorian Munz individual was a liar. Ms. Bollinger's not home, so you go to McDonald's to wait. You come back approximately thirty minutes later. You hear a moan inside. Door's unlocked. You take it upon yourself to enter, whereupon you find Ms. Bollinger bleeding on the bedroom floor."

"I'd say that about sums it up."

"But you didn't stab her, right?" Lawless said.

"Why would *I* stab her?"

"I don't know, Mr. Logan. I'm asking you."

"Time out. Is Lawless really your name? Because if it is, it's *awesome*. It'd be like me being a psychiatrist named Moody. Or Dr. Cockburn, your friendly local urologist."

"I asked you a question, sir."

"No, Detective, I did not stab Janet Bollinger."

"Would you be willing to sit for a polygraph examination to that effect?"

"Only if we can schedule it around *Dancing with the Stars*. I try never missing an episode."

"But you *would* be willing to take a polygraph?"

"No problem."

Rosario crooked a finger at her partner. They turned away to commiserate in a low murmur, not realizing their voices carried.

"He called it in," Rosario said. "What the hell kind of suspect does that? Plus, he's too, I don't know . . . sure of himself. I'm just not feeling it with this guy."

"Well, if he didn't do her," Lawless said, "who did?"

"Considering there appears to have been no forced entry," I said, "the perpetrator was probably somebody the victim knew. Possibly an acquaintance of Dorian Munz. After all, Ms. Bollinger did help put the guy on death row. Maybe it was a friend of Munz's. Maybe it was the man upstairs."

"What does Jesus have to do with this?" Lawless demanded.

I pointed to the second-floor landing. "The guy in the upstairs apartment. He was hanging out up there when I first pulled in, getting toasted in his skivvies—Charger boxer shorts with little lightning bolts on 'em. Very stylish."

"What did he look like, aside from his underwear?" Rosario said.

"Hispanic, twenty-two, five-ten, 220. Big tattoo of the Virgin on his chest. Gang tat on his neck. Girl's name. Esmeralda."

"Not every young Latino with a neck tattoo is a gangster, Mr. Logan."

"Agreed, but this guy was definitely playing the part. He wasn't real keen on me being here, either."

"You talked to him?" Lawless asked.

"Tried. He wasn't too chatty. Made a few choice observations about my ancestry, I think."

"Why would he do that?"

"Could be he thought I was one of you guys."

Rosario smiled. "We seem to have that effect on a lot of people."

She asked for my cell phone number, thanked me for my cooperation, gave me her card, and told me to keep in touch.

"If you do happen to come up with anything else while you're looking into this Dorian Munz guy," Rosario said, "I'd appreciate the assist. We can use all the help we can get these days. Department keeps cutting back on our overtime. Never know. Might be a tie-in somewhere."

"I'll keep you posted."

She shook my hand and told Lawless she was going off to canvass the neighborhood for possible witnesses. Lawless said he'd join her in a minute. He waited until Rosario walked off, then turned back to me and peered at me with one eyebrow cocked.

"Don't take this the wrong way, Logan," he said, "but I got a bad feeling about you."

I smiled and said, "Take a number."

Six

If you didn't know any better, you'd swear that there was some kind of cosmic force field buffering La Jolla and the people who live there from the blight and turmoil afflicting many of San Diego's other, lesser neighborhoods.

La Jollans are inordinately tan and fit. They spend their days seemingly unfettered by the economic constraints that bind the rest of us to our workaday worlds. They play golf and tennis and squash when they're not out sailing, and would never, ever, even think to uncork a Chardonnay that scored anything less than a 90 from *Wine Spectator*. They eat organic. They wear Tom Ford and Jimmy Choo. Rarely do they hack each other to death.

At first blush, a plainspoken son of the South like Hub Walker would have seemed the unlikeliest resident of La Jolla, among the swankiest enclaves on the Left Coast. But as I rapped the antique brass knocker bolted to the towering front door of his 4,000-square foot Spanish-style hacienda on Hillside Drive, taking in its moonlit tropical landscaping and bazillion-dollar ocean view, it was easy to fathom how he, or anyone, for that matter, would've wanted to live there. The place was paradise.

"Where'd you come in?" Walker asked, gripping my hand.

"Montgomery Airport."

"Figured you would. Montgomery's where I keep my airplane."

He insisted on commandeering my duffel bag and ushered me inside. The living room was bathed in the golden hue of antique wall sconces and original Tiffany lamps. Oil paintings from impressionists I would've been impressed by had I known the first thing about fine art hung in gilded frames on coved, whitewashed walls. The furnishings were Mission style. Elegant didn't come close to describing the place.

"Nice crib."

"Crissy has an eye for all this. Loves going first class. I guess when you grow up dirt poor like she did, all this stuff takes on added significance."

His wife, Walker said, was on her way home from the gym and a Humane Society board meeting.

"How 'bout a beer—oh, that's right, you don't drink. What about some chow? You hungry?"

"I could eat."

"Let's get you fixed up."

He led me into a kitchen nearly as big as my apartment. The fixtures were top of the line, stainless steel, industrial strength. A frail-looking girl of about ten wearing thick black-frame glasses and a Beauty and the Beast nightgown was perched on a stool at the granite-topped breakfast bar, absorbed in a laptop computer. She had curly blonde hair and a complexion so pallid as to be almost translucent.

"Ryder, can you say hello to Mr. Logan? He'll be staying with us for a few days."

She peered intently at the computer screen, acknowledging my presence not at all.

"My granddaughter, Ruthie's little girl," Walker explained, lowering his voice. "We assumed guardianship after her mama . . ."

I pretended not to notice the tears in his eyes. He shook his head and walked to the refrigerator.

The computer made noises like farm animals.

"What're you playing, Ryder?"

Ryder said nothing, tapping computer keys. The blue veins under the pale skin of her temples looked like freeways on a road map.

"Mr. Logan asked you a question, Ryder."

"A game."

"What kind of game?" I asked.

"A game."

"Ryder, how 'bout you go up and play in your room awhile, so Grampa and Mr. Logan can talk a spell, OK?"

She hopped down from the stool, grabbed the computer, and walked past me toward the stairs.

"Nice meeting you, Ryder."

No response.

Walker waited until his granddaughter left the room. "She never says hardly a word to anybody. They diagnosed her borderline autistic when she was three. All kinds of health issues. Poor kid. Seems like all we do is take her from one doctor to the next."

"Kids outgrow a lot of things."

"I surely hope so." Walker gazed at the floor, then brightened. "Anyway, what can I get you to drink?"

"Water's good."

"Water it is."

He dispensed ice cubes and chilled water from the refrigerator.

"Larry got your airplane working OK?"

"Better than new," Walker said, handing me the glass. "Home in time for lunch. He's a good mechanic."

"Snappy dresser, too."

I parked myself on a stool at the breakfast bar and watched Walker dig turkey cold cuts from a Tupperware container. He laid them on a stoneware plate between two slices of fresh sourdough.

"Mayo?"

"Mustard if you've got it."

"A mustard man," Walker said approvingly. He fetched a small ceramic crock from a cupboard, uncorked it, and meticulously painted each square centimeter of bread with a butter knife. "Bought this stuff at the duty-free last time I was in Paris. It's the horseradish. Knock your socks off."

I told him I'd gone to see Munz's lawyer, Charles Dowd.

"He do you any good?"

"He told me to read the file in court if I wanted any information on the case. Then his investigator told me to back off—I'm pretty sure it was his investigator, anyway. He accused me of stirring up trouble."

Walker set the sandwich in front of me.

"Thanks."

"I'm surprised Dowd reacted that way. He told me outside the courtroom one day how sorry he was for my loss, that he was only doing his job. Said he was angry he ever agreed to represent Dorian Munz in the first place, but that Munz's parents paid him to do it."

"Nobody likes a loser."

"You got that right."

I took a bite of the sandwich while Walker went to wipe down the counter with a sponge.

"I also went to see Janet Bollinger," I said.

"How's Janet doing?"

"Not too well. She was stabbed this afternoon. She may not make it."

Walker paused from his labors and looked back at me.

"Janet Bollinger was *stabbed*?"

I nodded and kept eating.

"Where was this?"

"In her apartment."

Walker turned away once more and stared down at his hands, spread flat on the counter. "Who would do such a thing?"

"One thing I'm wondering, Hub, is why you didn't tell me you and Janet were in a car accident the day after Dorian Munz was executed."

Again, Walker looked back over at me, eyebrows arched, surprised that I knew.

"Where'd you hear that?"

"A little bird told me."

He put away the mustard, formulating his words carefully. "Janet called me up out of nowhere. Said she wanted to talk. I agreed to meet her for coffee. She said she was upset about what happened to Munz. Felt like it was all her fault. Said she wished she'd never testified. I told her Munz deserved what he got for killing Ruthie. She wouldn't hear it, though. Kept saying she was to blame. Over and over."

"How'd the accident happen?"

"I rear-ended her car when we were both pulling out of the parking lot. Foot just slipped off the brake. Stupid. Police officer happened to be going in for lunch. He issued us a report number for the insurance. Nobody got hurt. Nobody got a ticket. That was about it."

A sour queasiness coated the back of my throat. Maybe it was the melodramatic way he'd responded to the news of the assault on Janet Bollinger, or the expression on his face when he realized I knew about the car accident, but I was left with the unswerving impression that Hub Walker somehow was already aware of what had happened that afternoon to Bollinger.

"How well did you know Janet, Hub?"

Walker shrugged. "We had her over for Sunday supper a time or two. Came to Thanksgiving one year, as I recall. Jan and Ruth were pretty close there for awhile. Then, after Ruth broke up with Munz, Jan started going out with him, and that was about it. She wrote me a note after the trial. Apologized for ever getting involved with him. Said it was a big mistake."

"Did you respond to her?"

Walker shook his head. "Wasn't nothin' gonna bring Ruthie back anyhow. Some things are best left alone. First time I heard from Jan Bollinger in years was when she said she wanted to meet for coffee."

He asked me if the police had any idea who might've attacked Bollinger. I said I didn't know. He said he wanted to send her flowers and asked what hospital she'd been transported to. I said I didn't know that, either.

"It's somewhere in Chula Vista. That's what the paramedics said."

Walker scratched his ear. "She was living down in Imperial Beach last I remember."

I nodded.

"Plenty of shady characters down there these days," he said.

"Plenty of shady characters everywhere these days."

I heard the low hum of an electric garage door opener kick on, and a garage door being raised. Walker ambled across the kitchen and opened a side door leading to the garage. A car pulled in and shut down. A car door opened and slammed shut. From inside the garage, Crissy Walker said, "We were out of milk. I stopped off on the way home. Whose Escalade is that in the driveway?"

"Mr. Logan's."

"He's here?"

"He is. Got in a while ago."

"Where's Ryder?"

"Upstairs, playing. I fed her supper."

Crissy Walker entered the kitchen lugging two cloth bags from Trader Joe's overloaded with groceries and set them on the counter.

"Welcome, Mr. Logan," she said. "So nice to see you again."

"Nice to see you, too."

I slid off my stool and asked if there was anything else to carry in. Crissy said no and thanked me for offering to help. She was wearing purple Nike running shoes, matching nylon warm-up pants and a silver leotard. The hair of her loose bun hung down in damp strands, like she'd been working out. Even sweaty, the former centerfold was a sight.

"Somebody stabbed Janet Bollinger," Hub said grimly.

Crissy's jaw fell open. "What?"

"This afternoon. In her apartment. Mr. Logan just told me."

She clasped a hand over her mouth. "Oh my God. How badly is she hurt? Is she gonna be OK?"

I shrugged. "She didn't look too good when they were putting her in the ambulance."

"Well, have they at least caught who did it?"

"Not that I'm aware of. One of the detectives working the case wants me to help them out a little."

Walker frowned, was none too pleased by my revelation. "What do you mean, 'help out a little'?"

"They want me to pass along any info I might trip over in the course of the work I'm doing for you, anything that might be relevant to their investigation. No big deal."

"I'm paying you good money to work for me," Walker said, "not the police." He rubbed the back of his neck. "Look, I feel terrible about what happened to Jan, and I'm not saying that it's her own fault, but she shouldn't have been living in Imperial Beach to begin with. It's just not safe down there."

"It's not like the sheriff's department deputized me, Hub. I'm doing my civic duty. You'd do the same."

Walker exhaled his disapproval, reached down into a cabinet and got out a bottle of Jim Beam.

"I suppose you can do whatever the hell you want."

A disconcerting thought came to Crissy. She looked over at her husband. "This couldn't possibly have something to do with Ruthie and Dorian Munz, could it?"

"I'm starting to wonder the same thing," Walker said, pouring himself three fingers of Kentucky sour mash.

AFTER I finished my turkey sandwich, Hub showed me where I'd be bunking, a small but comfortably appointed *casita* that doubled as a pool house out back. I dumped my duffel bag and drove to the Amtrak station in downtown San Diego to meet Savannah's train. I got there ten minutes ahead of its scheduled arrival. Chronically punctual. Another of my many character flaws. I planted myself on a bench trackside, with time to think.

Was there a connection between the stabbing death of Walker's daughter, Ruth, and the stabbing nearly a decade later of her former Best Friend Forever-turned-romantic rival, Janet Bollinger? I didn't know enough to proffer a reasoned opinion one way or the other. But if I knew anything, it's that most people go their entire lives without being violently knifed, or knowing anyone who has. The coincidence seemed more than coincidental.

People lie. Faces never do. The manner in which Walker responded to the news of the assault on Bollinger, as if he already knew, left me uneasy. Not that his response was a slam-dunk psychological assessment. Human behavior is always subject to interpretation. Failing to make eye contact, for example, does not automatically convey deceit. Nor does someone looking you in the eye confirm complete honesty. Those of us assigned to Alpha learned that we had to closely observe our enemies, taking note of their baseline behaviors—how they reacted when you *knew* they were lying or telling the truth—to accurately assess their nonverbal clues. Still, I couldn't shed the disquieting notion that Hub Walker, Medal of Honor recipient and living aviation legend, knew something about the attack that afternoon on his daughter's former friend that he wasn't telling.

It's just a job, Logan. You're only in it for the money.

I forced myself to think other thoughts. The sea air was cool and damp on my face, carrying with it a sweet fragrance I couldn't place at first. Pittosporum, maybe. Possibly jasmine.

Or pee.

A homeless teenager was using a bush not ten feet behind me as a toilet.

"Hey."

He glanced over at me, fear in his hollow eyes. He was about sixteen, garbed in a gray hoodie and jeans turned black with filth.

I started to read him the riot act, only I really don't know what the riot act is. The sugary odor of the kid's urine told me he was likely diabetic and dehydrated. He also looked hungry and scared.

"Step over here into my office, my man."

I reached into my pocket to hand him a couple of bucks, but he must've thought I was going for a gun, because he ran like a hunted deer.

I'm not my brother's keeper. I'm not convinced that we are the world. I believe that the world is filled with evil, two-legged monsters who would take from you what is yours in a heartbeat, including your life, if they thought they could get away with it; and that one's only assurance of safety is hypervigilance—that and a fully loaded weapon. Chasing bad people to the dark corners of the globe in the name of national security had only reinforced those convictions. But in civilian life, I'd come to realize, clichés aside, that there is something to be said for random acts of kindness. Not that such gestures necessarily make the world a better place. They make *us* feel better and, in the end, maybe that's what matters most.

I stuffed the cash back in my wallet.

From the north came a shrill whistle and the alarm bells of crossing gates lowering, followed moments later by a single blinding headlight that pierced the night a half-mile up the tracks. Savannah's train was in. For once, Amtrak was on time.

The locomotive slowed as it passed me and hissed to a stop. Savannah descended from the third passenger coach toting a cocoa-brown overnight valise while wrestling with a matching, oversized suitcase big enough that Houdini could've hidden in it. I grabbed it from her and maneuvered it down the steps, onto the train platform. The suitcase weighed eighty pounds if it weighed an ounce.

"Eisenhower packed lighter than this when he invaded Normandy."

"Eisenhower knew the itinerary," Savannah said. "I don't."

She was wearing calfskin, high-heeled boots that came up just below her knees, form-fitting skinny jeans, and a short-waisted, black leather jacket over a periwinkle camisole. On a scale of one-to-ten, she was close to infinity.

"How was your trip?"

"Long," Savannah said.

"You get something to eat?"

"A hot dog from the café car. They had an egg salad sandwich, but it looked more like a science experiment."

I had to smile.

We walked to my rented Escalade, Savannah shouldering her tote, me wrangling her rolling armoire, which kept pulling to the right. The SUV was in a pay-in-advance self-parking lot directly across from the tracks. I hadn't paid. Given the hour, I figured the meter maid would be off-duty. I was right. No ticket on the windshield. Good karma.

I pressed a button on the key chain remote control, unlocking everything, and opened the passenger side door for Savannah, before hefting her suitcase into the back.

"My, what a big car you have," she said. "Now the Saudis can afford to build another palace."

"Just be glad I didn't rent a Prius. We would've had to leave Houdini at the station."

We climbed in and pulled out of the lot, heading north on Pacific Highway. Almost immediately, I noticed headlights trailing behind us. A left onto West Ash Street, a right onto North Harbor Drive, along the all-but-deserted waterfront, then west on Laurel confirmed my suspicions: somebody was tailing us.

"Where are we going?" Savannah asked.

"The Walkers. They live up in La Jolla. Nice little guesthouse out by the pool."

"How many beds in that nice little guesthouse?"

I glanced over at her.

"I'd just like to know what the sleeping arrangements are, Logan, that's all."

"We'll figure it out when we get there, OK?"

"No, Logan, definitely not OK. The unknown equals tension, and tension in any relationship creates conflict. Or are you forgetting what our marriage was like most of the time?"

"Some of the time," I said, correcting her.

"It's one bed, isn't it?"

"I'll sleep on the floor."

I blew through a yellow light and hooked a left, back onto northbound Pacific Highway. A US Airways Boeing 757 thundered in less than 200 feet overhead on short final to runway 27 at San Diego's Lindbergh Field. The other car was still behind us, its headlights in my rearview.

"Why are we going so fast?"

"No traffic, open road. This is Southern California. Do you know how rare that is? I'm just enjoying the moment."

Savannah bought none of it. She leaned forward and checked the side-view mirror. "We're being followed."

"Really? News to me."

"C'mon, Logan. I can see the guy. He's right there."

Our pursuer was now all but hugging my bumper. I floored it. He floored it, drafting my rear like Dale Earnhardt at Daytona. Then blue and red lights swirled on his windshield. There came the whoop-whop of a siren.

Our pursuer was an unmarked police cruiser.

I pulled over to the shoulder of the road. The officer got out and advanced on my side of the SUV, silhouetted by the spotlight he'd purposely aimed at my mirrors to blind me to his approach.

His right hand rested cautiously on the butt of his holster pistol as he slowly scanned the SUV's interior with his Maglite. He looked young enough to have graduated that morning from high school.

"Any idea how fast you were going tonight, sir?"

"Obviously not fast enough to outrun you."

"You were trying to outrun me?"

"I was concerned you might be somebody who intended to do us harm."

"Why would somebody intend to do you harm?"

"My question exactly," Savannah said, eyeing me hard.

We would've been there all night, me attempting to justify to both of them my paranoia and flagrant disregard of California motor vehicle code.

"Just give me the ticket."

And he did.

SAVANNAH REMAINED largely silent on the drive to La Jolla, steamed by my unwillingness to explain what had prompted my latest run-in with local law enforcement. About the only thing she said was that the collapse of our marriage could be pinned to a large degree on my lack of "emotional honesty," as evidenced by what she condemned as my "chronic secretiveness." It started, she said, when I was unwilling to reveal anything to her about how I really earned a living when I worked for the government. And now I was doing it all over again, clamming up, refusing to tell her why I thought we'd been followed.

"I'm just going to say one thing," Savannah said, "and that is, the cornerstone of any healthy human relationship is open, honest communication."

"I thought you said the cornerstone was mutual respect."

She pivoted her gaze toward me, her mahogany eyes scorching me like a blow torch.

"Please tell me you're not mocking me, Logan, because if you are, you can turn around right now and drop me back at the train station. I'll be only too happy to go back to LA tonight."

"That was the last train tonight."

"The airport, then."

"I wasn't mocking you, Savannah."

End of conversation.

The Walkers' residence was dark and quiet—which made sense considering it was nearly one A.M. by the time we arrived. They'd left the back gate leading to the guesthouse unlocked. Somewhere far off, an owl hooted its salutation to the night. Savannah followed me as I maneuvered her suitcase up a meandering flagstone walkway and past the Walker's kidney-shaped pool. The backyard was not as lushly landscaped as Savannah's opulent spread in the Hollywood Hills, but lush enough. She paused and stooped, swishing her hand in the warm, glistening water.

"Perfect temperature. Reminds me of that night in San Francisco, remember?"

Did I remember? How could I forget? We were newly-weds, living in a tiny apartment without air conditioning in San Francisco's Mission District. One normally doesn't need AC in SF, but that summer, Baghdad by the Bay baked like, well, Baghdad. One night after midnight, we made our way to the downtown Hilton, passed ourselves off as guests who'd misplaced our room key, and went for a cooling dip in the hotel's pool, which we had all to ourselves. Then we got busy in the Jacuzzi.

"One of the best nights of my life," Savannah said.

I wanted to tell her that it had been one of mine, too. But, somehow, I couldn't. There were moments when I still struggled emotionally to get beyond that fine line between love and hate, the one that can consume a man after losing a woman like Savannah. Some moments remained more blinding than others.

"I vaguely recall we went swimming."

She shook her head and said nothing as she followed me inside.

The little guesthouse, like the gate, was unlocked. Turning on a brass floor lamp revealed a kitchenette and a small, bright bathroom done up in Mexican tiles hand-painted with yellow sunflowers. The sink was ceramic and shaped like half a clamshell. The faucet dripped. There was one bedroom and one full-size, four-poster bed. Savannah stared at it for several long seconds before I grabbed the bedspread and a pillow and tossed them on the terra cotta-tiled floor.

"You don't have to sleep down there," Savannah said.

"You're right. I can sleep in the car."

I started for the door. She grabbed my hand and pulled me toward her.

"Maybe we should just see what happens," she said.

"Meaning what exactly?"

"Meaning what you think it means."

"Seriously?"

She shook her head like she couldn't believe any man could be so slow on the uptake. "You know, Logan, sometimes you can be a complete buzz kill." Then she brushed her lips against mine.

Many things in life are incomprehensible. Soccer's offside rule, for example. Or Hollywood's insistence on continuing to cast Nicolas Cage in major feature film roles. But nothing is more inexplicable than fathoming what makes the average woman tick. And when that woman is anything but average, why even make an effort?

I kissed Savannah hungrily.

She melted into my embrace as we stood together, arching into me, her tongue softly probing mine, her fingers sliding down the back of my jeans. Her hair smelled like spring.

"You won't be needing this," she whispered, undoing my belt, "or this," tugging my shirt over my head.

I glided my lips along the side of her neck, savoring the silken sweetness of her skin, as I gently cupped her breast. Savannah leaned her head back and moaned.

"This could be a huge mistake, Logan."

"That's what they said about Alaska, and that turned out just fine last time I checked."

She laughed.

Call me a cornball, but a sweeter sound I've never heard.

Seven

My jeans were ringing on the floor beside the bed. I reached over, half asleep, and got out my phone.

"Logan."

"Mr. Logan, Gary Castle, Castle Robotics, returning your call of yesterday. My apologies for not getting back to you sooner. I was back in Washington on business. Got in last night. Hope I'm not catching you too early."

Savannah was snuggled into my back, her arm draped over my side, snoring softly. I glanced at the time display on the phone. It was nearly 9:30 A.M. The last time I'd slept that late was in a crib.

"Not too early at all, Mr. Castle."

"Hub Walker tells me you're doing some work for him."

"That's affirmative."

"Hub's been like a father to me. One of the finest men I've ever known, hands down—and unquestionably one of the greatest pilots who ever lived. I don't know if he told you: we met when I was working as a line boy at the Camarillo airport, gassing up planes, washing windshields. He flew in for an air show that summer. Quite a thrill. That was years ago, though, when I was still thinking about becoming a pilot myself."

"Never too late."

"It is for me, unfortunately. I've got some heath problems that would prevent my passing a flight medical." Castle's tone brightened. "In any case, Hub tells me you're a flight instructor. Must be a blast, getting paid to teach people how to fly."

"A total blast—if you don't mind shopping at the Salvation Army and eating ramen several times a week."

Castle laughed a little too hard. "How can I help you, Mr. Logan?"

"Actually, Hub wants me to help you."

I told him that I'd been hired to refute Dorian Munz's last-minute allegations. Any nuggets of information Castle could provide, however small, that hadn't already gone public could go a long way, I said, in restoring his good name.

"Needless to say," Castle said, "I wasn't pleased with the field day the press had over the lies Munz told, but I honestly don't know what more I can tell you that didn't come out during his trial."

"Hub seems to think there still may be a few apples left on the tree."

"Well, if that's what Hub thinks . . . I trust his instincts implicitly. Tell you what, Mr. Logan, why don't you swing by my office in an hour, if that's convenient. We can go somewhere, catch a little late breakfast."

He gave me the address. I said I'd be there.

I thought it odd that Castle hadn't mentioned Ruth Walker's name during our conversation. Ruth had been a loyal employee. She was the daughter of the man Castle said was like a father to him. But I let it go. I was naked and in bed with Savannah. It was impossible to concentrate on anything else.

CRISSY WALKER was standing at the kitchen counter, mixing a big glass bowl of batter, when Savannah and I entered through the patio door. Hub was sipping coffee at the breakfast bar, reading the morning paper. They were wearing matching blue terry cloth robes.

"This is Savannah."

"You didn't tell us she was so gorgeous," Crissy said, hugging her.

"You're the one who's gorgeous," Savannah said, her face radiant from our evening together.

Walker clasped her hand in his two. "Y'all make a fine-lookin' couple, if you don't mind me sayin' so," he said, his mood having improved appreciably from the night before.

"Actually, we *were* a couple," Savannah said, "and, while we may still *look* like one, we're really still more at the exploratory phase. We're hoping to determine whether a sufficient foundational framework exists to reestablish something potentially long term."

"Savannah's a life coach," I explained.

"Gotcha." It was clear by Walker's confounded expression that he had not a clue what a life coach was or did. I wasn't sure I knew, either.

"By the way," I said, "the faucet out in the guesthouse is leaking. Not sure if you knew that already."

Walker sighed, pouring us coffee in two ceramic mugs. "I replaced that whole sink not two years ago. Guess I'll have to get out there again with my toolbox."

"You shouldn't be getting out there on your hands and knees doing plumbing, Hub," Crissy said. "Hire somebody."

"I ain't paying somebody to fix something I can fix myself. We've been over this I don't know how many times."

"Well, maybe if you'd hired somebody to do it right the first time, you wouldn't have to be going out there to fix it."

The sudden tension between them was discomforting.

"So, I hear you have a very pretty granddaughter," Savannah said, playing referee.

Walker smiled. "Ryder. She's at zoo camp. Goes every morning. You'll meet her tonight."

"She absolutely adores animals," Crissy said. "We can't have any, unfortunately. She's highly allergic to all forms of pet dander."

"Crissy's a television producer," I said to Savannah.

"*Aspiring* producer," Crissy said. "I haven't actually gotten any projects on air yet, though I do have one that looks promising. Animal Planet seems very interested. Fingers crossed."

I told Savannah about *The Cat Communicator.* Savannah laughed and clapped her hands.

"What a great idea for a show," she said. "I'd definitely watch."

"With that kind of enthusiasm, you can come with me to my next pitch meeting."

"Maybe I just will."

Hub asked me if I'd had any more news on Janet Bollinger. I said I didn't.

"I couldn't sleep a wink, thinking about her," Walker said. "Finally had to take something to knock me out."

"We prayed all night," Crissy said.

Savannah over looked at me.

"Janet?"

"I'll explain later."

I told Walker that I was meeting Greg Castle for brunch.

"Excellent. You'll like Greg. Outstanding young man. Can't say the same for Ray Sheen, his No. 2, though. Smart fella. Something about that guy I don't trust." Hub shot Crissy a quick glance. She seemed not to notice as she poured milk into a batter bowl.

"Too bad you can't stay for breakfast," Crissy said. "I'm making Belgian waffles. With *real* whipped cream."

"I love waffles," Savannah said. "I just wish they didn't go straight to my hips."

Hub smiled. "Gotta die of something, darlin'."

I said I'd be back in a couple of hours. Savannah urged me to have fun, then kissed me goodbye. It was an awkward kiss, like new lovers, unfamiliar with each other. After so many years apart, I suppose you could say we were.

WALKER STEPPED outside with me to his driveway.

"Some looker, that ex-wife of yours. What's she doin' with the likes of you?"

"You have no idea how often I ask myself that same question."

The azure of Walker's ocean view melted into the cloudless heavens above, a cobalt that seemed to stretch all the way to Asia. The wind was out of the east. A desert wind. The promise of a warm day.

"I wanted to apologize for my behavior last night," Walker said. "I don't know what came over me. I just got a little tossed off my horse when you told me about what happened to Janet. I got no problems, you talking to the police about anything. I just want you to understand that."

Across the street, a squat, barrel-chested man in his mid-sixties wearing khaki walking shorts and a cinnamon-colored hairpiece you could spot from the International Space Station was watering pots of red and purple impatiens on his front porch and glaring.

"Cut down those trees, Walker!"

Hub waved like a good neighbor, then turned his back.

"My neighbor, Major Kilgore. Says my palms ruined his view. Keeps threatening to take me to court. Problem is, his house never had a view to begin with."

"Cut 'em down, Walker, or I swear to God, you're gonna regret it!"

"He's been harping at me like that ever since he moved in last year. Never took a shine to me 'cuz I was Air Force and he's Marine Corps. He's basically harmless, though."

Major Kilgore looked anything but harmless. He was scowling vengefully, fists clenched, shaking with rage.

Walker ignored him and squinted up at the sun. "High pressure's building in. I might drive out to Montgomery and do a touch-and-go or two. Crissy said something about wanting to take Savannah shopping."

I climbed into the Escalade. "You mind me asking you a question, Hub?"

He smiled. "It's not about the medal, is it? I thought we covered that ground yesterday."

"It's about Janet Bollinger."

Walker's smile faded. "What about her?"

"You wouldn't happen to know anything you're not telling me, would you?"

He ran a hand over his face, struggling to control his anger.

"All I know is what you told me."

I watched him stride up the driveway and back into his house, the door slamming behind him. I've spent a lifetime lobbing blunt-spoken questions, offending innumerable friends, relatives, bedmates, DMV workers, airline reservationists, one ex-wife, and, from what I was later told, the entire faculty of my high school. Hub Walker to my recollection was the first Medal of Honor recipient I'd ever pissed off.

FORTY-SOMETHING Gary Castle was everything Walker said he was. Clean cut. Athletic. Articulate. The All-American straight shooter. In his cuffed khakis and yellow golf shirt, with a hint of gray at the perfectly coiffed temples, he could've just as easily passed for a Republican seeking the White House.

"This is why I work so hard," Castle said, proudly handing me a framed photo of his exceedingly blonde wife and four towheaded boys, one of more than a dozen family pictures crowding his desktop.

"Good-looking brood," I said.

Less handsome was the view from Castle's second-floor office, located in a large, highly secure, two-story building with mirrored windows that overlooked a heavy equipment storage yard just off Pioneer Way. The "El Cajon Zone," as the locals call it, may be a mere half-hour drive inland from San Diego's La Jolla, but it is decidedly more industrial, a haven of machine shops, warehouses, fast-food outlets and guys driving jacked-up pickup trucks with oversized tires.

"Unfortunately, I realized after we spoke this morning that I have a meeting at noon," Castle said, "so I took the liberty of ordering in. I hope you don't mind."

A nearby credenza bore heaping platters of fresh pastries and bagels. There was a crystal pitcher of orange juice on ice and a silver coffee decanter. I picked out a chocolate doughnut with chocolate frosting, garnished with crumbled peanuts.

"These things," I said with my mouth full-to-overflowing, "should be outlawed."

"I'm sure you have many questions," Castle said. "I thought it might be helpful if you first got a brief overview of what it is we do here at Castle Robotics."

As if on signal, a slim man about Castle's age, with a slicked-back, receding hairline, sockless Weejuns, stylishly faded jeans, and an untucked black dress shirt rapped on Castle's open door.

"Come on in, Ray. I've asked my chief operating officer, Ray Sheen, to join us. Nothing gets done around here without him. Ray, this is Cordell Logan, the gentleman I mentioned. Hub Walker seems to think he might be able to help us out of this pickle."

Sheen had long, flared sideburns, like some nineteenth-century riverboat gambler, and a pronounced scar on his left cheekbone that reminded me of the Nike swoosh. In his hand was a Louisville Slugger, which he gripped as if it were a walking stick. An affectation if there ever was one.

"You must be a ballplayer," I said, shaking his hand.

"Second base. Started all four years at Arizona State."

"Ray and I roomed together in college," Castle said. "He got his pilot's license way back when, but it's been a few years since he flew."

"I have better things to do," Sheen said, "like helping this country defend itself."

Ray Sheen exuded an obnoxious, self-important air.

"Gentlemen, please." Castle gestured toward four wine-colored lounge chairs on the far side of his office surrounding a round coffee table upon which rested what looked like a mechanical hummingbird.

I resisted the urge to get myself another doughnut and sat.

"So," I said, "what exactly does Castle Robotics do?"

"Nano technology," Sheen said. "This company, Mr. Logan, stands on the brink of delivering technology to America's war fighters that will viably reduce unmanned aerial vehicles—more commonly known as 'drones'—to the size of this." He held up the hummingbird and showed it to me.

I remembered sitting in on a classified briefing in which we learned all about plans by the Pentagon's Defense Advanced Research Projects Agency to create such drones. The incentive was to reduce collateral damage from bomb strikes. High-orbiting Predator UAVs aren't always discriminate when lobbing Hellfire missiles. Target a terrorist who stops in for a quick bite to eat at the House of Hummus, and innocent people often get blown to smithereens with him. On the other hand, a battery-powered, remote-controlled drone packing miniaturized optics and a small warhead could buzz in through an open window at the House of Hummus, land unobtrusively, wait until the bad guy visited the men's room, *then* blow him to smithereens. That was the concept, anyway. Nano technology was little more than theoretical when I worked for the government. How times had changed in only a few short years.

Castle Robotics' relationship with the Pentagon, Sheen said, had taken a substantial hit following news reports of Dorian Munz's unfounded, eleventh hour assertion that Ruth Walker had been murdered in part because she supposedly had knowledge of malfeasance on Castle's part. The company had also taken a financial hit. In the weeks following Munz's execution, the value of the company's stock had tanked on the NASDAQ.

"The board is meeting next month in New York to hold a vote of confidence," Castle said. "If I lose that vote, I'll have no choice but to step down."

"That won't happen, Greg," Sheen said. "Not as long as I have any say in it."

Castle got up, patted Sheen on the shoulder and paced the room. "If Munz were still alive, I'd sue him for libel. To imply that I killed the daughter of the one man I most admire in this world, because I was somehow trying to protect this company, or that she and I had an affair and I impregnated her, is outrageous on the face of it."

"Can you prove Munz lied?"

"Absolutely. I took a paternity test."

"Voluntarily," Sheen added, "and passed."

"You took a *paternity* test?"

Castle rubbed his forehead. "I can't believe I just admitted that. I've never told anybody, except Ray. And Munz, of course."

I tried not to appear as surprised as I was.

"You told Dorian Munz you took a paternity test?"

"I don't recall the specific date," Castle said, "but it had to have been a few weeks before Ruth was killed. She told me Munz was running around town saying I was the father, so I offered to take a test, to prove him wrong."

"Where did Munz come up with the idea you were the father?"

"You'd have to ask him."

"Munz is dead. I'm asking you."

Castle poured himself some orange juice. "I don't exactly appreciate your tone, Mr. Logan."

I reminded him that I was there to help, and asked him again where Munz had gotten the notion that he'd sired Ruth Walker's child.

"Honestly? I have no idea. I'd always assumed that Munz was the father and simply didn't want to accept responsibility. All I know is, I went to a clinic ten years ago, they swabbed the inside of my mouth, and the results showed it wasn't me. I assumed that was the end of it. It never came up in Munz's trial. Then, ten minutes before he's put to death, he pops off with all these insane accusations, and the news media reports them like it's fact." Castle gulped his juice. "You have no idea, Mr. Logan, the strain this has put on my marriage. My wife's a practicing Roman Catholic. She can't understand how anyone could lie like Munz did, knowing they're about to face their maker."

"If you shared the results of that test with the news media," I said, "you'd be golden."

"Share the results? With those bloodsuckers? So they can boost their ratings or sell a few more papers? It's none of their damn business."

"It is if Munz's accusations ruin your company and take you down with them."

Castle looked over at Sheen as if for guidance.

"The press would probably just ignore it anyway at this point, Greg," Sheen said. "You know how that tune goes—never let the facts stand in the way of a good story."

"You mind if I have a look at the report?" I asked.

"I really don't see how this is any of your business, either," Castle said.

"Hub Walker hired me to help find a way to get you out of a jam, Mr. Castle. This could be that way."

Castle thought about it for a couple of seconds, sighed, then crossed the room to a four-drawer oak filing cabinet.

"Greg keeps *every*thing," Sheen said admiringly. "He's very well organized."

It didn't take Castle long to find what he was looking for.

"Here we go." He pulled open a manila-colored file jacket, gave the single sheet of paper inside a quick look, and handed it to me.

It was a report, dated August 21, 2003 and printed on the letterhead of SoCal Genetic Laboratories in nearby Kearny Mesa. It stated:

"Sixteen genetic loci were tested using DNA amplification with the Accu-track/16 system, an XY-300XL genetic analyzer, and second-generation, Geno-Chromosomal marking software. Based on the DNA analysis, GREGORY CASTLE is excluded as the father of the female child, RYDER WALKER, because they do not share sufficient genetic markers. The percentage probability of the stated relationship is zero (0)."

"I rest my case," Castle said.

I asked if I could have a copy to pass along to Walker. Walker would then distribute the results to the newshounds, proving that Munz had lied.

Castle rubbed the back of his neck. "I'd have to think it over. I don't know, I just don't know."

"If I could weigh in here for just a second," Sheen said. "Greg, my primary concern is that directors meeting in New York next month. I mean, do you *really* want to be having to explain to the board whether you did or didn't sleep with someone ten years ago?"

"I may have no choice, Ray."

"Maybe. But even if Munz's allegations were true, which of course they weren't, having a child out of wedlock reflects in no way on your ability or inability to manage this company," Sheen said. "The more onerous allegation, obviously, is that Castle Robotics was stealing from the government. No paternity test addresses that."

"An independent audit would," I said. "Send out a press release. Tell the world you've commissioned one, and that Castle Robotics has nothing to hide."

"I couldn't agree more," Sheen said. "The transparency of a fresh audit could do us nothing but good."

"And dignify the lies of a condemned killer who's gone to his grave?" Castle shook his head. "Our bylaws already require an annual audit of the corporation's books. A supplemental audit would be a waste of money—money better spent in product R&D."

Castle readily agreed that Munz's allegations had created a public relations nightmare for his company and him personally. He agreed that the federal government's confidence in Castle Robotics had been undermined, and that something had to be done public relations-wise if the company hoped to continue securing the multimillion-dollar defense contracts that were its lifeblood. But Castle was hesitant to get involved directly. Decorum, he said, prevented him from standing up in his own defense.

"It would look undignified," he said.

"Fair enough," I said. "All you have to do is get a copy of that paternity test to Hub. He'll do the rest."

"I'd have to think about it."

"It's your rodeo."

I got up to leave. Castle and Sheen walked me out.

"When we first heard that Ruth had been murdered," he said, "quite frankly, we thought it was the Chinese."

"Why the Chinese?"

"Because of the classified nature of the work we do," Sheen said. "Ruth was involved from a design standpoint in some of our most sensitive projects. Chinese intelligence has always been eager to pirate proprietary technology from U.S. defense contractors, especially here on the Pacific Rim. Who's to say they didn't kidnap her, then kill her when she resisted interrogation? That's what we assumed, anyway, before the FBI determined that Munz was the real killer."

"Ruth was a good employee," Castle said. "Boundless energy. Very ambitious. Highly intelligent. I probably would've hired her whether she was Hub Walker's daughter or not."

We paused at his office door.

"What about Janet Bollinger? I understand she used to work here, too."

"Janet Bollinger?" Castle smiled to himself. "I haven't thought about Jan in years. She was what we call around here a 'short-time friend.' I believe she was hired as an entry-level CAD operator, was she not?"

Sheen nodded.

"Her heart wasn't much in the job," Castle said. "From what I remember, she seemed more interested in meeting Mr. Right. I'm not sure she even made probation."

"She did," Sheen said, "but she didn't last long after that."

"How close were Janet and Ruth?" I asked.

"Close enough that she started seeing Munz after Munz broke up with Ruth," Castle said. "I remember that much. What either of them saw in that loser is beyond me. Tell you the truth, I was glad when they finally executed him. Why it took as long as it did, I'll never know."

"'Tis better that ten guilty escape than one innocent suffer."

Sheen and Castle both looked at me funny.

"William Blackstone, the English jurist—at least I think it was Blackstone. I doubt it was any judge in Texas."

Sheen scratched his ear. "What's your interest in Janet Bollinger?"

"Somebody stabbed her yesterday, in her apartment."

"Jesus," Sheen said, "She was *stabbed*? Do they know who did it?"

"Not yet."

Castle cupped his hand over his open mouth and asked me if she was going to be OK.

"I'm not a doctor."

I studied Castle's nonverbal gestures. Behaviorists commonly contend that covering one's mouth when speaking is a sign of dishonesty, a clue that somebody's covering up the truth. Others say it's a self-soothing gesture, an innate human reaction to unsettling news. I didn't know Castle well enough to speculate either way. As for Sheen, his response to the news didn't strike me as anything other than normal. He seemed genuinely stunned. Neither man said they had any idea who would've attacked Jan Bollinger, or why.

"Dorian Munz is put to death and a month later a woman he dated is attacked in her own apartment." Castle rubbed his chin. "I would think that's more than coincidental, wouldn't you?"

I shrugged. True Buddhists don't believe in coincidence. They believe that cause and effect rule the universe. This philosophy is personally problematic for aspiring Buddhists like me. I find little comfort in the notion that there is some logic hidden in the chaos of existence. Call me jaded, or call me a pragmatist. Anybody who's been kicked down the block a time or two recognizes that, sometimes, there's no "why" to the happenstance of life. It is what it is.

Was there a conspiracy involving the murder of Ruth Walker, the execution of Dorian Munz, and the knifing of Janet Bollinger? Possibly. Maybe even probably. But right then, all I could really think about was the glorious night I'd spent with Savannah—and those delicious doughnuts speaking to me from atop Greg Castle's credenza. I grabbed two on my way out— one for me and one ostensibly for Savannah.

Who the hell was I kidding? I wolfed them both down before I left the building.

WALKING OUT toward my rented Escalade, I caught a glint of sunlight coming from a pearl white Lexus idling at the far end of the parking lot. The car's occupants, two young Asian men, were snapping photographs of Castle Robotics' headquarters.

They noticed me noticing them, put down their cameras, and slowly motored on.

I told myself they were probably tourists.

Eight

I was driving back toward the freeway when I decided to try federal prosecutor Stephen Tassio one more time. Maybe he'd reconsider speaking out in Greg Castle's defense if he knew that Castle had voluntarily taken a paternity test before Ruth Walker was murdered. I called his office intending to leave a message on his machine.

"This is Stephen Tassio."

I waited for the I'm-unavailable-right-now-so-please-leave-your-name-and-number-and-I'll-get-back-to-you-as-soon-as-I-can part of his message, but there was only silence on the other end of the line.

"Hello?" Tassio said.

"The real Steve Tassio? Not the *voice* of Steve Tassio?"

"Who's this?"

"Cordell Logan."

"I already told you, Mr. Logan, I have nothing to say to you."

"I'm aware of that. But I came across something I thought you'd want to know."

I told him about Castle's paternity test. There was a long pause.

"Who told you Castle took a paternity test?" Tassio said.

"He did."

Another long pause, which gave me pause.

"Well," Tassio said, clearing his throat, "whether Mr. Castle did or didn't take such a test is irrelevant to the case. Dorian

Munz paid the price for his crime. Justice was served. That's all I'm prepared to say. Good luck to you, Mr. Logan."

He hung up.

Clearly, the prosecutor had been caught off guard by my mention of Castle's paternity test. Why had he reacted the way he did? I wanted to ask him if his office had ever considered Castle a suspect in Ruth Walker's death. Was Castle really the model citizen that Hub Walker made him out to be? Why had Castle balked at the prospect of an independent audit?

Inquiring minds wanted to know.

I'd done what Walker had hired me to do—uncovered information that could help clear Greg Castle. The paternity test confirmed that Dorian Munz had been lying when he claimed Castle had fathered Ruth Walker's child. All Hub Walker had to do was persuade Castle to go public with the results of the test. I'd draw the remainder of the $10,000 Walker still owed me, and spend a few days hanging out in San Diego, getting reacquainted with Savannah—maybe I'd even take her to Sea-World. Then I'd return to Rancho Bonita and my exciting life as a flight instructor, almost earning a living. I was fully intending to do just that, when Detective Alicia Rosario called.

"Guilty as charged," I said.

"Excuse me?"

"You caught me in the act, Detective. I'm currently under the influence of a highly addictive controlled substance."

"What substance would that be?"

"Processed sugar."

"Processed sugar is not considered a controlled substance under California law, Mr. Logan."

"Well, it definitely should be."

Rosario was in no mood.

"I thought you'd want to know," she said. "Janet Bollinger expired last night."

The lump in my throat came unexpectedly. I may not have known Jan Bollinger, but I felt her loss. Perhaps it was the way she looked at me when I entered her bedroom, searching my eyes for a glimmer of hope, when we both knew there was none. I pulled to the curb.

"She managed to regain consciousness for a few minutes before she passed," Rosario said.

"Did she say anything?"

"She kept mumbling the word, 'Money.' Over and over. 'Money, money.' That's what the nursing supervisor thought it sounded like, anyway. 'Money,' or maybe 'honey.' Something like that. The nurse couldn't really make it out, what with the tube in Ms. Bollinger's mouth."

Money. Honey. Funny. Sunny. Runny . . .

"Maybe she meant *Bunny*."

". . . Bunny?"

"He's a PI. Works for Charles Dowd, the attorney who represented Dorian Munz. Bunny's his nickname."

"Who's Dorian Munz again?"

"The guy who went out with Janet Bollinger after Ruth Walker dumped him."

"Dorian Munz, who got executed for murdering Ruth."

"One and the same."

I told Rosario about my run-in outside the federal courthouse with the Human Doberman, he of the squished scrotum, and his threat that I get out of Dodge or else.

"The dude's a stone-cold thug," I said. "Except for his ears. He looks like a jack rabbit."

"Which explains the 'Bunny' part," Rosario said.

"What keen powers of deduction. You must be a detective."

"I'll check him out."

I asked her if her department had tracked down the tattooed gangbanger I'd exchanged pleasantries with outside Janet Bollinger's apartment. Not yet, Rosario said. She promised to let me know when they did.

"The woman had lost a lot of blood by the time I got in there," I said.

"Nobody's blaming you, Mr. Logan. There wasn't much you or anyone else could've done."

Her sentiments were appreciated. But they didn't make me feel better.

————◦————

HUB WALKER seemed genuinely surprised when I told him about the paternity test Greg Castle had voluntarily taken to disprove he was the father of Walker's granddaughter, Ryder.

"Greg never told me he took any test," Walker said. "Neither did Ruth."

"Paternity tests aren't exactly something you post on Facebook, Hub."

We were sitting in Walker's home office, looking out onto the backyard. His wife and my ex were lounging poolside in bikinis, sipping umbrella drinks and giggling about something, their legs swishing playfully in the turquoise water while Ryder swam at the shallow end. Granted, I may be biased, but Crissy Walker, former Playmate of the Year, had nothing in the looks department when it came to the former Mrs. Cordell Logan.

"That test could go a long way knocking down Dorian Munz's lies, that's for sure," Walker said.

"Castle hasn't decided whether he wants to release the results."

"He will when he understands how important it is."

I glanced around. Had I racked up a combat record like his, my walls and shelves might've been crammed with shadow boxes touting all of my many citations and medals, but there were none on display in Walker's office. The decor included two framed photos of his granddaughter and a framed cartoon rendition of a bulldog wearing a red sweater—the mascot of the University of Georgia. Only the wooden model sitting on his desk of an O-2 Skymaster like the kind he flew in Vietnam conveyed any hint of his wartime deeds.

"Any news on Janet Bollinger?" Walker asked.

"She died last night."

He leaned back in his desk chair and gazed sadly out the window, shaking his head.

"Why in the world would somebody have wanted to do something like that to her?"

"I don't know, Hub."

He watched his granddaughter swim. "Sweet Jesus," is all he said.

Whether truly grief-stricken or guilt-ridden, his reaction again was tough to read considering I'd only known him all of three days. I wanted to believe that he had nothing to do with Janet Bollinger's death. Nothing pointed overtly to his involvement except some vague, ill-defined gnawing in my gut. When you're a skeptic, I suppose, all the world's a suspect. Sometimes even war heroes.

"The detectives'll probably want to ask you and Crissy a few questions. You might want to call them."

"Whoever hurt Jan needs to pay," Walker said, his gaze still directed outside, "just like Dorian Munz."

I dug Detective Rosario's card out of my wallet and slid it across the desk.

"THAT PRIVATE investigator you told me about? His name's Herbie Myers," Detective Rosario said when she called me back that afternoon.

"Herbie 'Bunny' Myers. Definitely has a ring to it."

"I ran his records. He spent twelve years as a special agent for the Navy's Criminal Investigative Service before getting his PI license."

"He worked for NCIS? That fits."

Despite what TV producers would have you believe, Navy criminal investigators are about as high speed as the Mayberry Police Department. At least that's the impression they left when I was with Alpha and we'd occasionally cross paths with them. Their primary mission back then was ferreting out closeted homosexual sailors who would then be deemed unfit for military service and automatically discharged. Bunny's files showed that his own naval career ended abruptly, according to Rosario, after he'd stabbed a reputedly gay gunner's mate in the hand during a bar fight in downtown San Diego's tony Gaslamp Quarter. Witnesses said it was self-defense—both men had blades—but the sailor's uncle happened to be an admiral. Bunny was threatened with a punitive transfer and loss of six months' pay. He quit instead. How he ended up working as a private investigator for Dorian Munz's defense lawyer, Charles Dowd, was not readily clear. What was clear, however, was that Detective Rosario was eager to question him as soon as possible in what had evolved overnight from an assault on Janet Bollinger to a homicide.

Only problem was, Bunny had skipped town.

"Dowd says he has no idea where he's at, and the only thing Bunny's neighbors know is that he left town in a big hurry," Rosario said over the phone. "We think he may be hiding out in the Yuma area with a cousin. And get this: the cousin? His name's Daniel Zuniga. Goes by, 'Li'l Sinister.' He matches pretty closely your description of the knucklehead with the neck tattoo you chatted up outside Ms. Bollinger's apartment."

"His name's Li'l Sinister and he wears boxers with little lightning bolts on them?"

"What can I say? It's a weird world."

"Indeed."

Rosario said she and her partner were concerned that Bunny was planning to cross the border with Li'l Sinister into northern Mexico, where the men had relatives to harbor them. She was unwilling, however, to contact authorities in Arizona and have them make an arrest for fear that the local cops might tip off the suspects instead.

"The Mexican drug cartels have a lot of reach out there," she said. "It's hard to know who to trust on either side of the border anymore."

"Hard to trust anybody anywhere."

Rosario didn't disagree.

Yuma is about 175 miles east of San Diego across the Anza-Borrego Desert. On a good day, the drive takes less than three hours, but this, the detective said, was not one of those days. An 18-wheeler hauling fresh eggs had collided with a tanker truck filled with extra virgin olive oil. Both big rigs had exploded. Aside from making the world's biggest frittata, the accident had shut down Interstate 8 in both directions. No one could say how long the freeway would remain closed.

None of that should've been any of my concern. Savannah and I were "napping" in the Walkers' guesthouse. No man with a lick of sense would've willingly left under those circumstances. But most pilots have no sense. What else explains the inclinations of otherwise sane individuals who trade the safety of *terra firma* for the ever-unpredictable wild blue, an inhospitable domain that can spit out anything ever built by man and send it crashing back to earth faster than you can say "terminal velocity"? Still, for all its risks, a true aviator will jump at any legitimate reason to aviate—even if it means extracting himself from a warm bed and supple bedmate. And so, when Detective Rosario said that a fugitive was at large in the Yuma area and that the road there was impassable, I said what the pilot of any small airplane would've said:

"I can fly you there."

"You can fly?"

"Not in the Peter Pan sense. But if your question is, 'Do I own a Cessna 172 currently parked at Montgomery Field, and do I possess the capacity on short notice to transport you and your partner to Yuma,' then I suppose the answer all depends on whether your department is willing to reimburse me for fuel and wear and tear on my airplane."

"I think we can arrange that," Rosario said, getting excited by the idea.

"Then I'd say we're good to go."

She said she and her partner could meet me at the airfield in forty-five minutes. I gave her the name of the jet center where the *Ruptured Duck* was tied down, told her I'd be on my way there shortly, and tapped the red button on my phone.

Savannah spooned into me sleepily, wearing my polo shirt and nothing else. Her hand draped over my hip and dangled over a particularly sensitive sector of my anatomy.

"What's so important in Yuma?" she purred.

"I'll tell you all about it when I get back," I said, and derricked myself out of bed.

Savannah rolled over on one elbow and watched me pull on my jeans, biting her bottom lip, pouting.

"You can't go later?"

"I only wish." I sat back down and laced up my hiking shoes.

She leaned over and kissed me softly on the small of my back. "If you stay, I promise I'll make it worth your while."

"I can't, Savannah. I'll take a rain check, though."

"This isn't Kmart, Logan. There are no rain checks. Supplies are limited." She flopped back on the pillows and exhaled in frustration. It took every ounce of conviction to go brush my teeth and not climb back in bed with her.

"You could at least tell me why you're going."

"The police need a lift."

"To Yuma?"

"To Yuma."

"Why?"

"They're investigating a murder. It's no big deal."

"Murder *is* always a big deal, Logan. Who died?"

"That friend of Hub Walker's daughter, Ruth. The one I told you about last night."

"She *died*? I thought you said she was in the hospital."

"People do die in hospitals, Savannah. Except maybe on *House*." I spat out the toothpaste and rinsed my mouth with water from a glass sitting on the pedestal sink.

"Do you think it had anything to do with Ruth's murder?"

"Dunno. Maybe."

"What do you mean, *maybe*? You worked for the CIA. They didn't teach you how to figure out all that stuff?"

"I never worked for the CIA, Savannah."

"Well, you worked for *some*body. You and Arlo."

"Can we not talk about this now? I really do have to go."

I pointed to my polo shirt. She took it off reluctantly and tossed it to me, gathering the sheets around her. I pulled the shirt on and reveled in her scent.

"When'll you be back?"

"Hopefully tonight."

"What should I tell Hub and Crissy?"

"The truth."

I leaned down and kissed her.

She kissed me back like she meant it.

"Be safe, Logan."

"Always."

I TELEPHONED Flight Service from my rented Escalade and got a weather briefing: the forecast called for unrestricted visibility between San Diego and Yuma. Winds below 12,000 feet were forecast to be light and variable. There were no pilot reports of any turbulence or other adverse conditions. Like the old beer commercial said, it doesn't get any better than that.

Detectives Rosario and Lawless were waiting outside Champion Jet Center in a white unmarked Dodge Charger when I pulled in. Lawless asked to see my pilot's license.

"Nervous flyer?"

"Just want to make sure you're legit," he said.

I removed the credit card-size certificate from my wallet along with my FAA-issued medical certificate.

"Five bucks apiece in Chinatown," I said.

Lawless glowered as he handed them both back to me. That he saw scant humor in my lame attempt to put him at ease hardly came as a surprise. Like most people who have little experience flying in small planes, both he and Rosario were nervous but trying not to look it.

"Let me assure you," I said, "that you stand a greater chance of being struck by lightning than expiring in the crash of a light aircraft. Small planes are relatively safe—assuming, of course, your pilot hasn't had his license revoked once or twice for minor heart problems."

"I'm sorry, did you say *heart problems?*" Rosario said, her eyebrows elevated.

I assured her I was kidding.

Lawless grunted and held the door open, following us into the jet center.

Kimberly, who'd made fun of my plane upon my arrival in San Diego three days earlier, was still hunched behind her computer at the reception desk like she'd never left work. Maybe it was my imagination, or the way the afternoon sun slanted in, but she looked even more Irish wolfhoundish since I'd seen her last.

She gave me one of those I'm-paid-to-be-pleasant smiles as I walked past her with the two detectives in tow. There was a glass door adjacent to the receptionist's desk leading outside to the flight line. I pushed on it. Locked.

"May I help you?" Kimberly acted like she'd never seen me before.

"That's my Cessna 172, parked out on your ramp."

"I'm sorry. Your tail number is . . . ?"

"Eight two four Charlie Lima."

She took her time typing the number into her computer.

"I landed three days ago," I said. "You rented me an Escalade, remember?"

Kimberly stared up at me blankly, milking the moment, like any memory of me was somehow beneath her.

"You may recall," I said, "you implied my airplane wouldn't win Miss Universe."

Kimberly brightened, pretending to suddenly remember.

"Oh, right," she said, "the homely beast."

Takes one to know one, Kimberly.

I told her that I'd be flying to Arizona and planned to be back that night. She asked if I wanted to keep the fuel charges and overnight parking fees I'd already accrued on the credit card I'd given her earlier. I said I did.

She reached under her desk and pushed a button, electronically unlocking the glass door.

"Have an *extremely* safe flight," Kimberly said as we walked out to the flight line.

Have a *good* flight. Have a *nice* flight. Those are among the standard salutations uttered by people in aviation. They might even say, "Have a safe flight." But to have an *extremely* safe flight?

I wondered if Kimberly wasn't some sort of visionary.

Nine

"Montgomery Tower, Four Charlie Lima is ready, 2-8 right."

"Skyhawk Four Charlie Lima, hold short 2-8 right, landing traffic."

"Charlie Lima's holding short, 2-8 right."

We were buckled in, the three of us wearing headsets, the *Ruptured Duck's* engine humming at idle, all set to go. Detective Rosario was riding shotgun. Lawless hunkered in the back. His white dress shirt was one big sweat ring.

"Make sure your belts are nice and tight," I said.

"I can't believe you talked me into doing this," Lawless said to his partner, glancing around the *Duck's* passenger cabin like a trapped animal.

"We'll be fine," Rosario kept saying as if to convince him and herself that we actually might.

"Relax, kids. I haven't lost a passenger yet."

"There's a first time for everything," Lawless said.

I could smell their adrenaline.

I triple-checked to make sure the *Ruptured Duck's* fuel selector was set to both tanks; that the fuel-air mixture control knob was all the way in; that the flaps and trim were properly set; that oil pressure was up and cylinder head temperature down; and that my window and both doors were closed and latched, then watched a red-over-white Cirrus float in on final approach. It crossed the numbers, flaring a bit high, before settling down on the runway. After the Cirrus turned off onto an adjacent taxiway, the tower controller radioed:

"Skyhawk Four Charlie Lima, wind two-five-zero at five, cleared for takeoff, runway 2-8 right, right downwind departure approved."

"Four Charlie Lima, cleared for takeoff, 2-8 right, right downwind departure."

I eased the throttle forward, just enough to get the *Ruptured Duck* rolling, and slowly taxied out, steering with rudder pedals and toe brakes until we were facing straight down the runway. I set the directional gyro to 280 degrees, aligned with the runway's magnetic heading, and checked the orange windsock to confirm that the wind was still more or less out of the west.

"Any final requests?"

"Not funny," Lawless said.

"Definitely not funny," Rosario said.

She made the sign of the cross as I advanced the throttle and we began rolling, picking up speed. I checked my engine instruments—all were showing proper indications—and rotated as we accelerated past sixty-five knots, pulling back gently on the yoke. The *Duck's* nose rose into the air, sniffing the sky, tentatively at first, and just like that, we were climbing.

And then we weren't.

Things went from "A-OK" to "Uh-oh" in about two seconds. The engine revved out-of-control and began screaming like a jilted lover. Oil splattered the windscreen.

"Is it *supposed* to do that?" Rosario said. Her eyes were as big as Kennedy half-dollars.

There's an adage in flying: "You don't have to take off, but you do have to land." We definitely had to land. We were 200 feet above the ground with substantially less than 1,000 feet of runway remaining below us. Past the end of the runway, running perpendicular to it, was busy Highway 163. I had a decision to make: either put down on what little runway I had left and try to stop before slamming into freeway traffic; or turn right, keep flying, and hope the *Ruptured Duck's* engine held out long enough to get us to the much longer runways at Miramar, former home of the Navy's famed "Top Gun" fighter weapons school, about three miles to the north. The decision was made for me.

The engine seized.

The propeller froze. The airspeed indicator swung down instantly to zero. I instinctively pushed the *Ruptured Duck's* nose hard over, avoiding the imminent stall, and dove. I probably should've said something classically pilot-like and reassuring to my passengers along the lines of, "This one might be cutting it a little close." Instead, don't ask me why, I blurted out, "Whoa, Nelly."

Any landing you can walk away from, as the old saw goes, is a good landing; any landing after which you can reuse the airplane is a great landing. I had a bad feeling this landing was going to be neither.

"C'mon, *Duck.* Don't do this to me now."

I wondered how many people on the ground were taking cell phone videos of us at that minute. Nothing beats an air crash when it comes to entertainment value. Ships sinking are like watching paint dry compared to planes going down. Likewise train derailments. Unless you're one of those creepy old dudes who wear Casey Jones caps and get turned on by miniature choo-choos chugging around and around through some fake little countryside they've constructed in their basement, does anybody truly care when real trains upend real grain silos out in the hinterlands?

I would've charged admission, but it all happened too fast.

I disengaged the master switch and flipped the fuel selector lever to "off" to minimize the chances of fire, then hauled back on the elevator at the last possible second, as far as it would go, raising the nose to something approaching a landing flair. The maneuver arrested our descent, but not by much. The *Ruptured Duck* belly-flopped, bounced limply back into the air like a corpse on a trampoline, then back down again. We quickly ran out of runway and skidded onto unpaved ground, heading for the freeway. I stood on the toe brakes. The Cessna careened sideways, ground looped, then pitched onto its back and slid in a groaning, grinding blizzard of dirt clods and dust.

And then, no more than twenty feet from the freeway frontage road, abruptly, mercifully, we stopped.

All was silent inside the airplane. I could smell gas fumes, but there was no fire. I made a quick inventory of my parts. Everything still seemed to be working. I looked over at Rosario, then back at Lawless as the three of us hung upside down in our seat belts. Except for a small cut on Lawless's forehead, both detectives appeared unhurt.

"Everybody OK?"

"What kind of stupid-ass question is that?" Lawless shouted. "No, I am not OK! You nearly got us killed!"

"Well, that's certainly one way to spin it. I prefer to look at it from the sunny side. Think how long you would've had to stand in line at Disneyland to get on a ride as thrilling as that."

"You think this is some kind of joke? Go fuck yourself, asshole. Now, get me the hell out of here!"

Yet another satisfied customer. Thanks for flying Logan Airways.

I could hear sirens approaching. I told Lawless to relax and that I'd help him and Rosario out of the plane.

Escaping the wreckage required nothing more than un-latching my door. I unbuckled my seat belt, sort of half-rolled out of the upturned airplane, then hustled around to the other side to give Rosario an assist as she crawled out on her hands and knees. Lawless was right behind her. I offered him my hand. He pushed it aside.

"I don't want your goddamn help," he said.

With my passengers safe, I surveyed the damage:

The *Ruptured Duck*'s right wing was crumpled from strut to wingtip. The tailfin and right side of the horizontal stabi-lizer were crushed. The prop was bent at one end like a pipe cleaner, and the nose wheel twisted at a grotesque angle that reminded me of Joe Theismann's leg after that sack by Lawrence Taylor. I tried to get mad at my airplane for having failed me, but I couldn't. The *Duck* had absorbed the force of the crash and saved our lives.

"Nice job, old buddy," I whispered, patting his scraped and dented fuselage.

"Now *that* was a rush," Rosario said, smiling and trembling at the same time. "Not that I'd want to do it every day."

There was no ready explanation as to why the *Duck's* engine had abruptly failed. I'd been meticulous in its maintenance. Never once had anything that would be considered a major problem. I knew that federal aviation officials would investigate to determine the cause of the crash. They would invariably blame it on me, if only to reassure other pilots who fly Cessna 172's, the most popular airplane ever built, that the same type of accident couldn't possibly happen to them because of mechanical malfunction. But there was no time to concern myself with that now.

A red San Diego fire engine pulled up, lights flashing. Three firefighters garbed head-to-toe in silver, Area 51-style hazmat suits climbed down from the truck. Two of them, armed with handheld extinguishers, began spraying down the plane even though there were no flames to fight. The third carried a medical kit and asked us if we required treatment.

"This man is a menace!" Lawless said, pointing at me as the firefighter tried to examine the cut on his forehead. "I'm placing him under arrest for attempted murder." Lawless pushed the fireman aside, reached for his handcuffs and ordered me to turn around.

"Kurt, it was an accident," Rosario said. "Be happy you're alive. I am. I'm ecstatic, in fact. Now, why don't you let the nice firefighter have a look at that cut?"

"He told us it was safe. Is that not what he said?" Lawless was breathing hard. "Well, it's definitely not safe! We could've died, Rosario. And he knew it."

Lawless grabbed my wrist to cuff me. I spun out of his hold.

"Listen to your partner, Detective. It was an accident."

"Resisting arrest *and* attempted murder. That's it!"

Again Lawless moved to handcuff me. Again I twisted free. Enraged, he pulled out his Glock.

"Turn around and put your hands behind your back."

"Whoa," the firefighter said, raising his own hands, "this is the freakiest plane crash I've ever responded to."

"You're being an idiot, Lawless," Rosario said. "I'm lead investigator on this case. Now, either holster your pistol, and I mean right now, or I swear, I *will* report you to internal affairs on an out-of-policy weapons draw."

Lawless eyeballed Rosario. He eyeballed me. Then, like some petulant little boy made to put away his playthings, he angrily holstered his gun and let the nice fireman patch up his face.

Rosario got out her phone and said she was calling authorities in Yuma to have them pick up Bunny and his cousin before they could hightail it across the border. She still didn't trust the cops in Arizona, she said, but under the circumstances, there was no alternative.

I gazed forlornly at the *Ruptured Duck* and wondered when, if ever, he would play again among the clouds. Considering my airplane represented my sole source of income, the same could've just as easily been asked of me.

THE CRASH led the nightly news on every TV station in San Diego. Three news helicopters orbited Montgomery Airport, relaying aerial shots of the *Ruptured Duck*, while reporters filed stand-ups live from the scene. They interviewed anybody they could find who'd claimed to have seen the crash, and even some who admitted they hadn't. One old guy, who wore a 56th Fighter Group baseball cap and was identified as a former airline pilot, said he was in his hangar overlooking the flight line and could tell from the strained pitch of the *Duck's* engine that a crash was imminent. But the most compelling eyewitness account came from a delivery van driver named Jay for "Pampered Bottoms Diaper Service" who said he happened to look over while cruising the frontage road to northbound Highway 163 with a truckload of soiled nappies, glimpsed the stricken *Duck* diving straight toward him, and "about crapped my pants."

The worst part of all was that the newshounds had apparently checked the *Duck's* tail number online and quickly determined my identity. Within an hour of my having debriefed various airport and local law enforcement authorities about the crash, yours truly was all over the airwaves. The story even led the news more than 200 miles away, in Rancho Bonita, where the local anchorwoman, a twenty-three-year-old former Miss Avocado Festival winner who couldn't read from a tele-PrompTer if the fate of the free world depended on it, got my name wrong, along with almost everything else:

"Topping the news tonight, a Rancho Bonita flight instructor identified by authorities as Cordell Hogan was seriously injured today along with three of his passengers when their small jet crashed while trying to make an emergency landing at a San Diego area airport. Witnesses said the airplane narrowly avoided hitting a bread truck."

Among those watching, only because it was summer and there were no football games on, was my landlady, who called to make sure I was still breathing.

"I'm fine, Mrs. Schmulowitz. All's well that ends well."

"Listen, I know you love flying, Bubeleh," she scolded me over the phone as I drove back to Hub Walker's house, "but if human beings were meant to fly, God would've made it a lot easier to find parking at the airport."

"People love to swim, Mrs. Schmulowitz, and I don't hear you squawking about gills."

"Swimming? Don't get me started. It's supposed to be such great exercise, low impact, good for your figure, blah blah blah. If all that's true, how do you explain whales?"

"I'm not sure I follow you, Mrs. Schmulowitz."

"They look like big blobs floating around out there."

"You don't like whales?"

"Do I like whales? I *love* whales. I love whales like nobody's business! But even whales drown—which is my point. Swimming is dangerous. Flying is dangerous. If I were you, I'd think about doing something less with the, you know, hazards. Square dancing. Now, there's something you're not gonna get killed doing."

"I can't make a living square dancing, Mrs. Schmulowitz."

"Well, you're not doing too good with the flying from everything I can see."

She had a point.

I told her I hoped to be home in a couple of days, just as soon as I could figure out what to do with my airplane, or what was left of it. Mrs. Schmulowitz promised to save me some of the brisket she'd cooked for Kiddiot.

"Did he come back?"

"Not yet, bubby. But I'm sure he will soon."

A melancholy settled over me. My airplane was a wreck and my Kiddiot was still gone. He may have been the world's most intellectually challenged cat, but he was still *my* intellectually challenged cat. The thought of life without him and the *Duck* left me feeling hollow inside.

"I'm getting my tummy tuck tomorrow," Mrs. Schmulowitz said. "I'll keep looking until then. He's around here somewhere. I'll leave some brisket out for him."

I wished her a speedy recovery and made a mental note to buy her white daisies, her favorite, when I got home.

CRISSY WALKER met me at her front door with a warm embrace. Hub squeezed my shoulder and said he was relieved I was still alive.

"It's a miracle you survived, from what I saw on the TV," Hub said. "You must have some damn powerful angels looking out for you, son."

In Buddhism, angels are known as *devas*. The only thing I knew about them is that they rarely intervene in human affairs. So maybe it was other angels who'd come to my rescue, like the workers at Cessna who, forty years earlier, had built into the *Ruptured Duck's* cabin the structural integrity to withstand an event like the crash I'd just lived through without so much as a hangnail. Whoever or whatever was responsible for my good fortune, I was alive. And that was good enough for me.

The Walkers stepped aside and there was Savannah. She approached me with open arms, like she was going to enfold me, happy that I'd returned in one piece—then socked me in the stomach.

"What was that for?"

"Scaring me half to death."

Once upon a time I would've seen a punch like that coming, slipped it easily and, had it not been my ex-wife, snapped the arm of whoever had thrown it.

You're getting old, Logan. That or civilized.

"I crash an airplane and you punch me?"

"You couldn't take two minutes and call me? I have to watch the TV news to find out you were nearly killed, and you can't understand why I'm upset? Jesus, Logan. Can't you think of anyone else besides yourself for once in your life?"

"I'm sorry, Savannah, I was a little busy."

"Busy. Right. Being self-absorbed. You have no consideration for anybody else. It's like the empathetic components of your thought processes are one step removed from a Neanderthal."

"So a Neanderthal deserves to be socked in the stomach? Think about that, Savannah. If I'd have punched you, the cops would be on their way over here right now."

"If you had punched me, Logan, we'd be done."

"I'm starting to wonder if we already are."

She turned in a huff and disappeared into the house.

Hub and Crissy watched her go.

"That's how they all are," Walker said. "Every one of 'em. Wired up funny as hell."

Crissy slugged him in the shoulder, feigning insult. He grinned and drew her close.

"Savannah was just scared, that's all," Crissy said. "We all were, quite frankly. I know she's relieved you're OK."

"She sure has an interesting way of showing it."

Across the street, Major Kilgore sat in a white wicker chair on his front porch, cleaning what looked like an M14 rifle.

I spent that night parked in the driveway in my rented Escalade. Savannah refused to talk to me and had gone to bed early. The Walkers, sympathetic to my plight, graciously offered me the use of their living room sofa, but I declined. I needed my own space to think things through.

Savannah, I realized, was a compulsion, if not an addiction. If I were to recover from that addiction, I would need to fall back on the same kind of twelve-step strategy embraced by alcoholics and gamblers. The first step of any recovery program is to admit that you can't master your addiction alone. It requires a higher power. This is where I ran into trouble. Buddha to my knowledge never addressed the issue of former spouses that you just can't let go of. I was also fairly certain that no support groups existed in the Rancho Bonita area specifically intended to benefit men with a problem like mine. "I Miss My Ex Anonymous"? Seriously, what guy would attend *that* kind of whine fest?

If I were at all honest with myself, however, the truth was that, painful as it was at times, I didn't want to escape my Savannah addiction. And, at the same time, I wanted her out of my life as much as I ever wanted to be rid of anything. Hell, I didn't know what I wanted when it came to her. I tried to focus on my missing cat. I tried to think about my broken airplane. Both made me feel worse.

My phone rang. I was hoping it was Savannah, but it wasn't. It was Eric LaDucrie, the baseball star-turned-death-penalty proponent Hub Walker had wanted me to meet with. He said he was due back in San Diego the next day. We made arrangements to meet at his condo on Coronado at two P.M. He seemed eager to talk.

I drifted off to sleep somewhere after midnight. Two hours later, I was awakened by the sound of chewing.

Raccoons had invaded Hub Walker's trash cans. Five of the critters were enjoying a late night feast of chicken bones and what looked to be leftover fettuccini Alfredo. I rolled down my window and yelled at the thieves in their cute little Zorro masks to scram. One of them paused, raised up on his haunches, and looked over at me as if to say, "Yeah? What're you gonna do about it, pal?," then continued chowing down with his buddies like I wasn't there. I rolled the window back up, reclined the driver's seat, and tried to go back to sleep.

Live long enough, you learn to pick your battles.

Ten

The sun was up. Savannah had locked herself in the Walkers' guesthouse bathroom. From the other side of the door, I could hear water running in the sink.

"How about we go to SeaWorld today," I said, "pet some penguins?"

No response.

"You're being unreasonable, Savannah."

"*I'm* being unreasonable?" she said from the other side of the door.

"Look, I'm sorry. I didn't mean to scare the hell out of you. Next time I crash, I'll definitely call you immediately afterward, OK?"

The door flung open. Savannah was wrapped in a towel.

"How can you possibly have the audacity to call me 'unreasonable'? Do you know how many nights, how many *years*, I cried myself to sleep, wondering where you were, wondering if you were alive or dead, knowing you were lying through your teeth whenever I asked you what you did for a living—what you *really* did—and all you'd tell me was, 'Marketing'? Yesterday brought it all back, Logan. The fear. The constant, terrible stress. I'm just not sure I can go through it all over again. Can you at least begin to understand that?"

She caught me staring at her legs.

"I'm trying to have an adult conversation with you. Can you please get your mind out of the gutter for once?"

"My mind is not in the gutter, Savannah. It's in the shower. I need to take one—unless you want to take one together. Conserve precious natural resources. Save the planet. All that happy stuff."

She rolled her eyes, tears streaming. Then she slammed the door, locking it once more.

Call me a dope. I'd probably deserve it.

"Guess I'll take a shower later," I said to the door.

Silence.

My phone rang as I walked outside to cool off. The caller identified himself as Paul Horvath from the Federal Aviation Administration's local Flight Standards District Office. He'd been assigned, he said, to investigate the "incident" in which I'd been involved the previous day at Montgomery Airport. His voice was nasally, like his nose had been clipped by a clothespin.

"My preliminary examination of your aircraft found something quite interesting," Horvath said. "How soon can we meet?"

"As soon as I can hire an attorney willing to represent me."

Most pilots have a keen distrust of the FAA. For better or worse, the agency's accident investigators are perceived as headhunters eager to ground any flyer for the slightest transgression. A meteor could sheer off your wings, terrorists could blast you out of the sky over Kansas with shoulder-fired missiles, and the FAA would still find some way to blame you for the crash.

"You're entitled to legal counsel, Mr. Logan," Horvath said, "but I should tell you, again preliminarily, that the causative factors leading to the catastrophic failure of your engine yesterday would appear to have been largely beyond your control."

"Meaning what?"

"Meaning that I'd prefer to show you what I found, rather than discuss it over the telephone."

He didn't sound like an evil government bureaucrat. He sounded like a government bureaucrat with an adenoid condition. I agreed to meet him an hour later outside the airport's terminal building.

Savannah was still locked in the bathroom. I told her I'd be back that afternoon, which would still leave us plenty of time if she wanted to go to SeaWorld.

"I'll think about it," she said through the door.

At least she was still talking to me.

CRISSY WALKER left a note for me on the kitchen counter: Hub was spending the morning with Ryder at zoo camp, and later attending a lecture at the San Diego Museum of Art. Would Savannah and I like to join them for lunch after they got home? I couldn't speak for Savannah, I wrote on the backside of the same note, but I was headed to the airport to meet with the FAA and to not expect me until afternoon. I added, "Thanks anyway." I would've included one of those little smiley faces, only I don't do smiley faces.

The mess the raccoons had left beside my Escalade was still there. The Walkers must've missed it when they pulled out. I cleaned it up as best I could while Major Kilgore trimmed his hedges across the street with electric clippers, pausing periodically to check his work with a carpenter's level. Backing out of the driveway, I gave him a thumbs-up, but he appeared not to appreciate the gesture. I could see him in my rearview as I drove away, getting smaller and smaller, glaring after me.

I called my insurance broker, Vincent Moretti, on the way to the airport and left a message, letting him know he'd be receiving a claim on my policy. A big claim. In all my years of flying, even in combat, I'd never once dinged an airplane. And of all the planes I'd ever flown, none was more reliable than the *Ruptured Duck*. I hoped to get him back in the air, but given his age and the damage done, I had my doubts that my old airplane was even salvageable.

Paul Horvath was waiting for me in the parking lot outside the terminal building at Montgomery Field, a professorial, gray-haired man in his late fifties with bifocals and a wispy,

Wolf Blitzer-style beard. A laminated FAA photo ID card hung from a lanyard around his neck. He wore a peach-colored, short-sleeve dress shirt, pleated khakis, and black, soft-soled oxfords. His left eye twitched with a pronounced tic.

"Your aircraft's been relocated to an enclosed hangar for closer inspection," he said, shaking my hand. "We can take my car."

"Lead on."

We climbed into a white government sedan, unmarked but for its FAA license plates. Horvath drove fifty feet to a chain link gate, swiping his ID card on the computerized badge reader and punching in a security code. The gate lurched open, beeping. After we drove onto the tarmac, he waited until the gate automatically slid closed behind us, then continued on toward a line of corrugated aluminum hangars that fronted the runway, not far from where the *Duck* and I had gone down.

"Your plane's in there," Horvath said, pointing to the westernmost hangar. "What's left of it."

I'd sat through more than a few postmortem examinations when I was with Alpha. You get used to them after awhile, even the stench, when you realize that the body on the autopsy table is there because you'd helped put it there, and because the individual it once belonged to posed a threat to national security. Dispassion comes easy when you watch a genuine bad guy being sliced and diced. But the *Ruptured Duck* was no bad guy. Inanimate object or otherwise, he was one of my best friends, who'd gotten me out of more scrapes than I cared to remember. Having to observe a clinical assessment of his remains by some federal paper-pusher like Horvath was hardly something I was looking forward to. Neither of us said another word as Horvath drove toward the hangar and stopped in front of it.

A padlock secured a side door. The FAA man dialed in the combination, then stepped inside to undo a couple of hinged bolts holding down the hangar's bifold door. He pushed a button, engaging an overhead motor, and the big door slowly began to lift, like a metal curtain on a stage.

There sat the *Duck*, scraped and streaked with oil, his right wing crumpled, tail assembly smashed, miscellaneous pieces strewn about the hangar floor. They'd turned him right side up, back on his landing gear, but it only made my dead plane look even deader. Something caught in my throat and I could feel my eyes getting moist.

"I've seen far worse," Horvath said, resting a hand on my shoulder.

"Me, too. At the glue factory."

"This is what I thought you might want to see." He strode toward the engine compartment. The cowling cover had been removed. "Your engine breather line was plugged," Horvath said, holding up a short length of black rubber hose. "You applied full throttle, as you normally would at takeoff. But with the line plugged, pressure inside the engine built up, the crankcase seal blew, and there went all your oil. No oil, no engine. Simple as that."

"You're implying that I should've checked the breather line during my preflight inspection. Which means I'm at fault."

Horvath smiled reassuringly. "No pilot would be expected to check his breather line on a preflight inspection, Mr. Logan. It's too deep inside the engine compartment to get at readily. Besides, you'd have to open up the tube itself to check for obstructions. The only person who's going to do that is your mechanic when the plane goes in for its annual inspection."

"So, you're saying it wasn't my fault?"

"That would be my supposition at this point."

I exhaled. "Then what caused the obstruction? That engine was overhauled a month ago. I've logged fifty hours since then without so much as a hiccup."

Horvath's eye twitched. He reached into his pants pocket and pulled out a plastic baggie. Inside was a small wad of duct tape.

"I found this inside the line," he said, stuffing the oily gray wad into one end of the hose to show me how snugly it fit. "Whoever put it in there must've done it intentionally."

"You're telling me that somebody tried to sabotage my plane?"

"Not *tried*, Mr. Logan, *did*. That's off the record, of course. We're not allowed to discuss any findings until our investigation is completed. But I did think you'd want to know at least preliminarily."

My eye began to twitch like Horvath's, and I don't have any tics. It was one thing to come after me by trying to bring down my airplane. It was quite another to do so without regard for the safety of my passengers, or for innocent people on the ground who also could've died. A rage burned through me like magma.

"Any idea who might've wanted to do something like this?" Horvath asked.

"I'll have to get back to you on that one."

You don't spend as many years as I did hunting rabid humans without rankling more than a few bent on payback. No names or faces, however, came readily to mind. Was there a link between that wad of duct tape jammed inside my engine and the execution of Dorian Munz? Had somebody tried to kill me because I'd somehow stuck my nose where it didn't belong in the employ of Hub Walker? My gut told me as much. There were a couple of things I knew with certainty at that moment, staring at the pathetic wreck of my airplane. One was that I intended to find whoever was responsible. The other was that I intended to hurt them. Granted, not a very Zen-like sentiment, but had the Buddha ever flown a plane like the *Ruptured Duck*, I'm sure he would've understood.

Horvath noticed my right hand. I had unconsciously balled my fingers into a fist.

"Looks to me," he said, "like somebody's spoiling for a dogfight."

There's an expression among fighter jocks that described what I was feeling, the adrenaline-fueled determination to close with the enemy and destroy him. They call it, "Fangs out."

"You're aware, Mr. Logan," Horvath cautioned, "that this may well be a matter for law enforcement."

"Whatever you say, Mr. Horvath."

He nodded as if he understood the vengeful thoughts bouncing around inside my head, then turned away to survey the *Ruptured Duck*. I could see he was anxious to get back to his postmortem. I didn't much feel like watching, and started to go. Horvath offered me a lift back to the parking lot, but I declined. The stroll would help calm me.

"You can't just walk around an airport you're not based at without an escort or proper credentials," Horvath said. "There are security considerations, Mr. Logan. You're a certified flight instructor. You should know that."

"What's the worst thing the FAA could do, ground me? I'm already grounded."

He didn't try stopping me.

I CALLED Savannah as I walked back to the terminal building. There was no answer. I hung up without leaving a message. I wasn't sure I wanted to talk to her, anyway, not in the mood I was in. Then my mechanic, Larry, called from Rancho Bonita. He, too, had caught my inadvertent appearance on television news.

"Please tell me that wasn't your definition of a landing."

"Whatever happened to, 'Hello, Logan, I thought I'd check in to see if you're alive or dead?'"

"If you were dead, you wouldn't have answered your phone."

"What do you need, Larry?"

"What do I need? I need my daughter to stop dating losers, that's what I need. I need my wife to stop talking for five minutes when I come home from work—just five lousy minutes—so I can enjoy one lousy beer before she starts in on everything that needs fixing around the house, and why she's feuding with that witch down at the nail salon. What do I need? I need to drop a hundred pounds. I need to be rich. I need *peace of mind*."

"You should try becoming one with everything."

"What is that, some of your Buddhist bullshit?"

"It means try loving your life, Larry, warts and all. But I'm guessing that's not why you called. So, before you ask me, no, I have not yet seen Crissy Walker naked, though I did see her in a bikini, and she looks as good as you think she looks. So you can go ahead and eat your heart out right now."

Did he appreciate vicariously my sharing with him first-hand observations of the former Playmate in her swimsuit? No question. But that wasn't why Larry was calling.

"From what I saw on TV," Larry said, "your insurance agent is gonna want to total out the plane, cut you some low-ball check and call it a day. But that airplane, Logan, is your livelihood. And, besides, I know how much you care about the piece of junk—like it's your little buddy or something."

"What are you telling me, Larry?"

"I'm telling you to tell your insurance agent to stick it when he gets out his checkbook. Tell him you'll take him to court if he doesn't give you every penny of what that plane's really worth. Then hire a flatbed, get the *Duck* back up here to Rancho Bonita, and I'll put it back together for you. We can work out the money later."

Hookers and nurses are supposed to have hearts of gold. But nearsighted, 320-pound airplane mechanics with bad knees and terrible outlooks on life are not typically known for their generosity.

"You're a credit to your species, Larry, whatever species that is."

"I'm trying to cut you a break and you call me names?"

He was right. My plane was in pieces, my ex-wife wasn't talking to me, my cat was AWOL, and somebody wanted me dead. But there's never any excuse for bad manners.

"I'm sorry, Larry. I'll repay you. Just as soon as business picks up. A few more students and I'll be back in the black. Every dime. I swear."

He snorted like he'd heard the same promise from me many times before which, in truth, he had.

"Listen," Larry said, "I'm just glad you're OK—but that doesn't mean we're goddamn engaged or anything. You'll still owe me. Let's not forget that."

"I won't forget, Larry."

I passed on my regards to Mrs. Larry and their teenaged daughter, neither of whom I'd ever met face-to-face, and walked into Champion Jet Center.

Kimberly the counter clerk was not scheduled to work until the next day, according to the young woman on duty who was garbed, like Kimberly, in a navy blue skirt and matching blazer. Her name tag identified her as "Rita." She claimed to know nothing of what had happened to the *Ruptured Duck* the day before. Any questions as to who may have had access to my airplane while it was parked in front of Champion would have to be directed to her manager, she said, and he had the day off. I asked her if Champion maintained any surveillance cameras that could've showed someone tinkering with the *Ruptured Duck*'s engine. She shrugged apologetically.

"I'm really sorry. I just started working here. Maybe you could talk to the airport director. I'm pretty sure his office is, like, in the terminal. He's, like, in charge of everything."

"That's, like, an excellent idea."

I left my card along with a request to have her manager call me as soon as he got in.

———— ✈ ————

THE AIRPORT's director was away for the day—does anyone in this country still work anymore?—but his assistant was in. He was a ginger-haired thirty-year-old with a pencil neck and baggy, tired eyes who said he'd heard about the crash and wanted to offer his condolences. His name, he said, shaking my hand flaccidly, was Andrew Gresham.

~ 139 ~

"Somebody tampered with my engine. That's why my plane went down."

"Geez. You're kidding. Hadn't heard that one."

I asked about the airport's surveillance cameras. Andrew said he wasn't authorized to discuss airport security measures. I asked whether the airport maintained a master list of people who had access to transient airplanes parked along the flight line. He said there was undoubtedly such a list but that I would not be allowed access to it.

"You're not helping much, Andy. In fact, you're the opposite of help. My airplane's in pieces because somebody at *your* airport decided to test the theory that what goes up must come down, and you can't—or won't—provide me *any* information that could help me locate the people responsible? What if this guy is some kind of deranged wacko who has it in for general aviation? Do you have any idea how many pilots could be at risk?"

Granted, I was laying it on thick, but I figured I had nothing to lose.

"Sir, I get where you're coming from," Andrew said, "and our office will cooperate fully with any investigation the FAA has going, or any other agency, for that matter, but I really can't—"

"What if it was your airplane, Andy?" I said, cutting him off. "What would you do, wait for some government investigation to play out? That could take years. Have you *worked* with the FAA? Look up the word 'bureaucracy' in the dictionary. Do you know what you'll find? A picture of FAA headquarters."

Andy reiterated that he empathized with my situation, but said his hands were tied. He simply was not authorized to release any information.

The words, "I understand," slipped from my mouth before I realized I'd even formed them. I found myself more pleased than upset. Understanding is the first step toward acceptance, and acceptance is the first step to achieving inner peace—even if there still remained a large part of me that wanted to wring Andy's bureaucratic pencil neck on principle alone.

I<small>T WAS</small> nearly noon by the time I left the airport manager's office. Inside the terminal lobby, I caught a whiff of Mexican food. Nothing quite whets the appetite like the fragrance of boiling lard, especially when you've missed breakfast. A sign pointed to a restaurant on the terminal building's second floor. I bounded up the stairs.

"Welcome to Casa Machado. Would you like a table by the window? You can see the airplanes that way."

"Bueno."

I followed the young hostess in her colorful Mexican skirt. The restaurant was Spanish baroque in décor. Models of airplanes hung from the ceiling. A busboy delivered water, salsa, and a basket of warm tortilla chips almost before I'd sat down.

"Would you like something to drink? Iced tea?"

"How 'bout an Arnold Palmer?"

The busboy nodded regally, almost bowing, and went to fetch my drink.

I scanned the menu, then punched in Savannah's number on my phone again. Still no answer. Her conspicuous silence weighed heavily. It's hard to reconcile with a former spouse when she's about as communicative as a terrorist on the lam.

"Have you had a chance to decide?" The waitress was big and brown, with a moist radiant smile.

"What is your expert opinion of the *chile verde* burrito?"

"*Muy delicioso.*"

"Sold."

She jotted down my order, scooped up my menu, smiled that smile, and left for the kitchen. I gazed out the window as a yellow airplane came in for landing.

Two old men, each pushing ninety, were sitting at the next table over, both finished with lunch, eyeing the same plane.

"What is that, a T-6?" one of them asked me, squinting hard out the window.

"It is."

"Thought so. Did my advanced training in one of those babies." His accent was straight out of Chicago. His wire-frame aviator bifocals seemed too large for his wizened face, as did his "56th Fighter Group" baseball cap. "Good airplane, that Texan."

"*Great* airplane, that Texan," I said. It took me a second to remember him. "Didn't I see you on TV last night?"

He grinned yellow teeth. "Sure hope it wasn't on *America's Most Wanted*."

"On the news. You heard the engine on that Cessna before it went down."

"Been near seventy years since I heard an engine like that. It was attached to the airplane I was flying at the time. Cost me two years, cooling my heels in a German stalag, courtesy of Herr Hitler."

He'd gone to work for Pan Am flying DC-3's after the war, he volunteered without me asking, and retired three decades later as a 747 captain, with more than 40,000 hours logged. I was impressed.

"The 56th flew Thunderbolts," I said, pointing to his cap.

He seemed pleased that I would know such trivia. "You a pilot?"

"I flew Thunderbolt II's in Desert Storm. Mind if I join you gentlemen?"

"That all depends," he said, teasingly. "Are you a *good* pilot?"

"You wouldn't have known by what happened yesterday. That was my Cessna."

"The one that went down? That was you?"

I nodded.

The old man leaned across the table and yelled at his friend. "That was his Cessna that went down yesterday!"

His friend, a frail-looking fellow with hearing aids in both ears, took a long moment to digest the information, looking over at me not unpleasantly, then finally nodded like he under-stood. "Glad you're still kicking!" he said to me loudly.

"He can't hear too good and I don't see too good," the old man in the baseball cap said. "Together we make one helluva pilot. I'm Ernie Holland, by the way. Everybody calls me Dutch."

"Cordell Logan."

I shook his knobby hand, grabbed my water glass and sat down at their table.

"That tin-eared crumb bum you're sittin' next to is Al Demaerschalk," Holland said. "Al's an ace. Flew Sabres in Korea. Bagged three MiG-15's in one day over the Yalu."

"Say again?" Al said cupping his ear.

"I said you're a crumb bum!"

Al nodded and gave me a modest shrug, his eyes twinkling.

"Al could tell ya how many rivets were on the underside of the wing, every detail," Dutch said. "Got one of those Kodak memories. Remembers everything, even if he don't hear too good anymore."

I shook Demaerschalk's hand. "It's an honor to meet you both."

"So what's the story on your engine?" Dutch Holland said. "What happened? Why'd it fail?"

"It was tampered with."

The old man leaned forward on his elbows and gave me a quizzical look. The irises of his hazel-brown eyes were clouded with cataracts.

"*Tampered* with?"

"Somebody plugged the breather line with a wad of duct tape. They say duct tape has a thousand uses? Make it a thou-sand and one."

Holland leaned across the table to Demaerschalk and shouted, "They tampered with his engine!"

"What?"

"THEY TAMPERED WITH HIS ENGINE!"

Other diners paused mid-bite to glance over.

Demaerschalk looked at Holland, then at me, then back at Holland, with a sudden desperation in his eyes. "I gotta use the john," the old man said, again too loudly, and got to his feet unsteadily.

Holland watched his friend totter away. Then he glanced over his shoulder, making sure nobody could overhear us. "I think I might've seen something," he said in a confiding tone. "I mean as far as your airplane goes."

"What did you see, Dutch?"

Holland leaned closer and lowered his voice even more.

"Somebody tinkering with your ship."

We waited for his friend, Al, to come back from the men's room, but he never showed.

Eleven

America's smaller airports are crawling with old pilots like Dutch Holland. Grounded after failing to pass their FAA-mandated medical exam, unable to shed their love of aviation, they continue hanging around the flight line, often living in the hangars where their airplanes sit rusting because their aging owners are no longer legally permitted to fly them.

Holland's hangar was located at the east end of Montgomery Airport. The remnants of my airplane were sitting in a hangar on the west end, nearly a mile away.

"Got your TV, your icebox, your hot plate; cot's over there, and there's a port-a-john down the way. All the modern conveniences of home," Holland said proudly, giving me the cook's tour, the central feature of which was an immaculately maintained four-seat, single-engine Piper Cherokee older than I was. "Airport administration doesn't care for us living out here—they're worried about liability—but as long as you don't make waves, they more or less leave you alone."

He was a widower, Holland said. The concept of living at the airport was so incomprehensible to his country club wife, he never once attempted to float the balloon while she was alive. After she died, he sold their home overlooking a golf course in suburban Poway and moved.

"I wouldn't trade it for all the tea in China," Holland said.

I considered for a millisecond hooking him up with my landlady, then quickly came to my senses. Mrs. Schmulowitz had chewed through nearly as many husbands as Henry VIII had wives.

"Dutch, you said you saw somebody tinkering with my airplane."

"Slow down, sonny," he said, raising the main door of his hangar with the push of a button. "I was in a rush, too, when I was your age. When you get to be ninety-one, and you can see the end of the road, you're not as much in a big hurry to get where you're going."

He offered me a cold bottle of water from his dorm fridge, which I readily accepted, then labored to unfold a couple of flimsy, aluminum-frame beach chairs. I knew enough not to offer my help; it would have only offended him. He set the chairs facing out toward the flight line, then slowly lowered himself into one of them with an arthritic groan. The worn mesh webbing sagged under his weight.

"Unless you're waiting for an engraved invitation from the King of Siam, might as well take a load off."

I sat down beside him.

The old pilot watched with rapt fascination as a two-seat Robinson helicopter swooped in across the field about a quarter-mile away and hovered over the tarmac.

"Always wanted to get a chopper rating," Holland said. "Never got around to it."

"There's a little known law of physics. Helicopters don't really fly, Dutch. They just beat the air into submission."

He looked over at me like it was the dumbest thing he'd ever heard, then looked back out at the flight line. "Your Cessna was parked over there, at Champion Jet Center."

I followed Holland's gnarled index finger to a small fleet of sleek Gulfstreams and Citations about fifty yards away, each easily worth the price of a Beverly Hills mansion.

"I noticed your ship right off," he said. "Most everybody who flies in here from out of town in small planes like yours, they tie down over on the transient ramp outside the terminal.

Cheaper to park over there. You must've been born with a silver spoon."

A silver spoon. Right. That's me.

As Holland told it, he was sitting exactly where we were, enjoying the cool night air and a bedtime toddy, when a small pickup truck drove onto the tarmac and stopped near my airplane. Wearing a baseball cap and mechanic's coveralls, the driver got out with a flashlight and opened the *Ruptured Duck's* cowling like he knew what he was doing. He rummaged around inside the engine compartment for about five minutes, then buttoned up the cowling, got back in his truck, and drove off. The truck was light in color, possibly white. It was too dark, Dutch said, to make out much detail beyond that.

"My eyes," he said apologetically, "aren't what they used to be."

I told him I appreciated the tip, and asked that he pass it on to Paul Horvath, the FAA investigator I'd met with that morning. Holland pursed his lips and said he'd have to think about it.

"There's nothing to think about, Dutch. With all due respect, somebody tried to kill me yesterday. You have an obligation to tell the authorities what you saw."

"I do that, I draw attention to myself. I draw attention to myself, airport management kicks me out."

"But you went on TV. How is that not drawing attention to yourself?"

"I-I don't know," Holland stammered, growing agitated. "I was just standing there and next thing you know, some pretty girl's pointing a microphone in my face, asking me what I saw. I probably shouldn't have said anything. I made a mistake. A stupid mistake."

He got up slowly out of his chair, painfully, bracing his hands on his knees, and said it was time for his nap. My cue to leave. I jotted down Horvath's number on a business card and handed it to him. The old man tucked the card in his shirt pocket without looking at it and started folding up the beach chairs. I asked him what happened to his friend, Al Demaerschalk.

"He never came back from the bathroom," I said.

"I don't know."

Dutch Holland suddenly seemed in a big rush to put distance between us. I had to jump clear of the hangar door as it came down, him on the inside, me looking in.

The story of my life.

LEGEND HAS it that L. Frank Baum wrote *The Wonderful Wizard of Oz* while staying at the Hotel del Coronado, across the bay from downtown San Diego. He supposedly modeled his "Emerald City" on the hotel's Queen Anne-style architecture. It was at the "Del," as the locals reverently call it, that an American divorcee named Wallis Simpson purportedly met a British prince named Edward, who would later give up the throne for her—just as Hitler's dark shadow began to spread across Europe. American presidents have vacationed at the Del for more than a hundred years. The biggest names in Hollywood have had trysts there. All of which is to say that the place is dripping with history. But former Padres pitcher Eric "the Junkman" LaDucrie, whose luxury high-rise condo overlooked the Del, didn't want to talk about any of that as I stood with him on his balcony, admiring the view from seven floors up.

"The truth," the Junkman said, literally thumping a leather-bound Bible. "It's all in here. 'Eye for an eye,' 'tooth for a tooth,' 'hand for a hand,' 'foot for a foot.' This is what the Lord decreed. You want proof? Read Exodus, and Matthew, *and* Leviticus—'Whoever takes a human life shall surely be put to death.' Look at Romans: 'For the wages of sin is death.'"

The bucktoothed, forty-something LaDucrie was just warming up. He went on and on with his preaching, barely stopping to breathe, half moons of perspiration staining the pits of his pink golf shirt. Everyone from Jesus to Gandhi to Mother

Teresa believed in the death penalty, he insisted, even if none of them ever said so openly.

I could take only so much.

"Mr. LaDucrie, I didn't drive over here to attend religious services. I came to talk about Dorian Munz and the murder of Ruth Walker."

"Ruth Walker. Right. Sorry. I can get carried away a little sometimes. The whole death penalty debate isn't just some political cause for me. It's my *life*. And I *know* I'm 110 percent right."

"Yeah, I picked up on that."

I asked him how long he'd lived there as I followed him back inside.

"Ten, eleven years. Bought the place right before the Padres wanted to send me back down to the minors. I'd been to the minors. So I hung up my spikes instead."

His living room, like the rest of his swinging bachelor pad, was a shrine to unchecked egotism and his Big League career. Framed game jerseys lined the walls along with magazine covers and the pages of newspaper sports sections featuring photos of the Junkman in action. Autographed hardballs in clear acrylic cubes shared shelf space with displays of Junkman rookie cards and Junkman bobblehead dolls. Over the fireplace was a vintage, larger than life LeRoy Neiman painting of LaDucrie on the mound in his Padres uniform, uncorking a knuckleball.

He asked me if I wanted a beer or a soda. I declined both as he disappeared into his kitchen. "Dorian Munz killed Ruth Walker in cold blood," LaDucrie said. "He deserved to die. Anybody who says different is misinformed."

He returned with a Diet Coke, and plopped down on an overstuffed leather chair shaped like a giant catcher's mitt. I parked myself on a sofa, the back of which was constructed entirely of Louisville Sluggers. Furniture design by Major League Baseball and the Marquis de Sade.

"Ruth Walker's father is looking for additional information, facts that didn't make the newspaper, that would help convince the public Munz was lying about Greg Castle."

LaDucrie gulped his soda. "I'd like to help," he said, wiping his mouth with the back of his left hand, "but all I know is what I saw on the news."

"I'm told you were interviewed on TV just before Munz was executed. You said you were 'completely confident' he was guilty. 'Completely confident' suggests to me you know a lot more than what you saw on the news."

"Let me put it this way: Fox News, they got me on speed dial, OK? Every time there's some death penalty case around the country and people are squawking about how the dude who's about to get it doesn't deserve it, I'm the guy who goes on camera and says he does, OK? Somebody's gotta stand up against all these bleeding heart pussies, unless you want 'em taking over the world."

"What you're telling me is, you have nothing to back up your 'complete confidence' claim that Dorian Munz was guilty."

LaDucrie looked off to his left and thought about it for a long moment. "Not really, no." He chugged the rest of his Diet Coke, strained forward in his catcher's mitt chair—his gut hanging over the expand-o-matic waistband of his tan golf shorts—and set the can down on a coffee table shaped like home plate. "What I know is that from everything I heard and read, the evidence against the douche bag was dead on. Ruth Walker should've never died the way she did, OK? She was a real nice little gal."

"How do you know that?"

"Maybe I met her once or twice."

"You knew Ruth Walker?"

Again, the Junkman gazed off to his left for no more than a second, like he was thinking about it, then looked back at me. "I said *maybe* I knew her. You meet a lot of babes in the show. They're all over the place, ya know what I'm saying? They all start blending in after awhile. You forget faces." I caught a trace of sadness in his eyes as he looked down. "Soon as you retire, they scatter like cockroaches."

I asked him if he'd ever met Janet Bollinger. Again, he looked left, then back to me.

"The name doesn't ring a bell."

LaDucrie's eye movement, his involuntary micro-expressions in response to my questions, had at least been consistent. Either he was telling the truth when he said he may have known Ruth Walker but not Janet Bollinger, or he was lying through his buck teeth about both. I hadn't known him long enough to accurately gauge which was which.

I asked him how he'd become so passionate about upholding capital punishment. He told me how his sister was murdered at thirteen, lured into a baseball dugout by his Little League coach, who swore he'd only meant to kiss her. Convicted of involuntary manslaughter, Coach Rapist was sentenced to four years in Folsom. He ended up doing half of that.

"The son of a bitch got hit by a car a week after he got out of the joint," LaDucrie said with a smile as he walked me to his door. "Sometimes, the good Lord has ways of setting things right. Deuteronomy 32–35. 'It is mine to avenge; I will repay. In due time their foot will slip; their day of disaster is near and their doom rushes upon them.'"

The Buddha believed that vengeance is pointless. Vengeance can only be met by more vengeance, force with force, bombs with bombs. But, then, the Buddha never knew the pure pleasure of dropping a 500-pound JDAM down the pie hole of an avowed Al Qaeda killer, or putting a 9-millimeter hollow point behind a terrorist's ear at Helen Keller-can't-miss range.

I walked through the parking lot of LaDucrie's condo to my Escalade. The sea breeze carried with it the cannonade of waves crashing onto the beach and the gleeful laughter of children chasing each other among the dunes. Nearly ten years earlier, less than a mile from where I stood, the body of Hub Walker's daughter had been found amid those very dunes.

I turned and gazed up at the Junkman's balcony. He'd been living there, I realized, about the same time Ruth Walker was murdered.

CRISSY WALKER was standing at her kitchen counter, making a smoothie. Her black short shorts showed off her toned tanned legs. The University of Georgia Bulldogs T-shirt she had on highlighted the fact that she was braless. Hub wouldn't be back until after dinner, she said, dumping banana slices into a food processor. He'd gone to play golf at Torrey Pines with Greg Castle, hoping to convince Castle for his own good to go public with the paternity test he'd taken years earlier. She asked me if I wanted a smoothie. Given that I am not the smoothie type, I politely declined and went to make amends with Savannah.

"She's not here," Crissy said before I got to the back door. "I took her to the train station about an hour ago. She said she wanted to go back to LA."

I couldn't say I was surprised. Angry women don't usually lock themselves in guesthouse bathrooms without also formulating escape plans. I recognized that my ex-wife had every right to be mad at me: I'd crashed my airplane and lacked the grace to let her know afterward that I wasn't dead. Had the shoe been on the other foot, I probably would've been just as angry. I wondered whether we would ever get back together, or whether it was even worth endeavoring to try. Staring down at the glossy, terra-cotta tiles of the Walkers' kitchen floor, I felt at that moment like a sailboat bereft of wind.

"Sure you don't want a smoothie?" Crissy said, cutting strawberries. "You look like you could definitely use a pick-me-up."

"I'm good, thanks."

"I bet you are."

When I looked up, she was smiling at me. I may be a few transistors short of a circuit board when it comes to picking up on the nuances of female communications, but I knew exactly the message Crissy Walker was broadcasting.

"Ryder's at a playdate until after dinner," she said, glancing at the digital clock on the microwave. "That gives us two hours."

"I have nothing but respect for your husband, Crissy."

"My husband is not here right now." She glided around the kitchen's center island biting her lip, her breasts swaying seductively behind her T-shirt, and stood in front of me, closer than was prudent. "No one ever has to know."

Her fragrance reminded me of scented massage oil. *This is what the Playboy Mansion must smell like.* She smoothed my collar, then reached up and stroked the side of my face.

"I never properly thanked you for saving our lives, Cordell."

I gently grabbed her hand and stopped her. "I'm flattered, but . . ."

Her lips spread slowly into a puzzled half-smile that conveyed something between surprise and self-doubt. "No man has ever said no to me before."

"I'm not trying to offend you, Crissy. I'm just down here to do a job, that's all."

She covered her mouth, embarrassed. "I must need my head examined. I don't know what I was thinking."

I knew exactly what *I* was thinking as I watched her hurry out of the kitchen. That a million other red-blooded American guys would've *killed* for the same opportunity I'd just passed up. The Buddha might've argued that I had followed a moral path, and that I was a better man for it. But turning down the chance to spend two hours alone with a former Playmate of the Year, no strings attached? Maybe I was the one who needed my head examined.

As far as I was concerned, my work in San Diego was done. All Hub Walker had to do was convince Greg Castle to make public the results of his paternity test, and I could collect on the five large Walker still owed me. I could use the dough to cover the cost of trucking the *Ruptured Duck* back up to Rancho Bonita. Whatever was left would go directly to Larry to pay down some of the back rent I owed him, along with seed money to begin rebuilding my plane ahead of whatever damages the insurance company was willing to cover.

I was toweling off from a shower in the Walker's guest-house when my insurance broker, Vincent Moretti, returned my call. I've never met the guy face-to-face, but I've always envisioned him as Vito Corleone because that's exactly who he sounds like over the phone. He'd reviewed my policy, he said, run some numbers, and scheduled a claims adjuster to tally up the damage. Assuming the *Ruptured Duck* was totaled, he said, which is what it sounded like to him, I was looking at about $20,000.

"That's laughable, Vinnie, and you know it. My plane's easily worth twice that much. I just got the engine overhauled."

"You're a serious pilot, Cordell, to be treated with respect," Vinnie said, like his mouth was crammed with Sicilian olives, "but your aircraft is old. It's tired. Trust me on this, my friend, when I say that I would be doing you a service, cashing you out at twenty large."

"I *owe* more than twenty large on that plane, Vinnie. I've got two notes against it. I settle with you for $20,000, I'm done flying. That means no more annual premium checks from me to you. This is the first claim I've ever filed. *Ever.* You're telling me that doesn't count for something?"

Vinnie heaved a Godfather-size sigh and said he would see what he could do, like he was doing me a huge favor.

After I got dressed, I settled back on the bed and tried to relax. I thought about checking in with Detective Rosario to find out whether Bunny the Human Doberman had been picked up by the authorities in Arizona, but I figured Rosario would've called if she had any news. I yawned, suddenly real-izing that I was tired, and closed my eyes to catch a short nap. When I awoke, four hours had come and gone. The guest-house was dark. I walked outside.

Ryder was in the pool, floating on an air mattress, wearing a Little Mermaid bikini. Crissy was reclined on a padded chaise lounge in a white, one-piece tank suit, sipping what looked like a Bloody Mary, and perusing a copy of *Millionaire* magazine. Hub still wasn't home, she said. He and Castle had gone to cocktails and dinner after golf. "Boys' night out," Crissy said with an irritated smirk.

"I'm a girl," Ryder said.

"Yes, you are, Ryder," Crissy said. "And you know what? You're lucky, because you'll be a woman someday, but men will always be boys. Silly little boys who have no idea what they're doing half the time. Isn't that right, Cordell?"

There was an edge to her words, a definite bitterness, as if in the interim between her having made a pass at me and my having rejecting it, she'd concluded I was a ball-less jerk.

"That's right, Ryder," I said. "All men are boys. And the trick for us boys is to always remember to think with our big heads, not our little ones."

"What's that mean?"

"It means Mr. Logan thinks he's being funny, but he's not." I gazed up at the night sky and tried to change the subject. "See the Big Dipper up there, Ryder?"

Ryder floated on her back with her twig-like arms outstretched and said nothing, rotating her wrists and making circular splashing movements as if her hands were pectoral fins.

"Well, anyway, if you follow those two stars," I said, pointing, "they'll take you straight to Polaris, the North Star. That way, you'll always know which direction to go."

"Ryder has eye problems," Crissy said curtly. "Congenital stationary night blindness. She was born with it. Everything looks blurry to her in low light."

"Can't say I've ever heard of it. Must be a rare condition."

"Only one out of every two hundred thousand people gets it."

Many of life's greatest gifts can only be enjoyed in the dark. The aurora borealis. The lights of Paris. The saliva-inducing way roasted pig looks in the glow of Hawaiian tiki torches. I felt sorry for Hub Walker's granddaughter, all she would miss in her life.

"One more reason Ryder's so special," I said.

Ryder said nothing.

My stomach was making noises. I checked my watch: half-past suppertime. Crissy seemed in no mood to offer me dinner, and even I am not so presumptuous as to go foraging through other people's refrigerators without an invitation. I told her I was heading out to grab some chow, and would be back afterward. Hopefully Hub would be home by then.

She sullenly sipped her drink, read her magazine, and said nothing.

THE VILLAGE of La Jolla at night is no cheap eats central. Unless your hankering is for coq au vin or wild mushroom raviolis in port wine sauce with a sautéed side of pomposity, you're pretty much out of luck.

Where's a taco shack when you need it?

El Indio still had to be open at that hour. It was fifteen minutes away, but definitely worth the drive. I wheeled the Escalade south onto Coast Boulevard and accelerated to something under Mach.

Bent as I was on my craving for something refried and wrapped in a tortilla, I didn't notice the headlights at first, creeping up on my tail. I switched lanes. The lights did, too, so close behind me that they disappeared from view altogether, leaving only an ominous, dark presence in my wake. The Escalade's illuminated speedometer registered close to fifty in what I assumed was a thirty mile-an-hour zone. The guy behind me had to be Johnny Law. My second traffic stop in three days. Damn.

A real Buddhist is supposed to be kind and considerate, even to traffic cops. I decided I'd save him the trouble of firing up his lights and siren; I pulled over without being prompted. He followed, aiming a high-intensity beam at my side-view mirror, blinding me to his approach, just as his fellow officer had done two nights earlier when Savannah and I were still on speaking terms. I turned on my dome light and put my hands on the top of the steering wheel to assure him that I posed no threat to him. But in heeding the Buddha and the Golden Rule, I forgot Rule Number One of the Official Special Operators Handbook, highlighted in boldface and printed all in caps on page one: NEVER LET YOUR GUARD DOWN OR YOU'LL HAVE ONLY YOURSELF TO BLAME WHEN THEY FIND YOUR SORRY ASS IN A DITCH.

The passenger door was flung open and into the Escalade climbed Bunny the Human Doberman with his .50-caliber Desert Eagle, the muzzle of which he jammed in my right ear.

"Drive," he said, slamming the door behind him.

"You mind if we stop at El Indio? I'm seriously jonesing for a burrito."

The blinding, high-intensity beam reflected in my side-view mirror had come from an LED flashlight like the kind police officers carry. Only in this case, the flashlight belonged to Daniel 'Li'l Sinister' Zuniga, Bunny's cousin, who came hustling up to the driver's side of the Escalade with the flashlight in his left hand and a Mac-10 submachine pistol in his right, which he proceeded to level at my head.

"You got him?" Li'l Sinister said, panting, sweat pouring off his pudgy face.

"Get back in your car!" Bunny yelled at his cousin.

I watched out of the corner of my eye in the side mirror as Li'l Sinister hustled back to his ride.

"I'm not gonna tell you again," Bunny said, pressing the barrel of his gun into me even harder. "Drive."

Twelve

"Turn left here," Bunny said.

I turned left.

"Make a right at the next corner."

I made a right, kicking myself at having left my revolver back in Rancho Bonita.

"Turn left at the stop sign."

We were meandering through the hills of residential La Jolla with Bunny's pistol aimed at my head. He glanced back every few seconds to make sure the only vehicle following us was the one driven by his cousin, Li'l Sinister. I thought about making a move, but I was worried Enterprise might charge extra if I returned the rented Escalade bloodstained. Any heroics would have to wait.

"You obviously have no idea the kind of gas mileage these things get," I said, "because if you did, we wouldn't be driving around in circles, expanding our carbon footprint. We'd be driving directly to wherever it is we're going and protecting the earth's delicate environment."

"I don't give two shits about the environment."

"Why am I not surprised?"

"Go left here."

La Jolla Scenic Drive South became Soledad Park Road. To the south, the skyline of downtown San Diego shimmered like a jewel in the night. We drove uphill, past a sign that said "Mt. Soledad Memorial Park" and into a cul-de-sac at the center of which stood a concrete Latin cross nearly forty feet tall, flanked by two small parking lots north and south. A red Honda Civic was parked in the southern lot, its windows fogged. Probably a high school kid and his date, enjoying more than the view.

"Over there," Bunny said, directing me to the unoccupied lot on the park's north side.

I maneuvered the Escalade as ordered into a parking space and switched off the ignition. Li'l Sinister pulled up on my left, driving a primer gray Chevy Caprice with low-profile tires and shiny, gangsta-style rims.

"Caught you on the news," Bunny said contemptuously. "You must be a pretty shitty pilot, you know that?"

"We all have our bad days."

"You're gonna fly us to Mexico."

The depth of his illogic was hard to comprehend. "I suck as a pilot and you want me to fly you to Mexico? That's like saying, 'I'm planning to go on a cruise. I wonder if the captain of the *Titanic* is still available?'"

"Like you said, asshole, we all got our bad days."

"Why not just *drive* to Mexico, Bunny? It's thirty miles away."

"Why? Because every cop from T.J. to El Paso is looking for me. Because they got surveillance cameras at the border. You don't think I don't know how the game's played?"

I was about to explain how the use of double negatives is never a good thing grammatically, but then Li'l Sinister jumped in behind me, breathing hard. "We're cool," he said, slamming the door. "Ain't nobody on us."

Bunny was giving me his best crazy, mad dog-killer look. "First thing in the morning, you're driving us to the airport. You're gonna rent a plane, and you're gonna fly us to Mexico. You say no, I put a bullet in you right where you sit. I'm a wanted man. I don't give a damn at this point."

"Not that I wouldn't enjoy some real Mexican food, but I have a better idea: why not give up? It won't matter where I fly you, Bunny. They'd find you. I mean, let's be honest, you guys aren't exactly Butch and Sundance."

Li'l Sinister jabbed the barrel of his Mac-10 into the back of my neck. "I say we cap his sorry ass right now, dawg."

Bunny ran his left hand across his mouth, still pointing his pistol at me. "I didn't kill that bitch," he said.

"Then why run?"

"Jesus, are you *that* stupid? I'm half-black, half-Mexican. The Navy boots my ass out on some bullshit assault beef, this Bollinger chick mumbles my name before she checks out, and you want to know why I'm *running*?"

"How is it you know she said your name?"

"None of your business, *puta*, that's how," Li'l Sinister said, jabbing me again with his gun barrel.

His act was getting old real fast.

"Ain't none of my DNA in her goddamn apartment, I guarantee you that," Bunny said.

"And you know this how?"

"'Cuz I was never in there, that's how."

Bunny's version of the story was that a distraught Janet Bollinger had called his boss, defense attorney Charles Dowd, a few days after Dorian Munz was executed to say she couldn't take it anymore. Whatever "it" was, Bollinger wouldn't say over the phone, only that she needed to get something off her chest concerning the testimony she'd given in Munz's trial, something that had been weighing on her for a long time. Dowd then instructed Bunny to go interview the woman.

"And she just happened to live in the same building as Li'l Lunatic, here?"

"That ain't my name, dawg," Li'l Sinister said from the backseat.

"Shut up, Daniel," Bunny barked.

Li'l Sinister flapped his lips in protest like a kid who'd just been admonished for chewing gum in class.

"I didn't know she lived in the same building as him, OK, 'til I went down there to talk to her, like Mr. Dowd told me to," Bunny said.

"So you go down there to just talk. Small world. Then what?"

"I knock on the door. No answer, so I go 'round back. Take me a look-see in the window. She's laying there, blood all over the place. My cousin, he's up on the second floor, in his apartment. So I go up there. Tells me he didn't see squat. He's on probation—agg assault."

"They knocked it down to a misdemeanor."

"Shut your mouth up, Daniel! I ain't gonna tell you again!"

Li'l Sinister exhaled and crossed his arms.

Bunny went on. "I'm thinking the cops, they ain't gonna buy me saying I had nothin' to do with it. They gonna put two and two together, come up with five thousand—"

"Like they always do," Li'l Sinister chimed in.

"Like they always do," Bunny said, "and one-eighty-seven both our asses. So we split, ditch my ride and jump in his. Trying to buy ourselves time, come up with a game plan."

"And that plan is, what, 'Let's kidnap a pilot and make him fly us out of the country?' That's not a plan, Bunny. That's a ticket to life without the possibility of parole."

"You gonna fly us down there, yes or no?"

"No."

His nostrils flared. "*Yes or no, asshole?*"

"No. Final answer."

"That," he said, pressing the barrel of his pistol to my forehead, "is the wrong fucking answer. Nobody grabs my balls and gets away with it."

"If I could make a suggestion before you decide to do anything felony stupid?" I gazed deliberately over his shoulder and nodded. "You might want to discuss things first with those nice police officers over there."

He whipped his head around reflexively in the direction of my sightline, as I knew Li'l Sinister would do behind me. I bent Bunny's gun hand back at an angle it was never designed for, snapped his wrist with my right hand and smashed him in the face with his own pistol. I pivoted in the same motion, reaching between the front seats while driving the clawed fingers of my left hand into Li'l Sinister's throat with just enough force to make him wish he was dead. The kid got off a short burst from his submachine pistol that went high and wide through the roof of the Escalade before his lights went out.

Bunny was out cold, leaned against the passenger door, blood trickling from the bridge of his nose.

"My bad. There were no cops. Must've been wishful thinking on my part."

Tires screeched. I glanced over as the red Civic parked in the south lot raced away, date night ruined.

Sorry, kids.

I scooped up Bunny's pistol and his cousin's Mac-10, and counted five bullet holes stitched in the Escalade's roof. I had no clue how I was going to explain them to Enterprise. Then I called Detective Rosario.

Li'l Sinister hunkered silently in the backseat of a San Diego Police Department black and white. I stood with Rosario and Lawless watching paramedics load Bunny the Human Doberman into an ambulance. He was screaming how it's against the rules of human decency to handcuff a man with a fractured wrist and broken nose.

"Stop whining like a little girl," Rosario said to him, "and be a man."

"Eat me, bitch!"

Rosario shrugged him off. "I'm a cop," she said to me, smiling. "You get used to it."

Lawless was convinced that with the arrests of Bunny and Li'l Sinister, the investigation of Janet Bollinger's homicide was all but complete. There was little left to do, he said, beyond tying up a few loose threads before presenting the case, heavy with circumstantial evidence, to the San Diego County District Attorney's Office.

I wasn't so sure.

"What was their motive?"

Rosario and Lawless both looked at me.

"What reason would these two clowns have had to kill Janet Bollinger?"

"You're a pilot, Logan, and obviously not a very good one, considering you nearly got us killed," Lawless said. "How about leaving professional law enforcement work to the professionals?"

"Janet Bollinger's purse was missing from her apartment, along with a few other valuables," Rosario said. "I'm sure we'll find things when we execute search warrants."

"Bunny said he had nothing to do with it."

"Wow," Lawless smirked. "An innocent suspect. That's gotta be a first."

I told the detectives what Bunny told me, how Janet Bollinger had telephoned attorney Dowd to say she had to get something off her chest about her testimony during the Munz trial, and how Dowd had dispatched Bunny to go meet with her.

Lawless checked his watch like I was keeping him from more important duties. "What's your point, Mr. Logan?"

"My point is that maybe you should go talk to Dowd, the attorney."

"Maybe we just will."

He walked back to his unmarked cruiser while a tow truck pulled into the parking lot and backed up to Li'l Sinister's Chevy. The truck driver hopped out in grimy coveralls and began hooking up the car.

"How's your plane?" Rosario said.

I pantomimed crocodile tears. She smiled sympathetically.

"You know, one thing I'm wondering," Rosario said, "is how these two jokers were able to track you down."

"Bunny knew I was doing some work for Hub Walker. He digs up Walker's address, establishes eyes-on, then waits until he thinks he has an advantage before engaging the target. I made it too easy for him, spaced out on my counter-surveillance measures."

"How do you know counter-surveillance measures?"

"I watch too much TV."

Her sideways look said she didn't know whether to believe me or not.

"Well, anyway," Rosario said, "I'm just glad you got 'em. Makes my job easier. Flying out to Arizona would've been a giant time suck."

"One's allotted life span is not disallowed the time one spends in the sky."

"Heavy. You just make that up?"

"Me? Nah, I read it in a men's room at the San Francisco airport."

Rosario smiled and stroked the side of her neck. "You married, Logan?"

"Was."

"Me, too. Twice." There was a pause, then she said, "Been forever since I got laid."

Two offers to get busy with two different women in the same night. The last time that happened to me was . . . well, I couldn't remember the last time. I'd be lying if I said I didn't harbor fleeting fantasies of spending the evening with a woman stripped naked down to her badge and shoulder holster. But I had a lot on my mind. Too much, in fact. I shoved my hands in my back pockets and watched as a twin-engine King Air flew by, pretending that Rosario's invitation, like the airplane, had gone right over my head.

"Well, that was awkward," she said with an embarrassed smile.

I wanted to tell her about Savannah. But that would've required me to think about Savannah, which I'd already spent way too much time doing.

Her partner flashed the cruiser's headlights impatiently.

"You'll have to come back down for the prelim," Rosario said.

"We'll grab lunch."

"I'd like that."

Lawless tapped his horn. "Time to go."

"I'll be in touch," Rosario said and began walking.

I didn't doubt she would.

Bunny Myers was still screaming injustice as the ambulance transporting him drove out of the park.

MIDNIGHT WAS long gone by the time the giant cross atop Mt. Soledad faded from view in the Escalade's rearview mirror. The odds of finding a decent Mexican restaurant serving at that hour anywhere in the San Diego area were minimal. Rolling down Mission Boulevard through Pacific Beach, I spotted a Taco Bell that was still open for business. It would have to do.

I maneuvered the Escalade into the empty drive-through lane and stopped at the sign where you decide what you want to eat. It didn't matter what I wanted because there's really no difference from one menu item to the next at Taco Bell. There's a big machine in the back that cranks out what looks like *gorditas* and *chalupas*, but it's all really essentially the same stuff.

"Welcome to Taco Bell. May I take your order?" She sounded Hispanic and young.

"I'd like two Burrito Supremes and a small iced tea, please."

"Would you like some cheesy nachos with that?"

"Only if they come with an all-expense-paid trip to the cardiac care unit."

"Did you say yes on the nachos?"

"That's a big negative on the nachos."

She gave me my total. I pulled forward to the window and handed over a ten-spot. Giving me back my change, she noticed the bullet holes stitched in the SUV's roof and cocked a tweezed, pencil-thin, nineteen-year-old eyebrow that said, "Like, what the hell are *those*?"

"If you're a fan of the Cadillac Escalade, you'll notice that this happens to be the Tupac Shakur Signature Edition. Bullet holes come standard."

She smiled nervously, handed me my supper-in-a-sack and quickly slid her window closed.

I ate on the drive back to Hub and Crissy Walker's house—checking this time, repeatedly, to make sure I wasn't being tailed. It dawned on me as I polished off the second burrito, mystery meat and sour cream glopping in my lap, that I'd forgotten to check in with Mrs. Schmulowitz to find out how her tummy tuck had gone. Too late to call. I'd ring her up in the morning. Maybe she'd have news about Kiddiot. I hoped they were both OK.

My plan was to catch a few hours' sleep back at the Walkers' guesthouse, secure the $5,000 Hub still owed me, and be on my quasi-merry way. I'd make arrangements to have the *Ruptured Duck* transported by truck, then hop a train back up to Rancho Bonita. All of the money I got from my work in San Diego, I knew, would likely go to paying the difference between the actual costs to repair the *Duck* and what my insurance was willing to cover. Without an airplane at my disposal, I couldn't instruct others to fly, and without students, I had no regular income other than my monthly pension check from Uncle Sugar. How I'd keep the lights on once I got home was a question I wasn't prepared to answer.

The feeling lingered deep in my stomach, along with two Burrito Supremes, that there had to be a connection between the execution of the man convicted of murdering Hub Walker's daughter, Ruth, and the stabbing death of Ruth's former romantic rival, Janet Bollinger. I didn't know what that connection was, but I found it hard to believe that Bunny Myers was the linchpin. Yes, he was unhinged. Yes, he had a hair trigger. Yet I had derived nothing from his body language or words as he held me at gunpoint to suggest anything other than the fact that he was being truthful when he claimed no involvement in Bollinger's death.

All the same, I remained conflicted by a gnawing sense that Hub Walker *did* know something he wasn't saying. Whatever it was, however, I wasn't particularly keen on finding it out.

Walker was a living legend. The world needs its legends. What it doesn't need is people like me poking holes in them. As far as I was concerned, the sooner I left San Diego, the better. I'd be doing the world a favor. The people of earth could thank me later.

There was still the matter of who'd sabotaged the *Duck*. Driving back to La Jolla that night, my desire to hunt down and punish the culprit took on phantasmagoric overtones as I fantasized over what I would do to him. Carve out his lungs? Play "Lord of the Dance" on his face wearing golf spikes? I don't dance and I don't play golf.

It would have to be lungs.

First, though, I had to find him.

Thirteen

The mockingbird's repertoire was impressive. I'll give him that much. He sang all night perched on a telephone wire outside the window of the Walkers' guesthouse, belting out tunes like the feathered incarnation of Frank Sinatra. Sleep amid his serenade was impossible. I finally gave up as dawn approached, did a few push-ups and crunches, took a shower, changed into clean clothes, and waited for the kitchen lights to come on in the main house.

Many Buddhists striving to become one with the universe meditate in the early morning when their minds are not yet cluttered with the trivial concerns of the day that lies ahead. I sat on the edge of the bed, closed my eyes with my hands loose in my lap, and tried to calm my mind and body, starting with my toes. But all I could think about was that stupid bird, crooning out his talented yet annoying heart. At 6:15, the kitchen door flew open and Hub bolted outside in his robe and slippers, waving his arms and yelling, "Hey!"

The feathered Sinatra flew away.

"If I sang that well, I wouldn't be giving flying lessons," I said as I exited the guesthouse, "I'd be working the main room at Caesars Palace."

Hub rubbed the sleep from his eyes. "You want some coffee?"

"*Need* is more like it."

I followed him inside and took a seat at the kitchen table while he loaded the coffeemaker with grounds and water. Neither of us spoke. It was still too early.

"Heard you come in last night," he said after awhile. "Out on the town, were we?"

"Something like that."

He got out two cups and a quart of milk from the refrigerator. "Hope you don't mind skim. Crissy won't let me have real milk."

"Skim's like water with a little white in it. I'll take it black."

I told him that the sheriff's department had arrested two suspects on suspicion of murdering Janet Bollinger.

"I heard," Walker said.

"How'd you hear?"

"A little bird told me."

He glanced at me over his shoulder and winked enigmatically. The coffeemaker hissed. Hub leaned his elbows on the counter and watched the ebony liquid stream into the carafe.

"Played golf with Greg Castle yesterday," he said.

"So I heard."

"He won't go public with that paternity test he took. Says it would embarrass his family. He did tell me, though, he gave some thought to what you said, about an independent audit. He agrees it'd help prove his company wasn't stealing from the government, like Munz said they were."

"Good deal. Then I'll just collect the rest of my money and be on my way."

Hub looked over at me again. "What money?"

"The other five grand I'm still owed."

"I don't owe you nothin'," he said sternly. "I said I'd pay you the other five after you dug up something to give the newshounds, to get 'em off Greg's back. You didn't do that."

Anybody can get bent out of whack when the bills come due. But it was the degree of Walker's vehemence that seemed out of character. For a man with an otherwise amiable, slow-to-boil disposition, he was being rather loutish.

"You didn't know anything about Greg Castle's paternity test until I told you about it, Hub. I think that counts for something. He also wasn't planning on commissioning an audit until I suggested it. That counts for something, too."

"That test don't count 'cuz Greg won't release it to the press. And he told me that audit was something Castle Robotics was probably gonna do anyway. From where I'm standing, that means you haven't held up your end of the bargain."

"I flew down here in good faith to work for you. I did the work, my plane now looks like something my cat coughed up, and did I mention I almost got killed? From where I'm standing, or sitting, as the case may be, that's easily worth five grand."

"A deal's a deal," Walker said coldly, "and you didn't hold up your end of the deal."

Crissy swept into the kitchen in black running tights and a gray, UC San Diego hoodie, her hair pulled back in a ponytail. Hub asked her if Ryder was still sleeping.

"Like a log."

She nabbed a bottle of fluorescent green energy drink from the refrigerator and asked me pleasantly how I'd slept, as if what had occurred between the two of us the night before hadn't.

"That crazy bird kept him up," Hub said before I could respond, "like it did me."

Crissy took a long swallow from her bottle. "He just needs a little comfort," she said, looking at me with a small, telling smile that Hub, waiting on the coffee, didn't catch. "Like we all do."

I pretended not to notice, and asked Walker again how he'd heard so quickly that arrests had been made in the Janet Bollinger case.

"I heard," Crissy said. "I got up early to do yoga and turned on the radio. It was on the news. I'm just so relieved they caught them."

Hub poured the coffee. "Janet was a nice girl," he said, "even if she did get involved with Munz. Nobody deserves to die like she did. Her or my daughter."

He stared out at the pool, pursing his lips. Crissy caressed his arm, said she'd be back from her run in forty-five minutes, and gave him a departing peck on the cheek. I waited until I heard the front door open and latch closed.

"There's something you're not telling me, Hub."

"I don't know what you're talking about."

"Janet Bollinger was stabbed two days ago. Somebody drove onto the flight line at Montgomery Field that night and tinkered with the engine on my airplane. That's why I crashed."

"And you think *I* had something to do with that?"

I said nothing and watched him.

Walker began pacing angrily. "You got no right saying something like that to me in my own house. No right at all."

"Did you go out that night, Hub?"

"I told you. I couldn't sleep that night. I took a pill."

He strode across the kitchen to a gumwood desk built into a small alcove and yanked opened a side drawer. Fearing he might be going for a weapon, I reached across the counter for a steak knife from a butcher block carving set—paranoia wasn't a mental disorder among Alpha operators, it was a job requirement—when I realized that Walker wasn't attempting to arm himself. He was reaching for his checkbook and a pen.

He scribbled out a check like he couldn't do it fast enough, tore it off, and slapped it on the counter in front of me. The amount was $5,000.

"Time for you to hit the road, Mr. Logan."

I BRUSHED my teeth, gathered together my kit, and returned to the main house. I wanted to apologize to Hub for casting aspersions, but there was no one home. Walker, I assumed, had driven his granddaughter to school, and Crissy was not yet back from jogging. I jotted a note that said simply, "Blue skies—Logan," placed it on the kitchen counter, and left through the front door, making sure it was locked behind me.

Across the street, Major Kilgore, U.S. Marine Corps retired, was hosing down a silver Lincoln Town Car sporting a bumper sticker that proclaimed global warming to be a hoax of the liberal left. He paused to watch me toss my duffel in the back of the Escalade.

"Your pal's no hero," Kilgore yelled. "He's a jerk."

"Thanks for the heads-up."

I climbed in, cranked the ignition, turned to look over my shoulder, and began backing out of the Walkers' long driveway. Kilgore slammed down his hose with the water still running and came storming toward the Escalade before I'd reached the street.

His eyes were like pinballs, bouncing around in their sockets. My sightline went instinctively to his hands, which appeared empty. But as we converged, he dug into the right front pocket of his Bermuda shorts. I had no intention of waiting to find out if he was packing or merely playing pocket pool. I cut the wheel sharply and drove off the driveway in reverse, onto the Walkers' lawn, angling straight for him. He was a half-second from being flattened by 5,800 pounds of Motor City metal when I cut the wheel again, just missing him, as he leapt sideways to avoid being hit, like Superman jumping through a window.

I stood on the brakes, slammed the SUV into park and jumped out. Kilgore was lying on the grass, stunned and gasping but otherwise unscathed. In his right hand was a piece of paper he'd removed from his pocket.

"You could've killed me!"

"The operative word being *could've*."

I tried to help him up, but the major would have none of it. He got to his feet, dusting himself off, livid. The paper in his hand was some story he'd snagged off the Internet detailing how Georgia's Congressional delegation had expended no shortage of political juice to help get Hub Walker the Medal of Honor.

"They call him a hero," Kilgore said, "but a *real* hero would never block his neighbor's view with his goddamn trees!"

I assured the major that I would blast off letters straight away to the White House, the Pentagon, and, time permitting, the International Court in the Hague, supporting his assertion that Walker be stripped of his medal given such egregious violations of neighborhood decorum.

"Thanks," Kilgore said, a bit surprised that I saw things his way.

"Don't mention it."

Hub Walker was right about one thing: his neighbor was crazier than a three-day weekend in Reno.

I called Mrs. Schmulowitz as I drove away. Her answering machine picked up. The message was unmistakably hers:

"You have reached the Schmulowitz residence. This call may be recorded or monitored for quality and training purposes. If you do not wish for this call to be monitored or recorded, then let this *facacta* machine—which has too many buttons and numbers that are too small for me to read them all—know that you do not wish to be recorded or monitored when you leave your message. Thank you for calling."

Beep.

"Hello, Mrs. Schmulowitz, Cordell Logan here. I'm calling to find out how you're doing after your surgery. Hope you're doing great. Also, I'm wondering whether that cat who lets me live with him ever showed up. Please let me know if you get a chance. You have my number. Shalom."

I found an ATM machine not far from the Taco Bell I'd visited the night before and deposited Walker's check before he changed his mind and put a stop-payment on it. It took me three tries to punch in my PIN correctly. I was more tired than I realized.

The beach was two blocks away. I hooked a right past Hornblend Street, found abundant free parking outside a CVS pharmacy, secured the Escalade with the key chain remote, and was soon lying on soft, warm sand. The ocean was sapphire. I closed my eyes and tried not to think. All I wanted to do was sleep. And I did, for five minutes, until retired airline pilot Dutch Holland called.

"I lied to you," he said. "I was running my mouth. I didn't see anybody tinkering with your airplane. I can't hardly see my hands in front of my face anymore. Macular degeneration. You got any idea what that feels like, knowing you'll never fly again?"

"No, sir, I don't. But I'm sure it's not pleasant."

"It was my pal, Al Demaerschalk. He was the one who saw your airplane that night. He can't hear worth a hoot anymore but his eyes are still sharp. He told me what he saw and I told you like I'd seen it myself. I don't know why. Maybe I wanted to feel like a big man. Been awhile since I was."

Holland said he'd been sitting outside his hangar the night before the crash, just as he'd told me originally, only he'd left out the fact that Al had been there, too. It was around nine o'clock, Holland said, when Al noticed the pickup truck drive onto the tarmac. Somebody got out, opened the *Ruptured Duck*'s cowling, did something to the engine, got back in and drove off. Vehicles of all kinds come and go on the flight line at all hours. Neither man thought much about it until the next day, Dutch said, after my crash. And even then, he and Demaerschalk failed to make a connection between the crash and what they'd seen the night before until after I happened to meet them at lunch.

"I couldn't tell you for sure," Holland said, "but with those eyes of his, I wouldn't be surprised if Al saw more'n he let on, even to me. Hard to say, though. He didn't want to get into it. You can't really have a conversation with him these days. He just can't hear."

"Why didn't you tell me all this before, Dutch?"

"Al keeps a room with his son and daughter-in-law, over at their house in Point Loma. They've been talking about taking away his car before he hurts himself, and putting him in the home. So he's been staying in my hangar with me. He didn't want anybody to know where he was at."

"I need to talk to him."

"He's not here."

"Where is he?"

"Took off. Says he's afraid whoever messed with your plane might come after him. He also thinks it'll make his kids madder at him than they already are, give 'em one more reason to put him in the home."

"I understand, Dutch, believe me, but Al's a pilot. You harm one pilot, you harm all of us. You damage one plane, you damage them all. I can't believe he'd sit by and let that happen, do you?"

The old man was silent for a few seconds. "Well, when you put it that way . . ."

I asked Holland if he had any idea where Al might have gone.

"The Eastern Sierra, probably. He's got a little cabin up in the Owens Valley. Got his own dirt strip. Hasn't flown in there for years, though. Not since he lost his medical."

I asked for driving directions.

"I couldn't begin to tell you how to drive there 'cuz I never did," Holland said. "We always flew. It's south and west of Bishop somewhere. I could probably find it from the air if I had to."

"We could take your airplane."

"My airplane?"

"Assuming it's still airworthy. I'll even pay for fuel."

"I can't fly," Holland said. "My medical's not current."

"Doesn't matter. I'm a flight instructor. You'll be flying with me."

Holland mulled my proposal. "It's a deal," he said with a rising excitement, "but I'm flying left seat."

"It's your airplane, Cap'n."

There was a doughnut shop just north of Montgomery Airport. I stopped off for a quick breakfast—two plain cake bad boys and one large coffee. Inside were six molded plastic tables and seats, orange-colored, scrawled with gang graffiti. I dunked my doughnuts and savored each soggy morsel. *If loving deep-fried dough is wrong, I don't want to be right.*

I was polishing off doughnut number two when I glanced out the window and spotted a young, thin Asian man with dyed red hair standing across busy Balboa Avenue, about thirty meters away. He was aiming a digital camera at me. Or, if not at me, at the doughnut shop in which I was breakfasting.

Under normal circumstances, I would've disregarded him. *It's a free country, pal, snap all the pictures you want.* But these weren't normal circumstances. Chinese intelligence was supposedly spying on Castle Robotics. Janet Bollinger, who'd worked at Castle Robotics, was dead. And someone had intentionally trashed my airplane. Was the Chinese government behind it all? I flashed on the two Asians in the Lexus I'd seen taking photos outside Castle's headquarters two days earlier. And now this guy with his camera across the street.

Call it coincidence—like when you read a word for the first time, and all of a sudden, you hear that word everywhere—but I was up and moving toward the door before I knew it.

By the time I burst outside, the guy with the camera was gone.

DUTCH HOLLAND's Piper Cherokee hadn't flown in more than two years, which coincided with how long it had been since the FAA yanked Holland's medical certificate, effectively grounding him. That, however, hadn't stopped him from putting the airplane through FAA-mandated annual inspections and running its engine at least once a week, if only to keep everything properly greased for its next owner.

By the time I got to Montgomery Field, he'd already penciled in a flight plan to the Owens Valley on a couple of aeronautical charts and telephoned Lockheed flight service for a weather briefing. Forecasts called for light winds out of the west along our proposed route, with clear skies and visibility unlimited—CAVU in pilot lingo.

"Good day to fly," Holland said.

"Is there any other kind?" I said.

"I like your style, Logan."

He took out a tow bar from the Cherokee's aft luggage compartment and hooked it to the nose wheel strut. I offered to pull the airplane from the hangar and he let me. The last thing either of us needed was Dutch Holland having The Big One.

His preflight inspection was textbook meticulous. It was also glacial. Rockets have reached high orbit in less time than it took Holland to walk around his airplane, checking control surfaces, draining gas to make sure the fuel tanks had no water in them, fiddling with this and that.

"Any chance we can get going sometime before the end of the year, Dutch?"

"I'm surprised you've lived as long as you have with that kind of get-there-itis," Holland said, peering at the oil dipstick through the lenses of his aviator frames. "You know what they say. There are old pilots, and bold pilots . . ."

"But no old, bold pilots."

It was a truism in aviation, and I deserved the reprimand. Nothing will kill a pilot faster than impatience. I'd drilled the very same lesson into every one of my students—but not before convincing them that flying a small plane, if done correctly, is inherently safe. The last thing you want is to terrify somebody before they've paid you.

I sat down with my back against the wall of his hangar, and waited for Holland to finish his walk-around inspection. What, I wondered, had I gotten myself into? Trusting a moth-eaten, half-blind pilot to fly me into the meteorologically unpredictable Sierra Nevada Mountains, hoping to find a remote dirt strip and another moth-eaten airman who might or might not shed light on who sabotaged my Cessna? Finding a roulette wheel in Vegas and betting my entire life savings, all three figures of it, would've made about as much sense.

"OK, all set," Holland hollered over to me.

Too late to back out now.

The old man grabbed the handhold bolted to the upper fuselage behind the Cherokee's right rear window and, with no small effort, willed himself up onto the back of the wing. He unlatched the airplane's only door, got down on all fours and crawled inside. The contortions it took for him just to reach a sitting position, then to slide over from the right seat into the left, were monumental. But any fear I may have had as to his piloting skills evaporated the moment I glimpsed the joy in his eyes. Holland was in his element.

I climbed in after him and latched the door. Even though he knew it by heart, Holland asked me to help him run through the engine start checklist. After we'd gone through the procedures, he asked if anyone was standing near the airplane. I double-checked and told him no. He reached down, toggled the electrical master switch to "on," rotated the ignition key to the left-magneto setting, planted his soft-sole old guy shoes on the toe brakes atop the rudder pedals, then cracked open a small hinged window on the pilot's side, and yelled, "Clear!"

A push of the starter button, a few pumps of the throttle, and the forty-five-year-old engine fired up as if it were factory new. Holland turned the ignition key to both magnetos, pulled the mixture control out an inch to avoid fouling the spark plugs, and retarded the throttle to idle. We donned headsets.

"Need to get the ATIS," he said, his gnarled, palsied fingers fumbling with a communications stack that was even older than mine.

"How about I work the radios for you, Dutch?"

"Good deal."

I dialed in the correct frequency for Montgomery's Automated Terminal Information Service, the regularly updated recording that provides pilots with the current weather, altimeter setting and other pertinent information on airport conditions. I listened, then switched over to ground control, glancing as I did at the two inch-long placards affixed to the instrument panel in front of Holland that showed the airplane's tail number, and pushed the mic button on the copilot's yoke.

"Montgomery ground, Cherokee 5-4-8-7 Whiskey. Ready to taxi, east end hangars with ATIS Foxtrot. We're a PA-28 slant Uniform. Requesting a right downwind departure."

"Piper 5-4-8-7 Whiskey, taxi runway 28 right via taxiways Hotel, Alpha. Advise run-up complete."

Holland repeated the directions back to the controller before I could, barely able to contain his enthusiasm.

"Your airplane," I said.

"A-OK," Holland said, smiling.

He couldn't see for squat, but he didn't need to. When you've wracked up more than 40,000 hours doing anything, as Dutch Holland had done piloting airplanes, skills become ingrained like they're part of your DNA. He steered the Cherokee perfectly along the centerline of the taxiway. When we reached the engine run-up area, he stood on the left rudder pedal, turned the plane deftly into the wind, and set the parking brake. He tested the ailerons and elevator controls to make sure the inputs were working properly, moving the yoke in and out, left and right, then pushed the throttle up to 2,000 RPMs, checking the carburetor heat control, the two magnetos, leaning over to peer closely at the oil temperature, fuel pressure, and a half-dozen other engine gauges. All were in the green. Holland pulled the throttle back to 1,000 RPMs.

"Montgomery ground," I radioed, "Cherokee 8-7 Whiskey, run-up complete."

"Cherokee 8-7 Whiskey, taxi to 2-8 right and contact the tower."

Holland released the parking brake and steered the plane toward the runway with his feet. "I love flying," he said. "I'd have no complaints if that's how I headed west."

In aviation circles, to say somebody "headed west" is to say they died. Where the euphemism came from I have no idea. But, personally, I could think of any number of other, more desirable ways to head west than in some hurtling piece of machinery. Having The Big One, for example, while celebrating your 100th birthday with three showgirls in the presidential suite of the Ritz. Or maybe just gazing into Savannah's eyes.

"Nobody's heading west today," I said. "We're heading north."

Holland laughed and seemed not to notice the approaching hold-short line for runway 28 right. I thought he would stop the plane but he didn't. I stood on the brakes to prevent the Cherokee from rolling without authorization onto the runway, just as a six-seater Piper Dakota touched down in front of us.

"Sorry," Holland said.

He felt bad enough without me saying anything, so I didn't. I switched the number one radio to tower frequency and announced that we were ready to go.

"Cherokee 8-7 Whiskey, runway 28 right, cleared for take-off, right downwind departure approved, wind 2-5-0 at 9."

"Cleared for takeoff, 2-8 right, with a right downwind departure." I turned to Holland. "Bit of a crosswind from the left. You *do* remember how to do this, right?"

A smile was his only response.

He steered the plane onto the runway centerline and advanced the throttle. We were rolling. In seconds, we were climbing. Dutch Holland may not have been able to make out anything much past the nose of his airplane, but he still knew how to fly like the old pro he was.

I looked left as we lifted off, hoping to glimpse the *Ruptured Duck*. But the hangar housing my airplane until the FAA completed its accident investigation was closed. I wasn't sure which made me feel worse: seeing the *Duck* all banged up again or not seeing him at all.

A pocket of turbulence rocked me back to reality.

THE 344-MILE route Dutch Holland had laid out on his charts took us east of the restricted airspace surrounding the Marine

Corps helicopter base at Miramar, then northwest, straight into the Owens Valley of eastern California. We'd first have to request permission to cut across Edwards Air Force Base, where Chuck Yeager in 1947 had broken the sound barrier, and where America's original astronaut corps demonstrated the Right Stuff before conquering space. Unless Edwards was test-flying some new super secret aircraft, chances were good that air traffic control would give us permission to overfly the base. Holland had calculated our projected time en route accordingly at two hours and forty-five minutes. That allowed us a fuel reserve of about an hour.

What he hadn't counted on was the Air Force saying no to flying over Edwards. Or to the winds picking up.

We were forced to turn northeast and cut across the high desert, halfway to Las Vegas, then north, then west again. By the time we penetrated the mouth of the Owens Valley and banked north once again, the gauges were showing less than a quarter-tank of fuel in either wing. Our ground speed had fallen to less than seventy miles-an-hour, while the unsettled air pushed the Cherokee around like a leaf on a millpond.

"We'll need to make a fuel stop," I said.

Holland leaned over to his right, our shoulders touching, raised his glasses and squinted at the gas gauges on the instrument panel in front of me.

"Damn wind," he said. "That's not what they forecast."

"Weather forecasting is nothing more than fortune-telling with a few random numbers tossed in."

"You got that right."

Twin ridgelines towered on either side of the plane like fortress turrets, the Sierra Nevada on our left and the White-Inyo Mountains to our right. Many peaks were still topped with snow, even in June. The charts showed there was a small public airfield located on the valley floor about seven miles ahead of us with a single north–south runway. Holland wanted to keep going, but I persisted. Airplane fuel gauges can be notoriously inaccurate. Who's to say we weren't already flying on fumes?

"I know my plane," the old man said.

"And I know you're not legally allowed to fly without a certified flight instructor on board, Dutch, which, according to the FAA, I am. I'm sorry to pull rank, but that makes me pilot-in-command, and I say we put down before we have no choice."

Holland looked over at the mountains to our left, then down toward the ground, a mile below us. The area was starting to look familiar to him. Al Demaerschalk's cabin and dirt airstrip, he said, were just up the way, probably no more than ten or twelve miles.

I was starting to worry about committing aviation's cardinal sin—running out of gas.

"Let's say we do find the cabin and land on Al's strip," I said. "By the time we take off, we may not have enough gas to get to someplace where we *can* refuel. We'd be stuck, unless Al could drive us somewhere. And we don't even know if he's there."

Holland rubbed his eyes. "Fuel's gonna be cheaper up toward Bishop," he said. "I say we land there, then go find Al's cabin. But you're the CFI. If you think we should put down, fine by me."

He held up both hands like he was surrendering the airplane to me. I took the controls and started looking for a runway on which to land.

Looking back, maybe I should have listened to him.

Fourteen

There was no gas at the Fair Vista Airport. There was no nothing. Just a couple of boarded-up, weather-beaten, World War II-era hangars, and a crumbling tarmac with milkweeds growing out of the cracks. A mangy-looking pit bull with swollen teats barked at me as I stepped off the wing, before racing off toward an empty two-lane highway that paralleled the runway, about fifty meters to the west.

Holland climbed down stiffly out of the airplane behind me. "Where's the gas pumps?"

"There are none."

"Then why did we land here, Mr. Certified Flight Instructor?"

Good question.

He shook his head and started walking toward the rear of the nearest hangar.

"Where're you going, Dutch?"

"The little boy's room."

We both knew what he meant. There was no public washroom at the Fair Vista Airport. But when you're male and you're outdoors, well . . .

A parching wind whistled out of the north. The place reminded me of the mountainous region east of Kabul, only without the charm. I'd flown into Afghanistan frequently with the government, the last time to visit the Taliban's leading manufacturer of quality suicide vests. We found him doing business behind a mud hut, hunched over an antique foot-powered sewing machine in a rusting steel Conex shipping container that doubled as his workshop. Eight vests laden with explosives were stacked neatly on the floor behind him. Our translator asked him his name. When he confirmed that he was the man we were looking for, we shot him. Two of his teenaged sons heard our muffled gunshots from their mud hut and came running, one armed with a Russian-made Makarov pistol, the other with a sword. We shot them, too. Then we shot a Taliban courier off his Honda trail bike as he rode in, presumably to fetch the new vests. We radioed for exfil, helicoptered back to Bagram, and got hammered on Wild Turkey, courtesy of a one-star from Joint Special Operations Command who said he couldn't believe that a couple of go-to guys had done in a day what all of his operators had been unable to achieve in a year.

A drunk member of my team told me that night that Echevarria, who assigned our missions, had been bedding my wife while sending me overseas, sometimes for weeks at a time. Granted, I'd given her every reason to find comfort in the arms of another man; nobody would ever pin a merit badge on me for marital fidelity while I was away—and even when I was home, I admit I was a distant presence emotionally, my head still in the field. All I had left to share with her were jittery nerves and lingering, combat-induced anger. But still . . .

I stopped drinking after that.

The sound of an approaching car derricked me from Memory Lane. I turned to see a faded gold Oldsmobile Cutlass lurch off the highway and onto the tarmac, toward the plane, streaming a thin contrail of oily smoke. The driver was about twenty-five, shirtless and skinny.

"How goes it?" He waved pleasantly as the car pulled up beside me. A pair of dice showing snake eyes was tattooed on his left deltoid. He was wearing dark wraparound sunglasses.

"Just living the dream."

"Saw you land," he said, shoving his transmission into park and stepping out. "We don't get too many planes coming in here. Usually they just keep right on flying up the valley, all the way to Mammoth. Why land here unless you got engine trouble or something, right?"

"We were running low on gas."

"Well, there's no gas here, that's for sure." He was missing two lower front teeth.

Tell me something I don't know.

He gestured with his thumb to a young woman slouched in the front passenger seat of his car, smoking a Marlboro red.

"Yeah, me and her, we live down the road, 'bout a mile thatta way."

She was as scrawny as he was. Her hair was long and unwashed and zigzagged down the middle. Nasty-looking skin blemishes ravaged what had once been a pretty face. If the Crystal Meth Manufacturing Association of California was looking for poster kids, these two were it.

"Nice airplane," he said, gazing at the Cherokee. "How much you think something like this sells for?"

"Hard to say. A lot depends on the radios, how much time there is on the engine."

He glided his hand along the wing. "Yeah, I was gonna be a pilot once. I don't know, man. Life, ya know?"

"I do indeed."

He snapped his fingers as though hit by a great idea. "Hey, you know what? There's a gas pump at the Independence Airport, just up the valley. Tell ya what, we could drive you up there. Got a couple jerry cans in the trunk. Fill 'em up, drive you back, get you on your way."

"We sure would certainly appreciate that, young man," said Dutch Holland, done with his business behind the hangar and walking toward us. He dug into the front pocket of his trousers and pulled out a fat roll of cash. "Be happy to pay you for your trouble."

The driver stared at the wad the way a hungry man stares at a ham sandwich as Holland peeled off a couple of twenties.

"Awful nice of you, Mister," he said as he stuffed the bills in the back pocket of his jeans. "Isn't that awful nice of the gentleman, Jodi?"

Jodi flicked the butt of her cigarette out the window and tried to smile.

"I'm . . . Mike, by the way," her boyfriend said, hesitating for a split second, like he first had to come up with the name.

"Pleasure. I'm Dutch Holland. This is Mr. Logan."

We shook hands. Mike's palm was as slimy as a mackerel.

"Well," Mike said, holding the left rear door open for Holland, "let's get 'er done."

Holland seemed to suspect nothing as he eased into the backseat of the Olds. I suspected plenty. "Mike" was way too eager to help us. Either he was an Eagle Scout, or he was up to no good. My money was on the latter.

There's a given in escape and evasion tactics. The odds of surviving a kidnapping decline radically the second you set foot inside the kidnapper's vehicle. Better to resist any abduction attempt, forced or coerced, on open ground, where you still have a fighting chance. I wasn't too worried about whether I could incapacitate Mike and his stringy girlfriend. Even armed, neither struck me as much of a threat. But there's that weevil that lodges at the base of your throat when you don't know what's waiting for you up ahead. It's the same feeling you get just before you touch down in a hot landing zone, or when you kick a door, not knowing who's waiting on the other side, and with what. The unknown. You never get used to it. You just learn to put it aside.

We needed fuel.

I climbed into the back of the Olds with Dutch Holland.

The highway was empty. Jodi sucked on her cigarette, staring straight ahead in heavy-lidded, narcotic-addled silence.

"So where'd you guys fly in from?" Mike looked up in the rearview mirror with his sunglasses on as the speedometer pushed past seventy-five.

"San Diego," Holland said.

"Nice. They got those big whales down there," Mike said. "Always wanted to see those whales."

I rolled down the window to vent Marlboro smoke and asked Mike what he did for a living.

"Me? Uh, construction. Framing, mostly. Yeah, it was pretty slow around here for awhile but things are starting to pick up. I've been working pretty steady lately."

He was lying. The local construction trade may well have been on the upswing, but Mike was no part of it, not with callous-free palms like his.

We passed Manzanar, where thousands of Japanese-American citizens were forced to relocate during World War II after the attack on Pearl Harbor. Long gone were the guard towers and barbed wire fences. Little beyond concrete foundations remained of the camp's tar paper barracks. That and the lingering air of injustice. Dutch Holland appeared to notice none of it.

"We're looking for my buddy Al's cabin," he said, squinting at the landscape whizzing by, trying to get his bearings. "It's just up the road, to the west, into those hills a little, I think. He's got his own airstrip."

Mike was quiet. Then he said, "I know exactly where that is. Just up the road, into the hills. We can cruise over there right now if you want."

Holland brightened. "You wouldn't mind?"

"Not at all. It's on the way." Mike glanced over at his girlfriend. "Isn't it, darlin'?"

Jodi stared straight ahead.

I knew one thing. Wherever Mike was taking us, it wasn't to see Al Demaerschalk.

There was a turnoff just south of the town of Independence. Mike hooked a left and headed west. The terrain rose quickly from the valley floor as we pushed higher into what soon became pine-dappled foothills.

Holland peeled off his glasses, polished them on a trouser cuff, and slipped them back on, peering out the windows. "This doesn't look very familiar to me at all. You sure Al's cabin is up here?"

"Just a little further," Mike said, his jaw set.

The pavement soon gave way to a rutted dirt road. Dust swirled behind us. We bounced over a cattle crossing guard doing fifty, suspension and tires chattering across the metal grate like machine-gun fire. Mike eased off the car's accelerator as we approached a metal mailbox mounted to a weathered four-by-four leaning precariously into the road. To our right was another road that led perpendicularly up a short draw, so overhung by a thatch of tangled vines as to be all but unnoticeable. Mike made the turn.

"I'm sorry," Holland said, "but this is definitely not the way to Al's place."

No kidding, Dutch.

The top of the draw gave way to a collection of junked vehicles, an unpainted Quonset hut, and a dilapidated, freestanding mobile home from which two long-haired men, both the approximate age of our driver, emerged on the run. The shorter and heavier of the two sported a scruffy beard and a pump-action, 12-gauge shotgun. The other man toted an AK-47.

Mike jammed on the brakes. He reached under his seat, then jumped out, waving a cheap .25-caliber pistol and yelling, "Get out of the car!" as the two men from the trailer converged on us with their weapons at the ready.

Holland looked left and right, confused. "Where are we?"

"In deep guano," I said, stepping out with my hands up.

The odor of ammonia wafted in the dry, hot air from the direction of the Quonset hut. Somebody was cooking a batch of crystal meth.

"Who're these jokers?" the guy with the shotgun demanded. He was wearing flip-flops, cargo shorts, and a John Deere baseball cap, backwards.

"Dude, they're Fort fuckin' Knox," Mike said. He pulled open Dutch Holland's door. "Get outta the car, Gramps. I mean it. Now!"

"You heard him," Jodi said from the front seat, almost like she was bored. "Get out."

Dutch got out.

"I don't understand," he said, confused.

"It's gonna be OK, Dutch."

"I saw 'em land, down in Fair Vista," Mike was telling the others. "Check this out." He jammed his hand into Holland's front pocket, holding up the cash roll like it was a scalp. "Plus they got their own airplane. Is that chill or what?"

"They got their own plane?" said the man with the AK-47. He wore a "Jugs, Not Drugs" T-shirt.

"Real nice one, too," Mike said.

"That means people must've seen 'em come in, you moron! They probably got tracked on radar or something. What the hell were you thinking, bringing 'em up here? Seriously, dude, I'd like to know."

"I thought . . ." Mike stopped to ponder the question. "I thought, you know, we could, like, I dunno, jack 'em, or somethin'. Take their plane. Whatever."

"Then what, shoot 'em?"

Mike looked down at the ground like he hadn't really planned that far ahead, then shrugged. "I guess. I dunno."

The guy wearing the backward John Deere cap smacked him on the side of the head.

"Just so you know," I said, "I'm an employee of the United States government. I work for one of those alphabet agencies you've no doubt heard about, and I just happened to be on a mission with my distinguished colleague here when your friend 'Mike' offered us a lift. Now, you probably want to know what kind of a mission I'm on, and I *could* tell you, but then I'd have to, well, I think you know . . ."

Jodi turned to Mike and asked, "Have to *what?*"

"Kill us," Mike said, rolling his eyes.

I went on. "One thing I *can* tell you, because most foreign intelligence services hostile to the United States already are aware of these things, is that I've been implanted with a microchip, which is standard procedure for operators in the field, by the way. My chip transmits a discrete transponder code. And that code," I said, unfurling a finger skyward, "goes directly to an NROL-25 satellite in geostationary orbit, programmed to monitor my every movement. The National Reconnaissance Office is actually watching you right now. Everybody say cheese."

They all craned their necks and gaped as if to see the aforementioned recon bird in orbit. Even Jodi looked up.

"So here's the deal, kids: my colleague and I will borrow Mike's car, and we will go about our mission here in the beautiful Owens Valley. After we've completed our mission, we'll drop the car back at the Fair Vista Airport, where you can pick it up tomorrow at your convenience."

The guy with the shotgun scratched his chin, pondering my offer. "What about the cops?" He gestured toward the hut.

"You mean am I going to tell them about your little chemistry project? Not as long as Mike here gives my colleague back all the money he stole from him and if you young gentlemen promise to consider contacting the Betty Ford Center."

Shotgun man thought about it, then said, "OK."

Mike returned Holland's cash. "Sorry, mister."

The old man struggled to come up with an appropriate response. "Just try to keep your nose clean," he said finally. "The mind is a terrible thing to waste."

I climbed in behind the wheel of the Olds. Dutch got in on the passenger side. The last thing I saw driving away was Jodi lighting another cigarette and the guy with the AK punching Mike in the face.

"WHAT THE heck was that awful smell back there?" Dutch Holland said, glancing back through the rear window.

"Drugs."

"What kind of drugs?"

"Bad drugs."

The old man was quiet for a minute as we drove along the dirt road.

"You really work for the government?"

"If I did, Dutch, do you really think I would've *said* I did?"

He mulled my answer.

"What about the computer chip, the satellite, all that. That made up, too?"

I looked over at him as if to say, *of course it was.*

"Well, you sure had me bamboozled—and those dope fiends, too," Holland said, smiling. "Boy howdy, now there's a story to tell the grandkids."

It took two hours cruising up and down the valley floor before we turned up a canyon west of Lone Pine that Dutch Holland thought he recognized, and found Al Demaerschalk's cabin.

It was located along a short, straight section of dirt road, which doubled as Demaerschalk's runway. Hewn from rough barn wood, the cabin itself was little more than an oversized shed, probably 200 square feet tops, with a flat, corrugated metal roof set at a steep angle so the snow could melt off. There was a raised wooden porch with a pole railing around. Flanking the front door, chained to the floorboards, were two rusting metal milk cans bearing clutches of fake black-eyed Susans.

I pulled off the road, parked in front of the cabin, and got out of the Olds.

"Al drives a Kia," Holland said.

The man shoots down North Korean MiGs and sixty years later drives a car made in South Korea. You've gotta love that kind of consistency.

There wasn't a Kia in sight, unfortunately. Or any other motor vehicle except the commandeered Olds we were driving.

I tried the front door. Locked. There was a double-hung window on either side of the little porch. Both were lashed tight and covered over from the inside with butcher paper. The cabin appeared to have been unoccupied for a very long time.

Holland took off his baseball cap, rubbed his smooth, pink crown, and said, "I don't know where else he could be."

We headed back to the car and were almost there when a loud crash erupted from inside the cabin. Holland froze and looked over at me in alarm.

"Stay here, Dutch."

I eased silently along a side wall and peeked around the corner, to the back of the cabin. No one was there. I stepped around an outhouse and past a decomposing wooden wagon wheel. A box spring stripped of fabric was leaning vertically against the cabin's rear wall, partially obscuring a back door.

Which was cracked open by about two inches.

"Al? You in there?"

Another loud crash from inside the cabin. I retreated and pried a spoke off of the wagon wheel—a makeshift weapon in the event that whoever was inside wasn't Al. I was heading toward the back door again when I sensed movement behind me, whirled with the club raised, and nearly took off Holland's head.

"I told you to stay put," I whispered, a little too loudly.

"I thought you could use some help."

"It would help if you went back to the car."

His shoulders sagged, his feelings hurt. He turned and started walking away.

"OK, hold up. Just stay there, Dutch. I'll call you if I need you, OK?"

"OK."

Whatever tactical element of surprise I once held was gone. I shoved the box spring aside, booted open the door to make what operators call a "dynamic entry," and stormed into the cabin.

Waiting for me just inside the doorway, aimed and ready, was a skunk.

The sneaky little bastard let me have it with both barrels.

Fifteen

"Mary Mother and Joseph," Dutch Holland said, craning his head out of the passenger window for fresh air, "you stink."

I drove as fast as the Oldsmobile would allow until we found a general store in the humble hamlet of Independence, our eyes watering from the overpowering stench of skunk that was me.

The cashier, a porcine blonde with black roots and an attitude, started coughing uncontrollably as she tried to find a price tag on the bottle of hydrogen peroxide I'd set down in front of her, along with vinegar, baking soda, liquid detergent, bib overalls, and a chartreuse "I ♥ California" T-shirt.

"Tell ya what," she said, gagging as she tossed the bottle into the bag, "thirty bucks for the whole kit and caboodle and we'll call it even."

"My day's just getting better and better."

I tried to hand her the cash. She backed away from the cash register like I had leprosy.

"Just leave the money on the counter."

I did as she asked, stuffed my purchases in a plastic bag, and got out of there before she threw up.

THERE WAS a run-down, eight-unit motel out on the highway south of town boasting "Free Cable TV!" Dutch paid for a room—the least he could do, he said, considering it was me and not him who'd been unfortunate enough to go *mano-a-mano* with Pepé Le Pew—then waited in the car while I went inside to de-skunk.

The bathroom sink was stained hard-water green. A centipede ran laps around the bottom of the chipped white bathtub.

"Moving day, crazy legs," I said, trapping the squiggling insect in a wax paper cup before turning him loose outside.

I plugged the tub's drain with a hard rubber stopper chained to the overflow and ran the water as hot as it would go, squeezing in the entire bottle of detergent. My skunky jeans and shirt went into the plastic bag from the general store, and from there, outside my room. When the tub was half-full, I poured in the hydrogen peroxide, most of the vinegar, and all of the baking soda. Then I lowered myself in and made like a submarine, grateful at having remembered an article in *Boys' Life* I read growing up that said vinegar and dish soap, not tomato juice, did the trick when skunked.

The scalding water helped steam the stench from my pores, but did little to resolve the conundrum that swirled in my head. Where was Dutch's buddy, Al Demaerschalk? What insights, if any, could he offer on who had tampered with the engine on my airplane, and how much of it, if any, was connected to the slaying of Janet Bollinger?

Four days had passed since Hub Walker had hired me to help clear the good name of the man his murdered daughter had once worked for. In that time, I'd crashed my airplane, been accosted at gunpoint by various assorted lowlives, and managed to dig the schism between my ex-wife and me only deeper. I'd also made a fast ten grand, but the money hardly seemed worth it.

The water was beginning to burn. I pulled the stopper and stood while the tub drained, slathering dish soap on a thin washcloth and scrubbing my scalp and body until it hurt. Then I showered off and scrubbed all over again.

Dutch Holland was snoring in the passenger seat of the Oldsmobile, his head back, mouth open, when I emerged a half-hour later and dropped my old clothes in a Dumpster behind the motel. I could've used some sleep myself, but I was eager to get back to San Diego before nightfall. No use tempting fate, flying a single-engine airplane over mountain terrain you can't see.

I checked the Olds' trunk for the jerry cans that "Mike" said were inside. Of course, there was none. He'd been lying the whole time. As if I didn't know that already. Dutch and I would have to land and refuel somewhere en route back to San Diego. That meant part of the flight would be in darkness. Hopefully, we'd be out of the mountains by then.

I climbed in on the driver's side, my hair wet and uncombed, closed the door as softly as I could, and turned over the engine. Holland barely stirred. He didn't wake up until we were on the highway southbound and well on our way toward the Fair View Airport. He yawned, rubbed his eyes and nodded toward the new T-shirt and bib overalls I was wearing.

"You look like you just stepped out of the Grand Ole Opry."

"I'll take that as a compliment."

I wanted to say that I was dressed that way only because I couldn't find anything else in my size at the general store in Independence, and that beggars can't be choosers. But I kept my mouth shut. I'd change clothes after we landed.

"At least you don't stink anymore," Dutch said, "though you do smell a tad vinegary."

I turned on the car's radio. An evangelical preacher was discussing why God intended for only men to mow the lawn, and how scrap-booking and cooking were lady-only activities.

"My wife couldn't cook to save her life," Holland said.

"My ex-wife is a great cook."

One more thing to miss about Savannah.

I changed stations and caught most of Jimmy Buffett's "Cowboy in the Jungle," a song about learning to trust your instincts while accepting life's inevitable ups and downs.

Listening to the tune, I decided, was worth more than an hour on any shrink's couch.

Fair Vista Airport was as deserted as when we'd first arrived. Even without security gates, Dutch's plane had been left untouched. He asked if he could fly left seat. After all, he said, it *was* his airplane. I checked my watch: the sun would be down in less than an hour. It would take probably half that to reach the Inyokern Airport at the valley's southern end, where we'd refuel before continuing on to San Diego.

"OK," I said, "you fly us to Inyokern. I'll get us back to your hangar."

He smiled and flew magnificently. We landed, gassed up, switched seats, and lifted off once more, just as the last of the sun slid into the Pacific.

At altitude, on a clear night, Los Angeles glimmers black and gold like a living thing. Freeways and major streets pulsate like arteries with the flow of red taillights, feeding dozens of city centers—the amorphous creature's vital organs. Electrified baseball and soccer fields festoon the body, their high-intensity stadium lamps burning holes in the darkness. Here and there, airport beacons rotate green and white. For pilots like Dutch Holland who are born and not made, it is a panorama that never gets tiresome. He gazed serenely to the west, watching jetliners bound for LAX hanging in the night sky like strands of fireflies. I knew what he was thinking because I was thinking it, too: that being able to fly an airplane, to enjoy that much beauty and freedom, was a privilege few others will ever know.

"'Evening, Los Angeles Center," I said, keying my radio push-to-talk button. "Cherokee 5-4-8-7 Whiskey, with a VFR request."

"Cherokee 5-4-8-7 Whiskey, Los Angeles Center, squawk 4-2-5-1 and say request."

I dialed in 4251 on the Cherokee's transponder and informed the controller of our location and altitude. I said we were en route to San Diego's Montgomery Field, and requested "Flight Following." That way, we'd be on radar—a good thing when you'd rather not scrape paint with other airplanes.

"Cherokee 8-7 Whiskey, radar contact, position and altitude as stated. Chino altimeter, 3-0-0-0. Maintain VFR."

"Triple zero, 8-7 Whiskey."

I glanced over at Holland. He was now slumped forward against his shoulder restraints, his mouth open, dozing contentedly.

Over the horizon, the lights of San Diego beckoned like an unsolved riddle.

WE TOUCHED down at Montgomery shortly before ten P.M. Fifteen minutes later, following a pit stop at the port-a-potty, Holland and his Cherokee were safely back inside their hangar home.

"Thanks for humoring an old man," he said.

"Thanks for letting me fly your plane, Dutch. You've got yourself a fine ship."

He patted the Piper's propeller spinner like the muzzle of a trusty mount, then offered to let me spend the night on the air mattress normally reserved for Al Demaerschalk.

"He's probably over at his son's house," Holland said. "We probably should've started there to begin with. We can go over first thing tomorrow, if you want."

My stomach reminded me I hadn't eaten anything all day except those doughnuts at breakfast.

"I appreciate the offer, Dutch, but think I might take off and catch something to eat."

"No need. I got plenty right here."

He led me to a large cardboard box sitting on a folding card table. Inside were food items that, it's safe to say, few women would ever put willingly in their mouths.

"How 'bout some Vienna sausages?" Dutch said, holding up a can for my consideration. "Got your pork rinds, your buffalo jerky, ahh, OK, here we go." He pulled a glass jar out of the box. "Pickled eggs. Wash it all down with a couple of root beers. It doesn't get any better than that."

It certainly got a whole lot better than that, but who was I to contradict a ninety-one-year-old man? My options were simple. Find a Taco Bell and bed down in the Escalade, or go on a junk food bender and camp out with one of the world's last remaining World War II fighter pilots? Holland waited on my answer like he'd just asked me to the prom. The old man was lonely.

"Who could resist pickled eggs?" I said.

He grinned and offered me the jar. I forked out one with my fingers. It had the consistency of rubber. Which is exactly how it tasted.

DUTCH HOLLAND could've set off fire alarms with his snoring that night, and I would have slept through it. Could've been because I was exhausted from lack of sleep the night before, or because I was bunking snugly under the wing of an airplane, something I hadn't done in a long time. Whatever the reason, I couldn't remember awakening more refreshed than I was that next morning.

Feeling fine lasted about as long as it took to change into fresh clothes and drive with Holland to the seaside neighborhood of Point Loma, where Al Demaerschalk shared a two-story duplex with Quentin Demaerschalk, Al's squat, sixty-something son.

"My father had a stroke," Quentin said without emotion, standing inside his front door. He wore baggy shorts and an oversized aloha shirt with little pink palm trees in a vain effort to camouflage his basketball-sized breadbasket, along with one of those ridiculous little Vandyke beards to hide his many chins.

"Al had a stroke?" Holland's voice caught in his throat. "Where is he? Is he OK?"

"Up at Scripps. He's not expected to live."

Holland tottered on the front steps like he'd been pushed by a gust of wind. I steadied him.

"When was this?" I asked.

"Last night," Quentin said as a dark-haired, wide-bodied woman wearing turquoise medical scrubs appeared behind him in the doorway. "Somebody found him in his car on the side of the road up in Escondido. God only knows where he was going. This is my wife, Blair. I'm sorry, you are . . . ?"

"My name's Logan."

Blair ignored me and scowled at Holland.

"Al wasn't fooling anybody, Dutch. We all know he's been staying with you out at the airport. We tried calling, but obviously you don't have a cell phone, which is no surprise. Nobody your age does. It's just too complicated, isn't it?"

Al Demaerschalk's daughter-in-law reminded me of the Wicked Witch of the West, only not nearly so nice.

Holland was starting to totter on his feet. I was afraid he might have a stroke, too.

"Can he sit down inside for a minute? He needs to catch his breath."

Blair looked over at her husband, pursing her lips, as if to say, "You decide."

Quentin shook his head and exhaled like he was none too happy about letting us inside his house, then reluctantly stood aside, holding open the screen door for us.

The living room was a tribute to tacky. I helped Holland to one of two purple chairs, which matched the couch. Wax blobs floated surreally in a lava lamp on a glass-topped coffee table held up by deer antlers.

"Would it be too much trouble to get him a glass of water?"

Blair sighed, put off, and headed into the kitchen.

"Look," Quentin said to me, "it's not that we're bad people. It's just that, maybe if my father had been in some kind of assisted care facility, where he belonged in the first place instead of hanging out at the airport all the time, the doctors could've done something to save him. But now . . ." He stared down at his sandaled feet, shaking his head.

Holland's chin trembled as he fought back his tears. "Al's a good joe. Even if he can't hear worth a hoot."

Blair arrived with a glass of ice water and handed it to him. "What did you say to him, Dutch?" she demanded.

Holland looked up at her with a confused look. "Say to him?"

"He's been behaving super weird the last few days," Blair said. "He came over here the night before last, went to his room, shut the door, and wouldn't come out. Said he was scared but wouldn't say why."

Quentin Demaerschalk rubbed his ear. "Did something happen to my father out at the airport, Dutch?"

Holland looked up at me as if to say, "Help me out here, will ya?"

"Your father may have seen somebody tampering with the engine on my airplane," I said to Quentin. "He apparently was scared that whoever did it might come after him if they knew he'd seen them. He also was afraid it would give you reason to put him out to pasture."

Quentin's eyes pooled. "Crap," he said softly, then turned and disappeared down a hallway.

The duplex's windows rattled as turbine engines roared overhead. An airliner was climbing out of Lindbergh. Al Demaerschalk's daughter-in-law kneeled next to Holland. Gone was her scowl.

"I'm sorry, Dutch. I know how close you and my father-in-law are." She took his hand. "I know he thinks the world of you."

Maybe she wasn't so witchy after all.

Quentin returned, fisting tears from his eyes and clutching a scrap of paper. "I found this on the carpet under his bed. He must've dropped it right before he left because I vacuumed that afternoon."

He handed me the paper. It was torn from an AARP mailer. Scrawled shakily in an old man's palsied hand were the letters, "CAPCAFLR."

"Maybe it has something to do with what he saw at the airport," Quentin said.

Maybe. Or maybe it was nothing, the erratic ramblings of an ancient brain verging on implosion.

I tucked the paper in my pocket.

Dutch Holland took off his glasses. Tears streaked his cheeks. "Al can't have a stroke. He's five years younger than me. It makes no sense."

"C'mon, Dutch. Let's get you home."

I helped him up and walked him outside. Quentin came waddling out after us on our way to the car.

"Wait."

Holland turned.

"I know my father would've wanted you to have this," Quentin said, putting something small in the palm of Dutch Holland's hand.

It was a military medal, a Silver Star.

The old man clutched it tightly, as if holding on to Al Demaerschalk himself.

AFTER DROPPING Holland back home and making sure he was squared away emotionally, I sat in the airport parking lot and called Buzz. He said he couldn't talk long. He and other analysts were closing in on a particularly virulent terrorist cell they'd been stalking for months.

"Screw flying 767's into skyscrapers. That's so last week. Now these douche bags are trying to poison the food supply," Buzz said.

"One more reason to say no to broccoli."

"Well, there is something to be said for that."

"I need you to check something out for me."

"Did you not hear what I just said, Logan? I'm trying to save the Free World over here."

"You can't do it on your coffee break?"

"There are no coffee breaks in the global war on terror, Logan, or whatever the President is calling it this month. Maybe you've been out of the fight so long you've forgotten that."

"I'll buy you another CD. Placido Domingo's greatest hits."

"I'm still waiting on The Three Tenors."

I told him about what had happened to my airplane.

"You still flying that rust bucket? Whadda you call it—the 'Pregnant Goose'?"

"The *Ruptured Duck*. And, yeah, Buzz, I'm still flying it—or was, until somebody tried to kill me in it."

"Who'd be stupid enough to try something like that?"

"That's what I'm hoping you can help me find out."

I read him phonetically what was on the slip of paper that Al Demaerschalk's son had found in his father's room.

"Charlie-Alpha-Papa-Charlie-Alpha-Foxtrot-Lima-Romeo," Buzz repeated, making sure he had it right. "What is that, some kind of acronym?"

"I have no idea. But a code breaker might."

Buzz sighed resignedly. "I'll get back to you when I can."

"Thanks, Buzz."

I went to push the red button on my phone.

"Hey, Logan?"

"Yup?"

"Screw Placido Domingo. If you're gonna get me another CD, get me Pavarotti's greatest hits. The guy makes Placido look like a talentless punk."

"Pavarotti it is."

I was hoping Buzz would reach out to his cryptologist contacts at the National Counterterrorism Center, geeky geniuses whose idea of happy hour was chugging Red Bulls while hashing out unsolved mathematical theorems. If anybody could figure out what "CAPCAFLR" meant, it was them.

Sixteen

I tried calling Mrs. Schmulowitz yet again to see how she was faring after her tummy tuck. A computerized voice said the memory on her answering machine was full and not accepting any more messages. My concern for her welfare was quickly escalating from worry to dread. Had there been surgical complications? Had she returned home and suffered an accident? What if she was lying on her kitchen floor with a fractured hip, unable to move? *Help, I've fallen and I can't get up!* My mind raced with the ominous possibilities. In my haste to jump in my airplane and fly down from Rancho Bonita to San Diego, I hadn't thought to ask for the name and telephone number of Mrs. Schmulowitz's physician.

Dumb.

Neither hospital in Rancho Bonita could find any record of her having been admitted. I sat in my rented Escalade, in the parking lot outside the Montgomery Airport terminal, and fretted. Somebody needed to check on her as soon as possible. Problem was, I was more than 200 miles away. Fighting my way through the log-jammed freeways of Orange County and Los Angeles would take six hours at least.

Larry's repair shop at the Rancho Bonita Municipal Airport was a ten-minute drive from Mrs. Schmulowitz's house. I called him, but there was no answer.

The only other person I could think of was my ex-wife. She could be in Rancho Bonita, depending on traffic, in less than two hours. She picked up on the third ring.

"It's me."

"Are you OK?"

"I'm fine. Still down in San Diego. You got home all right?"

"Yes."

Strained silence. She was clearly still irked at me.

"I need a favor, Savannah."

The health of any friendship or romance can be gauged in the response to that one simple request. If the answer is an automatic, "Absolutely," you can bet you've got a good thing going. If the answer is, "What is it?" it might be time to punch out.

"Sure."

My heart danced, even if I don't.

I explained that Mrs. Schmulowitz had undergone cosmetic surgery, that she wasn't answering her phone, and that I was worried. Would Savannah mind driving up to Rancho Bonita to make sure she was OK—and checking on the welfare of my cat while she was at it?

"You can be there in an hour and a half, Savannah. I'll pay you back."

"Pay me back how?"

"We never did make it to SeaWorld."

"C'mon, Logan, you can do better than that."

"OK, I'll throw in the Wild Animal Park, too."

"What if you just started being more sensitive to the feelings of others?"

"I suppose I could do that."

"Good."

"So you'll go?"

Savannah said she was just finishing her notes following a counseling session with a client, and could be on her way within the hour.

"I'll let you know what I find when I get there," she said. "I just hope she's OK."

I could've said, "That makes two of us." What I said instead was, "You're a good woman, Savannah."

She seemed pleased.

As I hung up, a black, unmarked police car rolled into the lot and pulled up beside my rented Escalade so that the driver's side windows were facing each other. Behind the wheel was Detective Alicia Rosario. She was alone.

"I was just over at Hub Walker's house," she said. "Wanted to ask him a few questions on the Bollinger homicide. He said if you were still in town, this is where I'd find you."

"What was so important, you couldn't just call me?"

She shut off the engine, got out of her cruiser, and got in on the passenger's side of my Escalade.

"Hub Walker won the Congressional Medal of Honor."

"It's not *Congressional* Medal of Honor, Detective. It's just 'Medal of Honor.' And you don't 'win' it. You *receive* it."

Rosario gave me a hard sideways look. She didn't like being lectured.

"Something doesn't smell right about your Medal of Honor *recipient*," she said.

I said nothing.

"Hub Walker and Janet Bollinger were involved in a car accident the day after Dorian Munz was executed. Are you aware of that?"

"I heard something along those lines. Doesn't make Walker a murderer."

"Agreed," Rosario said. "But when I was talking to him about what happened to Bollinger, he seemed a little, I don't know . . ." Her words trailed off.

"Like he knew something you didn't?"

She nodded as she gazed out at the runway, trying to piece the puzzle together. "Janet Bollinger starts dating Dorian Munz after her good friend, Ruth Walker, breaks up with him. Munz goes on trial for murdering Walker, Bollinger testifies against him, Munz is executed, then Bollinger gets stabbed to death— *stabbed*, not shot. Pulling a trigger, that's easy. But stabbing somebody to death? Feeling that blade cutting through flesh? Man, you gotta want that person dead pretty bad."

"So I've been told."

I asked her about the status of Bunny Myers and Myers' gangbanging cousin, Li'l Sinister, who'd tried to make me fly them to Mexico. Rosario said sheriff's forensics investigators had found both of their fingerprints inside Janet Bollinger's apartment. They'd also found two ceramic Hummel figurines in the trunk of Li'l Sinister's car that they believed were stolen from Bollinger.

"Bunny told me he never went inside the apartment," I said.

"He told me he did. Him and his cousin. They go in, see Janet Bollinger bleeding on the floor, and rabbit. Zuniga grabs a couple of Hummels on the way out the door."

"Why steal Hummels?"

"His mother's birthday was coming up."

"Nice."

"I don't know if Walker was involved in Bollinger's homicide, directly or not," Rosario said, "but if we end up going after a Medal of Honor *recipient*, the sensitivity of that, in a military town like this? . . ."

"You never answered my question, Detective."

Rosario looked over at me with her head cocked.

"What was so important, you drove all the way over here to talk to me in person?"

She hesitated, then turned and locked her eyes on mine. "I get the impression, Mr. Logan, there are things in this case you're not telling me, either."

I realized that if I filled her in on what Dutch Holland's pilot buddy, Al Demaerschalk, had seen that night at the airport, and what FAA inspector Paul Horvath had found inside my engine—that someone had purposely tried to bring down the *Ruptured Duck*, perhaps to thwart a homicide investigation—Rosario would call in the cavalry. That meant the FBI, the National Transportation Safety Board and, for all I knew, half the Marine Corps. And that, as far as my ambitions were concerned, was a nonstarter.

I learned serving with Alpha that there is not always strength in numbers. Too many hunters can trample the trail.

Often, the most effective way to locate a target is to be small and stealthy, and to leave as few footprints as possible. That was my plan, so that I might find and personally punish whoever had done me and my airplane harm. Vengeance may not be very Buddhist-like, I realized, but then again, neither are *chile verde* burritos.

"I've told you everything I can," I told Rosario.

"Can or will?"

She could smell the lie on me as easily as I did.

PAUL HORVATH was leaning into the *Ruptured Duck*'s mangled engine compartment, snapping close-up digital photographs of the carburetor, when I stopped by. I was anxious to have my plane trucked to Rancho Bonita as soon as possible so that Larry could begin piecing it back together, and I could get back to being a flight instructor whose business, putting it diplomatically, afforded abundant room for growth.

"Take a look at this," Horvath said. "I didn't notice it until just now."

He pushed on the head of the carburetor drain plug with the tip of his index finger. The plug jiggled in its socket like a loose screw.

"Whoever put this plug back the last time didn't tighten it down with a wrench. They just hand-tightened it. Engine vibration would've shaken it loose, I'd say no more than fifteen or twenty minutes after takeoff, and there goes your fuel supply. Not only that: now you've got flammable gas splashing on a crankcase operating at near 400 degrees centigrade. Gasoline ignites at 257 degrees. You literally would've gone down in flames."

First the engine's breather line. Now, the carburetor drain plug.

"One way or the other," Horvath said, "somebody meant to bring this airplane down."

~ 207 ~

"Somebody who knows planes."

The FAA man nodded and asked me if I had any enemies.

"How much time you got?"

Horvath smiled and snapped another photo, his eye twitching. He said he'd spoken with airport administrators and was frustrated to learn that surveillance cameras covered only about half of the gated entrances to Montgomery's flight line—and that of the cameras in use, many didn't capture images well after dark. No camera, he said, had been angled in the direction of my airplane the night it was sabotaged. Officials planned to go through what videotape there was, but it would likely take months. As for security gates, only about half were equipped with computerized keypads that recorded the comings and goings of authorized users whom airport officials had assigned individual pass codes. The other gates relied on old-fashioned, three-digit mechanical punch codes that rarely changed.

"The bottom line," Horvath said, "is that security at most small airports, including this one, leaks like a sieve."

Should I have shared with him the information that Dutch Holland had conveyed to me, about Al Demaerschalk having witnessed a man cloaked in coveralls and a baseball cap getting out of a pickup truck to open the *Duck*'s cowling? Probably. But, as with Detective Rosario, my desires did not revolve so much around seeing justice served as they did retaliation.

"How long before I get my plane back?"

"Not for awhile."

"Can you be any more specific?"

"Wish I could, Mr. Logan. It's not up to me."

Horvath said he would turn over a final report to his supervisors, detailing his findings on the accident, probably within two weeks. His supervisors would then review the report before kicking it upstairs to FAA headquarters in Washington, D.C. It would be up to the aviation bigwigs there to decide when to release the *Duck* back to my care. The good news, Horvath said, was that his report would indicate the crash was in no way the result of pilot error. It was unavoidable, the apparent consequence of a criminal act.

"If anything, Mr. Logan, you probably deserve a commendation. That was a fine piece of airmanship, getting back down without incurring any injuries to your passengers or anyone on the ground. You should be proud of yourself."

"I just want my plane back, Mr. Horvath."

He nodded like he understood what was in my head.

<hr>

DEFENSE ATTORNEY Charles Dowd said he had an urgent need to speak with me. About what he wouldn't reveal over the phone, but the anxiety in his voice was palpable as I walked from the hangar housing the *Ruptured Duck* to my rental car.

"Is there somewhere we can meet? I'd prefer it be away from my office."

"I'm at Montgomery Airport," I said "There's a Mexican restaurant inside the terminal, upstairs. We could meet there if you want."

Dowd paused. "I'm not too familiar with that part of town."

Not familiar with that part of town? San Diego may be a large city, but it's not exactly Beijing. Hadn't Dowd mentioned when we first met that he'd been practicing law locally for more than twenty-five years? How could he claim not to know his way around a community after living and working in it a quarter-century? Either he didn't get out much or he was lying. But why be evasive? Had Dowd been involved in what happened to my airplane and now wanted to throw me off whatever trail might lead me back to him? For his own safety, I hoped not.

"We can meet wherever you want," I said.

The attorney suggested a bar in Imperial Beach that was located, curiously enough, less than three blocks from the late Janet Bollinger's apartment. I told him I was on my way.

"I'll be there," he said.

I had no idea what Dowd wanted to discuss, or whether he posed a legitimate threat. Still, if I learned anything toiling for Uncle Sugar, it's that the quickest way to end up on the wrong side of the grass is to assume that anyone is innocent. That includes attorneys. Especially attorneys.

Driving from the airport eastbound toward the 805 freeway, I spotted a small scuba diving supply shop and pulled in. The manager was about my age. He looked like he'd spent about twenty years too long in the sun.

"Help you find something?"

I told him I needed a knife. He asked me with a grin if I was worried about sharks.

"You could say that."

He unlocked the back of a display case, unsheathed a knife, and laid it on the glass countertop.

"Top-of-the-line. Pure titanium for durability, sharpness, hardness, strength and abrasion resistance. One hundred percent corrosion resistant and guaranteed not to rust. That's why it's the official knife of Delta and the Green Berets."

Spoken like a true chair-borne commando. Anyone familiar with Special Forces knows that when it comes to knives, nothing is official. Operators carry whatever feels best in their hands. I counted among my friends any number of hard-chargers who never even packed a knife. Why get yourself all bloody, they reasoned, when the government issues you unlimited bullets and silencer-equipped firearms?

"How much?" I asked, hefting the blade.

"With tax, you're looking at about $115."

I peered into the display case and pointed to a virtually identical knife.

"What about that one?"

"No self-respecting operator would ever be caught dead using that knife."

"Humor me."

"It's on sale. Twenty-two bucks and change."

"Music to my ears. I'll take it."

I SLID in behind the wheel of the Escalade, lifted the left leg of my jeans, and lashed the knife still in its sheath to my calf, then tugged the jeans back down. My phone rang.

"I got your good news and your bad news," Buzz said.

"What's the good news?"

"I talked to a cryptologist I know over at NCC."

"And the bad news?"

"He told me he couldn't run your RFI."

Had my request for information come in through official channels, Buzz's code-breaking friend at the National Counterterrorism Center would've fed "CAPCAFLR" into the NSA's supercomputer at Fort Meade. The computer would've assigned each letter a numerical value correlating to its respective position in the alphabet, then played with more than 180,000 possible combinations. The numbers would've been fed through a dozen code-breaking software packages, reconverted back to letters, and the letters to potentially relevant words. But, because my request was for nongovernment purposes, the only assistance Buzz's buddy was willing to render was wild speculation that the "PCA" in CAPCAFLR possibly stood for "principal component analysis," a procedure that relies on something called an "orthogonal transformation" to convert correlated variables into linearly uncorrelated variables.

"Orthogonal transformation? Who's your friend? Mr. Spock?"

"Don't go getting your bun all in a twist, Logan. I'm just telling you what he told me."

Buzz said he had to get back to work. I told him I appreciated his efforts regardless, and that I was still working on snagging the opera CDs I'd promised him.

CAPCAFLR. Two vowels. Six consonants. I stared intently at the scrap of paper on which Al Demaerschalk had scrawled eight letters. Maybe it wasn't some sophisticated code. Maybe it was an abbreviation. Or an acronym. Like me, Al Demaerschalk was a former military pilot. The military loves acronyms. They use tens of thousands of them. My personal favorite was always MRE, which stands for "Meal Ready to Eat," unless you're forced to eat them for weeks on end, wherein they become known synonymously as "Meals Rejected by Ethiopians." But if CAPCAFLR was a military acronym, Buzz would've catalogued it inside his encyclopedic mind, and told me.

I hooked a right onto Convoy Street out of the dive shop's parking lot and braked to a stop almost immediately as the traffic signal on Aero Drive went red. Two twenty-somethings who looked like they belonged in a sorority pulled up beside me in a silver Porsche Targa, sound system thumping out a rap tune, the title of which, I believe, was, "Freaky as She Wanna Be." The passenger looked over at me.

I head-bobbed to the pounding rhythm like I was gettin' down with my bad self.

She smiled and blew me a kiss as the light turned green. I noticed the rear license plate as the Porsche zoomed away. It said, "MZBHAVN" and, below that, "ca.dmv.gov."

Something clicked in my brain. I pulled to the curb and hit the redial button on my phone.

"Sorry to bother you again, Buzz. I just had a thought."

"Those are fairly rare for you, aren't they, Logan?"

"What if CAPCAFLR's a license plate number? A vanity plate. Charlie Alpha stands for California. Papa-Charlie-Alpha-Foxtrot-Lima-Romeo is the plate number itself."

"You're asking me to run it for you?"

"Would you?"

"I'm not your goddamn slave, Logan. Just because you saved my bacon once or twice in the field doesn't give you the right to ring me up whenever you get an itch and expect me to scratch it. I'm a key player in the battle against international terrorism. Do you *know* what that means?"

"It means that anytime you go answering one of my back-channel RFI's, you run the risk of stepping on your meat and being charged with misuse of government resources."

"Correct. It also means I'm taking my eye off about fifty Mini-me Osamas who, if they're not trying to poison the food supply, are all running around out there with a brick of C-4 hidden in their turbans and a hard-on for mom and apple pie. The taxpayer is paying me to help introduce these guys to the seventy-two virgins. But am I doing that? No, Logan, I'm not. And you want to know why I'm not?"

"Because you're too busy helping me."

"There it is."

I told him I valued our friendship and that I was sorry for having distracted him in his hunt for terrorists. It wouldn't happen again.

Buzz grunted. "You're just trying to make me feel guilty for saying no."

"I am not trying to make you feel guilty, Buzz. I still owe you the CDs. I'll get them to you as soon as I can. I apologize for having wasted your time. The country definitely needs you more than I do."

He was quiet for a moment. "OK, you win—but this is the last time, Logan. Next time you want an intel dump, do us both a favor. Re-up and make the request through official channels yourself."

With my airplane out of commission for the foreseeable future and no immediate prospect of income in sight beyond my government pension check, I told him I'd definitely give his suggestion consideration.

Seventeen

Four Harley-Davidsons were angled on the curb outside the Drop Inn cocktail lounge where I'd agreed to meet defense attorney Charles Dowd. I parked down the block and had just stepped out of the Escalade when Savannah called.

"I'm here at Mrs. Schmulowitz's house. She's not home."

"Did you check inside?"

"The door's locked. I rang the bell. Repeatedly."

"You need to check inside the house, Savannah."

"Logan, I just told you. The door's locked. What would you like me to do, break in?"

"That's exactly what I'd like you to do."

"Logan, I am *not* going to burglarize your landlady's house."

"What if she's laid out in there and can't get to the phone? You're a life coach, Savannah. Here's your chance to save a life."

Savannah growled with her teeth clenched—that exasperated sound women make when they know men are right but can't admit it.

"I'll have to call you back," she said testily.

"Please do."

I walked toward the bar's entrance.

A bearded ZZ Top wannabe straddled backwards one of the motorcycles parked out front. He was wearing a sleeveless denim vest with "Mongols MC" stitched on the back and nuzzling a skanky blonde biker chick whose arms were draped around his beefy shoulders. They were both smoking unfiltered Camels.

"News flash," I said, striding past them, "cigarettes cause cancer."

"Fuck off."

That's the thanks you get, trying to do your fellow man a solid.

Wedged into a strip mall between a check-cashing joint and a cash-only dental clinic, the Drop Inn seemed right at home on Imperial Beach's Palm Avenue. Tacked to the front door was a laminated plastic sign, one of those red circles with a slash through it. Behind the slash was the silhouetted image of a pistol: no firearms allowed. I hoped attorney Dowd had paid heed. The last thing I needed was to bring a knife to a gunfight. I stood outside the door for a few seconds with my eyes closed, letting them adjust to the dim light that I knew awaited me on the other side of the door, then walked in.

The Drop Inn offered no surprises. Dark and foreboding, it smelled of chewing tobacco and abject failure. Three rheumy-eyed regulars were parked at the bar, deep in their cups. Charles Dowd hunkered alone in a small corner table near the back, tie askew, suit coat off, sucking down a Corona. He waved me over.

I watched his hands.

"Thanks for coming on such short notice."

"No worries."

He caught the eye of the bartender, a narrow-hipped young woman with a lip ring and a violet-colored tank top who was washing glasses, and pointed to his empty bottle. She nodded.

I pulled up a chair from a nearby table and sat down opposite him, with my back to the door. Putting your back to the door is never a good idea, especially in a biker bar, but it was either that or sit beside Dowd like we were going steady, and who knows how that would've been construed among the regulars?

"This arrived in the mail this morning." Dowd unfolded a sheet of paper and slid it across the table.

It looked like an amateur's hackneyed idea of a ransom note—multicolored letters in multiple fonts and sizes, clipped from magazines and pasted together. It read, "LEt it go or DIe like janET B."

"Let what go?"

"I was hoping you might know," Dowd said.

"Know what?"

"It."

"What is *it*, Mr. Dowd?"

"You tell me."

I felt like I was trapped in an old Abbott and Costello bit.

"Let's try this one more time," I said. "Who do you think sent you that letter and why?"

"I don't know who sent it, but it's obviously a death threat," Dowd said. "Somebody clearly wants me to back off the Munz case."

He repeated what his investigator, Bunny Myers, had already told me. That Janet Bollinger had called shortly after I'd been to see Dowd, claiming to have new information that she insisted would clear Munz of Ruth Walker's murder. Bollinger seemed hounded by guilt, the attorney said.

"Munz was dead and gone," Dowd said. "Nothing I could do about that, but he was still my client. I felt like I'd let him down in the end. I owed him something. So I sent my investigator to see Ms. Bollinger. He shows up, finds her bleeding to death, and now he's in the sheriff's lockup. But I know he didn't hurt her. He would've had no reason."

Dowd's prominent forehead and upper lip glistened with sweat. His knee bounced nervously, vibrating the table. I asked him why he thought I would know anything about the threat he'd received.

"You're digging around for some kernel of truth that would erase any taint of guilt on Greg Castle's part in the death of

Ruth Walker. Her father hired you for that purpose. Is that not what you told me?"

"Mr. Walker concluded my services were no longer needed."

"You're not working for him anymore?"

I nodded.

Dowd snatched the note away from me and sat back with a puzzled expression. "So, if you didn't send me this, who did?"

"I'm wondering if maybe you didn't do a little cut-and-pasting yourself."

"You think I *threatened* myself?" Dowd gaped at me. "Why the hell would I do that?"

"To deflect suspicion from you. Or your investigator."

"You're crazy."

The bartender arrived with Dowd's beer. He hastily folded the letter and stuffed it in his suit coat as she set the fresh bottle in front of him and snatched up his empty. A motorcycle was tattooed over her left breast, along with the words, "Live to ride, ride to live."

"Thanks, Roxie."

"Four bucks, sugar."

Dowd pulled a five-spot from his wallet and told her to keep the change.

"What're you drinking, player?" Roxie asked me, cracking her gum.

"I'll have an Arnold Palmer, please."

"Take a look around. Does it *look* like we got fresh-squeezed lemonade around here?"

"Got any juice? Preferably fresh-squeezed."

"How 'bout a beer? We got plenty of that."

"Ice water. In a clean glass."

Roxie shook her head in disgust and walked back to the bar.

Dowd waited until she was out of earshot. "This letter," he seethed, tapping his chest, "came in the mail. To my office. To me. Personally. I did not 'cut-and-paste' it to 'deflect' suspicion from either me or my investigator. Some son of a bitch threatened me and I want to know who it is."

"Could be the same S-O-B who tried to kill me and two sheriff's detectives a couple of days ago by screwing with the engine on my airplane. You wouldn't happen to have any insights on that, would you, Mr. Dowd?" I watched his reaction carefully.

"I don't," he said, avoiding eye contact.

The attorney gulped half his beer and blotted his forehead with the backside of his tie. The door to the bar creaked open behind me. Dowd glanced over my shoulder, jittery.

Something didn't feel right.

I leaned forward in my chair and reached down for the dive knife lashed to my calf just as a burly forearm crooked around my throat. I sprung to my feet and pivoted left, in the same manner a bullfighter slips an onrushing steer, sliding behind my assailant and grabbing his left wrist in one fluid motion, while twisting his arm behind his back and using his own momentum to slam him head-first into the table. He flopped from the sticky wooden tabletop like a Slinky onto the floor, out cold. My knife never left its sheath.

"That was totally badass!" Roxie said approvingly as she stepped over the guy and put a glass of water down on the table in front of me.

I glanced around for any other takers—there were none—then stooped to make sure that my assailant—the Camel-puffing biker whose passing acquaintance I'd made outside the bar—was still breathing. He was.

"His name's Dwayne Streeter," Dowd said.

"Friend of yours?"

"I used to represent him. Big pot grower. Feds popped him awhile back on an intent to distribute rap. I got it knocked down to straight possession. He was convinced I was Perry Mason after that."

Dowd said he thought I'd been the one who had sent him the threatening letter and wanted to confront me—but not without first arranging to have Streeter watch his back in the event I tried anything hinky.

"We exchanged pleasantries outside," I said.

"The idiot was supposed to wait ten minutes, *then* come in and make sure we were cool," Dowd said, gazing down at his unconscious former client. "You must've made him a little nervous. You make a lot of people nervous, Mr. Logan."

"One of my many gifts."

The attorney said he had no theories as to who might've murdered Janet Bollinger, and professed to know nothing of what had happened to my airplane. The fact that someone had sabotaged the *Duck*, Dowd noted, was affirmation enough that the threatening note he'd received in the mail was legit. He said he'd be skipping town for awhile and staying with relatives somewhere back East until things cooled off.

"Could be Greg Castle killed those two young women, could be he didn't," Dowd said. "But I'll tell you one thing, ain't none of this conducive to my blood pressure."

Nor to mine. A tried-and-true Buddhist would've accepted with equanimity such trifling concerns as a pair of unsolved homicides, a sabotaged airplane, an obstinate ex-wife, a geriatric landlady gone missing, and an AWOL orange tabby cat. I clearly was not yet a true Buddhist, not by a long shot. My throbbing headache reminded me I had a long way to go before attaining true enlightenment.

Streeter began moaning, rubbing his head where he'd smacked the table.

"He's OK," Roxie the bartender said. "Got nothing in there but mush anyhow."

Dowd said he'd call me if he heard anything new.

"I'd tread lightly if I were you, Logan," he advised me. "There's a lot of gators floating out there. One of 'em's likely to jump up and bite you on the butt, you don't watch out."

"Free legal advice. I'll take it."

"Ain't nothing in this world free, Mr. Logan."

"You've obviously never been to Costco."

We shook hands.

Streeter's girlfriend was sitting on another Harley as I walked out, smoking yet another cigarette, getting friendly with another motorcycle enthusiast. Neither of them paid me the slightest notice as I walked by.

There was a drugstore three blocks away. I bought a bottle of aspirin and chewed four tablets in the parking lot. Savannah called. She'd found a rock, smashed the window in my landlady's back door, and searched the house. The mailbox, she said, was full. There was no sign of Mrs. Schmulowitz.

I went to a locals' eatery that night not far from SeaWorld and the beach, ordered a charbroiled turkey burger and chili fries at the counter, then realized after I sat down outside with my meal that I'd forgotten mustard. By the time I returned to my picnic table, thieving sea gulls had made off with everything on my plate, including the pickle. The manager, who looked like he greased his hair in the deep fryer, said it was not the restaurant's fault I'd been ripped off by wild animals. If I wanted another burger, he said dismissively, I'd have to pay for it.

"Gulls will be gulls," he said.

In caveman times, I would have fed him to a T. Rex, then pried open the cash drawer of his computerized register and given myself a refund. The fantasy was short-lived. Cavemen, I realized, didn't exist in the time of dinosaurs. I'm also fairly sure they didn't have computerized cash registers. Still, I left without making a scene, pleased by my own restraint.

Taco Bell beckoned yet again.

Former baseball star and death penalty pitchman Eric LaDucrie was sitting alone near the drink dispenser, working his way through a super-sized soda and a twelve-pack of tacos, when I walked in.

"I know you," he said, pausing momentarily from his caloric orgy. Red hot sauce dribbled down his chin. "Logan, right?"

"Right."

I ordered my requisite two Burrito Supremes and an iced tea.

"Is that for here or to go?" the pimply kid behind the counter asked.

"To go."

He took my money and gave me back a plastic cup along with a receipt. I walked to the drink dispenser and filled my cup. The tea wasn't bad.

"Hey, I've been thinking a little bit about what you asked me the other day," LaDucrie said, "you know, about Ruth Walker? I have a confession."

"Wait, don't tell, lemme guess. You murdered her?"

The Junkman blanched. "What?"

A short guy in his mid-thirties wearing board shorts, leather sandals, and a gray San Diego State T-shirt approached LaDucrie deferentially, holding the hand of a shy little boy. Their rotund builds and black, curly hair were identical. Father and son.

"Excuse me, I don't mean to interrupt anything, but aren't you the Junkman?"

"I am."

The man's eyes gleamed like LaDucrie was Cy Young himself.

"Wow, this is a real honor for me. We used to watch you play at the Murph all the time when I was this little dude's age," he said, patting the top of the boy's head. The man got down on one knee next to LaDucrie's table, his arm curled around his son's waist, and nodded in awe at the former baseball player. "Jake, this man was one of the finest pitchers the Padres ever had. I watched him strike out Mark McGwire once on three balls. Old McGwire, he never—"

"—Autograph's twenty bucks, kimosabe, picture's fifty," LaDucrie said, cutting him off. "You can order off my website if you want."

The fan stared at the Junkman, appalled by his attitude. He got up off his knee and grabbed his son's hand.

"I remember when you used to be great, man."

LaDucrie snorted derisively, watching them walk out, then turned and eyed me with disdain.

"What makes you think I killed Ruth Walker? I've never killed anybody in my life. Dorian Munz killed her."

"According to the jury."

"That's right. According to the jury. That's why they stuck a needle in his arm. And that's why for you to say something like that to somebody like me is total bullshit."

"You're getting awful worked up, Junkman, for something that's total BS."

"Yeah? Well, you would, too, if some cocky asshole accused you of doing something you didn't do."

"Number 263. Two Burrito Supremes?"

My order was ready. I grabbed the bag.

"You were about to confess something," I said, "before you were so rudely interrupted by your adoring masses."

LaDucrie wiped his mouth with a brown paper napkin, wadded it up, and tossed it on his tray. "I was wrong, about what I said about Ruth Walker. I never met her. I had her confused with somebody else. You asked me about another chick, too."

"Janet Bollinger."

"Janet Bollinger. Yeah, that's right. I looked her up online. You probably think I murdered her, too."

"Did you?"

"No."

He was looking at me square in the eyes when he said it.

DUTCH HOLLAND was more than happy to let me spend another night with him in his hangar at Montgomery Airport. He was mourning the imminent loss of his flying pal, Al Demaerschalk, and said he welcomed the company. He waxed poetic about bombing Luftwaffe airfields for more than two hours while I nursed a couple of cans of root beer. We were both asleep by nine o'clock.

It was still dark when my phone rang.

"Rise and shine, sleepy head."

I checked my watch, rubbing my eyes. "Buzz, it's four in the morning."

"Not on the East Coast it ain't. You get me those CDs yet?"

"Not yet."

"Then good thing I called early. This way, you got all day to go find a decent record shop. By the way, those letters you gave me—PCAFLR? I ran 'em through California DMV registration. Got a hit."

I sat up, suddenly wide awake.

State motor vehicle records, Buzz said, revealed that a vanity license plate bearing the letters PCAFLR had been issued to a 2006 Ford Ranger pickup, silver in color. The truck's registered owner was one C.W. Lazarus, thirty-nine, male white, five-ten and 165 pounds, who showed an address on Via De La Valle in the affluent beach town of Del Mar, just north of San Diego. Buzz said he was unwilling to do any additional research using government databases for fear of getting busted by his supervisors. He did, however, check out Lazarus using open source databases during his lunch break, on his own laptop.

"I couldn't find anything online on the guy," Buzz said. "Nada."

"That's impossible. The Googles has something on everybody."

"The *Googles*?"

"That's what my landlady calls it. 'The Googles.'"

"I'll be looking for those CDs, Logan."

"They're on the way."

"Right. Like I haven't heard *that* before."

Dutch Holland was sleeping fitfully on his cot, mumbling something tortured under his breath. I dressed quietly, the dive knife strapped to my calf, and was out the door before the sun.

Traffic was sparse on northbound Interstate 5. Southbound was another story—not yet six A.M. and already clogged with commuters heading into downtown San Diego. I felt sorry for those drivers, the repetition of their nine-to-five lives. But not as sorry as C.W. Lazarus was going to be when I finally found him.

I passed a subdivision of high-end, cookie-cutter homes. Buff-colored stucco walls and red tile roofs. A swimming pool in every backyard. California dreamin'. On my left were the Del Mar Fairgrounds, where the rich sip champagne and place bets on little men riding big horses. The Escalade's navigation system directed me to exit at Via De La Valle. I got off the freeway and turned left, heading west.

The sun was beginning to show itself, trimming the edges of high cirrus clouds in scarlet and gold. It was the beginning of one of those perfectly promising mornings. I was hoping to catch my prey asleep, in bed, unawares.

Eighteen

C.W. Lazarus lived in a strip mall. Or, more precisely, his mail did. His Ford Ranger pickup was registered to the address of Letters and Whatever, a stationery store where one can get copies made, have passport photos taken, and rent post office boxes where your mail can be delivered when you don't want anyone to know where you live. The store didn't open until eight A.M. I had nearly two hours to wait.

Across the street was a McDonald's. I ordered two Egg McMuffins and a coffee at the drive-through window, then sat in the Escalade and ate breakfast, feeling as if my arteries were clogging with every bite. I read somewhere that the marketing guru who dreamed up the idea of slapping a fried egg on an English muffin, slathering it with weird orange stuff called "cheese" and dubbing it the "McMuffin" died peacefully in his sleep at age eighty-nine. *Who says fast food can kill you?*

I drove back across the street and backed into a space two rows away from Letters and Whatever, with a white BMW 700-series sedan parked between the store and my Escalade. I would maintain surveillance watching my side and rearview mirrors, the Beemer obscuring my presence should Lazarus pull in.

Then I waited.

Hunting is mostly waiting. Ask any sniper. You wait and watch without moving as minutes turn to hours, with nothing to do but think. The longer I sat, the more I became convinced that C.W. Lazarus, whoever he was, not only was responsible for what had happened to my airplane, but for what had happened to Janet Bollinger as well. What links, if any, did Lazarus have to Hub Walker? Why would Walker have hired me to delve into a criminal investigation that had already been resolved if he feared there was the slightest chance he might be implicated in it? I had no answers to those questions. But I most definitely intended to find them.

Hunkered in the parking lot of a commercial shopping center with plenty of time on your hands would seem the ideal opportunity to meditate, only my thoughts were too scattered. Plus I was tired. I thought about calling Savannah for any updates on Mrs. Schmulowitz or Kiddiot—or maybe just to hear her voice—but I figured she'd call me if she had any news to share.

And so I waited.

At 7:59, a banged-up, mud-splattered red Nissan Sentra turned into the parking lot sporting a bumper sticker that read, "The Dude Abides." The driver parked in a space directly across from Letters and Whatever, and jumped out, dragging an overstuffed backpack. She was a bespectacled brunette in her mid-twenties, all knees and elbows, with kinky, shoulder-length hair still wet from a shower. Hurriedly, she unlocked the store's front door and flipped on the lights.

It was getting toasty inside the Escalade. I rolled down the windows. Other cars began filling the lot, luxury vehicles mostly, shoppers coming and going. None of them drove a silver 2006 Ford Ranger pickup truck with the California vanity plate, "PCAFLR."

I waited another hour. Then I went inside.

The gangly young woman I'd seen earlier was sitting behind the cash register, engrossed in a copy of *Fifty Shades of Grey*. She put down her book and forced a smile. There were no other customers in the store.

"Welcome to Letters and Whatever. My name is Kathy. How may I help you today?"

Well, Kathy, for one, you can dispense with the canned corpo-
rate salutation that turns you into a minimum wage automaton and
sucks from you the kind of refreshing irreverence illustrated by the
bumper sticker on your car.

"Can I borrow your bathroom? I had a little too much coffee this morning."

"I'm so sorry, sir. Our restroom is reserved for paying customers."

I plucked a ballpoint pen from a nearby pegboard display, took a dollar from my wallet, and attempted to give her the money.

"Actually, sir, that pen is $2.49."

I slapped three bucks down on the counter.

"The restroom's through there," she said, pointing down a long hallway, "all the way in the back."

The hallway was flanked by small, built-in mailboxes, their doors solid brass, each numbered. I tugged on door 1756, the box registered to Lazarus. It was locked. There was a tiny glass window built into the door. Peering into the box, I could see a few envelopes.

Kathy was restocking shelves when I came back from the restroom. I unlimbered my new $2.49 pen and wrote PCAFLR on my palm.

"Recognize this?" I said, holding up my hand in front of her. She squinted, scrunching her face.

"Sorry, I don't."

"There's a gentleman who rents a mailbox here. He drives a Ford pickup, silver. This is his license plate." I showed her my palm again. "I'm trying to find him. It's important."

Kathy folded her arms defensively. "Are you the cops or something?"

"No, no, nothing like that. I just need to talk to him a little, that's all."

"I'm really sorry. We're not really allowed to give out the names of our postal tenants unless it's to the police."

"Do you recognize the license plate?"

Kathy shook her head no.

"What about the name, C.W. Lazarus? Do you recognize that?"

Another shake of the head.

"What time is the mail usually delivered?"

"You know, sir, I'm really, really sorry, but you're making me really, really nervous, and I really don't do very well with anxiety." She walked behind the cash register, dug through her backpack, and pulled out a prescription bottle. "I'm afraid I'm going to have to ask you to leave now, if you wouldn't mind."

She was starting to tremble.

"I'm sorry, Kathy. I didn't mean to frighten you."

I walked outside and queried neighboring merchants and shoppers to see if anyone recognized Lazarus's license plate, or had any insights as to the man himself. My efforts proved fruitless. Most people reacted as fearfully as Kathy had when I approached them. One lady dug through her purse, hurled a ten dollar bill at me, and scuttled toward her E-class Mercedes. I wondered if maybe I still smelled a little on the skunky side.

"I'm not homeless," I yelled after her, "but I soon may be at this rate."

I stuck around the parking lot for much of the rest of the afternoon, hoping not to be arrested for loitering, hoping that C.W. Lazarus's truck would magically appear, but neither the police nor the man I was tracking ever appeared.

By four P.M., my stomach reminded me that I hadn't eaten since breakfast, while my bladder reminded me of other, equally pressing needs. I went back across the street to McDonald's.

The men's room had no toilet stall door and no paper towels in the dispenser, neither of which deterred me from conducting essential business. I washed my hands and wiped them dry on the back of my polo shirt.

The Angus Chipotle Bacon Burger sung to me. But at 800 calories and 39 grams of fat, I couldn't pull the trigger, especially not after inhaling two McMuffins hours earlier. I went with the Ranch Salad and an unsweetened iced tea.

"Alejandra" was printed on the name tag of the friendly crew member who took my order. I paid with the ten-spot the frightened lady had tossed at me outside Letters and Whatever. Alejandra made change and counted it back to me.

"*Picaflor*," she said, smiling.

"Say again?"

She gestured to "PCAFLR" inked on my outstretched palm. "*Picaflor*. It means the bird who pierces the flower where I come from."

"*Picaflor*. Very pretty."

I took the tray bearing my not-so-happy meal and found a table by the window, where I could watch the strip mall parking lot across the street. I sat down and was squeezing out salad dressing when it hit me:

Picaflor. The bird who pierces the flower.

During my visit to Castle Robotics, Greg Castle and Ray Sheen had shown off a miniaturized drone their company was designing.

It was a hummingbird.

CRUISING CASTLE Robotics' employee parking lot proved fruitless. No Ford Rangers with PCAFLR vanity plates. There was, however, no shortage of fuel-efficient hybrids, economy-minded subcompacts and one yellow MINI Cooper convertible with a bumper sticker that declared, "Engineers solve problems you didn't know you had in ways you can't even understand."

By positioning the Escalade on a side street directly across from the company's headquarters, I could maintain eyes-on the employee parking lot and every avenue of approach. Workers began streaming out shortly before five P.M., nerdy-looking software engineers with cheap haircuts and baggy jeans. They shuffled to their cars with their heads down, noodling with their phones, oblivious to my presence.

Did C.W. Lazarus work there? There was one way to find out. I found the list of contacts Hub Walker had given me and called.

"You've reached Castle Robotics. Please listen carefully as our menu has recently changed."

Once upon a time, real-live receptionists answered company telephones. People actually talked to each other. Now it was that same saccharine female voice, with the same computerized voice mail menu that always seems to have "recently changed." I shook my head. Someday, human interaction will be but a faded memory. People will procreate virtually, online, in the name of corporate cost efficiency. Thank you, bean counters.

"If you know your party's four-digit extension, you may dial it at any time. For technical support, please press one. For sales, press two. For billing, please press—"

I pressed zero, hoping to connect with an operator.

"I'm sorry, I don't recognize that extension. For technical support, please press one. For sales—"

Again, I pressed zero.

"I'm sorry, I don't recognize that extension. For technical support—"

I hung up and rested my forehead against the Escalade's leather-trimmed steering wheel while trying to suppress the desire to kill something, anything. My phone rang a few seconds later. I assumed it was the automated voice, calling me back to continue our "conversation."

"Blow it out your mechanical booty."

"My booty's been called many things, but never mechanical."

"That wasn't intended for you, Savannah."

"As I understand it, Buddhists don't typically exhibit unbridled anger, Logan. They modulate their aggressive impulses."

"I'm more of a Buddhist work in progress. And, for your information, my 'aggressive impulses' just now happened to be directed at an inanimate object."

"It does matter. There's a fine line between putting your fist through a wall, Logan, and putting your fist through somebody's face."

"I'll try to keep that in mind."

"I located your landlady," Savannah said somberly. "A neighbor told me he saw Mrs. Schmulowitz being taken away in an ambulance. She's in the intensive care unit at Rancho Bonita Mercy. She had some complications after her surgery."

My heart sank. I had called the hospital and was told they had no record of Mrs. Schmulowitz having been admitted. Apparently no one had bothered checking the ICU.

"Any idea what kind of complications?"

"They wouldn't tell me. And they won't let me in to see her because I'm not a blood relative. I gave the nursing desk your number and asked that somebody call you. That's all I can do for now. I have to get back to LA. I have an appointment tonight with a new client, a TV executive who's stressing out about his job. I'm sorry, Logan."

"Don't be. I appreciate the help. At least I know she's in good hands."

I told Savannah I'd call her that night and we could talk further.

"I'd like that," she said.

The phone went silent.

Dear, kind-hearted Mrs. Schmulowitz. I never knew my biological parents. I have no one to compare them to, but I couldn't imagine a better or kinder parental role model than my wizened landlady. She had one child, Arnie, a history professor who lived back East somewhere. They talked sporadically. Whether he was aware of her condition, I couldn't say. Somebody, though, needed to be with her, to hold her hand and help her get past whatever medical issues she'd run up against. The world could ill afford to lose someone as special as Mrs. Schmulowitz. *I* couldn't afford to lose her. Maybe we weren't kin in the DNA sense, but we were definitely family.

My airplane wasn't going anywhere for awhile. Neither, hopefully, was C.W. Lazarus. I decided to head back to Rancho Bonita and help take care of Mrs. Schmulowitz until she was back on her feet, then I'd return to San Diego to wreak revenge on Lazarus. That was my plan, anyway.

I fired up the engine and started to make a U-turn that would take me back in the direction of the northbound 805 freeway, when an ebony Hummer with tinted windows came flying out of nowhere and blocked the Escalade's path. A middle-aged man with a billiard ball head and a top-heavy, weightlifter's build climbed down from the driver's side and strode toward me authoritatively. He was garbed in ballistic, military-style sunglasses and a well-tailored Italian suit, black.

"What're you doing out here, partner?"

"What's it to you?"

He flashed me some cop-like badge and wallet ID. "Frank Jervis, corporate security chief for Castle Robotics. We've had you under observation for over an hour. Answer the question. What're you doing out here?"

"Minding my own business on a public street."

"That's not what it looks like to me."

"What does it look like to you?"

"Like you're conducting corporate espionage."

"Is that right?"

"That's right."

"Actually, Frank, I'm looking for somebody named C.W. Lazarus. I think he works for Castle Robotics."

"Never heard of him."

"You sure?"

"Positive." Jervis stared at me hard behind his sunglasses. "I'm gonna have to ask you to step out of the vehicle."

"What for?"

"To make sure you're not packing any surveillance equipment."

"You're not the police, Frank. You're a corporate goon in an expensive suit."

"You wanna do it the hard way? OK, smart guy, c'mon, let's go."

He opened my door and went to grab my shoulder. Nobody likes a bully. I slapped his hand away.

"I said let's go, asshole." He pushed his suit coat back and unlimbered a 9-millimeter Sig Sauer.

I pivoted in my seat, shoving the door all the way open. The edge of the door knocked the pistol out of his hand. Stunned but for only a moment, Jervis staggered back as I emerged from the Escalade, then charged. He was a brawler more than a boxer, head down, off-balance. He threw a ragged left, then a right, both of which missed, before I stepped in and wobbled him with a roundhouse to his left cheekbone that scraped skin from two of my knuckles. I was about to drop him when I caught movement at my seven o'clock position—and turned too late. A blow crashed down from behind me with such force that I could've sworn I heard my own skull crack.

Constellations appeared before my eyes.

Then I saw nothing.

Nineteen

I awoke on a concrete floor, in blackness, to the mother of all migraines. Weird as it may sound, I was happy for the excruciating pain that threatened to explode my head. Pain meant my nerve endings still worked. It meant I was still alive.

Wherever I was, it was uncomfortably warm. The air was stagnant and stunk like wet cardboard. I was aware that my ankles had been bound together with duct tape, as were the wrists behind my back. My mouth was taped over. Gone was the dive knife I'd stashed under my jeans. I was glad I hadn't bought a more expensive knife considering what little use I'd gotten from the one I had purchased.

How long had I been lying there? An hour? A day? An entire week could've come and gone and I would not have known it. Trying to assess the passage of time, however, wasn't my priority. Neither was formulating an immediate escape plan. I didn't yet know enough about the forces arrayed against me to shift effectively into MacGyver mode. What mattered most at that moment was convincing myself that I would survive no matter what my captors had in store for me, so that I could dish it back to them in spades.

There are two types of individuals when it comes to enduring life-threatening hardship: those who rationalize death as an easy escape from their agony, and those who spit in the reaper's face, too ornery to quit. The latter *will* themselves to live. "Fighting spirit" is what our instructors at Alpha called it. A refusal to roll over and die.

I closed my eyes and vowed that I would prevail no matter what lay ahead.

Hours passed, or maybe it was minutes. I nodded in and out of consciousness until I was startled awake by the sound of an approaching motor vehicle. The engine died. Two doors opened and slammed shut. I heard a key sliding into a padlock and the lock clicking open, followed by a harsh, metallic clanking. Cool sea air rushed in on a tide of moonlight as a steel door rolled up, revealing my surroundings: cardboard packing boxes, a bank safe, a stack of automobile tires, and what looked to be a vintage Plymouth sedan.

I was being held captive in a self-storage unit.

In walked Castle Robotics' security chief Frank Jervis, followed by Ray Sheen, the company's self-assured second-in-command. Sheen was toting a baseball bat.

Jervis muscled the rolling door back down as Sheen yanked on a pull chain. A naked light bulb flickered on overhead, bathing the storage unit in a harsh, white glare. Then Sheen nodded to Jervis who knelt down and ripped the tape off my mouth. The security chief's eye was as purple as an eggplant where it had met my fist. He was dripping sweat.

Sheen squatted beside me.

"How're we doing, Mr. Logan?"

"Can't complain." I nodded toward the bat in his hand. "That's not Tony Gwynn's autograph, by any chance, is it?"

"It is. You know why Gwynn was such a great hitter?"

"Tell me."

"Because he followed through on every swing. Which is why I stroked you as hard as I did. Didn't mean to. I was just trying to be like Tony."

"Imitation is the highest form of flattery."

Sheen smiled, but there was no warmth behind it.

"We had to make sure you weren't spying on us," he said. "You can't imagine how many of our competitors are constantly probing us, trying to gain proprietary information. Some try to pass themselves off as innocent vendors and private subcontractors. Others as friends of friends."

"How long have I been in here?"

"A few hours. Hope it hasn't been too much of an inconvenience for you."

"Being clubbed in the head, hog-tied, then locked in a self-storage unit isn't inconvenient, Ray. It's felony battery and kidnapping."

Sheen offered another soulless smile. "So, I understand you're looking for a Castle Robotics employee named C.W. Lazarus."

"Know him?"

"Can't say I do. I don't recall anyone by that name ever having worked for the company."

He was almost certainly lying. Liars commonly try to avoid appearing dishonest by implying—"Can't say I do"—instead of making direct statements—"I *don't* know anyone by that name."

"So who is this guy Lazarus, anyway?" Sheen said.

"He's the guy who made my airplane crash. He was also involved in the murder of Janet Bollinger, but I'm still working out that part."

Sheen signed and stood. He looked over at Jervis, who was rubbing his left shoulder and wincing in obvious pain, his head shiny with perspiration.

"You told me you just wanted to scare him a little," Jervis said.

"It's too late for that."

"I didn't sign up for this, Ray. Cut him a check. Just pay him off, for crissake."

"He already knows too much," Sheen said. "Don't you, Mr. Logan?"

"First of all, whatever it is you *think* I know, I can guarantee you it's not as much as you're assuming. Secondly, I recently met a very attractive San Diego County sheriff's detective. I'm sure she'd be pleased to sit down with the three of us and sort this mess out—unless, of course, you just want to pay me big bucks to keep my mouth shut."

"You seem incapable of keeping your mouth shut," Sheen said.

He had a point.

Jervis clutched his chest, his face twisted, and he made a sort of repetitive grunting sound, like a pig rooting.

"I t-think . . . I t-think I'm having a h-heart attack."

And then, apparently, he did.

Knees shimmying like a newborn colt, he staggered, then fell, crashing into the Plymouth's rear bumper and shattering the glass of the left taillight with his head while Sheen just stood there and watched.

"Frank, you OK?"

"You need to get him to a hospital."

"Christ."

Sheen quickly re-taped my mouth, rolled the door back up and looked outside to make sure the coast was clear. Then, with considerable effort, he dragged Jervis to the yellow MINI Cooper convertible I'd seen parked outside Castle Robotics, muscling him into the passenger seat and hustling back to the storage unit.

"I'll be back."

Take your time, Terminator.

He pulled on the chain, turning off the overhead light, then rolled the door back down as he exited, bathing me once more in blackness. I heard the padlock latch outside, followed by the high-compression whine of the MINI's engine, racing away.

Soldiers and Marines are taught to "adapt and overcome" in combat. More elite warriors learn that prevailing on the battlefield often takes more than mere resourcefulness. It requires complete situational awareness—the ability to instantly assess one's tactical environment, to inventory any and all available resources that might be used to crush his enemy. To hone this skill at Alpha, we played a game called "Remember or Die."

The course instructor was a fiery little Army private turned Delta Force operator with chronic bad breath named Oren Ernstmueller who'd once escaped a Viet Cong jungle camp after slitting two of his captors' throats with nothing more than a sharpened lens from his eyeglasses. One at a time, over and over, Ernstmueller would lead us into rooms cluttered with incongruous objects. Cleaning supplies. Ammo boxes. A chess set missing two pieces. A dead crow. Photos of naked women. He'd pull off our blindfolds, give us five seconds to memorize everything in the room and the placement of each item, then slap the blindfold back on. Woe unto any go-to guy who missed the details of a single object, or got its specific location wrong.

"When your ass is on the line," he'd bark, his halitosis melting your face, "all you got to go on is knowing who's who and what's what and where's where. The more you see and remember, the easier it'll be for y'all to make it through any shit storm and come out smelling like a rose."

Nobody ever accused Oren Ernstmueller of being a poet, but he was one outstanding self-defense instructor. Thanks to him, though enveloped in blackness, I could still see in my mind what was what and where was where. My memory was all I had to work with if I hoped to live—that and the shattered taillight of a vintage Plymouth coupe. As fast as my bindings would permit, I rolled and inch-wormed my way toward the car.

Broken glass littered the floor below its left rear fender. I groped around blindly for a shard from the shattered taillight, accidentally stabbing myself in the palm of my right hand.

"Son of a . . ."

I grasped it as best I could, the glass slick with blood, and began working blindly at the duct tape binding the wrists behind my back. I lost all track of time as I poked and pulled, struggling to free my hands. Every other jab seemed to produce a painful new wound, but it was either that or die.

I still had a long way to go when I heard the MINI Cooper coming back.

Twenty

My wrists came free just as Ray Sheen's car pulled up outside the storage unit. Like a man possessed, I tore through the tape binding my ankles, flung open the Plymouth's passenger door, and, groping in darkness, found an ignition key on the floorboard. Amazingly, the seventy-year-old engine fired up like new. Then I smashed down on the accelerator, blasted through the metal roll-up door, and made good my escape.

Actually, that's not what happened. That's what I *wished* had happened.

My mouth, wrists and ankles remained taped as Sheen rolled up the door of the storage unit and strode in, leaving his car engine idling. Clearly, he was planning to stay only long enough to haul me off and do to me whatever he was planning to do. Everyone says a highlight reel of your life is supposed to flash before your eyes when death comes calling. But there were no highlights in my case, only lament. *Who would take care of Kiddiot? Who would fly the* Ruptured Duck? *Who would make love to Savannah?*

Sheen grabbed me by the shoulders and began dragging me toward his car as the glass shard from the broken taillight slipped from my grasp. Without seeming to notice my bloody wrists, he stuffed me into the Cooper's tiny backseat. I had to bend at the knees to fit. Then he ran back, rolled down the door to the storage unit, locking it, and jumped in.

After a series of sharp turns, we accelerated onto a freeway. The car crossed under a sign that told me we were eastbound on Interstate 8. He turned the radio on and dialed in a news station. The top story detailed a Predator drone strike on Al Qaeda's latest second-in-command.

"That number two guy gets blown up all the time," Sheen said.

I wanted to say, "If I was the number three guy, I'd definitely turn down the promotion," but it's hard to say anything when your lips are literally sealed.

The digital clock on the car's dashboard read 11:23 P.M. I strained to free my wrists, twisting and pulling at the tape binding them. By the time I looked up again at the clock, it was nearly midnight.

Sheen's phone rang with the opening bars to "Take Me Out to the Ballgame." He glanced down at the number displayed on the phone as he drove, then put the call on speaker.

"Hello?"

"Where are you right now?"

"You don't need to know that," Sheen said.

"Look, I just got a frantic call from Frank Jervis's wife. He's at Scripps Memorial. They think he had a heart attack."

I recognized the voice on the other end of the phone. It was Sheen's boss, Greg Castle.

"I dropped him off there," Sheen said. "I was with him when it happened."

"You should've called me, Ray."

"I'm trying to minimize your exposure in all of this. I'm trying to protect you, Greg. Plausible deniability. The less you know, the better."

"You're right. I certainly appreciate your efforts, Ray."

Castle indicated that his own wife was out of town with their children, visiting his in-laws outside Salt Lake City. He'd called Sheen, he said, hoping to get a lift to the hospital, to be with Jervis and his family.

"Take a cab."

"I suppose that's what I'll have to do," Castle said. "I just wish I could see well enough to drive myself at night."

Greg Castle couldn't see at night.

Someone else I'd recently met couldn't see at night, I realized as I lay contorted in the backseat of Sheen's clown-tiny car: Hub Walker's granddaughter, Ryder. *Congenital stationary night blindness.* Isn't that what Crissy Walker said Ryder had? I'm no geneticist, but I certainly knew what "congenital" meant—that the little girl had likely inherited the exceedingly rare condition genetically. If Greg Castle couldn't see well enough to drive after dark, and Ryder Walker could barely see in the dark, what were the odds that the two could be anything other than related by blood?

In the final moments of his life Dorian Munz claimed that Castle had murdered Ruth Walker, or arranged to have her killed, after she'd refused to terminate her pregnancy, and before she could spill the beans about what she supposedly knew of Castle Robotics' alleged financial improprieties. But hadn't Castle voluntarily taken, and passed, a paternity test? And why, if his company was dirty, would he have agreed to open Castle Robotics' books to an independent audit? My head pounded trying to figure it all out as Sheen continued driving east, toward that great dumping ground for dead bodies that is the Anza-Borrego Desert.

"I'll call you," he told Castle, "as soon as I'm done taking out the trash. Keep me posted on how Frank's doing."

"Just be careful, Ray."

"Oh, it's way past that," Sheen said, and hung up.

At first I thought it was my imagination, but it wasn't: the tape around my wrists was starting to loosen a little. I fought off the pain and kept twisting.

Sheen reached back and ripped the tape off my mouth.

"Tell me about the truck."

"What truck?"

"You know what truck, Logan. The one registered to Lazarus. How did you find out?"

I bluffed.

"Actually, the cops did. They're looking for you, Ray. You're just making things worse for yourself. Turn yourself in and let's call it a day."

"You're lying," Sheen said. "If the cops knew about the truck, they would've already tried to contact me."

I bluffed some more.

"They also know that C.W. Lazarus is an alias for Ray Sheen."

Sheen smiled up at me in the mirror.

"Now I definitely know you're lying."

"Then who is he?"

Sheen said nothing, staring straight ahead as he drove, his jaw muscles clenching and unclenching. I kept twisting and pulling at the tape.

"How much is Hub Walker involved in all of this?"

"Hub Walker is a has-been who has no idea how lucky he is to be with the lady he's with. Crissy deserves better. She always wanted kids, but he didn't. Said one for him was enough."

"You got any bambinos, Ray?"

Sheen said nothing.

"Your boss has a passel of 'em."

Stony silence. A few more tugs and my hands would be free.

"OK, maybe you can answer this one for me: how is it that Greg Castle and Ruth Walker's daughter can't see at night, but the paternity test showed Greg wasn't her father?"

Maybe it was the way Sheen looked back at me in the rear-view mirror and smiled smugly, but that's when I knew.

"You took the test for him. You passed yourself off as Castle."

Sheen cut the wheel and exited the freeway. We turned south onto a two-lane highway, wending past an Indian gambling casino and, within minutes, through dark, desolate hills.

"The least you could do is tell me where you're taking me to die."

"I don't owe you any explanations, Logan."

The duct tape binding my wrists tore apart. I was good to go.

"OK, Ray, be that way."

I sat up and rammed my elbow into his right ear, then nailed him with a knife-edged left to the right side of his neck—your basic judo chop.

The tiny car veered sideways, careened off the road and flipped over, coming to rest on its right side in a concrete drainage culvert. Only I was no longer occupying the backseat. I was sitting in a daze on the side of the road, about seventy-five feet behind the wreck, having been ejected through the MINI's now-mangled convertible roof. That I was uninjured beyond some scrapes, a pain in my lower left leg, and a throbbing left thumb, was not what amazed me. It was the fact that my ankles were no longer bound. The force of the crash had apparently ripped the duct tape clean away, along with my left shoe.

A bee buzzed past my head. Then another, this one closer. In my stupor, it took me a half-second to remember that bees navigate by the sun. They rarely fly at night. Casually, I looked down the culvert at Sheen and realized those weren't bees zipping past. They were bullets.

He was standing in a two-handed combat crouch beside his wrecked car, blasting at me with a .45 caliber pistol. Another round sparked off the pavement inches away.

I got up and hobbled for the cover of a copse of scrub oaks across the road, as Sheen climbed out of the culvert, firing at me on the run.

The Buddha teaches that all things in life are to be treasured no matter how mundane. This includes Saturday mail service, two-ply toilet paper, and, I came to realize as I fled, a matching pair of shoes. Outdistancing a gunman bent on killing you is no easy task with bleeding wrists, an aching lower leg, and a possible broken thumb; it's even harder in inky darkness over rock-strewn ground, when all you've got protecting one foot is a crew sock from Costco. I vowed never again to take shoes for granted. Assuming I survived the night.

A bullet clipped a low-hanging branch to my right, followed a split-second later by the sharp report of Sheen's pistol.

Turning to face an onrushing enemy is often the most effective means of defeating him. But given my physical condition, discretion at that moment seemed the better part of valor. I zigzagged through the trees, angling upslope toward a dense forest of pines.

Another gunshot. This one thudded into the trunk of an oak just as I passed by it, stumbling uphill, gasping for breath. When I glanced back over my shoulder, I could see Sheen, a shapeless form in the darkness. He was less than fifty meters behind me.

"Save yourself the trouble, Logan!"

Three more shots ripped past.

The pines towered above me on the steeply rising slope. All I had to do was get there and I'd be home free. Find a place to hide and regroup. Hell, maybe I'd even fashion a makeshift wooden spear and go on the offensive.

Thirty meters.

My legs and lungs were on fire.

Twenty meters.

Exhausted and dizzy, I began crawling.

The tree line was now less than fifteen feet ahead, the pines looming sentries, beckoning safety. They could have just as easily been fifteen miles away for all the good they offered me. I was spent. Out of steam. Done.

"You Can't Always Get What You Want," the Rolling Stones intoned, but once in awhile, life's got a funny way of giving you what you need.

"*Hombre.*"

The man was crouched just inside the tree line, motioning me frantically toward him, a young man in jeans and a black, oversized LA Kings hockey jersey. Perched on his forehead was a pair of night vision goggles. "*Vámonos, rápido!*"

My legs no longer worked. All I could do was look up at him. He and two others were on me in seconds, pulling me up the hill and into the trees, where four other men, older and

heavier, hunkered on their bellies behind a large rock formation like troops sweating out a mortar barrage.

None dared breathe as Sheen approached. He paused not
twenty feet away, breathing hard, listening.

One of the men lying beside me quietly picked up a rock
and held it at the ready, but there was no need. We were invis-
ible in the night.

Sheen moved on, deeper into the trees, as my new friends
and I waited, scarcely willing to breathe. About ten minutes
later, about a half-mile away, came a single gunshot. It sounded
smaller than a .45, but I couldn't be sure. I was too exhausted.

The man in the Kings jersey issued a series of hand commands as complex as any I'd seen in my service with Alpha.
The other men rose in unison and began moving in well-dis-
ciplined silence, away from the echo of the gunshot.

Somehow, I found a second wind and fell in behind them.

THEY NEVER asked why I was being chased or why somebody
was shooting at me. They were being polite, I suppose, which
made us even. I never learned what they were doing out there
at night, in the middle of a California pine forest, just north
of the U.S.–Mexico border, but it wasn't hard to guess. Up in
Oxnard, there were strawberries to pick and, out in Beverly
Hills, pricey cars to wax. There were construction ditches to
dig and buckets of scalding hot tar to be hauled onto rooftops.
And somebody had to do all that spine-snapping work because
no American ever would, not for the money his fellow citizens
were willing to pay.

One of the men gave me a sip of lime Gatorade while two
others gently bandaged my wrists by flashlight. The biggest of
the bunch reached into his backpack and insisted I take from
him a pair of Air Jordan knockoffs to replace the shoe I'd lost.
He wouldn't accept no for an answer.

"*Gracias.*"

He gave me a thumbs-up and a smile.

The "Air Jordans" were purple and black. They actually fit.

I shook their hands, one after the other, and watched them move off single file, silently, through the trees.

"Good luck, you guys."

"*Buena suerte, señor.*"

Every inch of me hurt. My left thumb had swollen to nearly twice its normal size. I sat with my back against a boulder. The night was warm. An 18-wheeler let loose its air horn somewhere to the north. In the woods nearby, an owl hooted greetings to its mate, who hooted back. I found comfort in their dialogue. The birds, I knew, would go silent if Sheen were approaching. I lay down on a bed of pine needles and closed my eyes, too tired to think. When I opened them again, it was dawn.

I had no phone, no wristwatch, no food or drink, and not a clue as to my specific location. I did, however, have two matching Air Jordans, and for that, I reminded myself, I was grateful. I began walking downhill because downhill is how water flows, and it is always near water where people will be found.

The pines soon thinned, giving way to arid, rolling chaparral speckled by manzanita and chamise. Below me and to the east, a Jeep Wrangler negotiated a twisting dirt road at high speed, kicking up dust plumes in its wake.

Getting down to the road was easy. Not only because both of my feet were now uniformly and properly clad, but because, with the sun up, I could now see where I was walking.

Daylight. Another reason to be grateful.

I picked up my pace. After what I guessed to be about fifteen minutes, I stepped out onto the road just as a Chevy Tahoe with a throaty muffler rounded a blind curve and came barreling toward me.

The driver was a teenaged girl with long dark hair and big designer sunglasses. Her left hand was hanging out the window, a cigarette between her fingers. She rumbled past me without slowing, ignoring my waving. I couldn't say I blamed her for not stopping, not after catching my reflection in one of those pole-mounted convex mirrors that help alert motorists to traffic converging from the opposite direction:

My face was a grotesque pastiche of cuts and abrasions. My hair was matted stiff with blood. I looked like an extra in a zombie movie.

I'm ready for my close-up, Mr. DeMille.

I headed northbound along the road without a trace of civilization in sight, when I heard a car coming up from behind me. I turned to see a San Diego County sheriff's cruiser approaching. The driver skidded to a stop, threw open his door and took up station behind it, leveling an AR-15 assault rifle at me. His partner was similarly positioned behind the black-and-white's passenger door with a Glock pointed in my direction.

"Am I glad to see you guys."

"Kiss the ground! Hands outstretched! Do it now!"

Odd questions can rumble through your head at such moments. Questions like, "Who kisses the ground anymore other than the Pope?" And, "What happens if I lie down in the road, another car comes by and I get run over? Do these guys *really* want to assume that kind of liability?" But I said nothing. They clearly meant business and I was in no shape to cross swords with them.

I got down. But I did not kiss the ground.

The deputy with the assault rifle covered me as his partner holstered his pistol, kneed me in the small of my back, and yanked my left wrist back to handcuff me.

"Don't move."

"My thumb's broken."

"Shut up."

He hooked me up, smelling faintly of Old Spice, and hauled me brusquely to my feet. His partner read me my Miranda rights.

"Do you understand these rights I have just read to you?"

I said I did. He keyed a coiled radio mic clipped to the left epaulet of his uniform shirt.

"Eighty-four Robert, suspect in custody."

"You're under arrest," Deputy Old Spice said as he led me back to the patrol car.

"Can I ask what for?"

"Does the name, 'Raymond Sheen,' ring a bell?"

"You mean the same individual who tried to kill me?"

"He said you tried to kill him."

I was too beat to laugh.

Twenty-one

My left thumb was fractured. Fortunately, an X-ray showed the break didn't require surgery. After my hands were swabbed for gunshot residue, medical staff at the downtown San Diego Central Jail cleaned out my cuts and slapped on a cast that went midway up my left forearm. They gave me a thorough neurological exam to assess the severity of my concussion and an MRI for my leg, concluding it was merely sprained.

Then they tossed me in the slammer.

Aside from being in jail, I was convinced that I had hit upon a brilliant solution to affordable national health care: get busted for a crime you didn't commit.

I had hoped I might be put in a cell with Bunny the Human Doberman and his cousin, Li'l Sinister. Granted, they were perverse and prone to violence, but they were entertaining, and I'll take entertaining over dangerous anytime. Unfortunately for me, my cell mate turned out to be the very definition of dull. He was a husky African-American chap in his early thirties with some sort of tribal tattoo on the right side of his face, who sat on the concrete floor with his knees drawn up to his chest, staring catatonically into space. The steel door locked behind me as I entered. He pretended not to notice.

"Welcome to the Rock," I said in my best Sean Connery, which is much worse that my best Humphrey Bogart, which some who've heard it have suggested should be banned as a crime against humanity.

Bad celebrity imitations aside, Chatty Cathy wouldn't even look up at me. Nor did he respond when lunch arrived a few minutes later—two peanut butter sandwiches on white bread and a disposable paper cup of cherry Kool-Aid. Not having eaten anything since the day before, I wolfed down both sandwiches in short order, then asked if he was planning to eat his.

"You touch my food," Chatty Cathy said, still refusing to look at me, "and I'll gut you."

I had considered asking him to sign my cast, but that offer was definitely off the table.

<hr />

A JOWLY, sad-eyed deputy who reminded me a little of Huckleberry Hound escorted me into an interview room where Detective Alicia Rosario sat behind a gray steel metal desk, text messaging on her cell phone. The room was Modern Inquisition. Soundproof cork tiles lined the walls and ceilings. Two large eye screws were bolted to the floor beneath an unpadded metal chair opposite the desk. Deputy Hound directed me to sit, then strung my ankle chains through the eye screws while Rosario waited for him to finish locking me down. He gave my chains a good tug to make sure they were secure, then left, pulling the door closed behind him.

"Long night?" Rosario said.

"You have no idea."

She yawned. "I've been up since two this morning, no thanks to you."

"What are friends for?"

Behind her, facing me, was a large mirror. I knew it was one-way glass, and that there was probably a video camera recording us on the other side.

"For the record, you've been arrested on suspicion of attempted murder. You've already been advised by the arresting deputies of your legal right to counsel and you've waived those rights. Is that correct?"

"Yup."

"I need you to say it a little more formally."

"Yes, I've been advised of my rights to legal counsel and I waive those rights."

Rosario sat forward in her chair, her ballpoint pen poised over a legal pad. "OK, how about we take it from the top?"

"From the top, and for the record, I didn't try to kill Ray Sheen. He tried to kill me."

I laid it all out for her. How Sheen's company was designing weaponized, hummingbird-size drones for the government. How I'd gone to Castle Robotics looking for the mysterious C.W. Lazarus, whose truck had been spotted near my airplane, how the plane's engine had been tampered with, and how I'd wound up in a self-storage unit with Sheen and Frank Jervis, before Jervis keeled over with The Big One.

"Hold up a minute." Rosario looked up at me from her notes with her eyes narrowed. "The engine on your airplane? What're you talking about?"

I told her about the FAA's preliminary findings, and about the pickup truck registered to Lazarus that had been spotted suspiciously close to the *Ruptured Duck* the night before I'd crashed. I told her that a man wearing a baseball cap and coveralls was seen from a distance climbing out of that truck, opening up the engine compartment, and doing evil things to the *Duck*.

"Why didn't you tell me about all this before?"

"I was sort of busy."

She gave me a knowing look and asked if I had a witness.

"His name's Al Demaerschalk."

"Spell it."

I spelled it.

"What's Mr. Demaerschalk do?"

"He used to be a pilot. He had a stroke. He's in the hospital. They don't think he's gonna make it."

Rosario tossed down her pen and glared at me. "And you were going to tell me all this *when*?"

"I'd hoped to track down Lazarus myself."

"To do what? Have a friendly little chat with him?"

I shrugged.

"This isn't the Old West, Logan. We have laws. And you just broke one: willfully withholding evidence in a felony investigation."

"If you were a pilot, you'd understand."

"Understand what? Wanting to tee up some guy because he jacked up your ugly old airplane?"

"Hey, let's not get personal here."

She folded her arms and sat back. "Look, if somebody *did* sabotage your plane with the intent of committing great bodily injury, that's a crime. I'm a sworn peace officer, Logan. I get paid to investigate crimes. You don't."

"You can get mad at me all you want, Alicia. I'm just trying to help you out here."

"Help me out? How is this helping me out? Tell me, please. I'd really like to know."

I told her how Ray Sheen had taken a paternity test posing as Greg Castle so that Castle could deny having impregnated Ruth Walker.

"How does that help me?" Rosario said.

"Dorian Munz was right about Greg Castle fathering Ruth Walker's baby. If he was right about that, could be he was right that Castle was upset because Ruth wouldn't get an abortion. Could be he was also right about Ruth having dirt on Castle's company. Either way, it would've given Castle the motive to murder her."

"Sheen told you he took a paternity test for Castle?"

"Basically."

"You told the arresting deputies you hit him and that's why you crashed."

I nodded.

"And that's when he started shooting at you?"

Another nod.

"Any idea what he was shooting at you with?"

"A .45, firing ACP ammo."

"How do you know that?"

"Because Automatic Colt Pistol rounds make a very distinctive sound when they're coming at you."

"What sort of sound?"

"Like fabric tearing."

"I take it you've been shot at before?"

I shrugged. Maybe yes, maybe no.

Rosario sighed in frustration, not sure how to read me, and jotted a few notes.

"Why not bring Sheen in here and compare everybody's versions of events?" I said. "We can see who's telling the truth."

"We're not sure where Mr. Sheen is right now. He called in a complaint against you, then said he'd be unavailable until he had confirmation you were safely in custody. He said he feared for his life."

"The guy tunes me up with a Louisville Slugger, kidnaps me, drives me out toward the desert intending to put a slug behind my ear, and he's in fear of *his* life? Go interview Greg Castle. He knew what Sheen was up to last night. So did Frank Jervis, Castle's security chief."

"Mr. Sheen said you shot at him."

"With what?"

"State records show you have a .357 Colt Python registered in your name."

"Which is currently up in Rancho Bonita, under my bed. Search my apartment. You have my permission."

Rosario wrote some more notes. Her poker face gave away nothing.

"Look, if I were a 'sworn peace officer,' I'd start by connecting the dots between what happened to Janet Bollinger and what happened with my airplane."

Rosario's cell phone played the refrain from that icon of bad '80's rock, Journey's "Don't Stop Believin'." She picked it up and read a text message that prompted her eyebrows to arch. She got up abruptly and headed for the door.

"Don't go anywhere."

"Oh, I'll be here."

If I were further along the path of enlightenment, I would've tried meditating. Jail, after all, is the ideal environment for contemplative introspection. But all I could think about was my ex-wife, and her snide reaction had she seen me decked out in chains and county-issued overalls.

It's said that most men think about sex every seven seconds and are virtually incapable of distinguishing love from lust. I won't argue with that. Sitting there, though, I found myself yearning for nothing more than Savannah's smile. If that's not love, I don't know what is. But I couldn't think about any of that now, not if I was going to figure a way out of my predicament.

Why had Sheen kidnapped me? Why had he shot at me? I replayed the DVD in my head from the night before.

It began and ended with C.W. Lazarus.

Sheen lied about not knowing who Lazarus was. Things had taken a definite turn toward Crazy Town after I'd intimated a connection between the slaying of Janet Bollinger, Lazarus's truck, and the sabotaging of my airplane. Lazarus was the Holy Grail. He had to be. Find him, I told myself, and all things would be illuminated.

The door to the interrogation room was flung open. Rosario strode in, along with her partner, Detective Lawless, whom I assumed had been watching me the entire time behind the one-way glass. He began unchaining me.

"This is your lucky day, Logan. You're being released."

"To what do I owe the pleasure?"

"You tested negative for gunshot residue. We also have witnesses who've come forward essentially corroborating your version. We're trying to find Mr. Sheen."

My lucky day, indeed.

"We just need to get some paperwork out of the way," Rosario said, "then we'll get you out of here."

"Any chance the good taxpayers of San Diego County could spring for another peanut butter sandwich? I'm starting to OD on Taco Bell."

"I'll see what I can do," Rosario said.

I tailed her out the door and down a concrete corridor, past several holding cells, including the one in which I'd cooled my heels. My sullen cell mate, Chatty Cathy, was still sitting on the floor, knees to his chest, still staring at nothing.

"Happiness is a choice," I said.

He flipped me off without looking up.

Rosario punched some numbers into an electronic keypad, unlocking a steel door that led into a long hallway flanked by the wood-paneled offices of ranking sheriff's administrators.

"Who were the witnesses?" I asked.

"The investigation's ongoing. I'm not allowed to discuss those kinds of things."

"I had a feeling you might say that."

Rosario held the door open for me when we reached the end of the corridor. I thanked her.

"*Para eso están los amigos,*" she said with a little nod as I walked past her.

What are friends for?

I grasped the meaning of her words: the witnesses were likely among the same illegal migrants who'd saved my life the night before. I mouthed them a silent *gracias.*

Rosario escorted me through a covered sally port and into the jail's out-processing center, where my personal items were returned to me.

"We towed your rental car," the detective said. "I'll drive you over to the impound lot after you've changed back into your street clothes."

"Thanks, Alicia."

"It's Detective."

"Detective."

Rosario was right about one thing. She and her partner were paid to solve crimes. I wasn't. I should've turned in my rented Escalade, taken the train to LA, and begged Savannah to take me back. But then Hub Walker called. He was weeping.

"I didn't know who else to call."

"What is it, Hub? What's wrong?"

"My wife," he said, barely able to get the words out. "She's disappeared."

Twenty-two

Walker paced the patio in his bathrobe, clutching a half-empty quart bottle of Jim Beam. It was four o'clock in the afternoon. He was drunk with worry. Or maybe just drunk.

"I've been trying her phone all day. She would've called if she got sidetracked. She's never done anything like this before in her life. It's not like her."

Walker's granddaughter wandered past where I was sitting at the patio table. She was wearing inflated water wings and her Little Mermaid swimsuit.

"Hello, Ryder."

The little girl jumped feet-first into the deep end of the pool without responding, bobbed to the surface, and began dog paddling, water splashing everywhere. Walker barely noticed her. He plopped down in the chair next to mine and gulped a swallow of bourbon.

"I drove all over town this morning, looking for her."

"You called the police?"

"They said they couldn't take a report. Said she had to be gone twenty-four hours at least." He gestured to the cast on my arm. "What happened to you?"

"Tripped on some stairs."

He seemed not to hear me, absorbed in his own worries.

"It's gotta be Ray Sheen," he said. "He's behind all of this. I *know* it. I can *feel* it."

I wanted to believe that Walker was beyond reproach. He seemed legitimately upset. But all I felt was a vague queasiness that his wife's sudden absence was the latest tangle in a web of deceit, and that a war hero I once idolized was somehow complicit in all of it.

"What makes you think Sheen had anything to do with your wife being gone, Hub?"

He glanced over his shoulder, waited until Ryder paddled to the far end of the pool, out of earshot, then looked back at me, struggling to keep his emotions in check.

"Sheen and Crissy have been carrying on for years."

"You know that for a fact?"

He nodded. "She left the computer on by accident one night a month or so back. I saw some emails. Crissy told him it was a mistake. She wanted to end it. Sheen didn't. He blackmailed her, threatened to tell me all about it if she broke it off."

"Did you confront her?"

Walker shook his head and gulped more whiskey. "Like I said, she was the one who wanted to end the affair. I figured she would eventually. Then we could get back to normal, like things used to be when we first got married. I know she'd never leave me. She loves this house too much."

I wondered whether Savannah and I would have still been together, had I embraced Walker's arguably admirable *laissez-faire* attitude after discovering she and Arlo Echevarria had been carrying on behind my back. Maybe. Maybe not. Every relationship is different.

"I can't swim!" Walker's screaming blasted me from my reverie. He was on his feet, running toward the far end of the pool. "She's drowning! My granddaughter!"

Ryder was hovering motionless at the bottom of the deep end, arms floating ethereally in front of her body, the two inflatable water wings lapping on the surface above.

I dove in, my eyes and cuts stinging from the chlorine, crooked my good arm around her waist and kicked our way to the edge of the pool. Walker pulled her out and sat her on the brick pool decking as I quickly hauled myself out of the water.

She lolled, lifeless as a rag doll. Her lips were periwinkle. Walker whacked her on the back a couple of times with the flat of his hand. There was no response.

"She's not breathing! I don't know what to do!"

I did. Every Alpha operator was certified in combat life-saving. We learned how to stanch arterial bleeds using live pigs that our instructors would anesthetize, then blast with shot-guns to approximate battlefield injuries. Performing basic CPR on a child was a cakewalk by comparison.

I laid her on her back, positioned the heel of my right hand on her breastbone, and began pushing down on her chest. After thirty rapid compressions, I lowered my right ear close to her nose, my cheek over her mouth, hoping for the whisper of breath. None came.

"Ryder! Ryder, it's Grampa! Wake up, baby girl! Please, wake up! Please!"

I tilted the little girl's head back, pinched her nostrils, and forced the air from my lungs into hers. Her thin rib cage rose and fell. One rescue breath, then another. That's all it took.

She coughed up water. I rolled her on her side. More water came out of her mouth and nose. Then she began wailing.

Walker scooped her up, hugging and rocking her in his lap. "Thank you, thank you, thank you," he kept repeating, as much to me as to his maker.

I sat back on my knees, dripping wet and relieved, when the patio door slid open. Out stepped Crissy Walker.

"What happened?"

"She's fine, she's fine," Hub said. "Just had a little accident is all."

Crissy hurried past me and swept Ryder into her arms.

"Are you OK, honey?"

Ryder nodded and burrowed her wet face into Crissy's chest, soaking her outfit. She was wearing gold high heels and a form-fitted, pale lavender skirt suit that showcased every reason why she'd once been Playmate of the Year.

"Where the hell have you been?" Hub demanded. "I've been calling you all day."

"I told you. I had an early meeting in Los Angeles, that I'd probably be gone before you woke up."

"No, you didn't. You said no such thing."

Crissy stared at him in disbelief. "Hub, we were sitting at the table, in *there*, having dinner. I said, 'I have meetings tomorrow with the Animal Planet people on *The Cat Communicator*. Unless traffic's bad, I'll be home in time to make dinner. Defrost some chicken. Make sure Ryder takes her medicine.' Do you not remember me telling you that?"

"All I remember is waking up and you were gone."

"Baby, I'm worried about you. You're starting to forget things."

"You could've at least called to check in."

"I turned my phone off for the meeting and forgot to turn it back on. I'm sorry, Hub."

Walker was little appeased. Angrily, he snatched Ryder from his wife—"C'mon, baby girl, let's get you dried off"—and marched into the house.

Crissy handed me a thick, plum-colored bath towel from among several stacked in a fancy basket near the patio door. I dried off my cast first. It seemed no worse for the dunking.

"A little partying down in Tijuana?" she said with a smirk, nodding toward my arm.

"How'd you guess?"

"What happened with Ryder?"

"One minute she was wearing her flotation devices, and the next minute, she wasn't."

"What was Hub doing?"

"Worrying about you."

Crissy folded her arms and gazed toward the house. Her acrylic nails were crimson. "He's been acting strange. Not his usual self. Ever since Dorian Munz died. I keep telling him he needs to go to the doctor, but you know how pilots can be. Need another towel?"

I shook my head no and asked her to tell me about Ray Sheen.

"I understand you know him pretty well."

She looked at me hard. "Who told you that?"

"Your husband."

Crissy calmly lowered herself onto the mauve cushion of a chaise lounge. If she was caught off-guard by my question, she covered it well.

"We've socialized a few times. Dinner, banquets, that sort of thing. Ray works for Greg Castle, and Hub and Greg are good friends, obviously. Beyond that . . . Why do you ask?"

"Ray tried to kill me last night."

"Ray Sheen tried to kill you?" She scoffed like she didn't believe me. "Why in the world would he do that?"

"I'll let you know when I find out."

I slipped inside the house and headed for the front door. Ryder was wrapped in a towel, sitting on the living room couch, absorbed in a laptop computer game with her grandfather. Hub was still drinking.

"I need to turn in my rental car."

"Send me the bill," Walker said. "We'll call it even."

I said I would and mentioned nothing about the bullet holes in the Escalade's roof. I was just glad I wasn't paying.

"Take care, Colonel."

"You do the same, Mr. Logan."

Across the street, a red Marine Corps flag flapped in the breeze from a flagpole in Major Kilgore's front yard. The major was rocking in his porch swing, eyeballing Hub Walker's elegant home with clear malice.

HAVING BEEN abducted and stripped of various personal possessions, including a cell phone, afforded me an excellent opportunity to visit my friendly cellular service provider. My personal communications "advisor," an earnest young man named Seth, explained megabytes and the differences between central processing units as if we shared a like-minded fascination with telecommunications minutiae, then tried to sell me a $600 smartphone. I explained to him as diplomatically as I could that unless the phone could beam me up and came equipped with a death ray to kill Klingons, I wasn't interested in blowing nearly that much on any phone. I walked out fifteen minutes later with a bare-bones, seventy-five-dollar unit that was anything but smart. At least I didn't have to enroll in grad school to figure out how the damn thing worked. Plus, they let me keep my old number.

Sitting in the parking lot, I plugged my new phone into the Escalade's USB power port, called the central switchboard at Mercy Hospital in Rancho Bonita, and asked to be patched through to the intensive care unit. I told the woman who answered, who I assumed was a nurse, that I was calling to see how Mrs. Schmulowitz was doing.

"Are you family?"

"No."

"I'm sorry. Unless you're a spouse, domestic partner, or immediate family member, we're prohibited by hospital policy from divulging any patient information."

"Actually," I said, "we're married. In a technical sense."

"Huh?"

I explained that Mrs. Schmulowitz and I shared the same address. As such, any good lawyer (an oxymoron if there ever was one) would argue that we lived together. And *that* made her my common-law wife. Which made it perfectly permissible, I told the nurse, to be briefed on her condition.

"Sir, I really don't have time to play games."

"OK, look, in the interest of full disclosure, I'm just her tenant. But Mrs. Schmulowitz is more than my landlady. She's my inspiration. Hell, she may be the best person I've ever known. All I need is a word. Just *one* word. Critical? Stable? What? I don't think that's too much to ask, do you?"

The nurse sighed, tired of my badgering. "Mrs. Schmulowitz is in serious condition. We'd upgrade her to stable, but she insists on getting out of bed every hour to do leg-lifts."

I thanked her and signed off, feeling as if one large rock had been lifted from me. Whatever lightness of being I felt lasted about as long as it took for my new, less-than-smart phone to ring. It was Savannah.

"You said you were going to call me."

"True."

"I waited, Logan, all night. Then I tried calling you. Because I was worried. Any idea how many times I tried calling? Go on, take a shot at it."

"Many?"

"I stopped counting."

"My phone died, Savannah. I had to get a new one."

Was it the whole truth? No. But being a Buddhist is all about not hurting others. Telling Savannah all I'd been through in the past twenty-four hours would've only inflicted pain.

"I'm sorry you were scared, Savannah. I'm fine. I promise."

She exhaled. "OK, apology accepted." There was a pause, then she said, "I just miss you, that's all."

"I miss you, too, babe."

There was a pause.

"You haven't called me that in a long time," Savannah said.

"What?"

"Babe."

"It just sort of slipped out. Again, my apologies."

"Don't apologize. I like it."

So much I wanted to tell her. That I ached for her. That I could do a better job, be a more thoughtful human being next time around. But I held back. The next step toward reconciliation was unconditional forgiveness. I was still working on that one.

"I talked to the hospital. Looks like Mrs. Schmulowitz is gonna make it."

"That's wonderful, Logan. She's one of a kind. I hope your cat comes home, too. I know how much he means to you."

"Why he does is beyond me."

"I think it's because you admire his sense of independence."

"It's not because of his selflessness, that's for sure. It's Kiddiot's world. We just live in it."

Savannah laughed. What I needed, she said, was a visit from *The Cat Communicator*, the reality television show Crissy Walker was hoping to produce at Animal Planet.

"My new client actually works at Animal Planet," she said. "He's having panic attacks over picking which shows to produce. He gets pitched hundreds of ideas every week."

"I can see it now: the guy sits in climate-controlled comfort all day, sipping lattes and having people beg him to make their shows, then wigs out because he can't decide between *Monkeys Gone Wild* and *The Real Rodents of Orange County*? I'm glad he's not taking flying lessons. I don't think he'd do very well."

"Just because you've never had a panic attack, Logan, doesn't mean they're not real. They can be terribly debilitating."

Only a minute earlier, I'd vowed to be a more empathetic human being. Now here I was, the same old insensitive me. Bad habits die hard.

"I'm sure your counseling will help him immeasurably."

"You're just saying that to placate me."

"You know me better than that, Savannah."

She blew air through her lips, flapping them. "What am I going to do with you, Logan?"

"I can think of a few things."

The phone made a funny beep in my ear. I ignored it. Savannah didn't.

"You have another call coming in," she said.

"I don't have call waiting."

"Yes, Logan, you do, because that beep's definitely call waiting. Could be important. I'll let you go."

I reluctantly admitted that I was "unfamiliar" with how call waiting worked on my new phone—or any phone, for that matter.

"You can fly the wings off anything ever built but you can't figure out call waiting?"

"If I were dyslexic, Savannah, would you make fun of that?"

"Of course not."

"Then why belittle a man who's cellularly challenged?"

"You're right. That was incredibly insensitive. You'll have to forgive me."

"I'm working on it."

She told me which buttons to push on my new phone to toggle between calls. I pressed a button, promptly disconnecting her along with whoever else was trying to reach me. The phone rang almost immediately. It was Detective Rosario.

"One of our patrol units located that pickup truck you were looking for," she said, "the one registered to C.W. Lazarus. We also located Mr. Lazarus."

I'd fantasized about finding the son of a bitch myself, forcing a confession from him, then enacting with my fists the damage he'd done to the *Ruptured Duck*. But that wasn't going to happen now. Life, I reminded myself, is full of disappointments.

"Did you ask him about my airplane? I'm hoping he spilled his guts."

"That he did," Rosario said. "But he won't be talking about your airplane anytime soon, or anything else. C.W. Lazarus is dead."

Twenty-three

Turkey vultures orbited high above Lazarus's remains as Detective Rosario and I ascended the hill where his corpse lay under a broiling, late afternoon sun.

Mountain bikers had discovered the body a few hours earlier about a quarter-mile from a trailhead in the Cleveland National Forest where Lazarus's Nissan pickup with its PCAFLR vanity license plates had also been found. The truck had been broken into and its radio stolen—not an uncommon occurrence these days among vehicles left unattended overnight in America's majestic outback. Authorities surmised that garden variety vandals were likely responsible for the ransacking of Lazarus's truck. As for the apparent murder of Lazarus himself, blame and explanation had not yet been apportioned.

"Ever wonder why vultures are bald?"

"Can't say I have." Rosario was breathing hard, trudging uphill. "But I don't think it's because Mother Nature decided that rockin' a bald look would necessarily enhance their appearance."

"No feathers means the gunk that clings to their heads dries faster and falls off quicker after they go Dumpster diving inside the body cavities of dead animals."

"I could've gone the rest of my life without knowing that."

Rosario stopped and bent at the waist, hands on her knees, trying to catch her breath. I paused and waited for her. She was wearing lace-up hiking boots, faded Levis with her badge and pistol clipped to the waist, and a pink tank top that, without her shoulder rig obscuring it, revealed ample cleavage I hadn't noticed before.

"You doing OK, Detective?"

She nodded. Sweat beads dripped from her short black hair onto the dirt. "I gotta start hitting the club more."

The club. Before the days of computerized incline stair-steppers and cardio monitors, they were called "gyms," unvarnished houses of pain where jocks and those who aspired to be jocks sweated, not preened. You went there to pump iron until your hands bled and your arms burned like magnesium. Nobody went looking to check out the local talent. I'd had my fill of gym workouts after four years of playing wide receiver for the Air Force Academy. Exercise for me these days consisted of a few tortured minutes every morning of stomach crunches and push-ups, followed by coffee and three ibuprofens. Call them whatever you wanted, health clubs or fitness centers, I'd no sooner join one than I would the Communist Party.

Rosario dug an inhaler out of her shoulder bag and sucked deeply. "Better now," she said after a minute, standing erect and finger-combing her sopping hair. "Adult asthma. This getting older thing blows."

"After the age of thirty, the body has a mind of its own."

"You just make that up?"

I shook my head. "Bette Midler."

"You don't exactly strike me as the Divine Miss M type, Logan."

"Are you kidding? I'm huge into musicals. Nothing finer in my opinion than a big Broadway production number."

"You can't be serious."

"You're right. I'm not. Musicals make my butt hurt after about ten minutes. I just remember random stuff. Pointless facts to know and tell."

"Like why buzzards are bald."

I smiled.

Rosario drew a deep breath and continued walking uphill while I fell in behind her. A half-mile or so below us, I could see the winding dirt road where I'd been arrested after escaping the clutches of Ray Sheen who, according to Rosario, was still on the lam.

I had persuaded her to let me look at Lazarus's body, to stare down at the face of the man who'd caused me to crash my airplane. She'd turned me down at first, saying department policy prohibited unauthorized civilians from entering designated crime scenes. I countered by pointing out that the guy hadn't tried to kill me; he'd tried to kill *us*.

"We survived a life-and-death experience," I said. "That makes us brothers—or sisters—depending on how politically correct you want to get about it. I just want to look down at the dirt bag for a few seconds and gloat. Call it a catharsis."

"What's a catharsis?"

"It's an arrangement. You let me have my little moment of satisfaction, I'll spring for dinner afterward."

The detective mulled my proposal, then said, "If anybody asks who you are or what you're doing, you let me do the talking. You touch nothing, stand where I tell you, do what I tell you. Understood?"

"Roger."

We made arrangements to meet in the parking lot of a church one block from the sheriff's department's Pine Valley substation, about forty highway miles east of downtown San Diego, just off Interstate 8. Rosario would then drive us to the scene, which was less than two miles from the substation. Her partner, she said, would not be coming along. Lawless's wife was in labor. They were expecting twins.

No way was it a date with Rosario. Of that I convinced myself. My having asked the detective out to dinner was nothing more than reimbursement for a favor asked and granted. And even if it was a date, what Savannah didn't know would never hurt her. Still, as I hiked up the trail, staring at Rosario's bottom, I couldn't help feeling that I was somehow cheating on Savannah. A tart taste rose up behind my tongue and stayed there.

THE BODY was draped with a yellow tarp and surrounded by yellow crime scene tape looped in a loose circle around creosote bushes on either side of the trail. A pair of uniformed deputies, one African-American, the other white, guarded the scene, wiping sweat from their faces and sipping from plastic water bottles. They both looked bored and overheated. On the slope twenty meters above them, a ponytailed civilian in a green windbreaker with "SDSD Crime Lab" printed on the back was sweeping over the mountainous terrain with a metal detector, searching for what I assumed were spent bullets.

"What's the story on the ME, Alicia?" the African-American deputy asked Rosario as we approached. "We've been here since before lunch."

"Medical examiner's swamped," Rosario said. "Murder-suicide in Carlsbad, and the trolley splattered some transient down in Chula Vista. They said they'll get somebody up here as soon as they can. Shouldn't be much longer, fellas."

Per protocol, the body was to remain untouched until a representative from the San Diego County Medical Examiner's office arrived to declare the victim officially dead. They would then determine the approximate time of death by making a small cut with a pocket knife and jabbing a meat thermometer into the deceased's liver.

Human beings begin losing heat at a rate of about one and one-half degrees Fahrenheit per hour as soon as they die. The warmer the weather, the slower they cool. Count down from 98.6, factor in ambient air temperatures, and you can get a reasonably accurate idea as to time of death. Rosario didn't have to explain that part of it to me; I'd learned all about meat thermometers when I was with Alpha. More than once, we determined how many hours behind our intended targets we were by measuring the core temperatures of their dead compatriots, whom they often left behind to lighten their loads, in the vain hope of outrunning us.

"Who's your friend?" the black deputy asked Rosario, dipping his chin in my direction.

"DA's office," Rosario said.

"Never seen him before."

"He's new."

"He got a name?"

"He's working undercover," Rosario said.

"Gotta log him in, Alicia," the white deputy said, pulling out a small spiral notebook from his back pocket. "You know the drill. Anybody who comes in or out of a crime scene—"

"Yeah, yeah, yeah," Rosario said dismissively, "they gotta get logged in." She looked over at me, drawing a blank. "What's your name again?"

"Jake Gittes."

The deputy wrote it down. I spelled it for him.

Rosario squatted beside the body and looked up at me.

"Ready to do this?"

I nodded.

She peeled back the tarp.

Lazarus was laying on his back, facing uphill, wearing a black dress shirt, untucked, his arms and legs splayed like he was making a snow angel. There was a baseball-size splotch of dried, rust-colored blood just below his diaphragm, and a hole the size of a dime in the center of the splotch. Half a button was missing where the bullet had nicked it before penetrating his torso.

"Entry wound?"

"That would be my guess," Rosario said.

"So, whoever shot him, shot him more or less from face-on position."

She nodded.

He was squinting and his jaws were parted. His lips were pulled back like he was grinning—and not one of those half-hearted grins, either, the kind you manage after enduring your father-in-law's oft-repeated favorite joke about the rabbi who walks into a bar. We're talking laugh your butt off like it's 1999. Who knew death could be so funny?

"How do you know this guy's Lazarus?"

"How do I know?" Rosario stood and pointed. "I know because his truck's parked a quarter-mile down the trail. I also know because he matches the description of C.W. Lazarus on file at DMV. Hair, eye color, height, weight, and age. Everything. Who else is it gonna be?"

"You check his driver's license?"

"The wallet's probably in his back pocket. We can't get to it. Not until the coroner shows up and signs off."

"So, you haven't run his fingerprints?"

"Like I said. Not until after the coroner's investigator signs off."

The corpse had dark, well-barbered hair and long flared sideburns. His left cheekbone bore a scar I recognized. It was shaped like the Nike corporate logo. A "swoosh."

"His name's not Lazarus," I said, staring down at the man's dead, laughing face. "His name's Ray Sheen."

Rosario blanched. "Ray Sheen, from Castle Robotics? You sure?"

I was.

From down the trail came the sound of somebody hacking up a lung. He trudged into view, pushing a rolling metal gurney upon which rested a folded green body bag and a brushed aluminum tool chest. He was a heavyset man in his late thirties with a shaved head, black polyester dress pants, and a short-sleeved white shirt, the tails of which refused to stay tucked. His forearms were a miasma of colorful tattoos. A digital camera was slung over his shoulder. His name tag identified him as "E. Schlosser."

"They don't pay me enough for this," he said, wiping his soaking florid face.

"The Medical Examiner," Rosario said, "has arrived."

Schlosser's first move was to de-tarp the body and snap about 200 photos. Then, wheezing, he got down on all fours, reached under the corpse, and extracted a red, eel-skin billfold, which he handed up to Rosario without being asked.

"At least we know it wasn't a robbery," Rosario said.

The uniform deputies both nodded.

She opened the wallet, pulled out a California driver's license, studied it for a second, then held it up for my inspection.

The name on the license read, "Raymond Francis Sheen." The photo matched the man with the distinctive scar on his left cheekbone who'd tried to murder me.

Swoosh, indeed.

Twenty-four

Rosario and I occupied a corner booth at La Jolla's Su Casa, an unpretentious, windowless bunker of a restaurant renowned for its verde crab enchiladas and *camarones al mojo de ajo*—jumbo shrimp sautéed in garlic butter and white wine. I'd ordered my usual *chile verde* burrito, but after two baskets of homemade tortilla chips, salsa, and multiple refills of spicy pickled carrots, I was about ready to call it a night. Not Rosario. She was still sorting through events of the day, eyes gleaming, eager to ponder the jigsaw puzzle that her homicide investigation had become.

"You know what I'm wondering?" Rosario asked, sipping her second margarita.

"Tell me."

"How big it's gonna get."

"Excuse me?"

"I meant this case."

"The case. Right."

Rosario licked the salt from her glass. "Why? What did you think I meant?"

"The case. Obviously."

Her lips curled in a wry smile. She knew exactly what I meant.

I reached uncomfortably for another pickled carrot.

After hiking back down the trail and dropping me off at my Escalade, Rosario had driven home to change for dinner. I'd done the same, stopping off at the YMCA in La Mesa where I'd paid the ten-dollar day rate to shower and try to look presentable. Now here we were, me in a semi-clean polo shirt and Levis, and her wearing a floor-length, leopard print sundress with spaghetti straps that were made to be slowly untied. The look was decidedly un-detective-like.

"We ran the VIN," she said. "The truck belonged to Sheen's cousin, Charles Walter Lazarus. He's a mechanical engineer. Used to work for Castle Robotics. Sold the vehicle to Sheen three months ago, after he got a job in D.C. Sheen also owns the MINI you went riding in, along with an Audi turbo and a '65 Mustang. He never filed an ownership change on the truck."

"Wanted to avoid paying state sales tax, probably."

"It happens."

Deputies, she said, had reached Charles Lazarus by phone earlier in the day at his home in suburban Maryland, where he'd just returned from a month-long business trip to Europe and Asia. His alibi, according to Rosario, was solid; Lazarus could account for his whereabouts literally minute-by-minute over the previous week, thus ruling him out as a suspect in the trashing of my airplane or in any recent San Diego County murders.

"So, you're back to square one," I said. "You don't know who shot Sheen. And you don't know who stabbed Janet Bollinger."

Rosario sat back, pondering what I said. Her arms were draped across the top of the booth, affording me an excellent view of her impressive superstructure that I tried to ignore as I reached for another carrot. If this was a date, it was among the strangest I'd ever been on.

"I keep coming back to Walker," she said. "He had ties to both Sheen and Bollinger. Plus, he keeps an airplane out at Montgomery Airport. I checked. He rents a hangar there. He would've had easy access to your airplane."

She theorized that Walker had borrowed Sheen's pickup and driven it to the airport that night.

"Trucks come and go at airports all the time," Rosario said. "He figured a truck would draw less attention on the flight line than a car."

"Walker paid me to fly down here and do some work for him. Why would he want to monkey with my engine?"

"No clue." Rosario tapped some ice from her drink into her mouth and chewed it. "But I do know he would've had ample reason to want to shoot Sheen. Sheen was sleeping with his wife. Men have been killed for a lot less."

Her dangly silver earrings sparkled seductively in the candlelight.

I closed my eyes and massaged my forehead. Hub Walker was the last man I wanted to suspect of anything.

We sat for awhile without speaking.

"It would help if we recover a bullet," Rosario said finally. "At least a shell casing."

"It'll be a relatively small bullet," I said.

"What makes you say that?"

"Because I heard it."

"You *heard* Sheen get shot?"

"Pretty sure."

Rosario was incredulous. "And I'm only hearing this now? I thought we . . ." She paused in mid-sentence as our grandmotherly waitress arrived with our meals.

"*Muy caliente.* Very hot. Please be careful." She set two platters heaping with steaming Mexican food on the table. "Is there anything else I can get you? Another margarita for the lady? More club soda for the gentleman?"

"*No gracias,*" Rosario said.

"No, thanks."

"Enjoy."

Rosario watched me ladle an ulcer-inducing amount of salsa while ignoring her food.

"Did I hear you right? You say you heard Sheen get shot?"

"Single discharge, approximately 800 meters down range, approximately ten minutes after we parted company. Definitely sounded smaller than the .45 he was carrying. Nine-millimeter would be my guess."

The burrito was excellent. I ate probably faster than I should have. It was impossible not to.

"For a flight instructor," Rosario said, "you seem to know an awful lot about guns."

"Like I said . . ."

"Yeah, yeah. You're into TV." She picked at her enchiladas, eyeing me suspiciously but also intrigued. "Ever used to watch *Miami Vice* back in the day?"

"Occasionally."

"Best cop show ever."

"I beg to differ. Andy Griffith was the best cop show ever."

"Andy Griffith wasn't a cop show," Rosario said.

"Andy played a cop, did he not?"

"A little before my time but, yes, I seem to recall he did."

"And do you concede that the word 'show' in the *The Andy Griffith Show* connotes that it was, in fact, a show?"

"I'll concede that."

"I rest my case."

She smiled and watched me eat. "Unfortunately, I don't have Andy Griffith. But I do have all five seasons of *Miami Vice* on DVD. You interested in maybe grabbing some ice cream at my place after this and checking out a little Crockett and Tubbs action?"

Airplanes rarely crash because of pilot error. They crash because of *multiple* pilot errors, small mistakes that become larger ones, until the only option left is to bend over and kiss your keester goodbye. The same can be said of monogamy. Drop your guard, surrender yourself to an extracurricular distraction, and before you know it, you're grocery shopping for one and trolling the listings on Match.com. It was a mistake to say yes to Alicia Rosario's invitation to dessert in the same way I knew it was wrong to have asked her out to dinner, but I did it anyway. Blame it on her sundress. I was dying to find out where she stashed her off-duty weapon.

SHE LIT candles. We sat with our shoes off, on a buff-colored chenille sofa, in the living room of Rosario's tastefully contemporary Pacific Beach townhouse, pounding down Ben & Jerry's Karamel Sutra while watching *Miami Vice* on a sixty-inch big screen. Armani-clad detectives Tubbs and Crockett were busting their humps trying to stop villainous arms dealer Bruce Willis (when Willis still had hair) from selling a shipment of stolen Stinger missiles.

The episode brought back fond memories of the time I flew into Zagreb with three other Alpha operators posing as Canadian arms dealers to meet with a former Croatian cabinet official who was offering to the highest bidder a batch of U.S.-made, Rockeye cluster bombs. The money exchange was to take place in the luxury suite of an über-stylish hotel built some eighty years earlier as a refuge for passengers from the Orient Express. Our orders were to take the Croat into custody and spirit him out of the country for criminal prosecution, but he had other plans. When he pulled a pistol and broke for the elevators, another go-to guy I'll call "Barnes" snapped his neck like a chicken. We chucked the guy's body out a sixth-floor window, left a conveniently pre-typed suicide note on his nightstand, and jetted home business class.

Good times.

I was thinking how fulfilling it felt, my mind drifting, when I realized that Bruce Willis was dead, *Miami Vice* was over, and Rosario was stroking my right thigh.

"Welcome back." Her dark eyes gleamed. "Have a nice trip?"

She was exotic-looking and alluring, and I'd be lying if I said my neuronal impulses weren't sparking with the kind of thinking that got Bill Clinton in big trouble.

"I've never been with a cop before," I said.

"Then that'll make two firsts tonight."

She clicked off the TV, set my half-eaten bowl of ice cream on the coffee table, and softly pressed her lips to mine.

Time and reason quickly blurred in a frenzy of hungry mouths, groping hands, and clothing that seemed to shed itself. There was nothing romantic about it. It was foreplay in the same way Olympic wrestling is romantic. The stall warning horn inside my head was blaring and I didn't care. My big head was on autopilot. And then, just like that, I came to my senses. Maybe it was the firmness of her touch, so different from Savannah's, or the way Rosario's skin felt under my own fingers—some nonverbal, subconscious *something*. All I knew was that I suddenly felt as if I had no business being there, on that couch, with Detective Alicia Rosario.

"I can't, Alicia. I'm sorry."

"Why? What's wrong?"

I stood, hiking my jeans back up, and re-buckled my belt.

She sat back, naked from the waist up, and stroked the back of her neck. Her breasts glistened in the candlelight. They belonged in an art gallery. I stooped onto one knee and tied my shoes.

"Was it something I said, or did?"

"No, nothing like that. I'm just dealing with some personal issues right now."

She clutched a tasseled throw pillow to her chest.

"You mean *ex* issues."

I didn't respond.

Rosario sighed. "Story of my life," she said.

"Let's talk tomorrow, OK?"

"Sure. Fine. Whatever."

I knew it wasn't fine. I stood, pulled on my shirt, and leaned down to kiss her good night. She raised her chin and offered me her cheek. I could taste the salt of her tears.

"Thanks for dessert."

"Thanks for dinner."

The street was quiet, the chill night air a tonic. I sat in my luxury SUV outside Rosario's place for a long time with the windows down and thought about how far I'd come from nights in my not-so-distant past when I would've made any accommodation, told any lie, to maneuver someone like her between the sheets. Chalk it up to maturity? Declining testosterone? Who knows? It dawned on me as I drove away that I never did determine where she stashed her off-duty weapon. I wasn't sure whether to feel proud of myself or disappointed.

It was too late to call Savannah and too early to turn in the Escalade. I'd do both come morning.

Mission Boulevard was dotted with budget motels, the kind with towels you can see through and walls so thin you can listen to the porn flicks the guests next door are renting. Tired as I was, I would've settled for a room in any one of them, but every vacancy sign was preceded by an illuminated neon "No." I pulled into a sparsely occupied parking lot a block from the beach off of Reed Avenue, behind a sign that said, "The Beach Cottages, Day Week Month." There was another, smaller sign below it that said, "Tenants Only. No Overnight Parking. Violators Will Be Towed." I rolled up the windows, leaned my seat all the way back, and dozed off.

I WAS dreaming about machine guns when I was awakened by a loud banging sound. The sun was up. A pudgy San Diego police officer was looking down at me, rapping on the glass with his baton. I raised my seat back and rolled down the window.

"Top of the morning, Constable."

He was Latino, young, squared away. "Did you not see that sign?"

"What sign would that be?"

"The one that says no overnight parking," he said, pointing.

"I did."

"And you parked here anyway?"

"It was late. There was no room at the inn. I just needed somewhere to catch a couple hours of rack time. I'm out of here right now, if that works for you."

I'm pretty sure it had been awhile since he'd had to roust any scofflaws camped out in $70,000 SUVs.

"Just don't let me catch you overnight here again."

"Roger that."

I watched him walk back to his patrol car.

It was 6:20 A.M. My phone rang. The man on the other end spoke with an impenetrable Indian accent. He said his name was "Khan," then repeated it when I said, "Who?"

"Jahangir Khan. Your student."

Not merely my student. My *only* student.

"Jahangir. Of course. How could I forget? What's shaking, buddy?"

He apologized for calling so early, but said he was anxious to know when I would be returning to Rancho Bonita so he could resume his flight training.

"As you are no doubt remembering, Mr. Cordell, I am keenly interested in obtaining my official pilot's license certificate because you see, sir, it is of the utmost interest to me that I—"

"—I get it, Jahangir," I said, cutting him off before he got really cranked up. "I'll be back this week. I'll call you. We'll get it going, OK?"

"Oh, thank you, Mr. Cordell, thank you. You are a most kind and generous man—and, might I say, a fine pilot. If I could one day be only half as skilled as you are, sir, I will regard myself as a lucky man. You know, in the city where I am from, very few people will ever know the joy of flight, being in the air, above the teeming masses, and I—"

It was *way* too early in the morning to be that enthusiastic about anything, including flying.

"You're breaking up, Jahangir," I said, running the phone up and down my beard. "I'll call as soon as I get back. You take care now, buddy. Talk soon. Peace out."

I rubbed my eyes, yawned and stretched. Almost immediately, my phone rang again.

"I didn't have much to do last night after you left," Alicia Rosario said, "so I started reading up on your friend, Hub Walker." Her tone was all business, tinged with the bitterness of a good woman scorned. "He carried a German Luger pistol in Vietnam."

"His father fought in World War I. He inherited the pistol from him."

"The Luger's not exactly standard U.S. military issue."

"I'll take your word for it."

"Walker, by chance, hasn't shown you the pistol, has he?"

"What reason would he have had to do that?"

I waited for Rosario to respond. She sneezed.

"*Gesundheit.*"

"Sorry," she said. "Must've caught a bug from somebody last night."

I let the slap pass. "Why the interest in Walker's Luger?"

"One of our forensics people recovered a spent 9-millimeter round last night from the Sheen homicide scene," Rosario said. "I just got a call from the lab. They think they matched the make and model of the weapon."

"Was it a Luger?"

"How'd you guess?"

Twenty-five

No county sheriff with career ambitions would ever rush right out and throw handcuffs on a Medal of Honor recipient suspected of homicide without careful tactical planning, especially in a military town like San Diego. You don't simply cordon off the neighborhood, break out the bullhorn, and demand that the suspect surrender or else. You set about your work quietly and unobtrusively, hoping not to alert the breathless bobbleheads over at *Action News*, because if things go sour, you'll never be elected sheriff again. Or anything else.

Detective Rosario's plan, which her chain of command apparently had approved, was that I go in first. She was certain that Hub Walker trusted me by virtue of having saved his granddaughter from drowning, and by my having guided him to a safe landing on that fogged-in approach to the Rancho Bonita airport, when his airplane was running low on fuel. I could talk some sense into him, Rosario reasoned, and persuade him to surrender peaceably. He would have fifteen minutes to ponder his options before the SWAT team took over and took him by force. First, though, I'd have to sign a waiver absolving San Diego County of any liability in the event rounds start flying and I caught one or more of them.

Arresting a legitimate war hero for murder, discreetly or otherwise, had national news story written all over it. As soon as the story leaked, the military bashers would use it to perpetuate the myth that every veteran who sees combat comes home messed up in the head. Some do, but certainly not all.

How much of Walker's alleged bloodlust, if any, was influenced by his exploits in Vietnam forty years earlier was unknown. I'd once idolized the man. Now, I didn't know what to think of him. The knot in my stomach was the size of a grenade.

"You *do* have health insurance, correct?" Rosario asked me as I waited in the backseat of her unmarked unit, two sun-splashed blocks up the street from Hub Walker's house.

"I'm covered by the VA."

"Good luck with that," Rosario's partner, Lawless, said derisively from the front passenger seat. He yawned, heavy-lidded, like he'd been up all night.

I asked if his wife had given birth yet.

"None of your business, Logan."

"And on that cheery note . . ."

I opened the door and stepped out.

"Just be careful," Rosario said like she meant it.

"Always."

Two black Chevy Suburbans with tinted windows hunkered on the opposite side of the street, facing in the direction of Hub and Crissy's house—the SWAT team ready to roll in should my efforts to diffuse the situation prove unsuccessful.

Just don't leave me hanging, boys.

THE WELL-HEELED residents of La Jolla tended their bug-resistant roses. They walked their little yapper dogs. They pulled out of their driveways in their fine, impeccably detailed Beemers and Benzes. No one said a word to me or looked my way as I strolled toward the home of their celebrated neighbor, a suspected murderer—no one except Major Kilgore, who watched me through parted blinds as I passed by his house, then crossed the street. I flashed him a peace sign. Kilgore just stared.

The brass knocker on the Walkers' towering front door echoed like gunshots.

"Who is it?" Crissy called from inside after a few seconds.

"Logan."

Locks were unlocked. The door cracked open. Crissy smiled at me as though relieved. She was wrapped in a Japanese print kimono, red, her hair up.

"You scared me. With all this *stuff* going on around here, you can't be too careful, you know?"

I nodded.

Hub was at the airport, she said, doing some work on his airplane in preparation for a flight they were planning to take to Mexico the next day. She expected him back soon. Did I want to come in and wait?

I said I did.

Crissy made sure to double-latch the door behind me. "Coffee? I just made some."

"Sure."

I followed her into the kitchen, the scent of lilac soap wafted behind her.

"So, Mexico, huh?"

"Hub just wants to get away for a few days. Says things around here are getting too stressful. He's right. Also, there's a pediatric ophthalmologist I found online in La Paz. American guy. Very innovative. He's supposed to know everything there is to know about Ryder's eye condition. We're taking her down there to see him."

Mexico. Where investigators would have a tougher time finding Walker.

"Where's Ryder?"

"Still sleeping," Crissy said.

"Been a awhile since I was able to sleep this late."

"You and me both. I can't seem to sleep at all anymore."

She poured me a cup.

"I was thinking over what you said about Ray," Crissy said. "I don't know if this matters but, for what it's worth, I do know he's extremely jealous of Greg Castle. Ray's convinced he's the real brains at Castle Robotics. Thinks he never gets any credit.

If you ask me, he'd stop at nothing to get his hands on that company."

"How do you know all that?"

"How do I know?" Crissy fumbled for a credible answer. "Ask anybody who knows him. They'll tell you. Ray's got a little bit of a nasty streak in him."

I sipped my coffee.

"So, what was it you wanted to see Hub about?" Crissy said. "He told me he already paid you what we owed you."

"I'd prefer to discuss that with him directly."

"Sure, whatever." She pulled the kimono tighter around her. "Well, like I said, he should be home any minute now, and I really do need to go get ready. I've got another big meeting at Animal Planet up in LA this afternoon."

"*Cat Communicator?*"

"They're making noises like they're actually going to pick up the series," Crissy said as she padded down a long hall. "Can you believe it?"

"I'll believe it when I see it."

I waited until I heard her bedroom door close, then called Rosario to tell her that Walker wasn't home, but would be back soon. She put me on hold for nearly a minute.

"Change of plans," she said when she came back on the line. "SWAT'll move into position and take him down when he pulls into his driveway."

"Works for me. Then I'm out of here."

"Just do me a favor and stay put until we've got him, Logan. If he's due back any minute and decides to resist, I don't want you walking outside into the middle of a firefight."

Getting shot before finishing one's first cup of morning coffee is no way to start the day. I agreed to hang loose until Rosario called me back with the all-clear. Besides, I wanted the chance to confront Walker and ask him why he did what he did. Better, I figured, to pose that question after he was restrained.

"Just so you know," I told Rosario, "there's a little kid in here. Walker's granddaughter."

"Thanks for the heads-up. We'll be extra careful."

My phone beeped with another incoming call. I told Rosario I'd wait to hear from her and pushed the green button.

"You disconnected me yesterday," Savannah said.

I had totally forgotten to call her back.

"There was nothing preventing you from calling me back, Savannah."

"You mean other than phone etiquette? You cut me off, Logan. Etiquette requires that *you* should've called *me* back."

"Duly noted. I'll try not to let it happen again. Anything else?"

"I didn't call to chew you out. I actually have some great news. I talked to the hospital. Mrs. Schmulowitz is being released today."

Great news, indeed, but I wasn't much in the chatting mood as I fretted about the pyrotechnics that I feared might ensue when Walker arrived home.

"I appreciate you letting me know, Savannah."

"You sound distracted. I'll let you go—oh, one thing before I forget. You know my client I told you about, the one who works at Animal Planet?"

"The panicky programming executive."

"That's a bit callous, Logan, don't you think?"

"I have to go, Savannah."

"OK, well, anyway, I mentioned that idea to him, the one Crissy said she was pitching, about the cat trainer. He said he'd never heard of it, or her."

"Could be she's dealing with some other panicky programming executive. There are probably lots of them in Hollywood."

"My client says Animal Planet has no record of her ever having been in for any kind of meeting. The weird thing is, he really likes the idea. He wants her to come in and talk about it."

I told Savannah I'd have to call her back.

The disquieting scenario that unfolded inside my brain made what had become a chronic headache only worse. Ray Sheen had been shot dead hours before Crissy Walker claimed to have left San Diego for an early morning meeting at Animal Planet in Los Angeles, and before her husband woke up. I wondered if the alleged meeting was intended as an alibi, to put time and distance between Crissy and Sheen's murder. She certainly would've had her own motives to kill Sheen. He'd refused to terminate their affair, and had threatened to blackmail her when she tried to end it.

I gulped down the rest of the coffee, hoping the caffeine jolt would help clear my mind, and tried to focus.

Someone other than Sheen had to have driven his truck into the hills east of San Diego that night. Sheen, after all, was driving his MINI. Maybe he'd called Crissy after we crashed and asked her to come pick him up. Maybe she'd realized he was out in the boonies, where no one would see them, took matters into her own hands, along with her husband's German pistol, and put an exclamation point on the end of her affair with Sheen—not to mention his life.

I still had more questions than answers. Who tampered with my airplane? Who stabbed Janet Bollinger? And why had Sheen come after me with such a vengeance?

On the counter to my left was a stainless steel toaster. On my right was a photo in a gilded frame of Hub and Ruth Walker embracing after her graduation from the U.S. Naval Academy. Next to the picture was the butcher block carving set I'd admired four days earlier, when Walker had paid me the final money due me. There were slots for thirteen pieces of high-end, black-handled cutlery, eight of them matching steak knives. I noticed that two of the steak knives were missing. I slid one of the remaining knives out of the block.

The blade was about six inches long.

The edge was serrated.

I remembered the fatal stab wound Janet Bollinger had suffered to her abdomen. The edge was jagged. The kind of wound a serrated blade would've left.

Plenty of knives have serrated edges. The fact that two of them were missing from Crissy Walker's carving set, I reminded myself, proved nothing. They were probably misplaced, somewhere in her kitchen. I began looking for them, if only for my own peace of mind.

"What do you think you're doing?"

I turned. Hub Walker was standing behind me. In his right hand was one of the missing knives.

"Crissy said you were out at the airport," I said, closing a drawer and hoping my surprise didn't register with him.

"I don't know where she would've got that idea," Hub said. "I've been out in the guesthouse all morning, trying to fix that drip you told me about."

"With a steak knife?"

"Water supply line's rusted out. Had to cut away some drywall to get at the angle stop. Just don't tell my wife. She loves these knives. She should. They cost a small fortune."

I stepped aside as Walker washed the knife off in the sink.

"You didn't answer my question," he said. "What are you doing here? I thought we were all settled up."

"Where's the other steak knife, Hub?"

He turned around and looked at me.

"There's one knife missing from the set," I said.

Walker toweled off the knife in his hand and fixed me with a frigid stare.

"What do you care where it is?"

Crissy strode into the kitchen just then. She was wearing black stiletto heels and an ivory pants suit trimmed at the neck and sleeves in mother of pearl. Slung over her left shoulder was a black crocodile tote easily worth more than everything I owned.

"There's some of that leftover casserole Ryder likes," she said, grabbing a bottle of water from the refrigerator. "You can heat it up for dinner. I should be home around nine."

Walker gestured to the carving set, but his focus remained intently on me.

"Mr. Logan wants to know where the other steak knife went off to."

Crissy shut the refrigerator door.

"It's probably in the dishwasher. Why?"

"It's not," I said. "Or any of your drawers. I checked."

She set the water bottle down on the counter. Her eyes flashed fire.

"You want to tell me what's going on?"

"Ray Sheen's dead."

Crissy gasped and covered her mouth.

"He was shot last night," I said. "With Hub's Luger."

"That's impossible," Walker said. "My Luger's in a locked box, in the back of my closet. I haven't even looked at it since I got out of the Air Force."

"You can tell it to the detectives. They'd like to talk to you both."

"Why would they think *I* shot him?" Walker said, then turned and glowered at Crissy. "Just because he's been having sex with my wife for years?"

She forced a laugh.

"Hub, you're imagining things."

"Stop, Crissy. Please. I'm not stupid."

"You need to go to the doctor. You need help."

"I read your goddamn emails!"

The blood drained from Crissy's lovely face. "You did *what*?"

Walker fought back tears.

"Oh, Hub. I'm sorry. My God, I am *so* sorry. I never meant to hurt you. It was just one of those things that got out of control. I never loved him. I love you. I tried to end it, but he wouldn't. He threatened to tell you. You have to believe me. Please. I'm begging you."

She reached out to him with both arms. He pushed her aside with the knife still in his hand, then turned to glare at me like I was Judas.

"The police sent you in here to flush me out, so I'd go peaceably, didn't they?"

I said nothing.

He turned his back and stared silently out at the pool. "It's crap. All of it. I don't know who killed Ray Sheen, and I don't know who killed Janet Bollinger. But it wasn't me."

He slid the knife back into the butcher block, leaving one slot still vacant. Then he turned and faced me once more, chest out, chin squared, like he was back in the Rose Garden of the White House, about to be presented the Medal of Honor all over again.

"Let's go," Hub Walker said. "I got nothing to hide."

His beautiful wife gazed at him admiringly for a long moment with her eyes pooling. Then she reached into her crocodile shoulder bag, brought out a 9-millimeter German Luger pistol, and leveled it at me.

Crissy Walker, as it turned out, had plenty to hide.

Twenty-six

"We're getting out of here, Hub. You, Ryder and me. Start fresh down in Mexico. Everything'll be fine. You'll see."

Hub stared at her slack-jawed.

"Put down the gun, Crissy. We can work it out, whatever it is."

"We should have never hired him," Crissy said, pointing the pistol at me. " 'Leave well enough alone.' Did I not tell you that? 'Who gives a damn what Dorian Munz said or didn't say before they put him out of his misery. Let Greg Castle fight his own fight.' But did you listen to me, Hub? Have you *ever* listened to me? You didn't marry me for my brains. Admit it. You married me because I took my clothes off once and stood in front of a camera because I was too young and too poor to know any better. A stupid hick with a face and a body. That's all I've ever been to you."

"Crissy, you know that's not true. I respect you, for who you are. Now, please, give me the gun."

Walker took a step toward her. She swung the Luger toward him. He froze and took a step back with his hands raised. Then she turned and aimed it at me once more.

"This is all your fault."

"Your father was an Air Force mechanic," I said.

"My father was a great man. A million times better than you'll ever be."

"What's her father got to do with this?" Hub said.

"He taught her about airplane engines. Crissy was afraid I'd find out that Dorian Munz didn't murder your daughter, Hub. So she borrowed Ray Sheen's truck, pinned her hair up, put on some overalls, and drove on to the flight line that night."

Walker gaped at me in silence, then at Crissy, waiting for a denial.

None came.

"The only problem was, I survived the crash. So Crissy tells Sheen that I found evidence confirming what Munz had said was true, that Castle Robotics was ripping off the government. Sheen told Greg Castle, and Castle ordered Sheen to shut me up, permanently."

"You've got it all figured out, don't you?" Crissy said.

"Not quite. I'm still scratching my head about who sent that anonymous letter to Munz, tipping him off to the scam."

Crissy's nostrils flared. "That was Ray's idea. He thought Castle would resign to avoid a scandal, then he'd be named president of the company."

"And Ray wasn't worried about being audited," I said, "because he'd already cooked the books by then, right?"

Crissy began to weep.

"You shot him," Walker said, steadying himself on the edge of the kitchen counter like he'd just been punched in the stomach. "You shot Sheen."

"Whatever I did, I did for us, Hub, for our future. You've got to believe me."

"And Janet Bollinger?" I said. "What about her?"

"She called me. She said she couldn't take it anymore. I didn't mean to hurt her. Janet came after me. I just went to talk to her, that's all. Just talk."

"Talk about what?" Hub asked.

Crissy swallowed hard.

"About what she knew."

"What did she know?"

Crissy couldn't bring herself to respond.

Walker's face was flushed. "Crissy, what did Janet Bollinger know that was so all-fired important you had to go see her in person?"

"She found out about Ray and me. I wanted her to keep quiet about it."

"How did she find out?" Walker demanded.

Seconds passed. Crissy was panicking.

"How did she find out about you and Ray? I want an answer, goddammit!"

"She found out," Crissy said meekly, "because Ruthie saw us coming out of a motel one night up in Carlsbad. Ruthie told Janet. I didn't want you finding out, Hub. I didn't want to hurt you."

Walker's mouth fell open as the horrifying realization of all his wife had done washed over him.

"You killed Ruthie," he whispered. "You killed my daughter."

Crissy glanced around the room wild-eyed, like a trapped animal.

"You also threatened Janet Bollinger," I said, "to make Janet change her testimony during Munz's trial. All those years, enduring that guilt, knowing she'd sent an innocent man to Death Row, and finally she couldn't handle it anymore. She told you she was going to finally tell Munz's lawyer the truth and that's when you went to see her. That's why you sent him that back-off-or-die note, wasn't it?"

Crissy's teeth were clenched. The pistol was leveled at my head. Her gun hand was shaking.

"He's lying, Hub. Don't you see? He's making up everything, to put a wedge between us. He tried to rape me. You weren't here. I . . . I had to fight him off. Ask him. Go on. He'll tell you."

"You framed Dorian Munz, Crissy," I said. "You stole his shirt and phone out of his locker and made hang-up calls to Ruth, to make it look like he was stalking her. Then you stabbed her, dipped the shirt in her blood, and planted it where you knew the police would find it, behind his condo. That's why Janet Bollinger kept quiet all those years. She was afraid you'd kill her, too. And that's exactly what you did."

"That's not true! She came at me! It was self-defense!"

Walker buckled and slumped to the kitchen floor. I moved to help him.

Blam!

Crissy squeezed off a shot that went high, shattering the glass cabinet over my left shoulder.

"Don't you understand?" she said, sobbing. "I didn't want to lose everything we had, everything we worked so hard to build. This life. Our home. Can't you *begin* to understand that?"

"You mean everything *you* had, Crissy. Being married to a war hero has its perks, doesn't it? Sure beats being a washed-up centerfold from the sticks."

Her crocodile tears evaporated like an airbrushed illusion. In their place was a face I'd seen in many less-than-pleasant corners of the globe. The hard set of the jaw, the eyes gone flat and reptilian, drained of compassion. Crissy Walker's exquisite countenance had morphed into that of a remorseless killer.

I knew by the angle of the weapon in her hand that her next shot would likely be in the direction of my head—most people unfamiliar with firearms tend to aim high—and that I had a second or two, at most, before she pulled the trigger.

I dove for her legs.

Blam! Blam! Blam!

She got off three quick shots that went high before I made contact, driving her back into the trash compactor. I had thought that my textbook tackle would separate her from the pistol, but it didn't. She rolled on the floor and swung the Luger's barrel toward me.

Time slowed to what seemed like a standstill.

There are two things I can truthfully say that I'd never done in my life until that moment. The first was that I'd never decked a woman before. The second was that I'd never decked a woman with my arm encased in a rock-hard plaster cast. I did both to Crissy Walker, clubbing her in the head. The blow rendered her instantly unconscious while the Luger went skittering across the floor.

Walker leaned over, picked up the pistol, and aimed it at me. "Nobody hits my wife, you son of a bitch."

"I had no choice, Hub. You know it as well as I do."

"Secure your weapon, Walker! Do it now!"

I looked behind me, expecting to see the SWAT team. What I saw instead was Major Kilgore from across the street. He was kneeling behind the corner of the breakfast bar, hairpiece askew like he'd slapped the rug on in a hurry, leveling his M-14 rifle at Walker.

"Do me a favor," I said "Don't ask him to cut down his trees. Now would not be a good time."

Walker slowly lowered the pistol.

I reached over and took it from him.

"You OK, Colonel?"

He nodded almost imperceptibly, then covered his eyes with both hands and sobbed.

Crissy was unconscious, but her pulse rate and respiration were normal. I saw no outward indication of injury.

"I heard shots," Kilgore said, standing and slinging his rifle. "Somebody want to tell me what the hell's going on over here?"

I stuffed the Luger in my waistband and walked past him without answering.

Outside, on Hillside Drive, the morning sun shone down warm on my face, like manna from the Buddha himself. Sea gulls circled lazily overhead. They looked suspiciously like members of the crew that had made off with my turkey burger and chili fries.

I decided to forgive them.

SWAT CHARGED in with their assault carbines and submachine guns locked and loaded like they were storming downtown

Fallujah. I'd called Detective Rosario to tell her that the situation inside the Walkers' home was secure, but you know what they say about boys and their toys.

I waited behind a sheriff's cruiser parked outside, along with Rosario, her partner, Lawless, and Marine Kilgore, who'd grudgingly surrendered his rifle to the detectives, while members of the tactical team made entry. They reemerged five minutes later without having fired a shot, with both Hub and Crissy in handcuffs, and Ryder, wearing a Cinderella nightgown, under the protective arm of one of the deputies.

The Walkers were led to separate patrol cars. Crissy appeared woozy but was apparently functioning just fine under her own power. Hub hung his head. Dozens of neighbors had come out to watch.

"Check it out, dude," said one young man standing near us in board shorts and an "I Scored High on My Drug Test" T-shirt. "That chick? She was Playmate of the Year, like, before the Civil War."

"I'd still totally do her," his friend responded.

Kilgore went to chase both of them off his lawn.

Hub and I locked eyes as he was driven away. He nodded. I nodded back. I'd like to think it was a gesture of appreciation on his part, and respect on mine.

"He had no clue who his wife really was," I said.

"What man ever does?" Lawless said, ambling toward his unmarked Crown Vic parked up the street.

Rosario turned to face me. "You did good, Logan—for a flight instructor. Maybe you should think about becoming a cop."

"I'm a little old for that, but I do love doughnuts."

She smiled.

"My department owes you big time."

"How 'bout buying me a new airplane?"

"Hey, I'd cut you the check, but we're hacking back right now on everything, what with the economy. They won't even pay us overtime."

I dug my hands into the front pockets of my jeans and nodded. After years of lurching along on life support, the economy remained a joke. I would've laughed, but I couldn't afford to.

"Anyway," Rosario said, "if you come up with any good ideas on how we could help you out, within reason, you've still got my number, right?"

"That I do."

"Can I give you a lift to your car?"

"It's only a couple of blocks. I could use the exercise."

"You and me both." She hesitated, searching my eyes. "You stay safe, Logan."

"You, too, Detective."

"It's Alicia."

I smiled.

She walked toward the Crown Vic as her partner cranked the ignition.

"Hey, Alicia?"

She turned to look back at me.

"If things don't work out for me on the ex-wife front, you owe me a burrito."

"Consider it done."

I watched her drive away just as the first TV news van pulled in. A reporter with big hair and too much makeup jumped out with her cameraman and began trying to interview anything that moved. She looked less like a journalist than she did a day spa receptionist. Hungry for their fifteen minutes, Hub Walker's neighbors were only too happy to fill her in on every salacious detail of what they'd just witnessed.

Not me.

I called Savannah and told her I was Los Angeles-bound. Would she mind picking me up downtown at Union Station? I hoped to be there in time for supper.

"Lucky you," Savannah said. "I'm in a rare cooking mood. What do you feel like eating?"

"Surprise me."

"You hate surprises, Logan."

"And you love them. The yin and the yang, the balance of life. The Buddha's all about balance, Savannah—as long as it doesn't involve borscht. You weren't thinking of making borscht, were you? Because I *hate* borscht. More than I hate surprises."

"Did I ever make borscht when we were married?"

"Not that I recall."

"I've never made borscht in my life, Logan. I'm not about to start now."

"Good. Just so we got that straight."

"Call me when your train's a half-hour out. I'll come get you. Come hungry."

"You can count on it. See you tonight, babe."

She sighed like I'd made her day.

San Diego may well be America's Finest City. I couldn't wait to leave it, though, not with a home-cooked meal and Savannah waiting for me in LA. I dropped off the Escalade at Enterprise's downtown office and hopped a taxi to the train station, but not before stopping off at a vintage record store on 6th Avenue where I snagged CDs of the *The Three Tenors in Concert* and *Pavarotti's Greatest Hits* for my spook buddy, Buzz.

I made a mental note to buy Mrs. Schmulowitz the grandest bunch of white daisies I could find when I got back to Rancho Bonita.

Twenty-seven

Time, scientists tell us, accelerates the older we get—or, at least, the perception of time. Makes sense. When you're three, a year is one-third of your life. When you're forty-three, one year is, well . . . Look, I was no math major, but you probably get the concept.

Nearly three months had passed in what seemed like the blink of an eye since the *Ruptured Duck* and I had made our "hard landing" in San Diego. Plenty had occurred since.

Formally cleared of any criminal wrongdoing, Hub Walker had filed for divorce. His wife, Crissy, remained in the county lockup, awaiting trial for the murders of Ray Sheen, Janet Bollinger, and her stepdaughter, Ruth.

Mrs. Schmulowitz had recovered from her tummy tuck. She'd called it correctly: except for the scar and a few stretch marks, her new abs could've passed for those on a prepubescent Nubian princess.

Sadly, my tired old Cessna remained grounded. Larry had made substantial progress putting the *Duck* back together, but he was still waiting on sundry parts, many of which were on back order. With no airplane, my only student, Jahangir Khan, had left me to enroll at "Air Worthy," the slick new flight school across the field, where would-be pilots learned to fly on shiny new Cirrus SR22's. They attended ground school in a real classroom, practicing on state-of-the-art computer simulators while swilling free coffee and munching free cookies from

Mrs. Fields. *Free cookies.* Whoever said life isn't fair sure knew what they were talking about.

And, as if that were not distressing enough, my cat remained missing, while the woman of my dreams continued to remain my ex-wife. Savannah and I had agreed to take things slowly, spending alternate weekends together in our respective cities, gingerly feeling our way toward what we both hoped would be an eventual reunion.

"I remember how you told me she was your sister when she first showed up here, and how I fell for it," Mrs. Schmulowitz said, refilling my glass of lemonade. "Boy, am I a *schlemiel* or what?"

I was hanging out in my landlady's living room, taking a brief break from painting the exterior of her house. In lieu of other viable employment prospects, she'd insisted on hiring me as her resident handyman until I could regain my financial footing.

"I just didn't want to offend you, Mrs. Schmulowitz."

"Offend me? Bubeleh, people in their seventies get offended. Folks my age, we've seen it all. Lemme tell ya, when you've been hitched to a man who insists on dousing himself every weekend head-to-toe in Chanel, who then goes traipsing around the basement wearing your girdle and brassiere, as my third husband was extremely fond of doing, nothing fazes you, and I mean, *nothing.*"

She turned on her ancient Magnavox television, picked up a pair of ten-pound barbells and began doing bicep curls in black Lycra bicycle shorts and a New York Giants athletic T-shirt that was knotted at the waist. An antediluvian Gidget.

"She's a very intelligent lady, that lady of yours—and that body of hers? *Oy gevalt*, I only *wish* I could've had a figure like that," Mrs. Schmulowitz said, grunting on the down-curl. "You know, normally, I'd say what's done is done. It's over. OK, so it didn't work out. *Az och un vai.* Tough luck! Wipe your hands and walk away. But I got a good feeling about you two kids. I really do."

"I hope you're right, Mrs. Schmulowitz."

"Of course, I'm right. I'm always right when it comes to love. I've been right five times."

I gulped down the rest of my drink.

"I'd better get back to work before my paintbrush dries out. Thanks for the lemonade, Mrs. Schmulowitz."

"Pitcher's in the 'fridge, bubby. Come in and get more whenever you want."

"I may do that."

As I walked outside, Mrs. Schmulowitz was knocking out a new set of preacher curls while Judge Judy was laying into some loser on TV for cheating his 300-pound girlfriend out of a Kmart gift card.

Kiddiot was sitting on the back porch.

A joyous whoop came rushing up from somewhere deep inside me as I gathered up my cat and hugged him.

"Where'd you go off to, buddy?"

Wherever he'd been, he appeared not to have missed many meals there. Kiddiot was as porky as ever. I kissed him repeatedly, and even though he was never one for public displays of affection, he kissed me back, licking me on the cheek. Then he remembered he had an image to maintain, dug his rear claws into my chest, and demanded to be let down.

"Mrs. Schmulowitz, look who finally decided to come home!"

She pushed open the screen door, looked down and gasped with delight.

"*Mazel tov*! The Moses of Rancho Bonita has returned! Wandering around forty days and forty nights—only a lot more than forty, but who's counting, am I right? Where have you been, you *meshugana butterball*? We've been worried sick about you!"

Kiddiot rubbed against her legs, rolled over on his back playfully—then ran off when she stooped to pet him. He hustled toward my garage apartment and hopped in through the cat door like he'd never left. For a butterball with fur, he moved pretty good.

"I'll tell you one thing," Mrs. Schmulowitz said, wiping happy tears from her cheeks, "that cat could stand to drop a few pounds."

I called Savannah to tell her the news. She was thrilled.

KIDDIOT WAS dozing on the small of my back that night when we were both jarred awake by the sound of someone jiggling our front doorknob.

I grabbed the .357 and rolled out of bed, while Kiddiot took cover under the box spring.

The door-jimmying got louder, more frenetic. Whoever was outside seemed little concerned that I might hear them. I cocked the revolver's hammer as quietly as I could, took a deep breath, let it out slowly, then flung open the door with both hands on the grips.

There stood Savannah, cloaked in a dark-colored trench coat with the collar up. In her hand was a door key. Her heart must've been in her throat given the terrified expression on her face.

"Jesus, Logan."

"My bad. It's OK, it's OK. You're OK."

I set the revolver on a shelf and pulled her close to me.

"I don't think this key works," Savannah said, breathing heavily, trying to calm herself after nearly getting shot.

"I'll get you a new one first thing tomorrow."

She pulled away from me, glanced down at my nakedness, and offered me a wry smile.

"You gonna invite me in, flyboy, or you gonna just stand there, whistling in the breeze?"

I let her in and closed the door.

"Not that I'm unhappy to see you, Savannah, but what are you doing here? I thought it was my turn to come down to LA this weekend. Or am I confused?"

"You're not confused."

"Then you must be."

"Why am I confused?"

"It hasn't rained in months, it's seventy degrees outside, and you're wearing a raincoat."

She undid the belt and let the coat fall to the floor.

"Who said I was?"

She was wearing nothing underneath but skin.

I watched her slip into my bed, the filtered moonlight highlighting her curves under the sheets like the bas-relief of a Greek goddess.

"I have an excellent idea," Savannah said.

"Better than that raincoat?"

"Why don't you come in here and join me?"

"That is an excellent idea."

She was soft and warm, and when she snuggled close, we melded perfectly. Some couples just fit together better than others.

"How's your cat?"

"He's great. Fat as ever."

"I'm so happy he finally decided to come back after so long. It must've been a big surprise."

"Huge surprise."

We lay together, reveling in the still of the night.

"I never did answer your question," Savannah said after awhile.

"What question would that be?"

"Why did I drive all the way up from Los Angeles to see you tonight."

"I'm assuming it was to help celebrate Kiddiot's home-coming."

"That was definitely part of it. But that wasn't the main reason."

"What was the main reason?"

"Another surprise. This one's pretty big, too."

"I think I'm starting to like surprises."

"You have to guess."

"I won the Publishers Clearing House Sweepstakes?"

"Nope."

"Los Angeles is finally getting an NFL franchise?"

"I'm serious, Logan."

"OK, I give up. What is the serious big surprise, Savannah?"

I could feel her heart thumping against my chest.

"You and I," she whispered deliciously in my ear, "are having a baby."